I0739089

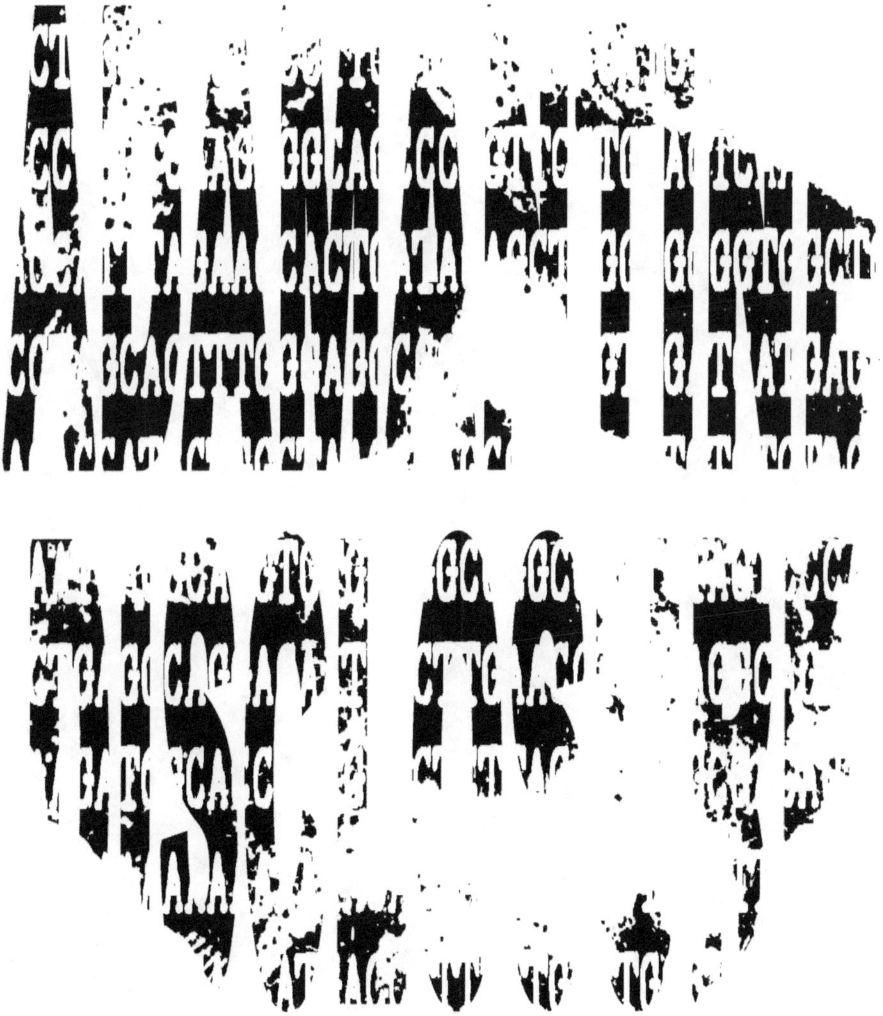

CGTG
CTAG
CCT AGAGGCAGCCCAGTCCTGTACTC
AGCATTTAGAAGCACTGATAC CTGGGTGCGGTGGCTG
TCC AGCACTTTGGGAGGC GGTGGATCATGAG
AGCGATCCTGGCT AGCG TCTCTC
A AGGTG GTGGCGGGC GGC
CTGAGGCAGGAGA TCACTTGAACC GGCAG
AGATCGCACCAC CTCTT CG
AAAAA
CCATGAGC TTC TGC

The Adamantine Disclosure

Published by Submariner's Map Imprint
An imprint of Submarine Media Pty Ltd
2nd Edition, June 2018
Malaga, WA, Australia
http://submarinemedia.com.au

The Adamantine Disclosure.

Chapter 1 — Canyon Crash

Nathanael Wayfarer was driving fast, too fast, around the corners of the Grand Canyon national park.

For some reason he had an ear worm, that old hymn, "Rock of Ages, cleft for me", going round and round in his head. He gritted his teeth at it — as if the rest of the rubbish in his head that he had to put up with wasn't enough.

His wife of twelve years had left six months ago, but that wasn't the cause of the implacable mountain of despair he was now facing down.

As far as Nathanael could see, they had been negotiating the divorce amicably, even in the last few weeks. She had seemed happy with fifty-fifty. It had all been going smoothly, she had acquiesced to all his requests. But now it was obvious that he had been completely mistaken.

Today, his house-cleaner back in Australia (he'd asked her to open his mail and email anything important) had sent him an iPhone photo of the interim violence restraining order.

That's the sort of thing that would have taken Debra eight or nine weeks to organise at least. She'd always said Nathanael was her rock. Well, now, he was her grindstone, but she still wasn't the sharpest tool in the shed. Didn't she realise they would both lose out if they started bringing lawyers into it? For God's sake, Nathanael had been in the U.S. for the last four months, he hadn't even talked to her for three. He had been doing the tour of the Grand Canyon he had wanted to do for years, the tour Debra hadn't wanted to be part of.

All he'd been waiting for now was for her to email him the divorce papers.

So she was getting at him. Was it because he was enjoying himself for once? He had never so much as raised a fist at her, barely even raised his voice even once during their marriage. No, his own anger and disappointment tended to be directed inward. In fact, Debra had been the one who liked throwing plates at the granite wall in the kitchen, destroying things, smashing cups on the stone floor tiles.

He pushed his foot down. He knew it was dangerous, couldn't be more so, nearly missed a corner, swerved past a car that had appeared out of nowhere, now here he was, skidding on the edge of the precipice.

Even as he was skidding, he glimpsed the glory that was the Grand Canyon, an ancient adamantine structure too big for his mind to take in, but he forced his attention back to driving.

He got control, skidded back onto the road. What had happened to the other car? Had he clipped it as he went past?

He looked in his rear view mirror and breathed a sigh of relief — they were sitting on the kerb, quite safe. He slowed down to the speed limit.

He didn't want to hurt anyone.

Not like Debra. She had wanted to hurt him. Is that why she had taken a VRO out on him? An act of spite, something a woman scorned would do, but the marriage had been dying of sterile fossilisation, not hatred or unfaithfulness. That was why Debra had found someone else, why she had left him.

Nathanael hadn't given her the child she wanted.

He looked in the rear view mirror again, still worried about the other car. They were fine, they were back on the road now.

He didn't see the elk until it was too late.

~~~

He woke up smelling clean linen. There was dull, indistinct pain everywhere — something was pushing his awareness of it away. Drugs, pethidine, or morphine, maybe.

A woman's voice in an American accent said, "You're lucky. They tell me it was fortunate the car rolled onto the left side. Even the barriers might not have stopped you going over the edge." Nathanael tried to open his eyes, but he couldn't manage it for some reason. The voice continued, "It was a good thousand feet to the bottom. They are saying you would have been little more than a smudge right now on the rocks, if you had gone over."

He tried to respond, but there was a tube in his mouth.

~~~

Someone was praying for him. An American woman's voice again. Was it the same woman? "Please, help this man. Forgive his sins, Lord Jesus, I know you already do, but help him to know that you do. Please save him. I don't know if he knows You, but heal him and help him and save him from death."

He didn't remember anyone ever praying for him before. It was comforting. God forgave him. Forgave all his sins. How about that...

~~~

The days and nights passed slowly after that, always in darkness, but the sounds became his friends, telling him everything that was going on. Sometimes the American woman's voice was there, sometimes it was just the television softly buzzing in the background, or the busy sounds of the hospital, or maybe it was different female voices, he couldn't tell. Sometimes it was someone in another room moaning or screaming, or people talking in the corridor. He could tell a lot from those other sounds, whether it was day or night, whether the other patients had lived or died, how stressed the nursing staff were, whose shift it was.

He imagined the ubiquitous 'beep, beep' of his own heart monitor was the sonar of a submarine, navigating in darkness between the underwater rocks.

And he began to wonder if he had gone blind. Why couldn't he see anything? The idea of being blind filled him with horror.

He found his arms free one day. The tube in his mouth had gone. He felt his face. There was a bandage over his eyes, which must be why he couldn't see. Then he fell asleep again.

~~~

A woman came in again, another American woman's voice, different from the other ones, "Nathanael? Are you awake?" He nodded and tried to speak, it came out as a hoarse croak, "Yes. Yes I'm awake. What happened?"

"You were in a car accident. You hit an elk. You're lucky to be alive."

"I know, I know. I mean, what happened to me. What injuries?"

She hesitated. That had to be bad. "The doctor will tell you everything when the bandage comes off." Then the fog returned.

~~~

Someone was shaking him.

"Wake up, Nathanael! Wake up!"

He said, "What's going on?"

She said in a voice shaking with panic, "You have to get up. We have to go. Get up!"

He pushed himself up, feeling butterflies in his stomach. Her urgency was contagious. She hastily shifted the bedrails, he felt them move.

She said, "Lean on me. I'm just going to pivot you around. The wheelchair is there. God, you are pretty big, aren't you? You must be six foot tall at least. That's alright, I can manage." He felt her gentle, strong hands moving him around, slipping him over the edge of the bed. He fell into the rock-hard seat of the wheelchair with a thump, arms akimbo, righted himself with some effort.

Was he paralysed? But he could feel his legs. That was where most of the pain was coming from.

She was pushing the wheelchair. She said, "Don't talk to anyone. Keep quiet." For some reason her tone of voice intensified his feeling of panic.

As she pushed him along, he moved his hand down to find out what was wrong with his legs. There were metal
~~~

things, like long, square screws or bolts or something, covering his legs, and they were attached to horizontal beams that felt cold and smooth, as though they were made of flint. Carbon fibre, perhaps. An external fixator? He must've broken his legs very, very badly.

When the wheelchair bumped over the floor cavities, he knew where they were — the door of a lift. Then the sound of a finger pressing a button and the lift bumped into action.

The pulling feeling in his legs was lessened — that was how he knew they were going down.

He said, "Where are we going?"

She put her finger against his mouth. Then he heard the other people in the lift, breathing, listening. The lift stopped and some of them got out. Then more came in and they were going down again.

Then they were in a carpark. That particular mix of smells, oil, gas, exhaust fumes, concrete, and the echoes that resounded as though they were in a giant cavern. The chair was rolling across the asphalt.

They stopped.

The sound of a car door opening.

She said, "You'll have to help me. You're too big, too heavy. I can't get you in on my own."

He tried to move his legs, he really did, but it was almost impossible. She started sobbing, whispering, "Quick! Quick! As soon as they realise you're not in your room, this is the first place they'll come to! Please, God, please!"

The genuine panic in her voice motivated him and he slipped one leg across and up to where he thought the car door was, then the other. The hospital gown got caught on one of the large screws on the external fixator and tore a little. Feeling his feet slip into the space beneath the seat, he pushed himself across from the wheelchair with both arms, with all his strength. A strong push from her as he pivoted across landed him in the seat.

He hardly knew how he did it.

She slammed the door and pushed the wheelchair off. He heard it careening away, hitting other cars and smashing against whatever was in the way, while she ran around, leaped into the driver's seat and started the engine. She revved the accelerator two or three times and then they were moving.

He could hear some men shouting, then another distant car engine starting up.

They turned around a corner and stopped again immediately. She leaned right over him and pressed a lever so that the seat back went down and suddenly he found he was lying horizontally.

She whispered, "Keep down! Keep your head down!" He could hear her breath — she was lying next to him on her seat. It was strange, with her close like that, so close that he could even smell her breath. Sweet, kind of appealing. A touch of spice. His heart, that he long ago thought had turned completely to stone, seemed to yield slightly. Like a small earthquake.

He heard the buzz of the window going down.

A car went past, tyres screaming, through the carpark up to the next level. One of the men was shouting at someone in an English accent. "Just now — a white Toyota Celica. Which way did it go?" The guy at the gate mumbled something. More shouting. "A small car — a two-door sedan. Oh, no. Kade, it's a one-way road, there in't no other way they could go." The car careened off.

The woman said, "Well, we can't take you back to the ward, can we? That's the first place they'll look." She wound the back of the seat up very carefully. "How are you feeling, Nathanael?" She spoke in an American accent, like the woman who had been talking to him in the ward.

He was alright. The legs were a bit sore still.

She started the car. "I can take you to my sister's place. But how the hell are we going to get that external frame off? Still, we can worry about that later. Are you alright? Nathanael? You're okay?"

He remembered to speak aloud this time. "Yes, I think so. A bit of pain but it's bearable."

"I'm just going to go out the entrance. So what, what the guys at the gate think." She paused, as though considering something unthinkable. "I think I might take us down a one-way street the wrong way today."

Nathanael groaned. "It was disobeying the road rules that got me into this trouble in the first place."

But the American woman said, "No, I think you were in this trouble before that. Well before that."

But she didn't elucidate.

CHAPTER 2 — NATASHA'S NOTIONS

The guys at the gate said, "Yeh, we knew you were still in there. Richards saw it all on the security cams, told me what was happening. Didn't trust those guys. Were they bikies? I've seen you before, though, you work here don't you? But you're not one of the nurses."

"I.T.," she said.

"You better turn left here," he said. "They didn't look like nice people. Turn left."

From the guy's tone of voice Nathanael deduced that this was the one way street the woman had been talking about. In his mind, he had seen it as a right turn, perhaps something to do with driving on the other side of the road here.

"Turn left," the guy said again.

She did.

Cars were beeping and people swearing at them as she switched lanes, pulling Nathanael from side to side in the seat. Then they careened around another corner and from then on it was a comparatively pleasant journey.

The meal that night was different from the hospital food, a curry, tasted genuinely Indian. Some kind of Tandoori chicken, strong, hot, and salty, with rice and dahl, and a few potatoes. He touched the potatoes with his fingers and could just about see them, sitting on the side like a pile of boulders. He wolfed the meal down then slept soundly.

Soon afterwards, it seemed, the American woman shook him awake. He had no clue if it was night or day. "We've got to get your bandages off. It will make it a lot easier if you can see."

Slowly she unwound the bandage around his head.

There were patches on his eyes as well. She removed the one on the right eye and light blazed in. He hadn't even opened his eyelids yet.

Then the one on the left eye. Gradually his eyes adjusted. It was a red light, the light that comes through closed eyelids.

"Open your eyes. Don't worry, the curtains are closed, the lights are off. It's not going to dazzle you."

He opened them slowly.

The room came into focus. It looked like a spare room and for a moment seemed extremely bright, although as his eyes adjusted he saw that it was actually fairly dim.

There was daylight peeking in through a gap in the curtains. It was daytime.

He had a fresh hospital gown on now.

She said, "Put that T-shirt on over your hospital gown if you're cold."

There was a T-shirt next to the bed sitting on top of a low bookcase. In the bookcase were a few books on geology and geography, a King James bible, a book called 'Foundations of Mathematical Reasoning', a jug of water and a plastic glass next to the t-shirt, and nothing else except the mirrored doors of a walk-in robe and the carpeted floor.

From his vantage point he had a glimpse out through the hallway to the kitchen's rock floors and fake marble bench top.

"Look," she said, "I've got your file here. You can read it if you want. See what you did to yourself."

He looked up at her and was mildly surprised. She was dark-skinned, Indian, probably, or Sri-Lankan, from the sub-continent, as they used to say. But she had a lot of tattoos, up and down her arms. She was wearing jeans and a loose tank top, but it looked elegant on her. Anything would, really. She stood in a relaxed, graceful way that seemed to say she didn't care what anyone thought of her, she didn't have to put on airs.

A beautiful face, and a nice figure. Late twenties? Even early thirties perhaps? Really sweet face, dark hair, brown eyes.

She said, "So what do you think?"

He looked up at her and smiled, "Sweet. Nice looking. Different from what I expected, but… beautiful. I look at you and feel… reverence towards your beauty." Damn it, he realised immediately it was a faux pas.

Her tone of voice seemed to tell him she was blushing. "Not me, stupid," she said. "Your legs."

He looked down at his legs. Each leg had external fixators, each with eight bolts, four in the upper leg, four in the thigh.

"Sorry. Been out of it for a while. Forgot my social graces. I'm not going anywhere just yet, am I?"

She shook her head. "I don't know how we're going to get those off, either, when it's time. I'm going to have to talk to the surgeon quietly, perhaps. I don't know. Leave it with me for now."

She handed him the hospital file and then picked up a cloth bag which had been lying on the floor next to the bed, where he couldn't see it. She took out his mobile, his wallet and passport and one or two other things he'd had on him when the accident had happened and placed them on the bookshelf next to the water jug. She showed him a 2 litre plastic bottle with the nozzle cut out and a pan.

"The bottle's if you need to pee. The pan's for the other. Tell Michelle afterwards so she can… flush it. Oh, and don't use your mobile yet. I don't know if they're tracking it. They probably are. The phone battery is flat at the moment. Don't recharge it — if someone's tracking you they will be able to find you as soon as the battery has even the smallest amount of charge in it."

"Thanks," said Nathanael a little bit numbly. He looked up at her again. "What's your name?"

"Natasha," she said. "Natasha Chase."

"Hi," he said. "I'm Nathanael."

She said, "I know."

They shook hands.

"Anyway," she continued, picking up her bag, "I have to go to work. I'll tell you everything tonight. My sister is at home today — she'll look after you. Michelle!"

A younger version of Natasha walked in, without the tattoos, in torn jeans and a tank top. She was wearing glasses.

Natasha said, "Nathanael is awake."

"Hello," she said, slightly sarcastically. "I am Michelle and I'll be your nurse for today."

Nathanael grinned. "Hello, Michelle."

She grinned back. "I'm looking forward to tonight, though. I still don't know what's going on, really."

Natasha snapped, "The less you know the better."

Michelle pouted in a peeved sort of way. "Well, it's only fair — after all he's in my house."

Natasha pressed her lips together and raised one eyebrow. "I'll tell you some, Michelle. But... it's a dangerous situation. It might actually be better if you don't know any of the other things I've worked out. Any more than you know already. Don't tell anyone, not even Mum, that he's here! And specially don't Facebook it. I don't want even a rumour getting out. I've got to go."

She picked up her bag and left.

"Well," said Michelle, "It looks like it's just you and me, Mister Mystery Man. Just call out if you need anything — I'll just be in the next room, doing my study."

Nathanael asked, "Can't you tell me anything?" His voice sounded so plaintive that he winced in embarrassment.

Michelle looked down at him and sighed. "Just that... Natasha overheard some men talking about how they were going to kill you. That's all I know, sorry."

Nathanael said, "So she really saved me."

"That's my sister. She's a rock."

CHAPTER 3 — ELUCIDATION AND ESCAPE

That night, after dinner, Natasha came into Nathanael's room and sat on the bed.

Michelle came in for a moment, but Natasha must have indicated, 'Not now,' somehow, because she said, "oh," and walked straight out again.

Natasha said, "Alright, Nathanael, I'll tell you everything that I know.

"I'm a computer programmer, I work for a group that contracts out work. I was contracted to work on the Flagstaff Trauma and Injury Clinic computers about six months ago. My job was basically to co-ordinate the updates on everything from the pay system to the rosters to email and the doctor's video conferencing systems.

"I had access to the email servers and was testing the anti-virus software when I noticed a strange trail of emails.

"The emails claimed to be coming from a relative of one of the patients in intensive care. It was the specialist hospital spam software that flagged these emails for further investigation — you see, the server the emails came from came up on a DNS blacklist, not for spam, but because the previous owner of the IP address had been arrested for drug trafficking.

"Hospital drugs are trafficked, sometimes, so I suppose that's why.

"I looked a little further into it. The server was owned by a bikie gang in Perth, Australia.

"I examined the emails. They had all come in the last two days, and were asking questions about one of the recently admitted patients. You. Which ward, which room, which bed, even funny things about the treatment. Fairly obscure questions, some of them. Was he on intravenous glucose or antibiotics? Was he conscious yet? Had he said anything about things that happened before he came to Arizona, to the Grand Canyon?

"I actually reported this to the Flagstaff Clinic administration but they seemed to think I had rocks in my head. They told me questions like these weren't that obscure. Quite frankly I don't think they fully understood what IP addresses can tell you — they said, 'Well, an email like that could come from anywhere.' They didn't seem to believe that I could narrow the source of the emails down to a single server, located at bikie gang headquarters in Bayswater, in Perth, Australia. People are surprisingly ignorant about this sort of thing.

"I even called the FBI but they told me there was nothing illegal about asking about a relative, even for someone in a bikie gang. And they warned me against excessive prying, implying that I might actually be breaking the law by looking into this. They seemed to resent me stepping on their toes, I think.

"I wasn't satisfied with this. I looked to see if you had had any visitors or phone calls. I examined the call logs — the system provides access — you hadn't had any phone calls at all. Surely if these people were your relatives they might have at least tried to phone you? There hadn't been a single phone call from Australia to your ward in the last four days, since you had arrived, and yet there had been fourteen emails.

"And not one of the emails said anything about telling you they had tried contacting you or that they were worried about you. Normally the family would be frantic. And they would want you to know that they were concerned about you.

"It really seemed odd. So I decided to keep an eye on you.

"When I had a free moment, I dropped in on you. There you were, lying there with tubes going in and out and machines keeping you alive — I felt sorry for you. You looked so pathetic."

Nathanael said sarcastically, "Thanks."

Natasha ignored him. "I started talking to you — you know, they say people in comas can hear, and all of the staff seemed to be too busy to be bothered — you didn't respond."

Nathanael nodded, "Yes, but you know I could hear you. It wasn't wasted effort."

Natasha continued, "I was there when you woke up. I hadn't intended that — I ended up saying some stupid thing about the doctor telling you when he comes in, or something — and rushing out. I think you went back to sleep though.

"At the same time I continued my investigations. I was worried about you, to be honest. I tried hacking the bikies' server. Their server wasn't secure at all.

Really looked like a hatchet job — hackers — not real programmers. The ftp protocol was dodgy, they hadn't even bothered to change the default password. Oh, there were a few websites on there, white supremacy, some kind of drug site, a 70s tribute rock site, another Harley Davidson site, but pretty soon I found the email folders on the ftp server. They weren't even encrypted, and no TLS or SSL. Incidentally, encrypted files are — "

"I know," said Nathanael, "They're files that have been turned into a bunch of numbers. Only if you have the key, which is a long prime number, can you unlock them and read them." He surprised himself, managing such a long sentence.

Natasha said, "That's basically it. But these weren't encrypted at all. I began reading through the email account from which the emails to the Clinic had been sent. I did a search for your name and some common terms and found the emails. By looking at the account passwords, I related that email address to one of the members of the club.

"Someone called Kade. And in his inbox I found two air tickets via Melbourne and LA to Prescott, which is the nearest airport to Flagstaff. It's about one and a half hours drive. They were registered in what I assumed to be fictitious names. Jonathan Johnson and Cameron Cameronson.

"And they were due in at Prescott Airport that day. Quickly I put into place some red flags on the hospital security system — you see, relatives have to sign in with ID these days, after we had a few incidents with ex-husbands breaching restraining orders, that sort of thing, so I put in an alert for anyone named Jonathan Johnson,

Cameron Cameronson, or anyone with a first or second name Kade.

"The alert came up pretty quickly, at the main reception, under the false names. I was in my office, which is nearby, so I raced down there and looked for them. There were two bearded men looking at the hospital map. They both had Australian accents, so I stood nearby and listened.

"They were talking fairly softly, but, you know, my hearing is pretty good. One was saying, 'Will it be hard? What do we do?' 'It's easy — I've done it before — detach the tube — put the syringe in — the potassium chloride will do the rest.' That was when I raced up the stairs — quicker than the lift if you're running — and got you out of there."

Nathanael's eyebrows raised. "Really? That's what you heard them say?" Nathanael knew that potassium chloride was one of the three chemicals they use in the lethal cocktail used to execute condemned prisoners on death row. He also knew that it was fairly difficult to detect in the body after death. "So you've saved my life?"

Natasha nodded. "I think so."

"So Michelle was right — you really are a rock, aren't you?"

She grinned. "I do rock." Then her expression went sombre again. "There are still some hurdles to get over, though, Nathanael. I actually discharged you — I'm rather proud of it actually, made a little circular thing in the database where the doctors can't be sure which one of them approved it — but you'll still need to get the external frame taken off. But there's one thing that might help — your Surgeon has a clinic here in Phoenix. I think I can get you booked in there through Health Services."

Nathanael said, "So we're in Phoenix are we? It didn't seem that long a drive."

Natasha said, "It was. Two hours. You fell asleep soon after we started. One other thing... Are you in pain?"

Nathanael said, "Twinges. Nothing too bad now."

Natasha shrugged. "Well — if you need some pethidine I could organise it..."

Nathanael grimaced. "I don't want you disobeying the law, Natasha. I mean, I can see you've... pushed the boundaries... but I'll be fine. The pain is not too bad. They'd been weaning me off, anyway, for the last few days. I just had a few pills in the morning yesterday. I don't think they were giving me any pain killers intravenously, just antibiotics and saline."

"Hmmph," Natasha raised her eyebrows wryly, "I've broken at least ten federal laws in the past week on your account. They won't miss the drugs, if I get them — I've got full control of the inventory. Never mind. As long as you're not in pain."

Nathanael said, "Why did you do it? Why did you save me?"

"I would have never forgiven myself if I had just left you there and then found your bed empty the following day..."

Nathanael took her hand in his and squeezed it. "Thank you. Natasha, thank you very much for what you've done. You really do rock." His brow knitted. "Now, if I could just work out why they're trying to kill me..."

Natasha squeezed back. "That's alright. Oh — there's something else, too. I was trying to hack their server again last night — using a Russian proxy, thankfully —

but I couldn't get in. It's well protected now. And they detected my attempted breach. They even tried to mount a counter-attack, a surprisingly sophisticated one. It just about brought down the proxy site's firewalls, they came perilously close to breaking into my computer. Ten minutes later my hospital mobile rang — the person ringing cancelled the connection when I answered. I presume it was them but I can't even imagine how they related my internet activity to the mobile. I've gotten rid of the SIM card, destroyed the phone, and immediately deleted any computer records of that number on the Clinic server. All of that is on a different level, Nathanael, it's why I told you not to use your mobile. Whoever is involved has some pretty sophisticated stuff — government technology, or telecommunications. There won't be any more hacking going on. That avenue's closed for now."

They were silent for a while, then she said, "You know, I was watching over you for several weeks — I feel like I know you — but I realise I really don't know the first thing about you. Do you have any clue at all why they might be intent on killing you?"

He shook his head. "No. No idea at all. But I'm going to start thinking about it."

Then Natasha put her hand on his arm, almost a conciliatory gesture. "Get your things ready, Nathanael. I'm moving you again. The fact that they located my mobile phone means that they may have connected me to you. This also means that you're not safe here. And Michelle's not safe either, while we're here. I'm sure it's not hard for them to find out where Michelle lives."

"Where are we going?"

Natasha said, "We have to go somewhere where no one knows us… Somewhere they would not think to look."

Nathanael felt more than a little grumpy about the idea of moving, just when he was starting to settle in. And how could he be certain that what Natasha was saying was solid? He really couldn't, despite the fact that he found he believed her. Was she really the rock her sister said she was?

But one could never be certain. Nathanael had learned never to trust his own perceptions of people completely. One could be wrong.

He resolved to check everything, as soon as he could.

CHAPTER 4 — REQUISITIONS AND ACQUISITIONS.

While Natasha was packing some things, Nathanael starting thinking over his activities in the last six months. What could possibly have happened, that had made him a target?

Since late June he had been on long service leave. Before that he'd been teaching high school science part time, as he had done for many years.

His hobbies surely couldn't have anything to do with it could they?

Could someone in the archery club have it in for him? Had he offended anyone? It was always possible — things had a way of slipping out and he had a way of inadvertently offending people — when he put the pieces of a puzzle together much more quickly than they could.

Or the chess club? Had he beaten someone recently who resented being beaten?

Or perhaps it was something he'd posted on the climate science websites he frequented?

But this was no matter of some individual person taking offence. Whoever was after him was either part of a high-powered organisation or a very wealthy individual. His online activities to do with climate science might fit the bill, but he was just a commenter on those sites, not even one of the bloggers.

What about his gambling? That might make more sense... But he hadn't been back to the casino since they blacklisted him because he was counting cards — he had heeded their warnings.

What about Europe? Over the Christmas holidays, which last for eight weeks in Australia, he had gone to the British Museum at the request of Jannah Heldlünd, one of his old school friends. Among his oldest friends his peculiar abilities were well known — his nearly perfect photographic memory — his talent at absorbing a massive amount of information and weaning it down to accurate conclusions — so, occasionally, they would ask his assistance when intractable problems arrived of a certain sort.

His friends had all been much more successful than he had, he reflected sourly. Wherever Nathanael had worked or studied he had sparked the resentment and hatred of his colleagues because of his intelligence and his off-hand habit of being right all the time. This had not been good for his career. But his best friends, those from his high school days, all knew and valued his gifts.

In this case Jannah had asked him to come across and keep an eye on requisitions and transport because some fossils and biological material had been going missing. She had not even been able to narrow down what was missing, because their server had been hacked, by someone with fairly high-level hacking abilities, actually. All of their requisitions databases, invoicing and payment records had been deleted, along with the records of all the British Museum's acquisitions and digital archives. They had kept it quiet, of course, and there were paper backups for absolutely everything (British thoroughness) so in the long run nothing was lost. They had begun the long job of transferring the paper records of the last hundred years back into digital, but Nathanael was tasked with identifying anything that had gone missing.

He discovered that it was prehistoric human remains that were being pilfered — not just any Stone Age remains, but Cro-Magnon remains, in fact — for many of the actual specimens had not been re-labelled 'human' since the DNA sequencing had revealed that these ancient hominids were in fact completely human. What was a bit strange is that it was only Cro-Magnon remains that were going missing, not Neanderthal or any other ancient human remains.

This really had seemed very strange to Nathanael — after all, scientifically speaking they knew now that Cro-Magnon and human were identical — why make any distinction?

Well, most of the fossils that were once called Cro-Magnon were now called Early European Modern Humans.

Nathanael had done it all from the old card catalogue, which took up two whole rooms in the basement. He had read through the whole thing in a week, a superhuman task, then had kept it all in his head for the next six weeks while he watched the comings and goings and went through the rooms checking off everything against the card catalogue.

If anything in the last year bore a similar mark to these events, it was that, at least in that high level hackers were involved and there was clearly illegality involved.

But if it was the same people, why would bikers want fossils?

And why would he be a target now? Why not…? Jannah…

She knew everything about it that he did. Well, apart from the complete card catalogue, but so far as results went. A pang of concern pierced his heart, sharper than a wooden splinter.

It didn't sound good. If they were after him, they were probably after her as well.

But why?

What was it about Stone Age fossils that someone very high up was prepared to kill for?

His jaw clenched involuntarily.

He had to get onto the internet. He had to know that Jannah was okay.

He had to warn her.

Michelle and Natasha came in to his room. "I've packed enough for two weeks. Michelle is coming with us — I don't know if I can manage to lift you in and out of the car on my own."

Nathanael said, "What about your studies?"

Michelle said, "I've deferred for a term. It's early enough in the year and it won't cost Mum and Dad any extra. I could do with a holiday anyhow."

Nathanael said, "Natasha — do you think I could use the internet before we go? I'd like to check up on a friend of mine. I'm worried about her — I think some events at the start of the year might be related to my…

situation." He didn't want to be too specific — he was a little worried that he didn't really know enough about Natasha yet to tell her about Jannah, in case he was putting Jannah in more danger. Or was he being a little too conspiratorial? For God's sake, one way or another he actually was in the middle of a conspiracy of some sort. It was stupid not to be careful.

Natasha said, "Look, I've got a company mobile phone with 100 Gigabytes of data, my laptop and a tablet, so we'll just use that — we can share the mobile's internet with the other devices. It's a lot harder for them to track, whoever they are. You can do it while I drive."

With some difficulty they got Nathanael into the wheel chair and from there into the front seat of the car. As they set off, Natasha handed him the tablet. "It's sharing the mobile's connection. Whatever you do, though, don't go onto your email. If someone's tracking you that is the first thing that will tell them where you are."

"Could they really do that?" Nathanael was skeptical.

"Yes, definitely," she said. "It was some pretty high powered hacking they did yesterday. I wonder if it was a government, actually? It would make sense, they already have a back door into most machines and most mail accounts — so please don't use your email. Once they know you're accessing it, they can put a trace on the mobile IP, track the phone, and within less than five minutes they'll know exactly where we are."

"How am I going to contact my friend without using email?"

"Just... google her. Find out if she's okay that way. Newspapers. Facebook should be okay so long as you don't log in. I don't know. You work it out. Nothing where you have to log in under your own name or account."

"Alright."

Michelle got in the back. Nathanael deduced that they must have put the luggage in the trunk already. Natasha started the car.

"Natasha," said Nathanael, "Where are we actually going?"

"Vegas. Good place to hide. Plenty of people there, lots of cash floating around. I took out some money from the bank — enough to keep us going for four or five weeks at least — we can stay there unnoticed I hope… Well, so long as we avoid any networked security cameras…"

"Isn't that going to be a little difficult in Las Vegas?"

Natasha snapped, "Look, it's the best I can do! We're getting you out of Phoenix, which is quite difficult on its own Nathanael. I'm already doing more than most people would. For God's sake, I'm giving up my holidays for you. I was going to go to Paris next summer, and the extra expense of this little jaunt is probably going to put that trip into jeopardy."

His face heated up and he felt sick to the stomach. Why had he doubted Natasha?

"I'm worried about you as well," he said. "Perhaps I should head off on my own. Perhaps I should… find my own way."

Natasha rolled her eyes and scoffed, "Don't be ridiculous! For starters, there's your legs. You can't even walk on your own yet. You need the external fixators taken off." She paused briefly and looked down at him the way people look at helpless children, charity cases and no-hopers. "Look, Nathanael, I'm sorry I snapped at you. This is a very difficult situation and quite frankly I've had doubts about why I even got involved in the first place."

"Why did you?"

Natasha paused again, then she sighed. "I struggled with it, to be honest, Nathanael, but I prayed, and helping you seemed to be what God wanted me to do."

Nathanael closed his eyes and massaged his temples. That was all he needed. He was stuck with a religious nut, completely dependant on someone who put their blind faith in Something Nathanael thought about as rational as an invisible pink unicorn. Things were even worse than he thought — someone who wanted to hurt him or exploit him he could understand. But religion — he'd never had any time for it. Never had any need for a crutch.

He snickered to himself. Well, until now. Now he needed a literal crutch. Or a wheelchair, in this case.

He turned his attention to the tablet. It was an iPad, luckily — an OS he was familiar with. He went to Safari and looked up the London Museum on Google.

One of the top results was a news item, "Museum Director Dies Suddenly." He gasped, clicked on it and his heart sank.

> Friday: Jannah Heldlünd, director of the British Museum, died suddenly of a heart attack on Friday while at work.
>
> The Museum issued the following statement: "The tragic death of Jannah Heldlünd is a great loss to the British Museum and the world

of archaeology and paleontology. For fifteen years she has worked at the museum and has been Director for seven years. She has supervised a large increase in acquisitions in the last four years and will be remembered as one of the most popular Directors the Museum has ever had, both with the general public and the staff at the Museum."

Rumours that stress was the cause were discounted in the press release. "While there was a recent situation involving a cyber attack on the Museum's computer infrastructure, Jannah had the situation well in hand and was dealing with the aftermath. We await the coroner's statement as to the cause of the heart attack."

Jannah used to go to church on Sundays. Did that mean she was a Christian, like Natasha? She would know now if there really was a God. If there wasn't, then she didn't know anything, and all that talent, all that beauty of character and kindness, was gone. Buried in the ground, rotting away with her flesh.

He could see the point of faith. Believing that something in us continues after death would be comforting. But what now, though? He had to deal with real life, life as it is, not some fantasy. And right now, his life might end up being a lot shorter than it might have been. As short as Jannah's, perhaps.

He sighed involuntarily.

Michelle said, "Everything alright, Nathanael?"

He was a little annoyed with himself — he hadn't really wanted to tell Natasha and Michelle. But he supposed he had to now.

"Yes. No. I googled my friend — she was Director of the British Museum — she's dead. Sudden heart attack. They must have got to her. You might be right, my life is in danger."

Natasha said, "I'm sorry, Nathanael."

"It's alright. No, actually, it's not, really. I just... can't believe she's gone."

The kilometres of desert passed and suddenly he was weeping.

They were going past one of the blue signs that herald a rest area. Natasha pulled over. He was dimly aware of Natasha opening the car door, holding his hand. He looked up through his tears. He seemed hyper-aware of the distance, the silence, the sight of the wilderness, seen over her shoulder.

There were no trees anywhere out here — it was the typical scenery from any Arizona highway, except in the canyon — desert stretching from horizon to horizon, low shrub, small angular rocks and pebbles on the red sand, no trees and nothing else to speak of, except for a patch of Mesas on the horizon purple with distance.

Natasha said, "It's alright, Nathanael." She sounded worried. Did he seem catatonic? He knew his reactions were sometimes strange — he didn't always know how to seem normal — he wasn't normal.

He said, "I don't know how to act. I don't know what to do."

Natasha repeated, "It's alright, Nathanael. No one knows how to act at times like these. You don't have to worry. There is no right or wrong way to react to news like this."

It was almost as if she understood him. Read his thoughts. He wept again for a short while and she embraced him rather awkwardly avoiding the two broken legs, then he pulled away and looked at her. He wasn't used to getting close to anyone. And she was…

A complete stranger.

He was horrified. What did he know about her?

She might be with them. With the people who had killed Jannah. Perhaps she was taking him to a lonely place to kill him.

She was closing the door. He forced it open, pushed her away. He was still strong. He could make it. She was crying out, "What are you doing?" but he ignored her.

He jumped out of the car, onto his legs — they were stiff, sore, bent at an unnatural angle, but he could walk if he tried to. He could get away!

His legs would only work by swinging them widely to and fro like a compass' clumsy feet, as though he was some sort of bandy-legged, stiff-jointed wooden pirate. He made it for about ten steps then his left foot hit a small rock and he plummeted down and smashed into the sand. He tasted gritty sand and pebbles in his mouth. He looked back — he had only got about five metres from the car. The rods in his legs had jarred as he hit the ground and they were throbbing painfully. Was there sand in the wounds where the rods penetrated his skin? That probably wouldn't be good. They had cleaned those every day in the hospital and here he was filling them with dirt.

Natasha came over to help him up. He looked up at her with the one eye that wasn't full of sand. A perspective that made him realise how crazily dependant he was on her. "I'm sorry," he said, "I'm... really sorry."

She said, "It's alright, it's just the shock of it all." She helped him up.

How stupid he was. If she was going to kill him, she would have done it already, right here. There was no one around. She could easily have shot him and left him here to rot in the middle of nowhere.

He tried to be more help this time as she walked him back and put him in his seat. He felt like an idiot.

She sorted his legs out, then closed the car door and they started off again, almost as if nothing had happened.

He stewed over it all for a while. He really had done the wrong thing. Natasha was not his enemy — he cast his mind back to the day she had come to get him — those men were real — she really had rescued him from them.

"I'm sorry, Natasha," he said. "I wasn't thinking straight. I don't know why I ran. I panicked."

"Nathanael, you can trust me. I'm not trying to harm you, I'm trying to help you."

"Good grief," said Michelle. "Why would you possibly run away from Natasha? When she's done so much for you."

"Don't be too hard on him," cautioned Natasha. "He's just had a big shock. His friend died."

"I just feel as though... I don't know what's going on. I can't trust anyone."

Natasha said, "You're grieving — you're trying to cope as best you can. People will go back to their lives. But you have to work out how to get yours back."

Go back to his life, get it back.

To act as if Jannah's life hadn't happened. As though her death was a thing of no account.

Everyone would go back to their tasks, their routine, and after a while it would be as if she had never existed...

What was the point of it all?

"Nathanael," said Natasha, "Are you any closer to working out why they're after you?"

"I think I know what it might be about," he said. And despite his earlier misgivings, he felt comfortable with her. Maybe she really was helping him out of kindness.

Maybe it was all a big mistake, but he told her everything about the Museum, the fossils, the hacking.

She said, "Thank you. Well, I think I know more now than I did before. Than we did," she added, rather hastily.

Nathanael noted the slip, but it didn't seem important at the time.

As Natasha pulled back onto the freeway, none of them noticed the black SUV that had just then parked on the slip-road behind them. It pulled out after them.

Chapter 5 — Degas in Las Vegas

As Natasha pulled into a small motel on the way into Las Vegas, she said, "I looked up the prices on the internet and I've chosen a motel that looks comfortable and is not going to cost us the earth. I think we can keep you well hidden here, Nathanael — get you out of the car without the security cameras seeing you — there is a parking lot with bays right next to the rooms."

As she pulled up next to the office, she said, "Of course that assumes that there are no security cameras in the rooms."

But there probably were. A friend of Nathanael's, who lived on the shady side of life, had once been a driver for prostitutes. Once he had told Nathanael that all the motel rooms had cameras in them, recording everything that went on in there, ostensibly so that people who did the wrong thing could be prosecuted. But it probably provided ample opportunity for blackmailers as well. And anyone else who might be willing to pay money to find someone.

And the other question was, were the cameras connected to the internet? Could someone hack them from outside?

He felt sick to the stomach. Let's face it. Probably are. And if they are, whoever was after him had the capacity to hack the camera system. His enemies had a lot of pretty high-powered technology at their disposal. They're connected. It's not a matter of if, it's a matter of when they found him. He had better start planning for that eventuality.

Natasha came out. She had two keys. She said, "Now we'll find another room."

She pulled into the parking lot. There was another car next to them, parked outside a room.

She knocked on the door. A big man answered the door, looked about twenty five, thirty, with curly hair. He looked angry at being disturbed. Natasha said, "Sorry to disturb you. It's just that — I'd like to swap rooms if we could. I'm willing to pay you for the discomfort."

His face lightened up considerably. He said, "Alright," and took the proffered bills. A few minutes later he emerged with a suitcase and a young blonde slip of a girl, eighteen or nineteen, if that. They hurried across the courtyard to another room and went in.

Natasha got back in the car.

Nathanael said, "That was smart, Natasha. It will give us some extra time if they find us on the cameras."

"Which they will," she said, shaking her head. "I'm sure they will. But how long it will take them? — that is the question. Do we have hours or days? How much power do these people have?"

Natasha parked on the footpath so that Nathanael's door was very close to the motel door. He climbed out as well as he could. Natasha and Michelle each grabbed an arm and a leg and carried him into the motel room.

It was a very unsteady, tentative journey and they didn't get as far as the bed before Michelle, whose hands were already slipping, shouted, "Here! Put him down here!" As he bumped down onto the floor sharp pain shot through his legs.

Michelle gasped, "Oh, I'm so sorry. Are you alright?"

He bravely said, "None the worse for wear." He pushed himself up and they helped him get onto the bed.

Nathanael looked around. The decor clearly hadn't been updated since the 1970s, with the faux stone accent wall, the orange lampshade, the old fashioned door handles on the two doors, the Degas print on the wall. The 1970s carpet must have been pulled up; the floor was polished floorboards. The room smelled of cigarettes, stale beer, dust and mould.

Natasha pulled something out of her handbag.

It was a handgun.

She said, "Have you ever used one of these before?"

He shook his head. "No."

She took the cartridge out and showed him how to aim and fire, which was a little artificial without the ammunition in. Then she showed him how to put the cartridge in. "I've got a spare cartridge here," she showed him where it was in her handbag. "And a few boxes of ammunition." She pulled out a box of ammo and showed him how to refill the cartridge. "Michelle and I need to go do some shopping. You should stay here. Keep the gun by your side. I'll knock this on the door when we get back," she tapped the rhythm for 'Star Wars' on his hand. "If hear that rhythm, then it's me, and it's okay. If not, get the gun ready."

He nodded and she put the gun back in her handbag. She took out her purse and left the handbag on the bed next to him.

He dozed off after they left.

A commotion outside, shouting and swearing, woke him up.

He pulled himself off the bed and walked clumsily towards the window, his feet clunking on the polished floorboards more loudly than a rock fall. He careened across and only stopped himself from overbalancing by grabbing hold of the windowsill like someone clinging to the edge of a cliff. He looked out through a crack in the curtains.

An SUV blacker than flint was parked outside the room across the parking lot. Two large men, wearing black trousers and white t-shirts with sunglasses, one carrying a gun, were standing outside the door of the room where they would have been. The big man with curly hair opened the door and after a short interchange started swearing and cursing at them. He waved over to where Nathanael was, in his vague direction, at least.

They nodded and turned around, began walking over.

Nathanael closed the curtains and thumped along the floor, his legs clumsy stick things that he had to balance on like stilts. He was making so much noise he was certain they would know which room to come to. He swivelled around unwillingly like a compass inscribing a circle and slammed into the faux stone wall, then shoved himself across, sliding and ripping his feet along the wooden floorboards. Then as quickly as he could he opened the broom closet door, bent down and jammed himself in.

He realised as he awkwardly pulled the door closed that he didn't have the gun. It was still on the bed, in Natasha's handbag.

In the suffocating darkness he began to panic. He thought of getting out of the cupboard, going back to the bed to get it but it was too late because he could hear the two men walking up to the door already. Thankfully, they walked past. They weren't going into his room, not yet at least. Should he try and get the gun? He heard them go into a unit somewhere down the corridor, talking, walking around, it was very muffled. He heard them leave that room, close the door behind themselves. Nathanael froze where he was. His heart pounded and he felt as though he was choking. He tried to get up. For some reason he couldn't manage it. They were closer now. He heard them using a key — did they have some sort of master key? No, they weren't opening his door, they were unlocking the door of the unit next to his, he could hear them traipsing in there, opening a door, then traipsing out. They were coming. Nathanael was pushing himself up using the shelving but was getting nowhere. What was wrong? Why couldn't he move his leg? Maybe he had hurt his spine with that ridiculous careening stumble across the floor.

They were unlocking his door. He could hear them, he could almost see everything they were doing from the sound. It was like being back in the hospital bed, listening, only hearing things, not seeing them. They had opened the door. They were looking in, looking around. He heard them talking softly.

One said in what sounded to Nathanael like an East End of London accent, "Well if they're not here perhaps they've gone somewhere."

The other spoke in a Southern accent. Arkansas? Texas? Nathanael didn't know his American accents well enough to tell. "They'll be back soon enough. Let's wait it out here in this room, out of sight from the parking lot. If the women get here first, shoot them. They're expendable. Easy enough to pin it on Nathanael anyhow."

Nathanael started to hyperventilate. He had to do something — he had to get back to the gun — he tried even harder to get up. He really couldn't move. But he could still feel his legs. He wasn't paralysed.

What was wrong?

His leg was stuck, he'd got it under the shelving the wrong way about. He tried moving it but it really was stuck.

That's the problem with external fixators — you don't have a sense of proprioperception about them.

He almost laughed. At least he wasn't paralysed. That was one positive.

It was so pointless — Natasha and Michelle were going to die because of something so stupid — getting his leg stuck in the shelving of the cupboard.

And to think they believed in God. What a joke.

Then he started shaking with rage. He prayed, for the first time in his life, silently, an angry prayer. "If you really are there, couldn't you help them by getting me out? I understand if you don't give a toss about me, but they're both good people. Really good people. They don't deserve to die."

He pulled his leg slightly and felt something large and cold next to his leg. That was what was stopping him from moving.

He leaned forward in the darkness and moved his fingers along the large, cold object and realised what it was. A tool chest. As quietly as he could he undid the latch. The first thing he put his hand on was a pair of pliers.

The thought that came to him seemed at once devastatingly stupid and temptingly brilliant. But the fact was, if he could just move his knees a little he was confident that he could make his way around at least a little better, maybe get out. At the moment his knees were fixed at an angle of about one hundred and sixty degrees, a most uncomfortable angle for walking.

It was what was stopping him from being able to get out. Without opening the door or bending his knees he couldn't get that leg out from where it was stuck.

How atrophied would the muscles be by now, anyway? His legs did look skinny, but he had been fairly fit before the accident, a bike rider, went to the gym twice a week, had muscular legs, surely the muscles hadn't atrophied that much? How many weeks had it been? He wasn't even sure.

He bent over in the darkness and felt his way down his right leg to the large screw that protruded from the bone. He tried to turn it gently, thinking the whole device might be able to be removed this way, but the screw didn't move and he could feel the turning motion moving the whole splint (if that was what it was called); the piece of carbon fibre that held the whole thing together.

Instead he looked for the device that held the splint onto the giant screw.

Righty tighty, left loosy. It came loose quite easily.

One by one he removed the smaller bolts that held the splints in place. The entire splint slipped off easily once he had done this. Then he took the pliers and began to remove the first giant screw from his leg.

Unlike the splint, this was agonisingly slow work. How do they do it in the hospital? Do they use some sort of power tool, a drill or something? Luckily it didn't hurt as much as he thought it would, although his skin had become slightly inflamed around the edges of the screws and so the wounds themselves were a little painful, but he didn't feel any pain in the bone, just a peculiar uncomfortable pulling feeling as the screws came loose.

He started on the other leg. Despite the darkness he was much quicker the second time. He had removed the splint and was just about to start on the first screw when he heard East End saying, "What was that?"

Nathanael stopped, completely still. He had almost forgotten they were there.

"What?" said the Southerner.

"That sound. It sounded like… someone unscrewing a screw or something."

"It's just rats in the cupboard. Keep your eye on the door."

"Rats don't use tools. They're just animals, Kade."

"Well… Could be someone in another room I guess."

"It could be… I s'pose." He sounded doubtful, but he seemed to have accepted the answer.

Nathanael relaxed for a moment but he didn't start unscrewing the screw just yet. He needed to rethink his plan.

Then he heard East End's footsteps walking towards him.

Nathanael reached into the the toolbox, felt around and found a large monkey wrench. He picked it up as the footsteps came closer and began pulling himself up slowly.

The footsteps went past him and another door opened.

East End's voice echoed — he must be in the ensuite, the bathroom, as the Americans called it. "Something definitely creaked — but there aint no one in here. Can't hear that screwing sound any more neither."

Kade, the Southerner, said, in the room, "You've got rocks in your head. They stopped working, didn't they?"

East End scoffed. "Right then? Right when I commented on it? That seems like too much of a coincidence, don't it? I mean, just when I say something, the person in the room next door stops screwing up whatever they're screwing up?"

"You're screwed up. Are you stoned again? I thought we'd put a stop to that. We should keep watching the door. What if that girl gets here? What if she's got a gun?"

"I know now. It wasn't in the toilet. It was over here."

East End's footsteps came closer.

Kade said, "Your brain is an empty cavern. I'm surprised you can't hear your own thoughts echoing in there, bouncing back off the rocks, hello, hello, hello! You smoke too much weed. There's no one in the cupboard. You're a rock-brained stoner."

East End said, "Well wouldn't hurt to check, would it? That guy with the broken legs could be sittin' in there with a gun, ready to pop one in each of us when we're not looking."

"You're just paranoid. Typical stoner. You got stoned one too many times, now you're permanently petrified." Kade was quiet for a moment, then he sighed. "Look in the stupid cupboard if you have to."

The door opened and light flooded in. Nathanael tossed the monkey wrench at East End's head and then kicked at his crotch with his left leg, that's the one that still had screws sticking out of it. A gun went off and Nathanael heard the bullet thud into the shelf behind him.

East End stumbled backwards, screaming in a high, girly voice, holding onto his crotch with both hands. Nathanael looked down and saw East End's black trousers staining blacker around the crotch, then he looked further down and saw the gun, sliding on the polished floor boards towards him.

Unthinkingly Nathanael bent down, grabbed the gun, then his left knee gave way and he stumbled and fell over. A loud report shattered the air and a bullet thudded into the faux rock wall. Nathanael rolled over, lifted the gun and shot at Kade.

East End was still giving forth a high, feminine wail, like some sort of banshee, backing towards the doorway.

Kade didn't seem as fazed, somehow, though. He snarled at Nathanael and took aim. Nathanael already had his gun up. Natasha said you aim for the body mass. He squeezed the trigger once, twice, and Kade's arm flung backwards, the shots went wild, more thumping into the faux rock wall, one after the other. Nathanael shot again and Kade stumbled backwards, not even screaming, groaning slightly but Nathanael could see he still had his wits about him. Nathanael rolled towards the bed, the screws bumping painfully on the floor as he did so. Shots ripped the waterbed to shreds, Nathanael was crouching behind it. The water spewed out over the floor and East End slipped in the puddle, which rapidly began turning dark red on the pale brown floorboards. Nathanael shot at Kade again, but Kade slipped on the wet floor and Nathanael's shot went wide. From his point of view on the floor about a foot from the bed Nathanael could see bits of fluff, a flak jacket maybe, poking out from Kade's shirt — that's why Kade didn't seem too fazed even though Nathanael had shot him at least three times in the torso.

Kade grabbed East End's arm and pulled him away.

Kade cursed, "You rock-brained stoner. Getting yourself shot." Then Kade paused, felt himself beneath the left shoulder and swore. "He grazed me too. Amateur. Beginner's luck. That hurts."

Nathanael heard them stumbling out through the door. Police sirens sounded somewhere in the distance. Nathanael lifted his head up above the bed, to see Kade and East End collapsing into the black SUV. East End was screaming something about, "You didn't tell me the Wolverine might attack us."

Kade said, "What are you blabbering about?"

East End was wailing hysterically, "He slashed me in the balls with metal bits that came out of his leg! What would you call it?" East End swore coldly and slumped, could barely drag his legs into his seat, he was definitely the worse for wear. East End was still pulling his legs in as the SUV screeched out of the exit, then the car door thumped shut as they pulled onto the road.

Nathanael looked down at himself. He was still in one piece. The holes in his right leg where he had removed the screws were weeping slightly, and the remaining screws in his left leg were stained black with East End's blood. He quickly found some tissues and wet them and wiped the man's blood off, anxious not to catch whatever diseases East End might have. Then he went back to the cupboard and found the pliers and began removing the other screws.

Just as he was taking off the last one Natasha walked in carrying two shopping bags.

Looking at the mess in the room she said, "You've been busy. Decided to do a bit of renovation did you?"

Nathanael got up, a little shakily, but his knees seemed to work fine.

Michelle walked in after her, and her eyes went wide when she saw Nathanael's legs.

Michelle and Natasha said together, "Oh my God…" "How did you do that?" "You took that thing off yourself."

And Michelle said, "You look terrible."

Nathanael looked down at himself. He didn't think he was that bad. A few weeping wounds on his left leg, dirty T-shirt, some tears and rips in his hospital gown. But he was still in one piece. He said proudly, "Yeah, a little worse for wear. But you should see the other guys."

Then Natasha said, "You are tall, though, aren't you? It's what I thought. Six foot at least. A bit hard to tell when you're laid up."

Michelle nodded. "He is tall. That's true."

Natasha glanced around at the bullet holes in the faux rock wall, the puddle of dark blood on the floor and said, "What happened?"

Nathanael explained, "They found us quicker than I thought they would. They were waiting here — talking about killing you both when you got here. An East End of London guy and an American Southerner called Kade. I think we should leave."

They got Nathanael into the car quickly and Natasha went back for a few seconds and retrieved her handbag. A few minutes later they were already on the road. A police car with its siren blaring came screaming around the corner and screeched past them into the motel parking lot.

Chapter 6 — Layers within layers.

Nathanael told Natasha and Michelle everything that had happened.

Natasha swore and said, "I can't believe I got involved in this. I'm so stupid. I don't know why I got involved in it."

Michelle said, "I don't know why you got me involved, either."

Natasha said, "Neither do I. I'm really sorry, Michelle."

Nathanael said, "No, I'm sorry. Drop me off somewhere. Get rid of me. It's no good either of you getting killed over me. I'm just not worth it."

Natasha took her left hand off the steering wheel and absently scratched her cheek. "But what is it all about? Why Cro-Magnon fossils, for goodness' sake? Maybe there's some sort of government involvement — they found us so quickly! Damn. I could drop you off, but I want to know what's going on. It's all so peculiar, none of it makes sense."

Nathanael said, "Someone is trying to hide something. Something that I know, even if I don't know that I know it. The question is, what is it?"

Natasha considered that for a moment. Then she turned the wheel of the car and they went off the highway.

She said, "I've got to do some hacking. The computer is the key. But first of all — we need a place where you can get changed, Nathanael. I can't take you into the public library looking like that."

"But I don't have any other clothes. And it's Saturday, isn't it?" He wasn't quite used to working out what day it was yet, but he seemed to remember someone yesterday saying it was Friday.

Natasha said, "Yes you do have clothes. We got you some. And the libraries here are all open on Saturday."

They found some public toilets. Two minutes later Nathanael walked out wearing jeans, t-shirt, a pair of boots.

He said, "You did a good job of guessing my size."

Natasha said, "I guess it's a female thing."

And a few minutes after that they were outside a large library building.

"Clark County Library," said Natasha. "Best public computer facilities in the whole state — this is a model facility. Come on, let's hack the British Museum."

She found a secluded corral, in the corner of the library.

Nathanael and Michelle sat on seats behind her.

Natasha put a usb into the computer. "Trojan," she said. "This handy little program will hide what I'm doing from the library administration system. Makes it look as though I'm on Facebook. Let's rock!"

In a few minutes she had found the British Museum site. A few minutes after that, she was logged in.

"Password 1," she said, "Most common password." She smiled. "Misspent youth. I had a few friends, when

I was at college. We got into everything. Used to read all the hacker bulletin boards, online discussions, we did everything, we were phishers and phone phreakers and hackers and crackers, we made worms and trojans, you name it, we did it. It was great fun."

Nathanael leaned over and clicked a menu item.

The British Museum catalogue filled the screen.

"Yes that's it. I thought it had been completely destroyed, no backups. They must have recovered it from a disk archive. But when?"

Natasha said, "Sit here. You do it."

Nathanael typed in a catalogue number.

A Chinese vase came up on the screen.

Nathanael said, "This one was acquired when I was there. Look at the catalogue number. It contains a date, 2016, marking when this item was added to the catalogue:"

2016,0524.994

"But you see, when you look further down the list, this vase was actually acquired in 2015, when I was there. I remember this because it was on a special list of new acquisitions to be put into the database when they rebuilt it. It's an anomaly, Natasha."

For a few minutes he went through the database, searching for old items and new ones.

He searched for several more Chinese vases and a few other recent acquisitions.

For anything earlier than 2015 the acquisition date matched the catalogue number. But for items that Nathanael knew were acquired in December of 2015, the catalogue number did not match the date of acquisition, but was 2016 instead.

He said, "I understand now. The database must have been a backup from November 2015. When the December acquisitions were added it was already 2016, so that was the date they ended up with on the catalogue number. Now, for the missing Cro-Magnon items."

He searched, 'Cro-Magnon.'

Three items came up; an end-scraper and two flint blades. The images were missing.

"Well, that's interesting."

"Why?" asked Natasha.

Nathanael shook his head. "Because in the card catalogue, there was a lot of European Early Modern Human remains listed as Cro-Magnon. I can even remember the catalogue numbers."

He typed in two or three catalogue numbers. None of them gave a result.

Natasha leaned forwards, looking over his shoulder. "Well... Maybe you haven't memorised the catalogue numbers correctly?"

Nathanael said, "The Cro-Magnon ones, yes I have, I was using those. And some of the others — the more interesting numerically."

She scoffed, "You can't remember the numbers, that's the simplest explanation. Occam's Razor."

He said, "Ostracon", typed in 1987,0227.144, and a piece of pottery came up on the screen with a large greek letter 'B' on it, labelled, 'Ostracon.'

"What's interesting about that number?"

"Oh, just the duplication of the 7, the 2, and the 4, and the fact that 227 is a prime and 144 is 12 squared. And 1987 is a prime."

"Oh, very interesting," said Natasha sarcastically.

He said, "Amulet" and typed in EA7337. A Sumerian Amulet showed up.

"Well I can see what's interesting about that — two 7s and two 3s."

"Yes, and 73 is 37 reversed, both are primes, 73 is the 21st prime, 37 the 12th prime. 73 was actually Sheldon Cooper's favourite number in Big Bang Theory. And A is the 1st letter of Amulet and E is the 2nd last."

"I see now," said Natasha, her voice still dripping with sarcasm.

He said, "Tobacco pipe," then typed in, Oc1919,.261, and a tobacco pipe appeared on the screen.

Nathanael said, "261 is interesting because it's boring. It's notorious in mathematics for being the lowest number not to have its own Wikipedia page. Also the factors of 1919 are 19 and 101, which is kind of neat. And Oct means eight, but is the tenth month."

Natasha waved dismissively, "Alright, alright I believe you. Try some more Cro-Magnon samples, then."

He typed five or six more numbers in. None of them gave any result.

He said, "That's very interesting. They're simply not there. Last December these remains were all listed as palaeolithic human remains, but in the description on the card catalogue they were listed as Cro-Magnon — in the electronic search Cro-Magnon should give a result, if it was simply copied from the card catalogue, as everything else was. But even if that doesn't bring up the result the catalogue numbers should. Clearly someone has changed the database — even though it was re-installed from a backup made in November 2015. All of the Cro-Magnon samples were 1980s, 1990s acquisitions, some earlier, but on the paper cards they were all marked as having been transferred to the computer catalogue. But they're gone."

Natasha said, "Why were they not listed as Cro-Magnon in the title, but only in the description?"

"It was actually in 2003 that the first mitochondrial DNA tests began to reveal that Cro-Magnons were actually fully human, a conclusion that was fully accepted by mainstream palaeontology by 2011 after further tests. This is why scientists prefer to call them European Early Modern Humans now, or upper palaeolithic, or just Early Modern Humans. I think they simply went through and changed all the titles, to upper palaeolithic or Early Modern Human after they had discovered that Cro-Magnon mitochondrial DNA is human."

Natasha said, "So what is mitochondrial DNA?" She sounded confused.

Nathanael said, "It's the DNA from the mother's line. It's… easier to recover from old bones than conventional DNA, because there is more redundancy in the copying, apparently. At least, that is how I understand it."

Natasha said, "Perhaps someone changed the catalogue numbers? The items might still be there."

Nathanael tried a few more searches, EEMH, European Early Modern Humans, Palaeolithic, Upper Palaeolithic, European Upper Palaeolithic, Human, Hominid, and came up with nothing for any of them.

Nathanael scratched the three-day growth that had been sprouting on his chin. Obviously they had been shaving him in the hospital; he had never even noticed. Now he was beginning to look like a tramp.

He said, "Well. It would appear those Cro-Magnon remains have totally disappeared from the database. As if they never existed. As though the museum never even owned these items. You know, when I was there, it was only five or six Cro-Magnon skulls and bones that had disappeared, and Jannah was always very careful to detail everything. Now, all the Cro-Magnon items have gone, with nothing about them ever having existed in the database. I guess the question is, who took them, where did they take them and why? And why have they tried to hide it?"

Natasha said, "I wonder if there are other museums that have lost their Cro-Magnon remains? Or other scientists or administrators who have died?"

Nathanael search for hominid and early homo sapiens fossils.

The first thing he noticed was that the Wikipedia page was different from the last time he had seen it. "When I was researching the problem in the British Museum, I looked at this Wikipedia page quite a few times. Some of the fossils are missing from this list." He was quiet for a while as he visualised the list of Cro-Magnon fossils. "It is, of course, the Cro-Magnon fossils that are missing... I'm going to do a search for Cro-Magnon fossils in the other institutions where they are stored..."

"Wait," said Natasha. She clicked to the edit history and shook her head. There was no sign of the fossils Nathanael was talking about, even there. "My God. To be able to change the Wikipedia page's edit history. That really is a pretty long reach they have, whoever they are."

Nathanael did his search. The Smithsonian, the Museo de la Evolución Humana in Burgo in Spain, the National Museum of Natural Science in Taiwan, the Heosphoros Foundation in Washington DC, the Anthropology

Museum at Tokyo University, the Australian Museum in Sydney, Direction Nationale de N'Djamena at the BEAC bank in Chad, the National Museum of Ethiopia and the Kenya National Museum.

A few places still had Cro-Magnon fossils on their websites. But for most of the places that had museum catalogues online, Nathanael found that the Cro-Magnon fossils were missing from the catalogues.

Nathanael shook his head. "This is very serious. It seems unlikely that anyone could hack the Wikipedia page, unless they've gotten rid of or silenced quite a few palaeontologists as well... Very strange. I'm looking up paleoanthropologists who specialise in EEMH fossils."

He typed in 'Doctor Piers Enderen,' and a report in the Guardian about his tragic death appeared. Nathanael shook his head. "He was one of the world experts in Palaeolithic DNA." He typed in, 'Professor Harrison Smith', and a news release from Yale came up, about his early retirement. "An expert in Palaeolithic bone structure — he was a maverick, claimed the Cro-Magnon definition was still important." He typed in, "Dr Milton F. Dryford". He was apparently still on staff at the Heosphoros Foundation in Washington DC, but there were news items in the Washington Post and some of the journals saying, "Milton Dryford withdraws from charity board membership," "Milton F. Dryford not attending the Champagne Social," "Milton Dryford to cease public appearances for a time, cites ill health." He typed in, 'Dr Andy Hawker', and a page from the Australian newspaper came up, lamenting the disappearance of the famous expert in Paleoanthropology and Archaeomagnetism. He typed in, 'Lazarus-Fox' and a news release came up again, early retirement. He typed in four or five more names. Early retirement, missing, dead prematurely, tragic demise.

Natasha gave an audible gasp. "I really thought you might have been imagining it. But there it is. That's very disturbing, Nathanael. Why hasn't this been in the news?" She was silent for a long while, then said, "We've got to go to London. We're going to need false identities, I'm going to have to get on the Dark Web. Right now. We need an open wireless connection so I can set this up."

Nathanael wasn't sure about going to London. He wanted to stall for time. "Um… Why can't you do it here, or on the mobile network?"

"If we use the library internet connection, or the mobile's internet for the Dark Web it's like lighting a beacon for the government saying, 'here I am, come get me.' There'll be cameras in here, you can be sure."

Michelle was quite distressed. "Why do we have to be involved? We can finish now can't we? We can go home?"

Nathanael nodded. "I agree."

Michelle seemed to change her mind. "I think you're both exaggerating — the government can't be involved. It's just one of your silly conspiracy theories. You're always going on about the NSA and all that." And she added in a smaller voice, "You're starting to scare me."

Natasha replied, "Why do you think it's always computer programmers who are paranoid about the NSA? We're the ones who know what they can do. And how do you think those men found the motel we stopped at so quickly? Only the government has the technology to do that."

Nathanael shook his head. "They could conceivably have worked out who you were, worked out where your sister lived and then gone there, waited till two or three people left in a car, and followed us."

Natasha said, "Yeah, but the only way they could have known who I was, was by hacking the hospital phone system."

Nathanael said, "Okay, okay. You're right about that. I have to admit that you must be right — government involvement — or some rich individuals on an international level — with some pretty hefty hacking at their disposal — who else could coordinate such a massive heist from the museum systems? And make all these people disappear or retire under mysterious circumstances? But I'm not completely convinced that the whole government is involved in persecuting us personally, Natasha. The precautionary principle might say we should assume they are, but… I'm just saying perhaps we ought to just go into hiding for a little while, assume they'll forget about us. What Michelle was saying."

Natasha's eyes flared, "We'd have to get totally off the grid, Nathanael! You don't seem to understand what they can do these days. How many ways they have of tracking us. Do you realise the government turns every call on every mobile in the country into text and stores it in a massive server in Utah?"

"Really?"

"Yes," said Natasha, "And that's just the start of it. People tend to think the internet is private. I'm telling you, the NSA has a back door into every major Operating System, piece of hardware, email server. There's no way of escaping their prying eyes. And that also means any security camera that is attached to the internet is vulnerable to their searches. Encryption really is useless if they can get into the computer at the end of the encryption process and view the unencrypted files. And they have facial recognition software they can use on all those hacked security cameras, though I can't believe it's always 100% accurate, it probably only takes small changes to fool it. It's probably useless to go into hiding unless you're going to completely give any hope of living the life you had before away. No, we have to go on the offensive. We have to find out what is happening and publicise it — turn what they're doing against them."

Nathanael nodded, but he wasn't really listening. "Well, we could go into the desert, maybe. Live somewhere far away from everything. Get off the grid in that way. It's probably the wise thing to do. "

Natasha looked at him. "I can't believe you're saying this. After I risked my life to rescue you. Now, we find out all these people have disappeared or died or been forced into retirement. Something is happening, Nathanael, and you're already part of it. I risked my life for you. The least you should be willing to do is risk your life to find out what's happening."

Nathanael said, "Yeh, I guess you're right. I can see your logic. It's a bit perverse but it makes a certain amount of sense. You risked your life for me so I should be willing to risk my life for others. A philosophical thing. Pass it forward." He was silent for a moment. "And I suppose there's Jannah. She was a good person, a dedicated scholar, a good friend. She didn't deserve to die. I investigated her little problem — the disappearing artefacts — but now, I'm looking for the reason of her untimely death. And I suppose it's probably the only chance we've got of getting our lives back. Sorry, I was being selfish I guess. Alright. Get on the dark net, get us some tickets to London — but why can't we do that here?"

Natasha scoffed, "We can't do it here, they'll have cameras. I told you, it's like lightning a beacon."

Ten minutes later they were driving through a leafy part of Las Vegas. She was driving along looking for something. "They're not that common these days," she said, pulling into a parking lot underneath some overhanging branches, a dark little space in the middle of the crowded city.

"What?" said Nathanael.

"Open wireless networks. Look — see that symbol?" There was a symbol, like a robot with radio waves above it, on the wall of a nearby building, "It means there is an open wireless network here. They're often run by town councils, or sometimes nosy individuals who want to pry into what people are looking at. I'm going to surf the dark web on it though — totally encrypted — no one will be able to see what we're doing."

She took the laptop from him and opened a piece of software. "This is Tor," she said. "It's a program that enables me to surf the dark web, to unpeel the layers of the onion. Darknet websites are completely encrypted and anonymous — to a degree. But the very fact that you are using Tor probably alerts the authorities to the fact that you're looking for something illicit — every security camera in Las Vegas will be looking for us. But it looks as though we're reasonably hidden here."

They looked around for security cameras, but couldn't see any.

She looked a little queasy.

"What's wrong?" said Nathanael.

"Well, I haven't done anything… like this… anything illegal… since I was in college. Since I became a Christian."

Nathanael rolled his eyes. "I don't think it's wrong if you need to protect yourself. And me."

She looked at him. "You're right. On principle I could perhaps allow myself to get captured, for the sake of truth. But it would be wrong to allow you to be captured as well, since I took you under my protection, by rescuing you from the hospital."

What a strange girl, Nathanael thought. What a strange way of seeing things.

"Well, I have to do it then," said Natasha. "First I'm going to find some fake some identity documents for us." Then she stopped fiddling on her laptop and looked at her sister. "Wait — Michelle. I don't think you should come. I think you need to… rent your house out. Go and stay with Uncle Clifford, or Mum and Dad. Get right out of this whole business."

Michelle burst into tears, and that really was the last thing Nathanael expected, he found himself coughing nervously.

Natasha said, "Well, you can come if you really want to."

Once she had calmed down a little, Michelle said, "I don't want to. I really don't. I'm not really strong enough to do this, Natasha. It really freaked me out, seeing the blood on the floor in the motel room. I've been meaning to say something."

Natasha said, "I thought you'd been a bit quiet in the last hour or two."

Michelle hung her head. "I'm sorry. I'm not good enough. I just don't have enough strength to stand by you."

Natasha gave her a hug. "You're only twenty one, Michelle, you haven't even finished college. For goodness' sake, I got involved in this knowing it was dangerous. I went into it with my eyes open. If something happens to me, well, I can live with that. You came in as an... afterthought — I didn't think it would go this far — I don't mean I didn't want you helping but, God knows, I just couldn't live with myself if something happened to you on my account. Or Nathanael's."

"Or mine," said Nathanael synchronously, "I couldn't live with myself either, if something happened to either of you on my account."

Natasha glared at him. "I chose to help you, Nathanael. Please don't."

Michelle clung sobbing to Natasha's shoulder for a while, then disentangled herself and found a tissue in her handbag and dabbed at her eyes.

Then Michelle said, "Do you really think I should sell my house? I only just bought it. They know where I live."

Natasha took Michelle's hand in hers. "Just rent it out for a little while. Uncle Clifford won't mind if you stay in his spare room for a few weeks. Neither will Mum and Dad. Whoever these people are, we don't want to make things easy for them. I think you'll be safer out of your house though for a little while. Get a real estate agent to rent it out for you, maybe for three months. By then at least we'll know where it's at."

Michelle seemed a little happier. "How am I going to get home, then?"

Natasha said, "We'll buy you a ticket on a coach. Under a false name. Get Mum and Dad to pick you up when you get there. Just… stay away from your house for a little while. I don't know, I don't think they'll target you anyway. They'll probably think you don't know anything. But… I think they might have been watching your place, as Nathanael says, that would be the simplest explanation for them finding us so quickly."

Natasha got back on the computer and began booking tickets, organising false IDs.

Two hours later, Michelle was on a coach heading home and Nathanael and Natasha were driving to an apartment block in downtown Las Vegas. The whole place stank of urine. They picked up their false IDs from an overweight, pimpled teenager who sniffled constantly and had needle bruises in his arms and the sunken eyes of a drug addict. Then Natasha said, "Right — now we go shopping, Nathanael. We need clothes for you, a few possessions, and a suitcase. Won't look right if you arrive in London with nothing."

"Yes," said Nathanael mournfully. "All my stuff is back at the hospital."

Three hours after that, Natasha and Nathanael had gone through airport security under different names and were sitting in an airbus A380 on the midnight run from Los Angeles to London, sleeping while the inflight movie ran.

Michelle's coach reached the coach terminal in Phoenix. When she got out, she realised her mobile phone was out of battery. She walked around some nearby shops until she found a pay phone.

She rang her Mum's mobile number.

"Mum?"

"Oh, hello, Michelle."

"I need you to pick me up. I'm at the coach terminal."

"Alright, my dear. Listen, your father and I are doing the shopping. We'll be able to be there in about twenty five minutes. Do you mind keeping yourself busy until we can get there?"

"No problem, Mum. Listen… I'll ring you again in half and hour and tell you where to meet me."

"Alright, my darling."

Michelle put the phone down. Oh, that was really stupid. Now, if the bad guys were listening in, they would know that she was going to be near the pay phone.

Would they even know that?

She went to a local newsagent and starting looking idly through magazines, trying to reassure herself that they wouldn't possibly be able to tell if she had rung from a pay phone. Would they? Unless it made a distinctive sound… Or maybe they could see the connections, if they had a way into the phone company… Which they would, if the phone company system uses any of the common operating systems… Which it probably would…

She shook the thoughts out of her head. "I'm starting to sound like Natasha," she mumbled to herself. "All paranoid."

Twenty five minutes later, Michelle went back to the pay phone and rang her Mum's mobile again.

"We're here, Michelle. We're waiting in the main carpark. We were a little worried, actually, the man at the kiosk said that there was no Michelle Chase listed on the manifest. We thought you might not have arrived, that something might have happened to the coach, but he assured us they have all come in on time."

"Mum, do you see the shopping centre across the road? I'll meet you just outside the burger joint."

"Alright, my dear."

Michelle put the phone down then glanced around nervously. It wasn't that anyone in particular was looking at her. It was that... she simply had that peculiar feeling that she was being watched.

It was then that she him. A man in a cafe, peering over his newspaper at her. As soon as she looked directly at him he looked away. A guilty look — discovered.

Her Mum and Dad rolled up in their four wheel drive; her Mum was driving. Michelle got in quickly, and then glanced back at the cafe.

The man was gone.

"Mum," she said, "Just... take a circuitous route. Somewhere with enough straight roads to tell if someone is following us..."

Her mother looked at her strangely. "What are you and Natasha involved in? And why has Natasha taken her holidays early? Something's going on, isn't it. I think you had better tell me and your father exactly what's going on."

Michelle stammered, "Alright... I'll tell you... but not now... please do what I'm asking you."

Her mother rolled her eyes. "Alright my dear. But you remember — you've promised me now — you need to deliver on that promise..."

Michelle had a sudden brain wave. Telling her mother what she wanted to hear might well be a way to keep away from the facts that her mother probably wouldn't want to have heard, not once they were keeping her awake every night worrying about Natasha. Well, a half truth was better than no truth.

"Mother... Natasha has met someone. He's a nice enough fellow, but... he was mixed up in some stuff beforehand..."

"Old girlfriend...? Ex-wife? A bit of a psycho?"

Natasha had had problems before with an ex-boyfriend who wouldn't leave her alone — so her mother's conclusion didn't seem completely out of the ballpark of possibilities.

"Yes... Something a bit like that, but not exactly like that. Well, it is... um... previous events that are impacting on their relationship... A bit of past conflict. Someone... A man... surveilling him."

"An old boyfriend?"

"Well, it involves men, anyhow. Look, Mother, I think it's better if Natasha tells you herself, don't you?"

Her mother shook her head. "My, my, but people are open minded these days. It's a wonder their brains don't fall out."

Her father simply tut-tutted, and that was the end of that conversation.

CHAPTER 7 — ONTOLOGY AND

PALAEONTOLOGY.

The fake passports seemed to pass the scrutiny of British Customs and soon they were in a London taxi cab driving towards a small hotel in Clerkenwell that Natasha had once stayed in before. She told Nathanael, "It's a bit expensive, but it is close to the Museum."

Once they had stored their luggage in their rooms they both slept until mid-morning on the following day. After a quick cup of coffee they were soon in a taxi cab, headed for the British Museum.

Natasha said, "You do the talking when we get there. You know the people."

About half-way there, Nathanael said to the cab driver, "Stop here."

Natasha said, "Why? We're not at the museum yet."

Nathanael said, "Well, you're always talking about lighting beacons and so forth. If we turn up at the steps in front of the British Museum, won't they immediately know we're here in London? And it just so happens that I know someone who lives a few blocks from the museum, who might be able to give us all the gossip. Come on!"

He leapt out of the cab, then stumbled on the pavement. Natasha jumped out and helped him.

"Damn that accident," he said. "My knees are not used to doing things yet." Once he had his balance again, Nathanael walked up to a large house which had been converted into an apartment block and rang the doorbell. Natasha followed him after paying the cab driver.

The day porter opened the door and Natasha said, "Thanks." He let them into the entrance hall, saying, "Oh, hello Mister Wayfarer. Yes, he's in, I'm sure he'd be pleased to see you. He always enjoyed your chats, last December. And I see you've brought an American friend." His nostrils seemed to flare slightly as he looked at Natasha, as though he disapproved of her, but he said, "I'm sure the Professor won't mind." He picked up the phone and said, "Professor. Mister Wayfarer is here to see you… Certainly, right away…"

Natasha followed Nathanael into a small lift, and soon they were knocking at the door of an apartment.

A man in his late seventies answered the door. He was wearing a tweed suit of the sort that was popular in the fifties and early sixties, and his balding hair was dishevelled. He carried a pipe, which was trailing smoke. "Nathanael, my boy! Come in, come in. I thought you'd finished all that research and gone home — and here you are, what a nice surprise! My, you are looking slim. And you have a friend with you. Do introduce me."

He embraced Nathanael and they walked in.

Nathanael said, "This is Natasha. She's a good friend of mine. Saved my life, actually, literally. Natasha, this is Professor Featherington."

The Professor said, "Call me Bruce. Everybody does. Hello, Natasha, pleased to meet you. I've told Nathanael plenty of times he needs saving."

The reception room was filled with old books, mostly in bookcases, some in piles on the floor, which extended down the hallway and into the other rooms. On seeing a rather large pile of newspapers next to the coffee table Nathanael said, "Bruce, I thought I'd got you out of the habit of saving the newspapers. This place was in such a mess when I arrived. Piles of newspapers, magazines, journals everywhere."

Bruce said, "Well, you never know when you might need to look something up, you know. I don't like to throw anything out. A bit of a hoarder, I admit, but you know, there are worse faults, aren't there?"

Nathanael eyed the pile. "I'll take them down to the recycling bin for you afterwards, alright?"

Bruce nodded, "Alright. Just sit there — I'll go and get you both a cup of tea. Milk? Sugar? Earl grey? English breakfast?"

"A coffee would be fine," said Nathanael. "You still have the coffee don't you?"

"Yes I — I do."

"...white with one sugar for me, black with no sugar for Natasha."

Bruce brought out the coffees a few minutes later on a tray with a cup of tea for himself, and some cucumber sandwiches. "Coffee. Blasted disgusting stuff. I ask you — what good ever came of Columbus' attempt to circumnavigate the globe? Coffee, tomatoes, and television, ultimately. Can't stand any of 'em meself."

"He's lying," said Nathanael. "He used to watch Neighbours."

"Well apart from that one. Ramsay Street did exercise a certain palaeolithic appeal I must admit."

Nathanael mused rather mournfully, "Palaeolithic…"

Bruce's expression turned serious. "So you heard what happened to Jannah?"

Nathanael nodded, afraid his voice would break if he spoke.

Bruce said, "A terrible, terrible loss. She was one of the few in the leadership team worth talking to. She always made time for me, you know. Told me everything about your battle to discover the apparent reason for the hack of the museum system — and she told me when you discovered that it was the old Cro-Magnon samples were disappearing."

"I didn't know that," said Nathanael, although he had known it — he didn't like to steal Bruce's thunder when he was in the middle of a story. He was a nice old bird.

Bruce continued, "Yes, all the way along. I never really talked to you about it — felt like I might be intruding — you had enough on your plate — I was happy just to have those cups of tea with you and her once in a while. But after you left, Jannah also shared with me her happiness when the back-up hard drive was discovered. It was one they had recently replaced, but the actual contents were still secure — it was the power supply, supposedly, not the drive itself that'd gone bung. And do you know, she also confided in me recently, just before she died…"

Nathanael's eyebrows raised. "Really?"

Bruce brushed a stray strand of white hair from his eyes. "About a month ago, she dropped in three or four times. She told me that there were still problems with Cro-Magnon samples disappearing and that they had hacked the database again but this time it was more subtle. The last time she dropped in I have to say she was very stressed and upset, muddled, rambling all the time. Her utterances were completely cryptic — she kept using the word, historicity, and when I asked her, in what context, she mumbled something about clay tablets, the Sumerians, the tower of Babel and Genesis and some organisation called the Lucifer Institute. And the antediluvian age of the patriarchs."

Natasha looked more alert. "The period of the patriarchs? You mean, the Bible? The book of Genesis in the Bible?"

"Yes," said Bruce. "To be perfectly honest, I could barely follow what she was talking about. By this stage she really was almost incoherent with stress and when I tried to get more out of her, she clammed up. That was the last time I saw her."

Nathanael clenched his fist. "I wish I could have been here for her."

Bruce said, "I looked up the Lucifer Institute, you know — it was an organisation associated with a number of Madame Blavatsky's disciples, I couldn't find their names. It was founded in the early nineteen twenties to research the antediluvian era, the giants and so forth, and the Lucifer Institute disappeared completely, insofar as I can ascertain, within five years of its founding, due to lack of funding. In other words, Jannah really was spouting nonsense."

Nathanael asked, "What about the other times you saw her? Was she any better then?"

Bruce pressed his lips together thoughtfully. "The second time I saw her, when she was a bit more coherent, she said she was thinking of calling you back in to look into it all, but that she was afraid this time. Afraid that they might find out how much she actually knew, and how much you knew, about it all. Told me there was something very, very peculiar going on. Very peculiar indeed. And she used to leave her mobile at home when she went to work. Not like her at all."

"No," said Nathanael. "She was always googling something on it, wasn't she? Or checking her emails."

"I was a bit worried even then, to be honest," Bruce admitted. "I thought perhaps the pressure of the last twelve months was getting to her, and when she came to see me the last time, babbling incoherently, I really thought my conclusions justified. She was evincing all the classic symptoms of paranoia, anxiety and delusions — first she's talking about the historicity of Genesis — and something about a creature in Surrey, some sort of big-foot or Yeti or Cro-Magnon wild man-beast and how it was living on some sort of country estate or mansion — ridiculous stuff — and then she starting going on about how 'they' were listening to her through her mobile and watching everything she did on the computer — she mentioned something called the Lucifer Institute then, too."

"It's possible," said Natasha. "The government can do all those things."

"Whether they can or not, I wouldn't have believed any Western government actually would do this sort of thing, if Jannah hadn't died so mysteriously. But now I think anything is possible. She told me to get rid of my landline — well, of course, haven't had one for years. All that technology — don't need it. Of course, while Alethea was still around, I had one, and a television. But really, that was for her. All I need are my books, a cup of tea occasionally, and the odd journal or newspaper that makes it's way here through the postal service. Don't understand all the fuss over the internet. Seems to be more trouble than it's worth. Foucault's Panopticon, finally realised."

Natasha nodded. "It has gone that way."

Nathanael commented, "Natasha actually knows what she's talking about. She's a computer programmer."

"Really? An American who knows what they're talking about?" said Bruce, with a twinkle in his eye, then his mood returned to sombre. "Well, there you are. Jannah feared for her life. And do you know, she had just had a doctor's checkup a week before she died. Fit as a fiddle. Blood pressure only slightly elevated, no heart problems at all, cholesterol ratio below four, absolutely fine, despite all the stress she was going through. And I discovered later that her doctor, who was her family doctor, he had known her for years, told her it's not paranoia if what you fear is a real thing, a legitimate threat to your well-being. In that case, to heed that fear is wisdom, not insanity. Sound advice, but given too late to help her, perhaps."

Nathanael said, "I wish she'd called me, or emailed me. Asked me to come back. Who knows. At least I could have got her out of here, found a safe place for her. I wish I'd done more."

"So do I," said Bruce. "She should have run. Why stick around if your life is threatened? Better a live dog than a dead lion."

Natasha said, "Book of Proverbs."

"No, Ecclesiastes 9:4 actually," said Bruce. "Wisdom literature though. Not far off. Know your Bible do you?"

"Kind of," she said, embarrassed that she had got the reference wrong.

"How about you, Nathanael? Do you know your Bible?"

"More less than more," he admitted, and he groaned to Natasha, "Now he's going to have a go at me." They had had quite a few conversations along these lines when Nathanael was working at the Museum.

"Nathanael, behold Natasha, an American, a computer programmer extraordinaire, even so she has read this book, though I presume she hails from the Indian sub-continent — which has a different literature, a different history. Nathanael Wayfarer believes of himself that he is an intelligent, worthy, cultured Australian. But if so why is he ignorant of the very wellspring of Western Civilisation, the inspiration behind the laws and customs and art of our entire culture, the raison d'être of all the values we hold dear, freedom and justice and faith and mercy? This book — or collection of books, rather, which it is, of many genres — ought to be the one thing every Western man reads."

"And woman," said Natasha. "I agree. But it is much more than that, of course. It is God's word."

Bruce winked at Natasha. "See, Natasha. I've been telling him for ages that he needs to get saved."

Nathanael scoffed, "He was saying, I needed to get married. Anyhow, Natasha, I can understand perhaps how someone obsessed with the past — like Bruce here — might like to read such an ancient, outmoded relic of lost civilisations," (In fact, Nathanael respected Bruce tremendously. But he was needling him, and he could tell he loved it.) "...but for someone in a rational field, like mathematics and computing, for instance..."

Natasha said, "I never told you my major was in combined number theory and computing. You googled me..."

Nathanael grimaced slightly. "Had to know whether my rescuer was a nutcase or not. Now that I know you're a Christian I might have to revise my assessment that you weren't. Why, to believe that something passed down from generation to generation like Chinese whispers could possibly contain even a grain of truth seems to me to be naive in the extreme, if not dangerously insane. To treat gospel as a synonym of truth seems an archaic folly to me."

Bruce rolled his eyes. "You really don't know, do you?"

Nathanael said, "What?"

Bruce said, "You're not even familiar with the documentary hypothesis, are you, which would be the only version of your Chinese Whispers theory that might even be slightly true? And yet, we've moved on from that. Why, the latest is that gospels are really bios, the ancient Greek genre of biography. The latest research says they four gospel writers used the same editing techniques as Plutarch."

Nathanael, "I'm sorry, I don't even know what you're talking about."

Bruce said, "The four gospels in the New Testament give four different, varying accounts of Jesus' life, death and resurrection. Luke is one of the four. Seems to be modelled on Plutarch's biographies, which were factual in intent. Also the prologue to Luke's gospel, for instance, is in literary Greek, and is similar in style to the prologue to Herodotus' Histories. Herodotus was the one Greek historian whose accuracy is proven again and again by archaeology. Much as the whole New Testament is, actually. Luke's prelude was written in a style that was intentionally designed to tell Greek speaking readers that this document is history. Not myth. Not a fairy-tale. History, my dear fellow. And if you wish to call these documents fairy-tales, Chinese whispers, if you will, then I think the onus is actually on you to tell us why they are so accurate archaeologically, why the gospel writers, even John, the latest, seem to know about locations and social customs that could not possibly have been known about after 70AD."

Nathanael said, "Why 70AD in particular?"

"Why? Because Jerusalem was completely destroyed, my boy. Anyone who was born 40 or so years after Jesus' death and resurrection would not know a single thing about the Jerusalem of Jesus' day, because it was not there any more. It was a pile of rubble. And the gospels describe Jesus' Jerusalem perfectly, especially John, the latest, down to peculiar architectural features and which street goes where and so forth."

Nathanael was a little perturbed by this line of discussion. "I've heard of scholars who doubt the historical reliability of the New Testament. Bart Ehrman, for instance."

Bruce said, "Well... Most of those scholars who would question New Testament historical reliability come from a position of a priori ruling out miracles and genuine prophecies. Which would mean they would have to doubt modern accounts of Jung and Churchill, because both of them predicted the second world war years before it happened."

Nathanael changed his tack. "Well there are plenty of apocryphal gospels. The gospel of Judas, the gospel of Mary Magdalene. Couldn't the four in the Bible be apocryphal as well?"

Bruce scoffed, "Discount the gospel of Mary Magdalene — a modern forgery. Clearly you haven't read either the originals or the apocryphal ones with an open mind, anyway, or you wouldn't even say that. I can't even counsel such ignorance — the difference is obvious if you had even read a little of Josephus."

"Alright," said Nathanael rolling his eyes, "Who is Josephus, then? I know you're going to tell me anyway."

Bruce gestured a broad, dramatic arc with his right hand. "See? Doesn't even know who Josephus is. Jewish historian, first century, eyewitness of Herod, Pilate, the Jewish leadership of the time, the fall of Jerusalem. Josephus tells us everything we know about the background of the gospels, Palestine in the first century. All of it supports, even agrees with, what we learn in the gospels and the rest of the New Testament. History, my boy. Not myth, not legend, not fairy tale, nor is it Chinese Whispers. Of course, that's the New Testament."

Nathanael groaned. What a fool he had made of himself. "Oh. You weren't talking about the New Testament, were you?"

Bruce shook his head. "No. We were talking about Genesis. That's an entirely different kettle of fish. Genesis is the first book of the Old Testament, the earliest part of the Bible in chronological terms. If the first six chapters of Genesis happened at all and weren't just divinely inspired myth as some theologians believe, then it all happened a very, very long time ago."

Nathanael said, "Well, how then do we know any of the Old Testament is true?"

"You know, it's not just one piece, the Old Testament, as far as archaeological evidence goes. For the more recent books of Isaiah and Jeremiah and the minor prophets, around the time of the Babylonian exile, we have plenty of archaeology, names and dates and kings and tablets and monuments and even the names of minor players recorded in independent sources — even the Biblical minimalists would agree with that. For the time of King David and King Solomon, one or two suggestive things, a pomegranate seal, the architecture of the Old Jerusalem and walls that might have been part of David's palace. For the time of Moses and Abraham before him, we have the laws and customs of the surrounding lands that clearly conform to the customs described, such as the various ways one might enter into a covenant, animal sacrifices, religious architecture, things like that. But what have we for the tower of Babel, for Noah, for anything earlier than Abraham, in fact? Nothing, my dear boy, absolutely nothing. Who knows, if the flood really happened then perhaps it washed it all away? (Well, apart from Babel, that was afterwards, but that is supposed to have fallen down.) (Oh, one peculiar exception, Gobekli Tepe — a very strange site — the oldest human construction ever found — on the very site where the Garden of Eden is supposed to have been — on a hill, just as Eden would have been — a bunch of standing stones with images of animals, made by people who seem to have had some sort of fascination with snakes, indeed… Almost makes one think of Romans one twenty five.) (But really, what does Gobekli Tepe tell us? No writing. Nothing, really. Who knows what was going through their heads when they made this?)"

Nathanael said, "So what you're saying is that for anything before Noah's flood, there is no proof, essentially?"

"That is exactly what I'm saying. But that is why Jannah's comment about the historicity of early Genesis is so surprising. In fact, so out of character. She herself knew everything I just told you. You know, she was an excellent historian, an excellent archaeologist, with a broad view of the discipline. A very mysterious comment, I can tell you, and one that, at the time, very nearly made me doubt her sanity."

They paused for a little while, Bruce blowing cool air across the top of his cup of tea, while Nathanael and Natasha sipped their coffees. Outside a raven cawed and clawed at the roof tiles of a nearby house. The sky was grey and overcast and a mood of dejection was seeping over them.

Nathanael said in mournful tones, "I really don't know where this leaves us."

Natasha looked at him, holding her cup of coffee precariously on the left arm-rest of the lounge chair, with her chin resting on the other hand. She looked to him like some sort of sparrow, with her head slightly to one side and her dark eyes staring back at him.

Finally she said, "It just leaves us with more questions than we started with, doesn't it? Why do these people want Cro-Magnon fossils? Why are they determined to silence anyone who knows anything about what they have been doing? And what has all this to do with Jannah's 'age of the patriarchs'?"

Bruce hesitated, "Yes — um — if we assume that Jannah's comments to that effect weren't just the product of a stressed mind that was about to snap. I'm still not certain that all the other stuff, the surveillance, hadn't simply got to her."

Nathanael said, "Where to now then? I really hoped you might have the answers, Bruce. I mean, you're still in the loop, you keep track of what's happening in the scholarly world, the journals, the Museum..."

Bruce shook his head. "All of this — it is out of my depth. I'm a scholar, Nathanael, and nothing more than that. But do you know — if I was you I might talk to Peter Lazarus-Fox. He came back to England, you know."

Nathanael said, "Is he working at the Museum again? Or has he taken a job at Cambridge?"

Bruce said ,"To my knowledge, he was offered both and declined. I actually heard from someone that he has bought a house in Basildon, it's a little village in Essex, about thirty minutes East of London, and is now actually working as a gardener. Can you believe it? One of the world's premiere palaeontologists? And a wonderful lecturer, apparently. I think you should go and see him and talk to him and find out what happened, why he retired and left the whole business behind."

On their way out, the day porter didn't open the door for them or shuffle them out as he was occupied with a phone call on his mobile. Nathanael noticed it and didn't think much about it initially, except that it was odd that the fellow would even leave his mobile on while he was at work. Maybe some day porters might, but this fellow had always been officious and dictatorial, in fact, he did his job with exacting, wearying efficiency. He was not the sort to shirk to have a bit of idle chit chat on the side. That particular day porter had been there for the eight or nine weeks Nathanael had been working at the British Museum over December to January — Nathanael remembered his name, now, Roger — and in all that time Nathanael had never even seen his mobile out before. Family emergency? Well, his family would have the number of the phone on the day porter's desk, surely. Surely they would ring him on that.

It just seemed a little odd.

~~~

A phone rang. The man in the chair sighed, put down his glass of neat fifty year old single malt Speyside Whisky and picked up the phone.

He said, "Yes?"

"We've found another leak."

"Where?"

"London."

"Could this one be useful? Or did you try seeing if you can… stop the flow?"

"Our source says this one's… old and stubborn. Won't be able to be used."

"Well, plug it then."

"Another one? We've plugged quite a few already, sir. Someone's going to start noticing."

"Yes. Plug it. There's an awful lot at stake here. And…"
~~~

"Yes sir?"

"Don't answer back again or you'll be replaced like the others."

"Yes sir. I'm sorry sir."

He put the phone down and returned to his whisky. He picked up the remote for the sound system. Bach's second Brandenburg Concerto filled the room, played by Nicholas Harnoncourt's orchestra. Civilised music. Divine music.

What a fool Bach was, the man thought to himself. Johann Sebastian never understood what real divinity could be.

Power over life and death.

Chapter 8 — Basildon Brush.

Michelle was walking down the road. She was headed for the local grocery store. Mum had asked her to get bread, milk, coffee and a few other things. She had tried to get out of doing it, but she couldn't, not without making her mother suspicious. And why should Mum bear the burden of knowing the truth? They were old, in their early sixties, not young any more, she didn't want them worrying about Natasha. Right now they simply believed that Natasha was on a holiday with a nice man she had met, a man with a troubled past. Michelle couldn't bring herself to tell her, not when she had described Nathanael in such glowing terms — the look of pleasure on her mother's face! — she couldn't bring herself to disillusion them.

God, they were thinking of grandchildren. And here Natasha was, playing with guns and using the Darknet. And some very bad people were chasing after her.

Michelle remembered how worried her mother had been when she had told her that Natasha had been hanging around with hackers at college, and now, this was a thousand times worse! A thousand times more dangerous!

Michelle forced herself out of her thoughts and started watching the people again, the cars going by, the faces in the shop windows and the parks, very carefully.

She had seen him two or three times in the past day or two, sitting in the car, watching her. Different cars, same man. And at the local café, reading a newspaper, watching her over the top of it, with his glasses perched on the end of his nose. Had she imagined it? He was so nondescript — could have been different men — perhaps she was getting like Natasha now, all paranoid, looking for shadowy figures standing in the dark alleyways?

~~~

Natasha and Nathanael were both still tired after the plane ride and their sleep patterns were disturbed, so they decided to find some dinner first and have a good night's sleep before they left for Basildon the following morning.

They found what turned out to be a rather pretentious pub near the hotel and each had an Angus steak and a glass of red wine.

It wasn't too loud to talk, and they felt secure in the anonymity of a crowd, so after a little while they began to discuss things, something they weren't always comfortable to do now in public.

After Natasha went up and bought two more glasses of wine, Nathanael said, "I've got money, too Natasha. I'm a bit concerned about you spending all of yours."

She said, "Look, I really don't mind. Anyhow, if you access any of your funds they will know we're in London, and that really wouldn't be a good idea."

"But it does grate against me to rely on someone else all the time. I don't like being indebted to anyone for anything."
~~~

Despite his moral objections, Nathanael happily sipped the glass she put in front of him, so Natasha waved his protests away with a dismissive gesture of her hand and said, "Pay me back later if you want, Nathanael. I'm committed now — I don't know, this whole thing sucked me in — I was getting so sick of sitting there all day long debugging code that other people had written and trying to make decisions on what software package would meet the hospital's needs, when there were really only two or three choices anyways. But this whole thing has piqued my interest. It's a different sort of puzzle."

Nathanael said, "It has piqued my interest too. But let's hope it doesn't kill us, as well."

Natasha rolled her eyes. "You're very dramatic. But we are stuck, Nathanael, aren't we? We don't have any choice. We have to keep investigating this if we ever want to get our lives back. The only way we can do that is if we can bring this whole conspiracy into the light of day — to let the world know whatever it is that's going on so that the legal authorities can punish the perpetrators."

Nathanael sighed. "Well, that might be unlikely, Natasha... First we have to uncover the whole thing. And then, if they have their claws as far up the food-chain as the NSA, surely they might also have insiders in the judiciary. Unless of course, we're looking at a business organisation that has deep pockets to bribe people, either way, the desired outcome at a trial or inquiry is not guaranteed. "

Natasha lifted her glass of wine up and took a long sip. Her frank gaze disturbed him somewhat, he didn't know why. "Well, what we are doing is right. Once we have the facts, then the people who killed your friend, Jannah, and the other scholars, might be brought to justice. We can't guarantee any more than what is within our own reach — we can only do our best to do what's right within our own sphere. If it all goes wrong after that because judges or magistrates choose to deny justice, well, at least we will know that we did the right thing. As Professor Fetherington's favourite book says, it's better to suffer for doing good than for doing wrong."

Nathanael smirked, "Is that in the Book of Proverbs too?"

"Do you know, I wouldn't be surprised if it was. I doubt if that quote comes from Ecclesiastes; that book sounds more like you talking. Normally I'd google it, but I can't really use my phone can I?" She finished her glass off. "Should we have another glass, do you think?"

Nathanael looked around. There didn't seem to be anyone suspicious in the pub — just people of all ages enjoying themselves. "I feel like we're letting down our guard, Natasha. Is that good?"

Natasha took his hand in hers. It was a little shock for him, actually, a gesture of affection that he hadn't expected. "We might need to let down our guard, Nathanael, when we can, otherwise we'll both burn out." She sighed and looked around as well. "None of these people look suspicious. I suppose we would know if they had found us."

That night they slept in the same room, in separate single beds; nothing had happened between them, despite sharing a third glass of wine. Nathanael didn't think he would have let it happen if Natasha had shown willingness, because if something happened between them he didn't want it to happen when she was drunk, although three glasses was hardly drunk. Anyhow, it was all academic, it had all been very chaste, but he wasn't sure if that was because she was a Christian or because she didn't like him in that way.

In the morning once they were dressed and ready to go they caught the train from Farringdon station, a short walk away from the hotel.

About twenty minutes into the train ride, Natasha said to Nathanael, "I think that guy's watching us." She pointed to a man in a black suit. They were at the front of the train and he was sitting near the driver's door. He did seem to be watching them.

Nathanael said, "Let's get up. Let's go to the next carriage and see."

They both walked slowly to the next carriage. As they walked into the second carriage, they saw the man get up.

Just as they sat down at the far end of the second carriage, the door between the carriages slid open and the man emerged. He was glancing around, looking for them. When his eyes rested on them he sat down again.

"He's definitely following us," said Nathanael. "Come on, we have to lose him." They both got up at once and went through the doors into the third carriage.

The pre-recorded voice said, "West Ham Station in one minute."

Natasha said, "That's where we have to get off." They ran through the third carriage. The fourth carriage was very congested with people. Nathanael shouted, "I think she's going to puke! She's about to vomit!" The people pushed over to the sides and gave them plenty of room, disregarding each other's personal space in the desire not to get vomited on. They ran through the middle and the people returned to their places. Nathanael looked back. The man following them was struggling to get through.

The pre-recorded voice said, "West Ham Station" and the train stopped. The doors opened and they slipped out. The doors closed again as they were walking away, and they looked to see the man, looking angry, watching them.

A little while later they reached Basildon station, a steel, glass and concrete structure with the customary sans-serif font and sparse, square decorations.

They sat down on the bench and discussed how to find Peter Lazarus-Fox.

Natasha said, "Well, where do people find gardeners in English towns?"

He said, "Where would a gardener advertise in an English town?"

She said, "On a grocery store bulletin board? In the local paper?"

He said, "On the gum-tree website?"

They both said, "The pub!" at the same time, and laughed.

"I could do with a drink, too," said Natasha, "After that little escapade."

Nathanael said, "I am glad you're not a teetotaller."

Natasha looked at him. "Why would you think I would be?"

"Don't know," he said, not willing to say, 'because you're a Christian.'

They asked at the retail shop in the ticketing hall where the nearest pub was and the girl told them it was the Beekeeper, just across the road. The building was a strange mixture of old and new, and looked as though the concrete shopping centre had been built around it. A double-layered metal fence ran around the roof, giving the building the look of a beehive, explaining the name.

In the pub they asked one of the bartender about gardeners. He pointed to a small business card and pamphlet display on the side of the bar. There was a small pamphlet for "Peter Lazarus Garden Designs, full service from conception to after care packages," with some attractive photographs of a well-manicured garden. They took one, had their lunch in the pub and then asked about a public phone.

"A public phone?" said the bartender; from his accent, he was a local. "Like, they've been gettin' rid of the public phone boxes roun' here. No chance, mate. Why don't you use your mobile?"

Natasha said, "Ah, it's broken."

"There's a mobile place about 5 minutes walk away, they'll fix it or you can get a new one, just go norf, across Roundacre, follow Market Square around and left onto Market Pavement. I forget what it's called. Mister Fone or somefink."

As they walked there, Natasha said, "No public phones any more. It's getting hard to get off the grid, isn't it?"

"We can get phones in our false names, though, can't we?"

Natasha nodded. "So long as we don't need a credit card… I wonder how long it will be before they find us on some security camera footage or something."

They got prepaid mobiles in their false names and Natasha bought them thirty pounds of credit each.

Nathanael asked about coffee shops, and there was a Greek coffee kiosk just around the corner, so they went straight there and sat sipping cappuccinos for twenty minutes, both of them dreading the next step.

After they finished, Nathanael said, "Well, it's now or never." He rang the number for Peter Lazarus Garden Designs.

Peter Lazarus-Fox answered; Nathanael knew his voice from when he had worked at the British Museum. "Hello. Garden Designs."

Nathanael said, "We're interested in meeting you about a project."

Peter said, "Well, it would be better for me to meet at your property. That way I can survey things, get a feel for the place. No charge for the first consultation."

Nathanael said, "We'd rather meet at yours, first, meet you, you know, see if we hit it off. Do you have any more photographs of your work? We've seen the ones on the pamphlet."

Peter said, "The ones on the website. There's about thirty there. Your voice sounds familiar. I don't know you do I?"

Nathanael said, "I don't see how. We can't look at the pictures on the website as we don't have the internet. You don't mind us meeting at your place?"

Peter said, "No, go ahead. I'll be free at about five o'clock tonight. 88 Southernhay road. Just knock on the front door."

Natasha googled the road, saying, "As long as we don't google his exact address, we should be alright. Mind you, we ought to get ourselves a street map of Essex, then we don't have to google. " Southernhay road was a semi-circular road that encompassed the eastern half of Basildon town centre. Then she said, "Mind you, we've rung him. That mobile phone is already compromised. You should get rid of it."

Nathanael said, "Really? It's got thirty pounds of credit on it. What a waste."

"Wipe your fingerprints off it and chuck it in the next rubbish bin."

He did.

Nathanael said, "So we've got a few hours to kill. What should we do? Buy another phone to throw away?"

They went back to the phone shop and bought another phone in Natasha's false name this time, and they found a street map of the area at a gas station. Then they discovered another pub and spent the afternoon there drinking coffee and eating a platter with Turkish bread and various dips.

After that, it was a ten minute walk to Peter Lazarus-Fox's house. They arrived. It was a relatively large country mansion with at least a quarter-acre of garden around it. They knocked on the door.

The door opened. Peter was standing there — a tall, thin man in neat, expensive looking casual clothes, not looking much like a gardener. His cheekbones were as hollow a skull, his hair was dishevelled and sparse and his bony left hand was holding a pistol pointed right at Nathanael's face.

"I recognised your voice, but I couldn't remember who it was till I thought about it for a little while. Nathanael Wayfarer. So are you with them? I can't see how you would have found me otherwise."

Nathanael shook his head.

Peter rolled his eyes. He indicated with the gun barrel that they should go to their right and guided them around to the back yard. There was a garden table there with four chairs. "Sit down," he said, sounding despondent rather than threatening.

Nathanael said, "Why the gun?"

Peter said, "I'm still holding the gun. It's under the table, pointed at you. What reason can you give me that I should trust you?"

Nathanael said, "Why shouldn't you?"

Peter snorted. "Come on, why the act? I think they sent you to test me, to try me out. See if I'll keep obeying their instructions. I mean, you were the newcomer at the British Museum. Perfect cover — investigating the disappearing artefacts — you couldn't have been in a more compromising position for the Museum if you had been one of theirs."

Nathanael frowned. "Yes, but you knew that I was a childhood friend of Jannah's. You know that. It's not as though I was some consultant who appeared from nowhere. I was someone from outside, someone not in the system."

Peter said, "That's the only reason I brought you out into here the backyard. The chance, the tiny chance that you are legitimate. But in that case, I didn't want them knowing you're here, if they don't already, because once they know, your lifespan will be very short. Just like the others. The house is bugged, you know. There's probably cameras around too, but I haven't any clue where."

Nathanael said, "All we want is to find out what you know. What's happening. Why they were taking the artefacts, why they have been killing people.

Palaeontologists, for God's sake, innocent people. And why you're still alive."

Peter said, "Go and hide. Get out, get away from here, get off the grid. They're murderous beasts, Nathanael, and they can find you wherever you are. God knows, they probably know you're here already."

Nathanael said, "But why didn't they kill you?"

Peter said, "Please go. Please leave me. If they find out that I'm talking to you, I'll be next on the hit list."

"Why, Peter? Why didn't they?"

"Leave! Nathanael, I don't want you to be harmed on my account! Leave, now! Or I'll call the police and then they will know that you're here."

Natasha brushed Nathanael's arm. "We'd better go. I think he means it."

Nathanael put his two hands up in a conciliatory gesture. "Alright, alright. We'll leave. As soon as you tell me why they didn't kill you."

Peter's face screwed up into a mask of distress and horror. "Because I'm still of use to them, Nathanael. That's why. That's why I'm still alive when the rest of them have died. That's why I'm a danger to you! Now, please, please go! I'm begging you! Leave. Leave before they find out you're here!"

"Of use to them? How?"

Peter said, "Just go. Anything more that I tell you can only endanger your life more — and mine. Just go."

Natasha said, "Let's go, Nathanael."

They left Peter sitting at the garden table, cradling his head in his hands, the gun still dangling from his left hand.

They walked back quickly to Basildon train station and arrived at five minutes to six. The London train was due at 6:01.

Natasha said, "Do you think we should go back?"

Nathanael nodded. "Why not?"

Natasha stared at him again, in that disconcerting way of hers. "Don't you think we should watch him? Find out where he's going?"

Nathanael shrugged. "Not sure. What? Watching two weeks of gardening?"

Natasha said, "Well... If he's of use to them, then perhaps he could be doing things for them. Perhaps he goes to their research base, or whatever it is, and does some research."

Nathanael said, "Unless it's all online. It often is, these days."

Natasha ran her finger along the seat. "Well, there might be ways around that, too. You know, we could work out some way to bug the computer..."

Nathanael said, "So you're saying, stay in Basildon?"

Natasha said, "Stay for two or three days... I have limited funds..."

Nathanael said, "Maybe we need to find a way to access my funds. Perhaps my sister can do it for me, and get the money to us some way that's under the radar."

Natasha nodded. "But we can manage on my funds for quite a few weeks yet before they run out. I just don't want to waste weeks watching Peter Lazarus-Fox, if he's not giving us anything useful."

Natasha quickly found a bed and breakfast about half a mile from the town centre on her smart-phone, and they made their way there and slept the night. She rang up the place in London and booked her and Nathanael out. She had left enough deposit to cover the extra day so they didn't mind her cancelling the booking.

The following day they booked a hire car and drove round to Peter's house again, and parked on the side of the road within sight of the driveway. Peter left about half an hour later and they followed him to a job about fifteen minutes away in Colchester. He spent the whole day landscaping a garden, and Natasha and Nathanael started to doubt the wisdom of their decision to stay in Basildon.

That night, over a glass of wine in their room at the bed and breakfast, they discussed their options.

Natasha was in favour of hacking his computer. "We can break into the house tomorrow, when he's not home. I'm pretty sure I can get a trojan together that would do the job — connect it to the USB, some kind of an auto-run .exe file — with the right piece of software I can get his computer to upload everything to my cloud backup account."

Nathanael shook his head. "Come on, Natasha, it just doesn't bear thinking about. Think of all the risks. Firstly, his house is bugged and possibly has hidden cameras in it too. There is a good chance they will know we are here in England, and then they'll be looking for us, if they catch us on the hidden cameras. Then there's the fact that you're uploading the file to your cloud account. Then they'll know it's you for sure."

Natasha smirked at him. "No, no, the cloud backup account is in the false name, not my real name."

Nathanael said, "You've been busy, haven't you?"

"Thought I might need it. Organised it the afternoon after we bought the smart-phones."

Nathanael folded his arms rather patronisingly. "Well it's still too much of a risk, though, isn't it? Just the fact that there might be hidden cameras in his house ought to be enough to discourage us. I think we should wait and see. Decide tomorrow afternoon if he doesn't go anywhere tomorrow."

The third day, which was Friday, Peter didn't drive to work the same way. He left half-an-hour earlier and took a circuitous route through the side-streets; it was lucky Nathanael was driving because he had had some experience following people and was able to do so clandestinely, without Peter noticing anything, or at least, as far as they could tell he had not seen them.

It was also lucky that Natasha had bought the street map because she was able to tell Nathanael which way to drive to head Peter's car off.

They followed him for much of the morning, weaving through the side streets of Essex, through Chigwell, Epping, finally joining the main roads in Harlow until they finally reached the village of Saffron Walden. It was a one hour journey that took two hours.

"Saffron Walden," said Natasha. "It's the name of a hymn tune, actually."

"Hymns? You mean, Anglican, Catholic? How do you know that?"

"I go to a small church in Phoenix," she said. "Evangelical Episcopalian. It's a small congregation, about half Latin American, actually. They have services in Spanish and English."

He said, "Huh. Always pictured you in one of those big churches with a stadium and a rock band, thousands of people all praising the Lord."

"Well, you were wrong about that, weren't you?"

In Saffron Walden Peter's car wandered through the streets again seemingly at random until they reached an attractive, leafy street with old cottages behind large, high, brick walls entwined with vines and roses hiding gardens overgrown with hedgerows gone feral, high poplars and ash trees overreaching their boundaries.

Natasha said, "This is Audley street."

Peter's car pulled into a driveway. Nathanael drove past and watched in the rear-view mirror as Peter spoke into an intercom. The gate opened and he went in, disappearing behind the high wall.

Nathanael drove the car around the block. He said, "I think we should leave it for at least half an hour before we do anything. Anyway, perhaps he's just doing a gardening job? Got lost on the way?"

Natasha shook her head. "Come on, Nathanael. I mean, he drove straight to the other jobs, very certain of the way there. Today he took the most circuitous route possible. No, whatever this place is, it has something to do with whatever it is that we're trying to find out. Mind you, it might not be a bad idea to wait for half an hour anyway. Look at the maps, find out if there's an alleyway behind this place or a way in through the back."

Nathanael said, "Let's go and find ourselves a coffee in the town and work out our plan." And he drove past the house again and went into the town centre, only a block away.

They parked on the side of the road found a small coffee shop nearby. They sat inside and Natasha examined the map. "There's not really enough here on this road map. We need more detail." She got out her phone and looked up the internet, and sighed. "This map app has more detail. I suppose it's natural for tourists to look up Saffron Waldren, while we're here. I don't think this will catch the attention of whoever has been watching us."

She worked out that there was a lane that went beside the house. "We can go along here," she said. "Though surely they will have cameras."

Outside the weather had turned sour and rain was starting to drizzle down. Nathanael looked out. "It's turning miserable. Let's get ourselves some large umbrellas, hoodies, maybe, as well, the sort of clothes we can remain anonymous in. The umbrellas will hide us from any cameras they might have on the house."

Natasha nodded. "Well, at least we can walk past. You know, I have an idea."

She looked up, "Saffron Walden music store", and a place came up. She pointed to it. "Once we've got our umbrellas and clothes, we're going there."

Nathanael was puzzled. He didn't want to ask why they were going to a music store, because he was thinking perhaps the stress had got to her. Maybe this was all too much for Natasha and she had reverted to some kind of fantasy that they were on a happy holiday where they could just go shopping in music stores whenever they wanted.

They finished their coffees. Once they had been to a local shop that sold umbrellas and hoodies, where

Natasha bought a large bag as well, they set off to drive to the music store.

As they were leaving the town centre they passed a medieval pub, the Keys Hotel. Nathanael commented that it looked nice, rather wistfully thinking if they really were there on a holiday instead of trying to discover the truth about this conspiracy it would be the sort of place he wouldn't mind staying at.

When they got to the music store, Natasha said, "I'm looking for some sort of USB preamp and a microphone?"

The music store proprietor was a grey-haired man in his early sixties with long hair and a beard. He said, "Well, I don't have much here like that. Look around, it's mostly just guitar strings and second hand instruments."

Natasha said, "It's okay if it's just for hire. We only need it for the day. Oh, we could do with a pair of headphones too."

He said, "Well, let me look out the back, then. My partner's got a little studio there we use for recordin' our songs. I think she's got something like that. We'll need a decent deposit, mind."

He came back about five minutes later with a microphone. "It's a Rode NT-USB mike. This will do both jobs in one. You plug it straight into your computer. It's worth two hundred pound, though, so we'll want a a hundred and ninety deposit plus ten pound for the day."

"How much for the headphones?"

"Oh, they're just cheap ones. I'll chuck them in for free."

"Okay," said Natasha, handing over two hundred pound. "We'll bring it back tonight or early tomorrow morning."

"Alright then. Pleasure doing business with you."

Nathanael and Natasha drove back to the town centre. They parked in the main road. Natasha plugged the USB microphone and the headphones into her laptop and started up the software. Then she put the microphone and the computer in her bag. She winced.

"What's wrong?" said Nathanael.

"I've got the compression up pretty high, and those cars going past are very loud." She took the headphones off her ears and hung them round her neck. They took out their umbrellas, put on the hoodies, with the hoods down for now, locked the car and began walking.

It was an eight minute walk to the laneway. Natasha put on the headphones again.

Nathanael said, "How will I hear?"

Natasha took them off. "What?"

"How will I hear what you're hearing?"

"I'm recording it. I've got some basic audio recording software on my computer. We can listen to it later. Place the umbrellas so that if there are any cameras on the right they won't be able to see us."

They walked down the laneway.

Natasha stopped. "Here. Stop here."

She stood there for a while, apparently listening.

Nathanael tapped her shoulder. He was concerned that they were rather conspicuous. She shushed him, listening intently.

Natasha's expression changed. Her eyebrows went up in astonishment. Then she looked at Nathanael. She nodded, as if to say, we've got something.

He badly wanted to listen, to hear what it was, but when he mimed putting the earphones on, she shook her head, definitely not. What a selfish girl she is, just keeping it to herself. Very spoiled.

They stood there for about ten minutes. Suddenly Natasha said, "Oh. Quick! Go!" and she started jogging back the way they had come. He ran alongside her. As they reached the end of the laneway, she ran more quickly. He followed, looking around to see what the threat might be. Two men in suits came around the corner into the laneway at the other end, from somewhere near the driveway where Peter Lazarus-Fox had entered the place.

Nathanael wasn't sure, but it looked like the Southerner, Kade and his East End mate, but they were already out of sight because they'd turned the corner and Natasha was sprinting now.

A voice cried out, "Hey! Stop!" It might be Kade's voice, but Nathanael couldn't be sure with hearing only two words. Natasha had turned a corner into another laneway. "This will get us to the car," she said, and sure enough, they came out onto the main street quite close to the car. They leaped in and Nathanael said, "Quickly!" and started driving, even while Natasha was still closing her door. He skidded on the wet road, in front of a truck which was forced to put its brakes on and skidded itself, almost ran onto the footpath, beeped at them. Nathanael looked in the rear view mirror. The two men in suits came running around the corner — they'd come the long way — they were already disappearing in the distance as he rocketed the pedal and rounded the road onto the highway.

They were heading north. "Go to the music shop," said Natasha. "Maybe we can hide out there for a bit. I might be able to use some of their gear, too, especially if they have decent monitors."

At the music shop, Nathanael stopped outside and went in. He asked the proprietor if they could park in the yard — they wanted to hire the studio. He seemed agreeable, though a little puzzled as to why they didn't want to park in the street.

After Nathanael parked, the proprietor closed the gate behind them. He said, "Come this way," and led them into the barn. The door was a proper soundproofed double airlock, and he said, "The whole barn has been fitted out with proper soundproofing, sand in the walls and ceilings, as well as a double layer of insulation, and we managed to virtually eliminate reflections in the mixing booth. We've got Genelecs, too, for monitoring. Good speakers."

Natasha raised her eyebrows in approval. "They're good."

He nodded. "They are. By the way, my name's Andy. You are...?"

"Natasha and Nathanael."

"Listen, Natasha, I'll give you back your other hundred. It'll be a hundred pounds for the day, and that includes the hire of the mike which you've already returned, and me on the desk, if you want. I know my way around this equipment."

Natasha looked at Nathanael. "What do you think?"

Nathanael shrugged. "I don't even know what you've recorded. You decide."

Natasha said to Andy, "Can you be discrete?"

Andy nodded. "Local private dick sometimes uses my studio. Cleaned up some fairly sensitive stuff for him, you know, a recording of a bloke's missus getting it on with his best mate. And I know them both — small town, this one. Forensic audio is my specialty," he said proudly.

Natasha said, "Well, we're paying you to be discrete. Keep the other hundred. Do you know, it wouldn't be worth your while to talk about this job at all, with anyone, and that's not a threat, by which I mean, it's not Nathanael and I you need to worry about. It's the people on this recording."

Andy nodded and swallowed. "Alright. I'll run with it." He looked at them again, funny. "I aren't going to regret getting involved with this am I?"

Natasha said, "I hope not."

Andy closed the door behind them and sat at the mixing desk. "Well, curiosity killed the cat, as they say, and you've hooked me in now. I simply have to know."

There was a computer console on the mixing desk with a large monitor, about forty channels each with a large fader for volume and parametric e.q. as well as high, middle and low. The two massive Genelec speakers framed the window that looked in on the sound booth.

Natasha and Nathanael sat behind him on a big couch.

Natasha took out her laptop and put the audio file on a usb to transfer it over to Andy's system.

He opened it up and pressed play.

"...you're saying. You don't think you can make the test for 4977-bp deletion any quicker?" said a voice Nathanael hadn't heard before.

Peter Lazarus-Fox's voice said, "No, I don't think so."

"You were sure you could."

"I told you we could if we already knew we were dealing with complete samples. Well, the thing is, we're dealing with mitochondrial DNA that might or might not be complete. Until we've evaluated the entire sample, it's impossible to know. And the fact is, 4977-bp deletion is the absence of something, not the presence of it, so until we've evaluated the entire sample we can't test for 4977-bp deletion reliably."

"Well you see, Peter, we already have some adults ready to start the splicing. They're putting a lot of money into this."

"We're still a long way from that. I've been telling you all the way along, we can't do that yet, even using the AIDS virus as a carrier. Too much risk that something will go wrong. Do you want your benefactors getting cancer? Do you want them getting AIDS for goodness' sake? You don't listen to me — stop making promises you can't keep. This isonly for their children. How is the number one going, by the way?"

"He's... doing fine. We're a little worried about him though — smart bugger that he is. We gave him a computer, Peter, just to make sure he can integrate, you know, when we get to stage three. He had Microsoft Word on there and a redacted encyclopedia, a few ebooks and games and so forth. We just wanted him to know how to use a mouse and navigate through pages on a screen. But he seems to have worked out how to surf the net. Got onto Wikipedia, for God's sake! Working things out for himself, it seems. But that's okay, we can contain it. There's lots of good software for controlling and monitoring web access these days, we'll just use that. We've got the staff to keep an eye on him."

Peter's voice laughed. "You can't contain it. Typical hubris. You think you can control, contain, everything. But it will backfire in your faces. So where is he?"

"He's here. We keep him locked up most of the time. We've taken him up north once or twice, to an isolated part of the country side. He keeps asking to see his parents."

"Really?" Peter's voice sounded strained. "But you told him that's impossible, didn't you?"

"Not… exactly. We told him… they're not in the country, that they… won't be coming home soon. I can't understand it — the environment has been so controlled. The books he read, the stories he was told, the people he was allowed to see. But somehow he worked it all out, at least to that degree. It's a very strange thing. Like he has a gift for putting disparate facts together."

"That's exactly what I've been telling you. Still, with the number twos you won't have that problem. But you will have other problems, you can count on it."

There were some sounds in the background, a bump, something clunking, distant talking or shouting. There was a long period of silence, and some inconsequential talking about cups of coffee, the toilet, that sort of thing.

A door opened. A different voice said, "We've got a situation, Clive. You might need to intervene."

There were some more sounds in the background, behind the talking.

"Alright, I'm coming." The door closed again.

Another voice, more muffled, was saying. "Look at this." It sounded like Kade to Nathanael.

"Wot?" said another voice. Was that East End?

"These two. Just standing there in the laneway for the last twelve minutes. Not even moving. And it looks like she's got headphones on."

Then Natasha saying, "Oh. Quick! Go!" and sounds of running, deep thumps as the microphone bumped inside the bag, footsteps, it was deafening so Andy hit stop.

He said doubtfully, "Hope you didn't damage my baby." He looked at the microphone. Grudgingly he admitted, "Looks alright."

He fast forwarded a bit to when they were getting in the car. After the loud bump of the car door closing, an exceptionally clear recording of Nathanael saying, "Quickly!" then turning the car key came through the speakers..

Andy smiled, "It's fine." Then he sat back in his chair and said. "Geeze. That's heavy stuff, innit? Do you want me to go back and boost those quiet, distant sections? Those two bits wiv other sounds in the background."

After a quiet moment Andy added, "It might be the little boy talking."

"Yes," said Natasha. "Boost them, please."

Andy said, "I've got some great software for doing that. Let's start with the middle section though. That probably just needs a little bit of gain."

He selected a part of the audio and pressed a few buttons on the keyboard, then pressed 'Play.'

The sound of a large thump, then something clunking, then talking, a lot louder but still muffled. Andy pressed a few more keys then selected the piece of the audio and slipped it down onto another track. "I'm going to e.q. it — if that doesn't work, I've got some software that could clarify the speech."

He fiddled with some knobs on the mixing desk, then pressed 'Play' again. The audio came through the speakers.

The thump sounded, much clearer. It sounded like someone pushing themselves into a door — they could even hear the door move. Then something in a room being pushed over, a table or maybe some chairs. Then it was clearly a boy's voice, shouting something, but still a little unclear because there were other sounds, traffic, background noises muffling it. It sounded like he was saying, "Lemon Goat Cheese Lemon Goat" or something.

Andy clicked on the audio and a screen opened up with a multicoloured picture. "It shows the spectrum," he said. "Here's the voice here," he showed a yellow section about half way along, in the middle. He selected the yellow section. "I'm going to highlight this, get rid of the extraneous noise. You know a mathematician at the CIA designed this algorithm, for separating out a single voice from a crowd in a recording. Now every audio engineer in the world has it."

A horizontal bar came up on the screen. After about eleven seconds it finished processing.

He pressed 'Play' again.

It was a child's voice. Quite a young child, by the sound of it.

"Let me go! Please! Let me go! Please! I want to find my mother and father! I don't belong here! I know that everything here is wrong. I should be at school, I should be with my family, like other children. You are not supposed to kidnap people! Yes, that's what you've done to me. I know. I know everything now! Children shouldn't be kept away from their mother and father, kept locked away, imprisoned. It's wrong, and I know you've done it since I was very young, I want freedom. You are very bad people! Bad people! Let me go!"

Another voice sounded, a man's voice. This time Nathanael was certain it was Kade.

"I don't want to have to do it. Don't make me do it you little-"

The child screamed, for at least ten seconds, then Kade's voice sounded again, "Alright. You forced me to do it." Then the scream faded into a sigh and another bump.

Andy said, "That boy's being locked away. He's being kidnapped and drugged. We should call the police right away."

Natasha said, "No! We're going to get him out. But we have to keep the police out of it."

Andy said, "You've got to tell the police."

Nathanael shook his head. He almost said, 'the kidnappers said if we contact the police they'll kill him' but what he found himself saying was much closer to the truth. "The thing is, Andy, it's… someone associated with the MI5 or one of the other agencies keeping him locked up. We're not really sure who it is, but believe me, they have the sort of high powered surveillance only MI5 or the CIA has access to. It's a giant conspiracy. If you decide to call the police they'll intercept your call and you'll be on a terrorism watch list before you know it. That's if they can't find you. If they can you'll be locked away for weeks without a trial while they pump you for everything you know. I simply wouldn't recommend taking that sort of action — you can try it — but I wouldn't recommend it."

Andy said, "Really? Are you serious? The government shouldn't be allowed to do this sort of thing. God, it's like JFK. You know that was a conspiracy. And the moon landing — you realise that was faked? Definitely fake — did you ever see that flag flapping on the television feed? And there are so many other conspiracies. Queen Elizabeth is actually one of the reptilians — you knew that didn't you? Wouldn't surprise me if that child was a human alien hybrid or something and that's why they're keeping him locked up. You're like… Mulder and Scully!" Clearly they had struck a chord with Andy. He continued, "Somebody needs to do something about it!"

Natasha put her hand on his arm. "We are doing something about it, Andy. And you can help us if you want. We want to get him out of there. Will you help us?"

Andy's expression darkened. "Mind you, who are you two anyway? Are you part of the conspiracy? An American Paki and an Australian man. Are you two spies as well? For all I know you are the terrorists. One of those guys in ISIS was an Australian, wasn't he? Not even Middle-Eastern."

"I'm not Pakistani. My parents were from Sri-Lanka, but I'm American."

Andy said, "Well who are you then? Why are you interested in this?"

Natasha took a punt. Well, she told a massive lie, actually.

"We're the boy's parents. Please don't call the police. We want to get our son back."

Chapter 9 — Michelle's Mistake.

Michelle's small group of friends were having a girls' night out at the local bar and grill, it was all over Facebook. She'd already said she was going months before, before the present… inconveniences… before the trip to Vegas, in other words — and she was determined to go. Why, if she let these worries stop her from seeing her friends, what next? She'd have to give up her life entirely and live like a recluse. Who had ever heard of a twenty one year old recluse?

But now she was wondering if she'd made the right decision. Mum and Dad had gone to the Symphony Orchestra, the orchestra was playing David Bowie tonight, or maybe it was Cirque du Orchestre, she couldn't remember. In any case, Mum and Dad had taken the car.

So she had caught the bus from their house.

The man was waiting at the next stop. Michelle sat there, petrified, looking at him out of the corner of her eye.

He got on the bus. She tried not to breathe too hard, tried not to let her chest rise and fall too quickly, tried not to show the man how afraid she was.

He sat in her line of sight and began reading the newspaper again, looking over his reading glasses, staring at her.

She looked past him, but she was constantly watching him through the corner of her eye, staring past him, trying not to make it look as though she was aware of him.

The mental effort of it almost made her miss her stop.

She leaped off, and looked at the bus as it left — the man had gotten up — but he hadn't seemed in any hurry to get off at her stop. Somehow that worried her even more.

It wasn't raining at that moment, but it had been. The air chilled her lungs. The obsidian sky above her with its blacker than black clouds, the patch of sky above the city centre, grey streaked through with dark and light layers like geological strata, the streetlight, struggling in its lonely, heroic effort to light up anything more than a few inches away from its pathetically tiny filament, her footsteps echoing frantically on the wet asphalt, bouncing off the tall, bland walls of the buildings; it was hard not to feel how alone she was, how solitary. It wasn't far to the bar and grill, but the distance seemed to stretch out like a tunnel in a horror movie.

Of course, they knew where she was going. They could look at Facebook, couldn't they? Her whole on-line life was an open book to them. Damn it, she was stupid, they probably had other people waiting at the bar and grill to keep an eye on her there as well.

She hurried down the street. It was only a few hundred metres, but there was that same car there, parked less than a hundred metres beyond the bus stop. It had its lights on. The bar and grill shone before her, a safe haven, a public place, its lights inviting and friendly. She had worn running shoes, just in case, and she began walking fast when the car pulled out behind her, then running, they were coming closer, she sprinted but couldn't get away.

Then they just drove past. She glimpsed them in the car, talking to each other, not even looking at her, a man and his wife or girlfriend, out for dinner or something.

She looked back.

There was another car parked there, with a man in it, watching her. The same make and model. Was he really watching her? She didn't know.

He certainly looked like the same man who had been on the bus. Could he have driven back? Or was she just imagining it all?

God this was hell. She was so sick of living like this, watching everyone, afraid, wherever she was. She clenched her teeth together. She wasn't going to let fear control her. Damn it all, she was going to enjoy herself tonight. She was with her friends and no one, no one, was going to stop her from having a good time.

She walked into the bar and grill, an aggressive bounce in her step. After the greetings, the kisses and hugs, they ate and then they were all saying, "Come on, Michelle, have a drink. You never abstained before? What's wrong with just one drink? We're here to have fun, let your hair down a bit, we're your friends, we'll look after you. What, now that you're finishing college, you have to be responsible?" Then Isabella said, "Come on, here, I've bought one for you, you can't not drink it," and plonked the glass down in front of her.

Michelle couldn't think of any more excuses, so half-reluctantly she took her first sip of the apple cider. No, she wasn't going to let fear control her.

It was delicious and as she drank her way through the glass she found that for the first time in three weeks that she was forgetting about Natasha, Nathanael, the bad men and all the paranoia and anxiety that had filled her life since their trip to Las Vegas.

A few minutes after she finished that glass someone brought her another glass of cider and she began to feel like things were back to normal. She was in the same zone as all her friends — the happy friend-zone — that delightfully inebriated place where conversation, friendship, mutual happiness was everything and all the unpleasant thoughts were becoming pleasantly fuzzy, disappearing into the fog.

It all went so delightfully after that, and she even remembered to ask Isabella to take her home. She wasn't taking the bus home — that had been too scary!

Isabella asked Michelle to drive. Michelle had only been drinking for half the night, really, a lot less than Isabella, so it made sense, so Michelle agreed.

It was all fine and Michelle's heart swelled as she pulled out from the parking spot, just outside the restaurant. She had outsmarted them!

Then there came the sound of a police siren. "Pull over, Ma'am."

Or at least, they certainly seemed like police at first.

"Ma'am," he said, "You were driving erratically." Then again, there was something odd about their uniforms, but Michelle's brain was too fuzzy to care.

The other man asked Michelle to blow into the little plastic, white pipe, attached to the little yellow machine and when she did the machine said she was over the zero point oh eight limit. They asked Michelle to park on the kerb. She parked Isabella's car on the kerb and Isabella was crying and sobbing and saying, "Sorry, Michelle, I'm really sorry, oh it's all my fault." Michelle was trying so hard to reassure Isabella that she didn't notice that the van didn't have the usual police insignia on it, and no seats inside or equipment, just an empty van, open at the back. Well, it registered on some level, or she wouldn't have remembered it afterwards, but she didn't really notice as much as she should have at the time.

The men came over and said to her, "You're coming back to the lockup with us," and they grabbed her. Then they confiscated Isabella's phone and said to Isabella, "Don't you drive, mind, you look drunk too."

And then they were escorting Michelle into the back of the white van and she was going as docilely as a lamb, thinking, well at least I'm in the hands of the police right now, so I'm safe from the criminals, and in the background Isabella was saying, "But don't you have to actually arrest her? And don't you have to wait half an hour before you do a urine test?" But the men said in a tone of voice that struck some part of Michelle's brain as suspiciously sarcastic for a policeman, "No, that law doesn't apply in this case. We are taking her under an entirely different set of rules. You just step back and watch out and keep yourself out of this."

At that moment Michelle started to panic. "No, no, it's not right," but the man held her by the upper arm and his grip was very strong. He threw her in and the back doors closed and locked.

She sat in the empty van, bumping up and down and watching Isabella's miserable face disappear into the distance as the concrete highway came between them.

It was then that Michelle puked. Her little white-walled prison began to stink and she was slipping on her own vomit as she started sobbing and cursing.

Then she was beginning to sober up. Regret began to take hold, a pang in her stomach that was physically painful, surprising her with its visceral reality.

After a while she began to get angry instead. How dare they do this to her. They had no right! She banged the window into the front of the van and said, "Where are you taking me? What are you doing?"

But it didn't matter how much noise she made, how much she shouted, kicked and cursed, the two men in the front ignored her and the van just kept on driving.

Eventually she accepted that there was nothing she could do. For now, she was stuck.

She sat down on the slippery floor and closed her eyes and started praying. "Dear Lord Jesus, you are real, you are Lord, be my rock and my shelter, my hiding place. I know you are dependable even when I'm in this situation, even though I made a terrible mistake. I'm sorry about my mistake, I shouldn't have gotten myself drunk. Please forgive me it was such a dumb thing to do when I believed those men were watching me. I just come here before you, just as I am, without any excuses, I'm not a good person, but please save me from these bad men and whatever it is they're planning to do with me. I'm sorry for not paying enough attention in church. I promise if you save me, I'll build my life on you, Lord Jesus, my rock. My shelter. Please help me."

Chapter 10 — Myth and Meth

Andy brought out some blankets and a couple of mattresses and let Nathanael and Natasha stay in the studio for the night. "Can't have you two wandering around in the streets, being surveilled now, can we?" he said. "I should have the plans from Essex some time tomorrow morning."

"Well then we'll sort what we're doing in the morning," said Natasha. "Thanks a lot, Andy."

"Anything I can do to help."

~~~

Someone somewhere in a secret office somewhere in London said, "I've got two names here that might be aliases. Can't find anything much in the way of records. They flew in from the US."

Another person replied, "Where are they now?"

"Well… They bought some phones and hired a car in London a few days ago, but the NADC has them in Essex. Actually, they went through Saffron Walden last night, so they might still be there."

"Well, start monitoring communications then in Saffron Walden. Isn't that where Room Raquel is?"

"Yes it is."
~~~

"Keep a special eye on anything in that street. Where is it?"

"Audley Street."

"Keep a special eye on anything that happens in Audley Street."

~~~

The previous night, Andy had emailed a friend at the Essex Record Office. Early that morning he received a reply and within ten minutes he had a printout of an 1850 map of Saffron Waldon showing the block plans of all the buildings and houses, including the Audley Street house where the boy was being held.

Natasha and Nathanael were already up when Andy brought the map in to show them. Natasha said, "I think we're going to have to call you Handy Andy." They printed out an enlarged copy of the house, and Andy said, "I'll help you as much as I can. The government has no right to take your boy."

Nathanael said, "Thanks, we appreciate it."

"It's a Listed Building," Andy said as he showed them the map, "So that means they can't really do too many renovations. Unless of course there were changes between 1850 and 1947, when the Town and Country Planning Act came in."

Natasha asked him, "And how do you know all this, Handy Andy?"

Andy put on a modest look. "Just… just smart I guess. And me mate in the Record Office told me. More of the second, really. But I don't mind if you think I'm smart, though, love."

Handy Andy also knew someone else who knew someone, and by two thirty that afternoon they were
~~~

sitting inside the back of a covered truck in the yard of the house next door, pointing three large microphones at the house they were surveilling.

They were at least five metres further away than Nathanael and Natasha had been when they were in the laneway, but Andy more than made up for that. And they were getting more audio footage and covering more of the house.

Andy was recording all three tracks onto his computer. He also had a small mixing desk, which he used to isolate one or the other of the microphones as they listened. Nathanael wasn't clear on how it all synced up with the computer, but apparently it did so he didn't question it.

Andy told them, "These people were moving stuff out just a few weeks ago, so a removal van parked here won't be suspicious."

There wasn't much going on in the house next door at that time on a Saturday, but with the few things they could hear happening they began to form an idea of the function of the parts of the house that corresponded to the rooms on the 1850 map.

Two men were talking softly in one room on the left of the house, the back. They both had English accents, London, East End, maybe. Nathanael didn't think either of them were 'East End', though, the guy from Las Vegas.

"...Just the same day to day. Then something happens and you're in trouble if you don't get it right. I hate this job."

"Me too. Still, well paid innit."

"Yeah, but what's going on? You know, there's something strange going on. They're government, too, but not really. I don't get it."

"We're not paid to get it. We're just paid to keep our eyes glued to the screen and catch anybody that's cottoned on to the fact that this isn't just your ordinary house with two parents and one point eight three little nippers."

"Well, there's been no one come down the laneway for at least three hours, none since that couple yesterday, who look like they might be doing anything suspicious. There's that removal van next door, though."

"Don't be ridiculous, they were moving stuff out last week as well. Now you're gettin' paranoid. You on a downer? Haven't had your shots lately?"

"No, every day, like you, I have me little spoonful of crystal rocks. They don't let you not take 'em. How do you think I keep so alert, day after day?"

"Hate to see you if you weren't on the Billy Whizz. You'd probably be a vegetable, wouldn't you?"

"You should see me after these gigs, when I'm amping out at home. I am a vegetable. Only feel normal now when I'm working. Can't even get a stonker on with the missus now unless I'm fully loaded."

Nathanael said hesitantly, "I think they might be using drugs to keep alert."

Natasha said in a sarcastic tone, "Really?"

Nathanael said, "Is it Cocaine?"

Andy said in a condescending tone, "Billy Whizz is Methamphetamine, actually... He was a character in the Beano comics who ran around everywhere, and crystals and crystal rocks means the same." He added, "I don't use but I've known plenty who have gone down that rabbit hole. D'you know I reckon that room's the kitchen."

The microphone was pointed to the far left, and from the volume level they deduced it was fairly close to the laneway, so they agreed it must be the kitchen of the old house. Then the men talked about making a cup of tea, then there was a humming sound and a ding, the microwave, probably, which seemed to confirm their assumption.

One of the men said, "I'll be back in a sec." Footsteps out.

Nathanael marked the leftmost back room, "Kitchen. 2 Guards. Surveillance screens. Microwave."

A muffled sound came through, the sound of a toilet flushing. Then a tap being turned on. The sound of the old plumbing creaking was louder than the tap. Andy said, "It's definitely at the back. That sound is not coming from the other two mics, either."

Nathanael marked those rooms, 'W.C.' and 'Bathroom.'

Pointing to the 'W.C.', Natasha said, "No, that one's the bathroom and that's the washroom."

Nathanael said, "Americans! W.C. means toilet, actually; bathroom means, well, washroom."

Then they listened to the middle microphone.

All they could hear there was the soft humming of a child.

Andy, though, was listening more intently. "That's curious."

"What?" said Nathanael.

"He's hummin' the harmonic series, moving up and down the intervals. It's the Pythagorean scale, essentially."

Natasha said, "Oh, I see. You're right. Like, the notes you get when you whizz one of those plastic pipes around."

Andy said, "Or a bullroarer; same thing, really. Like he's working music out from first principles. You've got a weird boy there. Was he always like that, from birth, or is it something weird they're doing in there?"

Natasha almost said, 'Strange,' but remembered at the last moment that the boy was supposed to be their son. "Well, just look at us," she said instead, "Nathanael and I are not exactly what you'd call normal, are we?"

Andy nodded.

A louder noise coming through the monitor speakers interrupted them, someone talking. It was Peter Lazarus-Fox's voice — he was still there, then — talking on the phone to someone.

"Yes, sir. Yes I fully understand that you are funding all of this. And I get it — but — I'm very sorry we don't have the technology to do that yet. Pressuring me won't help — you understand that we really can't even experiment on someone, it wouldn't be... a fruitful exercise. Well I think people would get ill, people would die, that would be the consequence, and you don't want that with this calibre of client. The likelihood of failure is far greater than the likelihood of success. And with such high powered individuals... Yes, sir. Well, I can only do my best. My advisory role ends in two months. Well, it did leave me without any means of earning an income when I was forced to leave the museum, that's why I started the gardening business. No, I enjoy it. Well, if you could see to it that I'm paid more, that would be agreeable. Very agreeable really. No, I wouldn't object to giving up the gardening if you had a better paid position. Of course I haven't told anybody. Yes, two people came to see me a few days ago, but I didn't tell them anything. Yes we met in the back yard, because I thought they were clients, the house was messy that day and I thought the yard might be a more agreeable place to meet. Alright. No, I'm not trying to fool you."

There were two rooms there. They marked the one closer to the laneway, 'staff room, telephone?, room for working in? Peter.' and they marked the one on the far side, 'boy.'

The last microphone was pointed to the right, the front of the house facing Audley Street.

At the moment, there was no sound coming from the front rooms. On the 1850 map a hallway, a bedroom or guest room and a front sitting room were outlined. They put question marks in each of those rooms.

A distinctive knock came at the back doors of the truck. Andy hopped up and opened the door.

A pleasant-faced woman in her sixties stood there, holding a tray with a cup of tea, two coffees and three pieces of cake.

Andy said, "Oh, Nathanael, Natasha, this is Marjorie. We're parked in her back garden. She's a good friend of mine." Andy took the tea tray and said, "Thanks, Marjorie." He put the tea tray down on a spare chair.

"No problem," said Marjorie. "Enjoy."

Andy closed the doors behind her. "I trust her implicitly," said Andy, answering an unspoken question. "She's not got loose lips. Won't be going round town gossiping like some would."

They sipped their coffees and began to consider their course of action.

Natasha said, "What we really need is to know how they… um… react to various stimuli… Then we know what to do to manipulate the situation to our advantage."

~~~

A little more than half an hour later, Andy was knocking at the front door of the house where the boy was being held. He was holding a package wrapped in brown paper and a folder, with a printed invoice ready for a signature.

One of the East End guards answered the door. "Hello?"

Andy said, "I've got a package here for a Mister…? Sorry, it's just got the address, don't know who it's for."

The guard said, "I didn't realise anyone had ordered anything. Just hold on a second, will you?"

He closed the door again.

~~~

In the van, Nathanael and Natasha were listening. The East End guard's footsteps traipsed through the house, to the end room where the other guard was. "Did you order a package?"

"No."

"What should we do?"

"Sign for it. Maybe it comes from him."

Nathanael said, "So, the one who answers the door is the underling, the one who stays in the back room is his boss. But they're both underneath someone else, the person Peter was talking to, presumably." He considered it for a moment. "Actually, it's the same as Kade and East End, over in Vegas. Kade was the one in charge, but I suppose they were both answering to the same boss, whoever he is, wherever he is."

~~~

The guard came back to the door.

"Alright," he said, and signed the invoice. "Unusual that you come on a Saturday. Anything owing on that?"

"No," said Andy, "It's all paid for. All you have to do is sign."

"Righto." He took the package and closed the door.

~~~

Nathanael and Natasha listened to the guard's footsteps walking to the back room.

They could hear them unwrapping the package and tearing open the box.

One of the guards said, "What? It's a book. Bones and Ochre: The Curious Afterlife of the Red Lady of Paviland."

"They must have ordered it for Lazarus-Fox. Put it here — when he comes out for dinner we'll give it to 'im. Funny that they sent this by express innit? Must need it for his research."

When Andy came back in, Natasha said, "I've got another thing to try. We've just got to wait a few minutes."

She waited until about a quarter past four, then checked outside. It was dark — the sun had set about fifteen minutes before. Natasha said, "Right. Let's see how they respond to a power outage."

The Tor opening page came up on her compter, 'Congratulations! This browser is configured to use Tor.'

Natasha typed an address in and said proudly, "I've been saving this one up. Worked it out when I knew we were going to England."

A fairly nondescript login page opened up. Natasha logged in.

She told them, "The system I'm taking advantage of is called BushGuard — it's a device that tests the integrity of a power transformers' insulation in an electricity substation. The insulation around the transformer is called bushing, you see, and when the bushing is failing BushGuard sends a message to the central SCAFA server. If the insulation fails, the transformer's temperature soars and it breaks down, often quite dramatically, and is very expensive to replace, so it is something the electricity company would like to be forewarned about so they can forestall any problems."

Nathanael watched Natasha working — she typed a few numbers and a new window opened up. She continued her monologue, "This is a rudimentary trojan I installed months ago. You see, there's a flaw in the SCAFA's online security protocol. Everything is encrypted in the messaging, but when it gets to the server the information is stored unencrypted in the buffer. Once I had worked that out it was actually quite easy to write a program that intercepted the buffer and changed the data before it's passed through. Watch."

A list of numbers came up, with street names and postcodes next to them, and another set of numbers with a small graph and a paragraph of text. Natasha typed "CB10" into a search field, and another list, all with postcodes beginning with CB10, came up. She opened up another page, a map showing all the power transformers and substations in Essex. She matched the numbers. "This transformer is in the substation on the grid that feeds their house."

She altered the second set of numbers and the graph changed, dipping at the end. Then she pasted in some different text into the paragraph. "Now the electric company thinks that the insulation on this transformer is failing," she explained. "They'll send out a truck within the hour and replace the insulation on the transformer, even if the BushGuard hardware display doesn't show any problems any more when they get there. Our friends are going to lose power for anywhere between one and three hours. In fact, I would almost be surprised if they don't shut down the entire substation immediately."

"Um…" said Andy. "What about…?"

All the lights went out.

"Oh," said Natasha, her sheepish expression clearly visible by the light of her laptop screen, which was the only piece of electronic equipment still working, "I forgot about that."

"Bloody hell," said Andy. "Just a second." He pressed a button. The whining sound of hard-drives and computers starting up turned into a low hum as the screens flickered into life. "Battery backup. Always have it ready in case someone trips over the extension cord at a wedding or an important concert we're taping. With any luck a clever edit can cover over a second or two of lost audio. Let's see what we've got."

The audio software opened up on the screen and he pressed, "Record," and immediately the sound of the two East End guards swearing came through the speaker. "Where's that torch?" "It should be on top of the fridge." "Well, it aint on top of the fridge. Where else would it be?"

Then the sound of Peter Lazarus-Fox's voice came through the monitors, saying, "Oh, no. A blackout." His footsteps sounded, rather slowly as though he was feeling his way along the corridor, then his voice again a little more faint. "It's just a blackout."

"I know," said the boy's voice, "I know. The electric power is off. It will pass soon."

"It will," said Peter, sounding a little more tremulous than the boy. Nathanael wasn't sure who was comforting whom.

"It will pass soon," said the boy, "These things do." He had a strange way of talking.

Andy's dark eyes flicked over their faces, as though he was examining them for some sort of clue. "Your son talks in a strange way, doesn't he?"

~~~

Somewhere in London in a secret room, someone was saying, "You remember you told me to keep an eye on Audley Street? There's someone been using Tor on a wireless network, right next door to Room Raquel."

Someone else said, "Notify the yankees."

"They already know. Oh, damn. We've lost it."

"Were they onto us?"

"No. Damn. Just a power blackout."

"Might be able to intercept them if they switch over to a mobile data network. Set Boundless Informant to look for Tor startups on the mobile network in the general vicinity. Oh, and notify the yankees anyway. Someone high up will want to know anything suspicious anywhere near Room Raquel."

"Do you know...why is it called 'Room Raquel?'"

"That's above my pay grade. In fact, it's so far above it that I wouldn't even like to hazard a guess. Some kind of American thing I suppose."
~~~

~~~

Eventually the guards found the torch in the backyard, went back inside and found some candles and matches.

For the entire blackout, Peter Lazarus-Fox talked softly to the boy, who seemed to be confined to his room.

The power came back on about two hours later. Natasha had a theory that the repairmen couldn't find which transformer was faulty, because none of the BushGuard indicators showed anything wrong, and in the end simply made a guess and replaced one of them. "It's only a theory," she said, "But if I'm right we can use the same trick again because they'll be suspecting that they didn't get the right one the first time round."

Andy said, "Well, it's all good, isn't it? We can certainly take advantage of darkness. Someone could go in and get your boy while they're all busy fossicking around trying to find the torch and such, especially if we take it off the fridge early on. Then it's only that scientist you have to worry about, and he doesn't seem that much of a threat. I presume that's what he is, isn't he? That's why you got that book? A palaeontologist?"

Nathanael said, "We need to make our move tonight, then. It always seems more likely when you have another blackout following the first. Now — here's a plan, see what you think. Natasha, you're needed in the truck at the start to cause the blackout. So when Natasha causes the blackout, I'll rush in, steal the torch in the dark if I can, and I'll keep going through until I'm at the boy's room. If Peter Lazarus-Fox is there we offer to bring him too. If he refuses to come, then I wallop him (he's pretty frail, I don't think he'll cause me any problems). I continue
~~~

through with the boy and emerge at the front. Natasha, you and Andy will need to drive your hire car through the front — smash the gate if necessary, it doesn't look that strong. The boy and I will meet you at the front and we make our getaway."

Natasha frowned, "Well... It has the advantage of simplicity, I guess."

Nathanael said, "Well, you are the only one who can make the blackout happen. And we need to do everything quickly once the blackout begins."

Natasha nodded. Andy said, "Okay, sounds good. I think we should be able to make it work. After dinner, then, are we agreed? I think Marjorie is bringing something out for us."

A few minutes later Marjorie brought them some dinner and they ate in silence. A strange mood had come over them, a peculiar melancholy. Nathanael couldn't put his finger on what it meant, what it was. It was as though the reality of all this skulduggery and and telling lies and sneaking about had started to sink in. And for him, the thought that his friend Jannah was gone. Murdered by men who hid in the shadows.

Andy said, "Come on, let's get this show on the road. Let's get your child back."

Natasha and Nathanael looked at each other. Nathanael assumed that they were both thinking the same thought: what would they tell Andy if they actually succeeded? This charade that they were the boy's parents could hardly continue once they had rescued him, once he was with them.

They would have to tell the truth, then — they may as well tell him now — he opened his mouth to start but

Natasha, frowned, shook her head. No, don't tell him yet. Nathanael shrugged. Maybe she was right. They would work out a way afterwards, then.

Natasha started preparing the hack.

At that moment Andy turned up the kitchen mic.

It sounded as though one of the guards was finishing off a phone conversation. "Gambling debts. Really? So that's how they did it. Next half hour? Alright. We'll be ready."

"Come on, whatever that is it doesn't sound too good."

Natasha said, "Right, I'm getting into the electricity company's server." Her computer gave a pinging sound. "Wait a second — something's going wrong. That's my trojan alarm. Someone's trying to take control of my computer!" She started typing furiously. The screen on her computer went blank and Nathanael gasped. She looked up at him momentarily. "It's alright — I have virtual servers. They infected the virtual server with some sort of Linux-only worm. I've still got the connection, I've just transferred it to another server. I'd better be quick though."

She was typing faster now.

The same screen appeared with all the postcodes and the small graphs and all the numbers. Natasha worked twice as fast as she had before. Another pinging sound came out of her computer. Natasha hit enter, and the screen disappeared.

She said, "I don't know if it went through. The worm got control again, even faster this time, so the detector program shut down that virtual server." She paused. "I don't know what to do. Should we wait and see, or should

I make another connection and check the buffers to see if my changes went through?"

A few seconds later the power went down. This time, Andy's screens and computers didn't stop. He said proudly, "I was ready this time."

Natasha's computer screen was still blank. She said, "I'm not going to restart another virtual server — it's too risky — it's unlikely but they might be able to break through the virtual barrier. Let's assume that it went through and that this isn't just some elaborate ruse..."

Her computer screen started up again.

"What are you doing?" said Nathanael.

"That wasn't me," said Natasha, frowning angrily. "I think they have a back door into my computer. You'd better go. Do what you have to. I'm going to fight this. No one owns me."

She looked up for a moment longer and threw her car keys to Andy. "Andy will have to drive the car. It's got a full tank. I'll be alright, if the worst comes to the worst I'll fry the hard drive and they won't be able to get anything. You'll have to get the boy, Nathanael. I'll meet you at that pub we went past when we were driving to Andy's — remember you said it looked nice? The Keys Hotel or something — I'll walk there once I've sorted all this out — I will know, Andy's gear is still recording." Then she returned to her computer. As she typed frantically she was mumbling, "God knows, it would be a disaster if they got in. They'll know we're here in the UK. They'll know our aliases. They'll know everything about me and my family. Even my contacts are on this computer. God, help me." She kept typing.

Nathanael said, "We'll meet you at the pub — it's called the Keys Hotel."

Natasha said, "Wait a second. Here's fifty pounds, you'll need some money at the pub if I'm running late. I don't know how long this will take." She took out a fifty pound note from her purse and gave it to Nathanael.

Nathanael and Andy leaped out of the truck. Andy hopped into Natasha's hire car and gunned the engine.

Nathanael ran along the wall, through a small gate into the alleyway then into the front garden of the house behind the house where the boy was being held. The garden gate was open. He ran through and had to climb a small tree to get over the fence. Nathanael's legs jarred when he hit the ground, but he managed not to fall over. He saw the back entrance to the house. The door was closed. Nathanael ran towards it, leaped at the door. It was flimsy and old and came off the hinges. He fell through into the laundry area. He knew exactly where the kitchen was.

What a stupid plan, to get the torch before they got it. Instead he ran straight up the passageway and ran into Peter. Peter fell down, protesting and cursing.

Nathanael grabbed him by the arm, pulled him up and said, "How do we get the boy out of that room?"

Peter said, "What? How? Who? Nathanael?"

Nathanael said, "You're coming with us, too, Peter. How do we free the boy?"

"Okay, Okay, Okay. Alright, I'm coming."

Peter stood up and used his mobile phone as a torch. There was a small keypad next to the door. Peter typed in nine numbers grouped in threes, "187-782-969", and the lock on the door clicked. Idly Nathanael noticed that the first two numbers, 187 and 782, added up to the third number, 969.

Peter said, "Battery backup for this door, in case there's a fire. They really don't want to lose him. They'd rather him get away than let him die."

Peter shone his mobile phone in there and said, "Meth, we're taking you out of here. Hold my hand."

It was a strange name for a boy. Meth. Methamphetamine? Was he named after an illicit drug? Nathanael couldn't think of any other meaning, but he supposed it might be natural if his guards were using Crystal Methamphetamine. Or was the boy on it too? Surely not...

And another weird thing — the boy looked younger than Nathanael had assumed he was from the type of language he had heard him use — perhaps only five at the most, perhaps even younger than that, barely more than a toddler. His vocabulary had sounded about ten or twelve, in Nathanael's opinion, for what it was worth. He was a teacher in another life — a high school teacher — but a teacher, nonetheless, he was familiar with the developmental stages of childhood. Was this a child prodigy of some sort?

Nathanael had read of child prodigies, children with high IQs. Often one of the earliest signs is complex speech at an early age. Was this what Meth was? Some sort of genius?

The child was very, very pale. His hair was more white than blonde and his eyes were strangely intense, and there was something strange about the fine cheekbones and finely honed jaw structure that Nathanael couldn't quite put his finger on.

He pushed those thoughts away — any hesitation might be fatal. He said to Peter, "We're being picked up out the front."

Peter said, "Come on, Meth." The boy grabbed Peter's hand and they ran up the hallway to the front of the house.

There was dim light coming through from the hall window and more light coming from the front room even though the curtains were shut. There was a hatstand next to the door, with a few umbrellas hanging from it.

Nathanael tried the door. It was locked. Peter reached up to the hatstand and produced a key.

Behind them, a commotion started up — the two guards had come out into the hallway shouting, with the torch flashing everywhere. On seeing Peter unlocking the door they shouted, "Stop!"

Nathanael ran at them, trying not to think about what he was going to do once he got there. He swung a punch at one of the men, but the man ducked. Nathanael kicked out blindly and managed to get a lucky strike, kneeing the other one in the nuts. The second guard doubled over in pain. The first guard shouted, "Stop!" and from the corner of his eye Nathanael saw he was holding a pistol. Right in front of Nathanael's face, though, was the first guard's elbow, and the hand at the end of that arm was holding the torch. Nathanael grabbed the man's forearm with one hand and twisted and forced it into the wall palm outwards, making him drop the torch. Then he punched the guard's elbow, crumpling it the wrong way inwards. There was no doubt the man was burly, but with the particular angle of Nathanael's attack his elbow gave a sickening crack and he gave a shriek of terror and pain. Nathanael kicked the torch into the wall, the plastic shell splintered into pieces and the light flickered out. The two guards were still crouching on the ground keening in pain, but probably not for long. Nathanael turned and ran back to the front doorway, which was standing open.

Outside Andy was sitting in the car with the engine running and Peter and Meth were both sitting in the back of the car. It struck Nathanael again how tiny the boy was. He leaped across the porch, across about three metres of garden, ripping through a rose bed, and jumped into the car.

Gunshots sounded but Andy had already floored the accelerator. They were screeching away. A few shots thudded into the car's trunk, but nothing higher. Nathanael looked back as they zoomed out through the broken gate to see the guard taking aim again with his left hand (his right arm was hanging uselessly, broken at the elbow), but the other guard pushed his left arm so that the shot went wild. Nathanael reasoned that he didn't want the boy to be harmed — they would rather him be free and alive than dead — he supposed it was because there was still some chance they could get him back.

~~~

Natasha had regained control of her computer and fought off the hackers. It was her own program that had made the difference — something she had written that monitored everything happening on the computer and detected any program that was rewriting its own code or attempting to access any communications protocols, in other words, anything likely to be a virus, trojan or worm — as far as she knew they hadn't gotten anything. None of the logs showed any significant transfer of information.
~~~

Just as she was finishing, the wireless network failed. No problem, she connected her computer to her mobile internet instead, and just as that was happening her mobile ran out of battery.

Oh, well, that's the end of doing anything right now. She may as well pack up and go to the café.

Clunk — the back door of the truck made a sound. Nathanael and Andy weren't coming back — was someone else trying to get in? The door was open a crack. But nothing happened. Then something at the other end of the trailer was tugging or moving, then sort of popped. The extension cord went whizzing past and the back door of the truck shut. Clunk. Was that the external lock on the truck doors being secured?

Natasha got up, her heart racing. She said, "Marjorie, is that you?"

Marjorie said, "Nothing to worry about, love. Just sit tight. They'll be here soon."

Natasha felt a twinge of suspicion for some reason. Was it something in Marjorie's tone of voice? Something was definitely wrong. She needed to clarify what Marjorie meant. Natasha said, "Who will be here soon?"

Marjorie was silent.

Natasha got up quickly and tried the door but it wouldn't budge.

Natasha's stomach sank. A bitter taste of betrayal came into her mouth. Natasha wanted to convince Marjorie to let her out but as she spoke her tone of voice sounded plaintive to her, begging, pathetic, "Please don't. What are you doing, Marjorie? Please, Marjorie, what are you doing?"

"I'm sorry love," said Marjorie in a tone tough and condescending; she had had to harden her heart to do what she did. "You don't understand, Natasha, we were about to lose the house. Ronald had so many debts, hundreds of thousands of pounds, debts to the casino in Montreal, the races, debts to online betting companies, even drug dealers, everybody, really. It's wonderful really. Ronald's debts will all be wiped off. A clean slate. We keep the house. And all I have to do is lock this door and walk away."

Marjorie's footsteps receded. The back door of Marjorie's house creaked open, then shut softly, and Natasha was left sitting in the back of the truck, alone.

Chapter 11 — Mirror, Mirror.

Nathanael, Peter and Meth got to the Keys Hotel and waited for Natasha to turn up. Meth was fine with drinking hot chocolates — a drink he had never had before, apparently — so he was occupied. And Peter had told him to keep quiet in public for now, and for some reason the boy respected the paleogeneticist's opinion so he didn't embarrass them in the pub speaking too eloquently for his young appearance.

They waited there for three hours for Natasha, but she didn't turn up, and by the end of that Nathanael was pacing frantically, and some of the other patrons were looking askance at him.

Andy whispered frantically, "Don't pace like that, Nathanael. You're making a scene. I'm sure it's all alright. There was probably something interesting happening in the house and she decided to record it. I'll ring Marjorie and see what's happening."

He kept ringing Marjorie's number on his mobile, both her home phone and her mobile, but she wasn't answering.

Andy said, "That's a bit of a worry."

Nathanael said, "We've got to go back to Marjorie's place."

"Yeh," said Andy, a knot of concern now on his brow. "All my stuff's still in the back of that truck. What if something's happened to it? I hadn't wanted to make a scene near the house, straight after that incident, but now… If Marjorie isn't answering her phone and neither is Natasha…"

Peter said, "What about us?"

And Meth said, "Yes. What about us?"

Nathanael said to Peter, "You wait here with the boy. Is that okay? Can I trust you?"

Peter scoffed, "Of course you can. We'll still be here. Where am I going to go? They've probably got all their cameras primed to send them a picture of my face wherever I am." He looked around nervously and whispered, "You're sure there's no cameras in here?"

Andy said, "Yes, I checked carefully. We couldn't have been seen — there are no cameras between the car and here. It is a quiet street where we parked. God I can't believe how paranoid you lot are." He hesitated and said, "But perhaps it's not unjustified."

Nathanael gave the fifty pound note Natasha had given him to Peter, "If we have any problems, spend the night here and meet us in the morning at that cafe in town."

Nathanael and Andy left the Keys Hotel and drove back to the house. It was only a short drive. They went through the back entrance and parked next to the truck.

The back door of the truck was wide open but Natasha wasn't in there. All of Andy's gear was still in there, though, and he heaved a sigh of relief. "I've to get all this back to the studio. If I didn't have all my gear, I'd be stuffed — couldn't make a living." Nathanael felt his temper rising, but he pushed it back down. Andy had no reason to want to find Natasha, she wasn't his friend.

Nathanael forced himself to see things rationally. It was obvious where Andy's priorities lay, and clearly it was time to let him loose.

"Andy," said Nathanael. "Take it all back to the studio, take your stuff back. Listen — I don't want you to risk your own neck, mate — you've done enough for us. Just watch your back for the next — I don't know — month or two, alright? I don't want you disappearing or something like those paleoanthropologists."

Andy said, "Wait a sec. I've got something else for you. The perfect gift for the paranoid man on the run."

He handed Nathanael a pair of number plates and explained, "These were on my Dad's car, somehow never got round to returning them. Paid the rego ever since he died just in case I needed them. You know, a little backup measure, in case I lost me license or something, pair of number plates can be mighty handy. Happens sometimes with us musos, you know, an unfortunate night on the booze, a random drug test."

Uncomfortable because he had no more money on him, Nathanael took out his empty wallet and said, "How much do I owe you?"

Andy said, "Nothing. I can see what you're trying to do is good. I know that boy Meth isn't your son — but he damn well deserves a better life than he's getting there. And from what I can tell, you and Natasha are good sorts. You're rocks, you two, real rocks. The salt of the earth." He unplugged a hard drive and handed it to Nathanael.

"Look, here's all the audio we recorded while we were here today, as well as the other lot yesterday that you and Natasha recorded in the laneway."

Nathanael took the hard drive. "Thanks."

"I hope Natasha's alright, hey, I can see that's what you're worried about." Andy grasped Nathanael's shoulder. "Do you know, she's a clever girl. I don't think she'd let herself get stuck in this truck if trouble was coming. I reckon she's somewhere out there, in hiding, looking for you or waiting for you to work out where she is. Oh, by the way," he took out a screwdriver from a toolbox and handed it to Nathanael. "If I were you I'd change those plates over right now."

They shook hands. Andy gave him forty pounds from his wallet too, something Nathanael accepted because he really wasn't sure where they would get money from.

Andy hopped in the truck and drove off and after switching the plates Nathanael quickly looked around the property. There was no sign of Natasha in the back yard.

The back door of the house was ajar. He took out a handkerchief and pushed the door open. What if Natasha was in here?

Marjorie was lying on the floor, prostrate, not breathing, clearly dead for a while, for her skin had gone pale and it looked as though rigor mortis had set in. A few yards away, her husband lay, dead also. There was no sign of trauma.

Did these people really think the police would believe a couple could die of a heart attack, one after the other, just like that, and not do an autopsy? He supposed they probably would. There might be a newspaper story out of it, the curious fact that a couple both died within minutes of each other, but not much else.

Nathanael felt sick. He got in the car and drove back into town and parked behind the Keys Hotel again.

He went in. Thankfully, Peter and Meth were still there.

He said, "No sign of Natasha. I think we need to make a hard decision... I have the hard drive of all the audio. And I have new number plates. I think we can escape detection for a while." He weighed his options for a moment. "I think we have to leave. We have to assume that if Natasha is captured, then it's all over for her. If she's free then she'll find some way to contact us. Come on, we're going to London. We're going to find a place to stay. I think Bruce's place would be agreeable. And I think Natasha would know anyway that London is where we're headed."

"Who's Bruce?" said Peter.

"Bruce Fetherington at the British Museum."

"Oh, that old guy," said Peter. "Is he really still around?"

"I hope so," said Nathanael. "I really hope so."

~~~

On the way to London Nathanael decided to find out as much as he could from Peter and the boy.

"So... Peter, why are you in on this? Why did you leave the house so willingly?"

"I'm... fond of the boy, Nathanael. And I knew I was the only person who had his best interest at heart. No one else did. Those guards just wanted to bully him. The man on the phone — the man who runs things — he just wants to exploit him, to exploit his... humanity."
~~~

"What do you mean?"

"I'm unique," said the boy. "That's what he means. I'm very unusual and there is something in my blood, in my genetic makeup, that they believe might be medically very useful to them. Unfortunately they have not been able to replicate the magic ingredient yet, or else they might have let me go."

Peter said, "I don't think they ever would let you go, Meth, if the choice was up to them."

Nathanael asked Peter, "Why does Meth talk in such an advanced fashion for his age? I mean, he uses a vocabulary far in advance of a — what is he? — a five year old?"

Nathanael saw Meth and Peter looking at each other in the rear view mirror.

Meth said, "I have an... endocrine disorder? Something like that, anyhow, I look a bit younger than I am, that's all. That's why they can't just send me to a regular school."

Nathanael said, "How old are you?"

Meth said, "I'm not completely sure. It seems to me that I have been here for a very long, long time."

Nathanael asked, "Are you still growing?"

Meth said, "Yes. By all accounts they expect me to keep growing until I reach a height of around five foot eleven, six foot one, perhaps, somewhere around that height, but at a much slower rate than a normal person. They don't know when I will reach adult height, exactly, but possibly many years yet, based on how slowly I am growing."

Nathanael said, "And where are your parents? How do we get you back to them?"

Meth sounded sad. "I don't know where my parents are. A long, long way away — that's what they have always told me for the years of my imprisonment. I have never seen them. I would like to see them. It is good that I am free now, I can try to find them. They must be somewhere in this wide world, somewhere out there."

Peter said, "Now, Meth, I've told you not to pine for that. It may not happen. It will be very difficult to find your parents, that's all I can guarantee. Perhaps impossible."

Nathanael had a feeling that Peter knew more, but he didn't want to push him just yet, not with the boy in the car with them.

He said, "Peter, do you know who's calling the shots here? The man you talk to on the phone. Your boss, the bloke telling you what to do and paying you."

Peter looked at Nathanael sharply, then said, "Oh, yes, I remember, you were listening in from next door, weren't you? I don't know his name. All I know is that he funds this type of research, has been for many, many years."

"But the real question is," said Nathanael, "What does all this have to do with paleoarchaeology?"

Peter said, "Not now, Nathanael, not now. I don't want to upset him."

Meth said, "Upset who?"

Peter said, "Upset... Nathanael. He doesn't need to know the whole truth yet."

Meth's face went red and he blurted, "That's not what you meant. You mean me. I don't need to know. Exactly the same as them. That's exactly what they told me. Exactly what you told me, Peter. Are you going to be my new jailers now? Do you know I found books on the internet before they found out I knew how to surf the net? The Man in the Iron Mask was my favourite. Now there's a good book for you. I think I have simply exchanged one set of jailers for another."

Peter pleaded, "It's not so, Meth, it's not so. You know I have your best interests at heart. Please believe me. I really do."

Meth looked up at him. "You don't care about me any more than any of the others."

Peter shook his head. "That was such a cruel, unfair thing to say. I gave up my position at the British Museum, to make sure I could look after you, Meth. Then I was ready to give up my gardening business too — probably will have to, now — and I was even ready to sell my soul to the devil, just about, even, to take a job with those creeps, just so I could keep an eye on you."

Meth said, "Alright. I believe you, Peter. I believe you."

Nathanael looked in the rear view mirror at Peter and Meth. Certainly a lot more going on right now between these two than meets the eye. What sort of relationship was it? Was Peter Meth's father? Was Meth his son? It certainly appeared to be something like that.

~~~

As they were coming into London, Nathanael said, "Got any cash on you, Peter?"

Peter said, "Yes. Always carry two hundred pounds, in case of emergencies."

"We're going to need to stay in a motel overnight. We won't be able to get into Bruce's apartment if the day porter is not there."

Peter nodded. "You realise we call them motor inns here?"
~~~

They found one a few miles down the road with a free three bed room. They stayed there for the night.

~~~

It was just after nine in the morning when they reached Bruce's apartment block the following morning. Nathanael quickly found parking about half a block away. They walked swiftly, the three of them, and went in.

The first thing they noticed was that the Day Porter wasn't there. They made their way up quickly in the lift, Peter and Meth following him out into the corridor.

Nathanael's heart sank when he saw that Bruce's door was ajar.

Bruce was lying on the floor in the entry hall. A small medical spray was next to his mouth.

His heart medication. Back in December Bruce had told him, if he found him like this, spray the stuff in his mouth, under his tongue, and it might revive him. He had also told him everything about the drug — it's a nitrolingual pump spray, the active ingredient is nitro-glycerin. Yes, the same chemical as the explosive. Restarts the heart, apparently, Bruce had said.

Nathanael opened Bruce's mouth. He didn't seem to be breathing, but Nathanael lifted his tongue slightly and sprayed the chemical underneath it.

Bruce woke up, coughed a little. He didn't move much, just tilted his head a little so that he could see who was there.

Nathanael picked up the hall phone, an old model with a dial still, and rang triple nine and called an ambulance.
~~~

"Oh, here you are Nathanael," said Bruce, smiling. "Wondered when you would get here. I managed to hold on… Despite what they did to me."

Nathanael said, "Who? What did they do?"

Bruce said, "They must have injected… Must have been potassium chloride… The nitrolingual spray helped. Wait — I have something I must… to tell you. Do you know, I don't mind dying. I have hope because of Jesus' resurrection. A historical fact."

Bruce's eyes began to close. Nathanael said, "You're not going to die. I've called the ambulance. Hold on."

Bruce coughed a little. "Bosh, Nathanael. Of course I'm going to die! Everyone does, you know. Do you know…" Bruce's voice was getting weaker. "I was wrong when I told you we have nothing. We have the colophons. The colophons. The toll of death." He gripped Nathanael's hand.

Then his eyes glazed over and his grip on Nathanael's hand slackened. His mouth was still moving — he was still talking, very softly. Nathanael put his ear to Bruce's mouth and heard him saying, "Hesperus is Phosphorus and Phosphorus is… what's that Latin name…? Isaiah. Look. Isaiah! The Rescuer will come."

A thin dribble of blood came from Bruce's mouth.

Nathanael couldn't hear him breathing any more so he started pounding on his chest to keep the heart pumping. The ambulance arrived eight minutes later.

He told the paramedics what Bruce had said about potassium chloride and at once one of them said, "Quick! Epinephrine, then 125 mL of a 4.2% sodium bicarbonate solution."

With the first injection, Bruce's body spasmed for a moment. With the second, he stopped moving and his eyes were still closed.

One of the paramedics opened his eyelids and looked at his eyes. "He's not responding." They brought out a defibrillator and placed the electrodes on his chest. 'Stand clear' — the machine shocked him. "Still not responding." They put him on a stretcher and carried him out.

Nathanael went to follow them, but Peter cleared his throat. Nathanael turned — he had forgotten that they were were — the boy had seen everything. Meth seemed strangely unperturbed. Peter said softly, "We need to get Meth out of here. Nathanael, I'm sorry for your friend, but at the moment, I think the more important thing to do is to run. After all, your voice is on the record now making that emergency call. How long before these people send someone here to finish off what they couldn't finish back in Arizona? Bruce is in good hands. If he's going to survive, he will survive, but you can't do anything more."

For a moment Nathanael was torn. Another problem — he needed the toilet.

He walked through into Bruce's ensuite and quickly did his stuff, then he stood for a moment, looking in the mirror.

What on earth was he doing? His friend, Bruce, needed him right now. Why had Nathanael been on this crusade for the truth? Was he crazy? He was following Natasha, following her agenda. It was her enthusiasm that had kept him going. Her Christian principles. Nathanael wouldn't normally be so irrational, but, you know, Natasha was a pretty face, and… And now she had abandoned him, or had been captured. Either way it didn't speak volumes about their probable chances of success.

Better to abandon this whole crusade, stay by his friend's bedside in the hospital, watch him, keep him safe.

But Peter was right. Even if he stayed by Bruce's bedside — and that was assuming they had saved him, which certainly didn't look certain — he couldn't protect him. They might come in the night and both of them would be dead. Nathanael couldn't stay awake for twenty four hours a day.

He could protect Bruce more by finding out what was going on and exposing it.

A painful feeling rose in the pit of his stomach until it seemed to be sitting at the top of his throat. He looked at himself in the mirror. His face was grimacing, his palms were sweating. Nathanael didn't always have insight into what he was feeling but this feeling was anger.

It was personal now. He was on a crusade for justice. They had killed his friend, Jannah, and now they had tried to kill Bruce as well. Nathanael didn't have that many friends. He couldn't afford to be losing them. He wept for a moment, about Jannah, then controlled himself. He had to get control of himself — they couldn't stay here for long.

He felt as though he had travelled a million miles, since the moment he had entered the small ensuite, as though he had been in there for millenia.

He washed his hands and came out and looked at Peter and Meth. Without a doubt, they were the key. If he abandoned them to look after Bruce, he might well fail completely at achieving both goals.

Whereas he was certain Peter knew more than he had told him. In fact, with Bruce spouting gibberish as he was dying — just as Jannah had been, not long before her own death — Peter and Meth were the only clues Nathanael had left. And if he could expose this whole thing then maybe, just maybe, Nathanael could protect Peter and Meth as well.

"Alright. I'm going to use Bruce's phone, quickly, though."

He rang the international call code, and rang his brother's number in Australia. He hadn't talked to him in months, they usually didn't talk for three or four months at a time. His wife answered. He asked for his brother.

Nathanael said, "Hamish. I need you to do something. Access my bank accounts. I've got about fourteen thousand dollars in saving. Use Western Union or someone like that, or American Express, wire the money here to this account. .Peter, what's your account number? I suspect they think that I'm coercing you — it means that they won't have put a stop on your accounts. If Natasha got caught, then they will almost certainly have a stop on mine."

Peter said, "Do you really trust me that much?"

Nathanael looked at him. "I think I do now. And that question in itself shows a... sensitivity about the issue of trust, that I trust, anyhow. I have to trust you. Who else do I have to trust now?"

Peter told Nathanael his bank account number and Nathanael told Hamish.

"Hamish — please do it as soon as you can. Right away."

Hamish started to protest.

Nathanael said, "It's a matter of life and death."

Hamish stopped protesting. "Really?" He knew Nathanael didn't exaggerate about things like that.

Nathanael said, "What time is it there?"

"It's just after five. The bank has just closed."

"Well, go to the bank at eight thirty, or whatever time it opens. You know my bank password, don't you?"

Hamish said, "Yes, I do. The usual one you use."

"Yes. Well, do it, please. If you don't, someone may well die. Don't worry, though, I'll tell you all about it when I get back."

"Alright. I'd better go then. I've got to change some plans for this morning. I'll get it done, right when the bank opens."

Hamish ended the call.

Nathanael reflected that Hamish didn't even know about his car accident, yet even so, he was ready to drop everything at a moment's notice to help him without even knowing the details.

Nathanael said, "Peter. We've got to go to the nearest bank first thing tomorrow morning. About seven thousand pounds is being wired through. In the meantime, do you have any money on you? We need to book ourselves a motel, a place to sleep for the night."

Peter had some money on him. They looked up homestays and motels in Bruce's yellow pages, found a couple a good half hour away. Nathanael didn't book a room — they decided just to turn up and see if any rooms were available. Using the phone wasn't really an option. Nathanael said, "I'll take the yellow pages with me. If the first place doesn't have any rooms, maybe the next one will."

They tidied the place up a little then Nathanael locked Bruce's door behind him.

As they were driving, Nathanael began wondering about Bruce's last words. Knowing Bruce, it might not all be gibberish. Whatever Bruce had been going on about, a colophon, Hesperus, these things might well have something to do with Natasha's last conversation with Bruce — knowing Bruce it was some sort of clue as to what was going on. Bruce had been so insistent that he had to tell him, before he died. Colophon. Hesperus is Phosphorus. Isaiah. What could it possibly mean?

~~~

"Money was just wired from the account of Nathanael Wayfarer in Australia."

"Where to?"

"Peter Lazarus-Fox's account."

"Do we stop it?"

"No. See which branch Lazarus-Fox withdraws it from. Then start surveilling that area."

"What do we do if we find them?"

"Watch. Wait. Tell the people upstairs. I have no doubt they'll send in the muscle."

~~~

There were roadworks on the way and they got held up a little, so it was past midnight by the time they reached the first homestay. They had only one room but it was available — a room with three comfortable beds and a bookshelf on the wall stuffed with classics and spy novels, and the three of them slumped down and slept soundly.

The next morning Peter went to the nearest branch of his bank and discovered that the bank transfer had gone through. He withdrew the whole amount, which came to eight thousand four hundred and seventy eight pounds and fifty two cents, and handed it over to Nathanael. The pound had strengthened, actually, since Brexit, much to the chagrin of all the doom-mongers. Actually, the rise of the pound was bad for Nathanael, though, going from Australian dollars, which were quite weak at the moment. Nonetheless, this pile of cash was still a significant amount. It would keep them on the run for three or four months or more if they needed to.

Peter had emptied his bank account too, converting it all to cash. That was another seven thousand pounds at least. They could get new identities with this, perhaps, or at least hide out for an appreciable while.

~~~

They decided to stay at the homestay for a few more days. Meth was absorbed in reading some of the books that were on the bookshelves and Nathanael and Peter both needed to rest. Nathanael's legs still ached when he was tired, the pain was insistent, lingering longer than usual. He hadn't realised how exhausted he was until he stopped.

Still, there were things he could do here.

The people they were staying with had the internet and they were happy for Nathanael to use their computer to surf the net from time to time. He stayed away from email or social media, but he did look up some facts, things he didn't think the people following him would know he was looking up. Things that wouldn't alert their systems to Nathanael's identity or location.

Such as the last thing Bruce had said.

"Hesperus is Phosphorus."
~~~

Chapter 12 — Gunter, Glieben, Glauchen, Globen

As the van bumped along the road, Michelle was praying, God help me, give me guidance, asking for him to save her.

Eventually they ended up on a smoother road, a freeway, she reasoned, and in the middle of praying she actually fell asleep.

When she woke up, they were still driving. It was dark, night time and the van was going on a very bumpy road now. The vomit had dried up and no longer smelled.

For some reason she started thinking about some Bible studies she had been doing at church lately. A verse from the Bible came to mind, "I tell you, my friends, do not be afraid of those who kill the body and after that can do no more." It was something Jesus had said, in Matthew's gospel, or maybe it was Luke. They had been studying Luke. Could this be God's way of talking to her? It certainly seemed applicable to her present situation. Was she going to be alright, then?

Then another verse came to mind. "Love your enemies." It seemed to her that God had breathed it into her soul, as though that was what He wanted her to do.

The van stopped.

The two men who had abducted her opened the back of the van. Michelle stepped out — she decided to keep her poise. It was about all she had. They roughly tied her hands behind her back with a luggage tie.

It was the middle of the night. They were somewhere in the middle of a forest with very high trees, they were probably redwood, and a lot of scrub and ferns at ground level, on some sort of park road. It looked like somewhere in California to her.

"How peaceful she seems," said one of the men, in an American accent. "Most of them are begging and crying and weeping by now."

The other spoke in some sort of British accent. "Wouldn't be so peaceful if she knew what was going to happen to her, most likely. Have we had the call?"

"Not yet. Who knows, maybe they still have some use for her?"

"Look at her. Doesn't even know what to do."

Michelle said, "Yes, I do. Love my enemies. That's what I have to do."

The British one said, "Well, I wouldn't say no. She's quite cute. What are you love, eighteen? Twenty? I'd go for it. In fact, maybe I will."

The American one said, "You may as well. Get your rocks off. Your wife'll never know."

"You reckon?"

"Well, I'll never tell her. And I'd lay bets that this girl won't be telling anything to anyone soon enough."

"How about it love?"

Michelle was simply revolted by the thought that some poor woman was going to sleep with a pig like this, that the poor woman was married to this pig. A flash of anger went through her and she kicked him in the left knee as savagely as she could.

He actually stumbled, in fact, something in his knee had snapped, Michelle was sure she had heard it, as clear as day. It really didn't sound good. Inwardly she smirked. Outwardly she tried not to show how pleased she was.

He tried to stand up but his left knee wouldn't hold his weight. "What have you done to me, you witch?" he cried out. "Look what you've done. You've injured my leg. You've hurt my knee and now it doesn't work properly." He tried bending his knee but it wouldn't bend properly.

"Good," she said, and spat at the ground in front of him.

He stumbled around a bit and then the American one said, "Get yourself together. Here." He walked to a nearby tree and tore off a long, straight branch. "Use this as a crutch."

The British man took the crutch and leant the weight of his left side on it — it seemed to hold. Then he snarled, "Kill her now."

"Oh, come on," said the American man. "You know we can't do anything until we hear from you-know-who. They might want her alive. She might be a useful bargaining chip. Or she might know something they need to know, maybe they'll need us to question her first."

The American's mobile rang. "Geeze, I didn't think we'd have coverage out here, but we do! Yes, sir? Oh, you don't want us to? So where are we taking her to? Alright."

He said to the English one, "Give her some water and something to eat. Bundle her back in the van. We're going to D.C. now."

~~~

She was sleeping soundly, when she was rudely awakened by someone saying, "Gunter, Glieben, Glauchen, Globen!" No, it wasn't a person, it was the stereo system in the van, playing music.

It was the start of a rock song.

> "All right!
> I got somethin' to say
> It's better to burn out
> Than fade away
> All right! Ow!
> Gonna start a fire"

~~~

There were speakers here in the back as well. She found the speakers. Perhaps she could pry them out? Use something as a weapon, or a tool? But they were protected by metal grills that seemed to have been welded in.

> "Rock of ages, rock of ages
> Still rolling. Keep on rolling."

Rock of ages. Somehow it was comforting.

Perhaps Jesus had chosen for them to play that particular song, because He was the Rock of Ages. She slept properly this time, despite the bumpy ride and the hunger and thirst. The Lord was still looking after her.

~~~

About twelve hours later, as far as she could tell, they'd gone through a drive-through, McDonalds or something. She had tried shouting but no one outside seemed to hear her. They stopped another hour after that after driving over some roads that definitely weren't highways. It was the American one who opened the back of the van and let her out.

It was now the middle of the day and the sun was very bright, wherever they were.

Her eyes adjusted and it looked to her as though they were in the middle of Utah. There was nothing for miles around but hayfields and pasture, with a few flat hills in the distance. What was it with flat hills in Utah and Arizona? Some sort of geological thing, she imagined. The type of rocks, the way they developed in prehistory.

Why was she thinking about hills and rocks and so forth when she was pretty certain she was going to die soon?

The British one stumbled out of the van, still using the branch as a crutch. Clearly his knee hadn't healed yet. Michelle was glad.

The American guy said, "Throw that branch away. How do you expect your leg to heal if you aren't using it?"

But the British guy answered, "No. I need it. Me leg's not working properly. I told you, that's what the Doctor said."

The American guy said, "You're such a wimp. That last phone call means I've got to go into town. Can't have her in the van — need to get some stuff and they'll need to put it in the back for me, so I can't have them peering in and seeing her cowering there can I? You'll have to stay
~~~

out here with her and look after her, by which I mean, don't let her get away, until I get back."

The British guy sort of sneered, "How can I look after her when I can't run? She could just run away."

The American said, "You work it out." The British guy was leaning on the crutch, glowering at him. It seemed like a power play to Michelle.

The British guy won.

The American sighed and took a small handgun out of his pocket and put it in the British guy's hand. "Just try not to kill her. They need her back at the ranch, apparently."

He hopped in the van and drove off, leaving behind dust clouds to billow and disappear.

Michelle looked at the British guy, limping over, leaning on his crutch to where she was sitting on the grass.

He said suspiciously, "Don't try anything I've got the gun."

Michelle rolled her eyes. She felt like being sarcastic but she couldn't think of anything to say.

Leaning on the crutch at an increasingly acute angle then making a controlled fall for the last foot or so, he sat down next to her with some difficulty. Once there he began dangling the gun on his knee, its barrel slightly oriented towards her, like some sort of macabre toy. They sat for a while like that, in silence, with the slight breeze ruffling her hair slightly and the sun shining down, making her feel warm inside, despite the fear that was inside her as well. Sitting here with that bad man reminded her of something she'd read once, she couldn't think what it was.

"You've really stuffed me up, little missy," British guy said finally. "I can barely walk. Do you realise I've got a vacation coming? I'm going to see me two boys for the first time in about six months, they're just toddlers, twins. Every time I see me two boys I pick them up and whirl them around, gives them a real thrill! Now do you realise when I see them I won't be able to do that, because of what you did to me knee? Christ, I probably won't even be able to pick them up at all, or carry them, or put them on my knee ever again. I'm in such a mess now."

In that warm sun, the thought came to her that it would be gracious to offer to pray for his knee for him, but she ignored it again.

"Well," said Michelle, "You were going to kill me. God knows, perhaps you still are. You kidnapped me. I mean, I hurt your leg. A little perspective here."

"Yeah, well. I'll be glad to kill you after what you've done to me. But, you know, we ain't never killed a young lady before. I was hoping that we wouldn't have to. Still hoping we won't have to. Dropping thugs is one thing, but I never wanted to hurt you. I was just... managing the situation, see? If you're scared it's easier to manage you. Not going to kill you if I can help it. I might be a thug, but I don't hurt women."

Michelle thought for a moment. "Kade probably wants you to hurt me."

"Kade's a bully," he said. "Pushes me around all the time. For years he's been threatening me, telling me what to do. He's a bastard."

He paused for a moment, and Michelle realised he was gnashing his teeth. He began rubbing his knee.

"I've been to the Doctor, you know," he said. "You wouldn't think we would've had time to do that, what with rushing across the countryside and zipping from here to there, but I managed to get dropped off to a Doctor's surgery when Kade was getting lunch at that burger joint. So, the Doctor says, 'Buddy, your knee is stuffed. It's the ligament, not the tendon or the muscle, and if you ask me, it's not going to just heal on its own. I've seen injuries like this. They don't just heal spontaneously. Time is not going to do it. You're going to need a big, very expensive operation,' he says, 'Get them to pay for it.'

"I says, 'Who?'

"He says, 'The sporting club of course. You got the injury playing soccer, that's what you said, isn't it? Get your sports club to pay for the operation. Surely they've got insurance?' It was then I started to think about what a crap job this is. I always knew it but it really is. Alright the pay's good, but no insurance, no sick leave, no worker's comp — and the likelihood of getting injured is pretty high. Actually, who gets out of this job alive? I've got so many friends who've been put away. There's Charlie, old Mitch, Big Rob, Teddy. All rotting in the ground now, not one of them died from old age, every single one of them put away, died of lead poisoning."

Michelle realised he was saying his friends had all been shot. She actually found she was feeling sorry for the man, despite herself, despite her fear of what he might be capable of. It was like being in a cage with an injured lion. If she helped him or showed some sympathy, how did she know he wouldn't turn on her afterwards? She prayed again, this time that God would give her words to say.

Before she was even aware of what she was doing, she found words coming out of her mouth, "Do you want me to pray for that knee?"

"What?"

"Pray for it. Do you want me to pray for God to heal it?"

He laughed. "You're crazy, love, innit? You're joking me."

She rolled her eyes. Here she was going out of her way to show him kindness and he didn't even believe it. "I'm serious."

He said, "I dunno. What would God want to help me for? I'm not exactly Mister Nice Guy. I'm not going to win the Saint of the Month award, I'd say. Maybe villain of the month. Thieving, murdering madman of the month." He laughed again and it chilled Michelle a little. "God would never want to help me. Naw, when I'm topped I'm gonna end up in hell, burning for all my sins. So I may as well enjoy life now for what it is, cause I can't help what I am..."

Silently she prayed for words, words from above. She felt naive as she heard herself saying. "God wants to help everybody. Jesus loves everyone, even very bad people." She didn't really want to say it, but it came out nonetheless. "God even loves you."

He stopped looking her in the eye and his voice broke. Michelle thought it was as though his pride had broken as well. "Me Mum used to go to church, you know. Every week, and she'd take us kids. Before she died she made me promise, 'Davo, go to church when you grow up, take your missus and your kids to church, the family that prays together stays together. Jesus loves you and forgives your sins, so you need to go to church so you don't forget that,' and I was a good boy then and I said, 'Yes Mummy, I promise.' She said, 'Good boy.' Them was her last words to me. You wouldn't believe it but I really was a good little boy back then. I used to do all me homework and did everything the teacher asked me to. But when I got older I took after me father instead. After Mum died he lost his way — she was always a light to him — he couldn't get a decent job, too sad and cut up over her passing away, so he became a bouncer at the local pub, a standover man, used to collect debts for the bikies, an all round thug really, and from when I was about eleven he'd take me off on his jobs. I thought it was great, being part of the tough guys' club."

He paused. "It really ain't so great, is it? I don't know what happened to my life. It's all gone wrong. I can't even tell me wife about what I do for a living, and I'm away from home for months on end. This job is the pits, it's a deep hole and every time I try to get out of it I just dig meself deeper in. It's been making me do things even I thought I'd never do. And the drugs start playing with your mind. I was a good boy as a child but look what's happened to me if me wife knew even half of it she'd be horrified and it's affecting our marriage anyway because I can't talk about half the things and the guilt is driving me crazy. I'm so stressed I can't even fulfill me marital duties." He started sobbing. "Please pray for me. And me knee, so I can lift up me kids."

Feeling it was all quite absurd, Michelle put her hand on his shoulder.

"Loving Father," she prayed, "Please help… Davo… He is a lost child of yours, but he's coming home to you now. I ask you to heal his knee. And please reassure him that you really do forgive all his sins and love him still. Father, you love him, please reassure him that you'll accept him back as a son, even after everything he's done."

Davo was really sobbing now. "I've been so bad. I've done so much wrong. How can God possibly forgive me? I don't want me son to go to hell, but if he follows in my footsteps…"

"When Jesus was being nailed to the cross," Michelle said, "He prayed for the men who were hammering in the nails, 'Father forgive them for they know not what they do.' If God could forgive the people nailing Him to the cross, don't you think He could forgive you? After all, you haven't done anything as bad as that, have you?"

Davo didn't talk any more for a little while, he was sobbing too much. "No… maybe… yes… But if He's as kind as that, then… I guess He'll forgive anything I've done… This is what I believed as a kid. That kind of Jesus. The forgiving kind."

"Davo," said Michelle, "Do you believe Jesus rose from the dead?"

"Yes, Michelle. Always did really." It was the first time he'd used her name. He laughed bitterly. "Ha ha. What a stalwart Church of England parishioner I've been."

Davo pushed himself up, stood up without thinking, without using the branch as a crutch. "Hey, look at that! Me knee's better. It just got better! I suppose it might be psychological, do you think?"

Michelle actually thought it might, but she felt it wasn't necessarily in her best interest right now to say so. Instead she said, "It might be a miracle. I think it's… quite possible that God healed you, Davo, because He loves you and forgives you."

Davo started stretching his leg, tried bending it out and back in again, then he jumped on that foot, up and down, and began laughing. "No more pain. It's bloody brilliant! Thankyou, Michelle! Thankyou, thankyou, thankyou!"

Michelle nearly pointed out that she had hardly done anything, really, God had done it, anyway, (or his subconscious) and she was the one who had caused the injury in the first place so it was a bit silly to thank her, but she wisely kept her mouth shut this time.

Davo said, "Cor, I'm going to look after you, little Missy, I'm way better than I ever been. You done for me what fifty counsellors, psychologists, psychotherapists and doctors couldn't do. God bless you!"

At that moment, the van appeared on the horizon. Michelle was praying still, praying now that God would get her out of this situation.

She might've made friends with Davo, but maybe that was just Stockholm syndrome. She wasn't out of the woods yet.

The drive over the hayfield seemed to take forever. Finally Kade got out.

Davo didn't hand him the handgun.

Kade said, "The things are in the back and I've got some lunch for us."

Davo stuffed the gun in his pocket while Kade brought out three bags of takeaway.

They sat there eating fried chicken and french fries. Michelle was really scoffing it down, it was only the second meal she had eaten in two and a half days and she was starving. Kade and Davo ate silently.

It looked to Michelle as though Davo wanted to say something, but he didn't know where to start.

Finally Davo said to Kade, "Do you ever think about religion?"

Kade said, "My grandma used to push it down my throat. She'd say, 'Kade, God is kind and patient, but He won't wait for you to repent of your sins forever. You must turn to Him before you die. Then He'll look after you.' I used to laugh in that old woman's face. I'd say to her, 'What, like the Almighty looks after you? You are as poor as a matchstick and nobody cares about you, and you're old and shrivelled and ugly as a prune. No,' I'd say to her, 'Once you're dead you're dead, and that's it. You got no hope in life, so you put your hope in fairytales.' She was very sick in her last years, ain't nobody looking after her neither. That's how God looks after his own. Then one day she up and died. Can't say as I missed her none." He bit into a piece of chicken and some of it dribbled down his face.

Michelle's disgust at Kade's attitude showed in her face. She said, "Didn't you ever visit her to help her or see that she was looked after? I mean, she was your grandmother after all."

Kade snorted. "Are you kidding? She was depressing. Always talking about death and people's sins. I think she wanted to die. No, never visited her if I could help it, never wanted to. Old bag."

Davo said, "Maybe you… should have listened to her. Maybe there's something in it." Michelle was worried. Davo seemed to be doubting.

Kade said, "Oh by the way, Davo, I got another phone call. Apparently they have someone else they can use as leverage now so they don't need her. So we can do her now. Hope you're ready." He smiled a ghastly smile at Davo. "I told you, I won't tell your wife."

Davo said carefully, "Kade, we don't have to do that now. I never done in a girl. I been faithful to my wife, Kade, despite what else we done. In fact... I won't be in on it." Then his voice took on a complaining tone. "She's just a girl, Kade, a young woman, we can't hurt a girl."

Kade's face turned red and he stood up and lifted Davo up by the arm and started swearing coldly. Then he bellowed in Davo's face, "What? Do I believe my ears? Are you disobeying me? Do you think you're better than me? Are you telling me you're better — better than him? Better than our boss? Better than him?" Kade grabbed Davo by the throat and slapped the side of his head with the back of his hand. "You are not to behave like this. Insubordination is not allowed in this organisation and if you won't apologise to me right now I'm going to beat the apology out of you. We're doing that girl and that's it."

The years of abuse he had endured from Kade finally made Davo snap. He shouted, "Get lost!" and shoved Kade's arms away with some sort of martial arts move and reached back with one huge fist. He threw a massive punch straight at Kade's jaw. Kade stumbled backwards blinking. A trickle of blood started dribbling down from his mouth. Kade shook his head and a tooth flicked out, and he looked disoriented. Davo moved in closer but Kade reached out quicker than a death adder and grabbed the handgun from Davo's pocket.

Kade laughed. He pointed the gun at Davo and said in a low, threatening growl, "I don't mind doing two for the price of one. You've been a disobedient dog, all the way along."

Davo shouted in his face, "What, I'm supposed to be your best mate and you'd pull your gun on me? I done everything you ever said until now. You been pushing me around ever since I started working for you and I've had enough of it. Don't you dare pull a piece on me!" Davo pushed his finger into Kade's forehead.

Kade twisted the gun on his finger and said, "Look it's not even loaded, you fool." Michelle noted that — an interesting fact that might get her free — but Kade was laughing like a man possessed with a Banshee. "There's no ammo in it. You're an idiot. You guarded this girl with an empty gun. Stupid. She's stupid. Both of you are idiots. You could have run away from him at any moment." Kade was waving the barrel at himself and laughing insanely. "See? You're an idiot. No ammo in it. Watch." He pulled the trigger.

The gun gave a huge explosion.

Kade looked down with horror at his shirt.

A large red stain had started to form on the left side. The blood was darker than Michelle had expected, but there seemed to be bright red blood mingled with it.

Davo said, "Kade, you just shot yourself in the heart. You idiot."

"Davo, I did. It looks as if I did. Well, glory be."

"Kade, put your trust in Jesus before you die! You want to go to heaven don't you? Give your life to Jesus and let him forgive you."

"What? What are you saying, Davo?"

"You can be forgiven. Your sins can be forgiven."

"Are you a Christian? You're not telling me you're a Christian?"

Davo hesitated, a little confused, "I..."

Kade starting laughing hysterically. "I can't believe it. Hahaha!" He gasped and spluttered and continued laughing hysterically, blood still leaking and spurting out of the wound in his chest and staining his shirt red. He began leaning over in a rather unnatural way, his limbs not quite sitting right. "Davo! After everything you've done, and you're a Christian. He's a Christian. Hahaha! Hahaha! He's a Christian! Davo's a Christian! He's a Christian!" His chuckles turned into intermittent gasps as he tried to breathe. He was lying on his side now and a small eruption of blood came out of his mouth. Michelle watched, horrified, not sure if the sounds Kade was making were more laughter or the sound of someone choking on his own blood.

Kade gave one last paroxysm and stopped, his eyes still open, his face still fixed in a grotesque open-mouthed parody of a grin.

Everything was quiet. The feeling of the wind blowing across the grass, silently, was the only sensation that touched Michelle. And the sight of the man's body, completely still, with that terrible grin on his face.

Davo looked at his dead friend and wept for a moment. As if to explain he said, "He was a monster but he was still my mate."

He took out a large spade from the back of the truck and started digging a hole.

He said, "I think this spade was supposed to be for you, for your grave, Michelle. That's what he went into town to get."

After two or three hours of digging, the hole Davo made was big enough to bury Kade in. He dragged the body over into the hole and began spading dirt over him.

It was now late afternoon and the sun looked as though it would be heading over the horizon soon. The whole world was very, very silent.

After a long while, there was nothing but an insignificant mound, and Davo covered it over with hay.

Then he said, "Well, looks as though it's you and me now Michelle. I suppose we need to have a chat about where we're going. One thing I know. We can't go back to your home, and I can't go back to my home neither, not without me delivering proof that I killed you to D.C., so I suppose we need to find a different alternative."

And saying that he slid a small knife out of its sheath in his boot and grabbed Michelle's arm rather roughly and she gasped as he swung her around so that she was facing away from him. It was completely impersonal. All of that effort, trying to show love to the man, it was all for nothing. He was going to kill her anyway, poke her in the kidneys with the knife, or something, slice open her heart, do it that way, in the back, so he didn't have to look her in the eyes as he killed her.

But he slit the luggage tie on her hands and freed her, and slipped the knife back in its sheath and said cheerfully, "So, where are we off to then?"

Chapter 13 — Natasha's Noncompliance

Natasha sat for a moment. What was she going to do?
This was a no-win situation for her, a dead end.

All she could think of was to pray…

Having done this, she began to go through her assets.

She was healthy, fit, active, no injuries, and she had the advantage of surprise.

She had some money on her, a few thousand pounds at least.

She had all of Andy's gear with her, but none of this was of any use, really, because there was no power in here.

Her laptop was fully charged. But her mobile was dead.

But she did have Skype on her laptop. Of course, without an internet connection that was useless.

She had a USB in her pocket with a few hacks, trojans and so forth on it.

She had her charger but no power.

She looked on the computer for any wireless networks nearby.

The local library had an open network that had one bar. Maybe it was strong enough to send an email.

She closed every computer program that might conceivably access the internet and went through her preferences to see if she could turn off 'receive' emails or anything else that might chew up bandwidth.

Once she was set up she logged in to the network and opened up the email app.

She thought of emailing the police but was afraid that they might just hand her over to whichever branch of intelligence services had abducted the boy. So she emailed the local locksmith. She headlined the email, 'Emergency Situation! Please help!' "It's an emergency — someone locked me into the truck and I... am due to pick up my children at the hotel from my ex-husband, per our access arrangements. Please help me!"

Within five minutes someone was opening the door of the truck.

"It was just the latch on the outer door. Not even locked. What sort of cretin would do this?"

Natasha said, "It doesn't matter." Over the locksmith's shoulder, Natasha saw the curtains move. Marjorie was peering out.

Natasha hopped out and paid the locksmith's attendance fee, forty pound, thanking him for coming out on Saturday night. She was still counting out the money when she heard the footsteps coming up the laneway.

She grabbed her laptop and handbag, with her mobile in it and used her cheeriest

"You couldn't give me a lift to the pub as well, could you? Since you just got forty pounds for doing nothing!"

"Sure. Which one?"

"The Keys Hotel."

"Okay. Hop in." He opened the door to his locksmith's van.

She jumped in and said, "Please er... make it quick. I was due twenty minutes ago."

He leaped in to the other side, gunned the engine and the locksmith's van screeched out of the rear yard, careening along the laneway towards the centre of town. The two men walking down the laneway had to leap out of the way. She looked in the rear view mirror and saw them chasing the van down the laneway, shouting and cursing. One of them pulled something small and black out of his jacket pocket, but they were already turning the corner, she didn't even have time to notice what it was.

She heard the gunshot, though it was soft, silenced perhaps, but the locksmith didn't even notice. If you weren't listening for such a sound it probably seemed like an engine backfiring or something.

They reached the pub three minutes later, but just after he had driven off, leaving her standing out on the kerb in front of the pub, she noticed the black car pulling up at the end of the street. That was High Street, she remembered from when she had been driving through the town.

There were two men in it.

They were watching her.

What now?

If she went into the pub she was just leading them to Nathanael and the boy. What else could she do?

She was standing at the end of a T-Junction. She turned and sprinted down King Street.

Just past the hotel was a short alleyway to the right. She ran down the alleyway, through the car park at the back of the hotel, leaped over a fence and ended up running through another alleyway.

She was back on High Street. She looked around — no sign of the black car. She supposed they had followed her down King Street and lost her.

She hailed a taxi that was passing slowly, presumably looking for passengers from the hotel.

The taxi driver wore the turban of a Sikh, and seemed glad that she was not drunk.

He said, "Where to, then?"

Natasha considered it. "Andy's place — the music shop. Saffron Music, other end of High Street. And there's an extra ten pound in it if you can get me there quickly while taking the side streets."

The taxi driver took off down a side alley immediately and they ended up going through a residential area. He said, "I'm taking you round the long way, past the golf club. Tell me, why are you doing this? Is someone following you?"

Natasha nodded. "Yes. A black car with two men in it."

The taxi driver said, "Oh, forgive me, but that is rather exciting. Ever since I started driving taxis I thought, how wonderful it would be to be part of such a chase." He put his foot down and glanced in the rear view mirror. "I don't think they are following us. Do you mind if we go a little slower? I don't really want to get a ticket."

Natasha sighed. "Yes, that's fine."

Within a few minutes they were driving through the countryside. The trip took about twenty five minutes and there was no sign anyone was following them.

When she reached Andy's place she had misgivings. He had expressed a desire to be done with all of this. She told the taxi driver to keep driving until they reached the nearest hotel or tavern.

He said, "There's one just up the road, Miss. See? — right there. The Golden Lion." He went slowly along and pulled up in front of him.

She paid him, including the extra ten pounds, hopped out and knocked on the door.

The owners were happy to have an extra guest for the night.

It was a comfortable bed and she slept very soundly.

The following morning she got up at eight o'clock, had breakfast and had the hotel call her a taxi.

The taxi arrived just after nine.

On the off chance that the others were still at the Key Hotel, she told the taxi to head for the town centre.

As they were driving, she was watching the side of the road for the black car. She didn't think she had left any trace of her activities, but all it would have taken was one stray security camera.

Then she saw it, on the main street coming into town, parked by the side of the road with the two men in it. As they passed, the black car pulled out onto the road, following close behind.

Natasha said, "Turn around, please, I forgot something. Oh, could you go via that little Greek coffee shop on High Street?" No point leading them straight to Nathanael and the boy, assuming that they were still at the Key. The way she had told him to go, he had to make an awkward U-turn. They went through a laneway and Natasha said, "Oh, I changed my mind. Just go past the golf-club would you?" She was getting to know the streets around here now.

After she apparently changed her mind three or four times they went back to the Golden Lion and had the taxi drop her off. She booked herself into the hotel for another day and spent the day reading books and thinking of how to evade the black car if it turned up again.

The following morning Natasha got up at seven o'clock.

She called another taxi.

The black car was waiting about fifteen minutes down the road, much closer than before. Did they know where she was staying?

Natasha clenched her fist on the hand rest in the door and said, "Go to the church primary school, please. I've just had… a message — need to pick up my children."

The taxi driver said, "No problem."

In a few minutes they were there and she paid her fair.

The black car parked where they had a clear view of the school. Natasha knew she couldn't run away, not there, too many cameras these days around schools.

She walked into the school office, reasoning that whoever they were, they wouldn't do anything to her in a public place, particularly not at a school.

The receptionist was busy with parents, thankfully. Natasha got out her laptop.

She needed a disguise. And a lift out of here.

One of the parents the receptionist was talking to was wearing a hijab. She had her two children in two, and was just finishing whatever business with the school she was conducting.

As she walked out, Natasha said, "Excuse me."

She said, "Yes?"

Natasha assumed what she thought was a passable Pakistani accent. "My husband is picking me up and he tends to get very upset if I don't wear my hijab. Do you think I could borrow yours? In fact, I'd be prepared to pay you for it."

"Really? Look — we're in England now. You mustn't let him treat you like that." She took the hijab off and gave it to Natasha. Natasha offered her a ten pound note, which she refused.

Then Natasha went up to the receptionist. "Hello. I'm considering enrolling my children in the school here. Would you be able to run me through the costs involved, the requirements and so forth? We are recent immigrants from Pakistan." The school receptionist began to tell Natasha the details, but then Natasha said, "Oh, one other thing. You wouldn't have a suitable mobile phone recharger handy? I left mine in the car and I'm supposed to ring my husband when I'm ready to get picked up." They did indeed have a phone recharger and agreed to charge Natasha's phone for her while the receptionist went through everything.

Twenty five minutes later, Natasha's phone was on 45% and the receptionist had finished answering her questions. She called a taxi and gave the same false name she had used with the receptionist. She asked the taxi driver to come into the reception when he arrived.

The taxi took forty five minutes to arrive, something Natasha was not particularly happy about, but there really was very little she could do about it. The taxi driver was Pakistani, as Natasha apparently was too, but he was quite rude, probably because it was only a short journey to the coffee shop and he wouldn't be getting much for it.

Natasha glanced out of the back window.

The black car with the two men was following them.

She told the taxi driver to forget about the coffee shop. She flipped out a fifty pound note, not many of those ones left, unfortunately, but she gave it to him anyway. "Lose those guys tailing me and there's another fifty pounds in it for you."

CHAPTER 14 — LEVIATHAN ON A LEASH

Davo was driving. "Well, obviously we can't go back to my place. I'm pretty sure my bosses are watching my place. And for now, we can't go back to Washington DC, because it will be pretty bleedin' obvious if I turn up wiv' a girl who conforms to the description of the one I should have topped. I suppose I could top them all of course. I'd just have to kill... Ah, about seven people, they're the only ones in the organisation who know who I am. I'd be scot free then. We'd be scot free then!" He turned to her and smiled momentarily.

Michelle felt a wave of nausea and discovered that she was screwing up her face. She consciously calmed her features; she didn't want Davo to know how concerned she was. Then she managed to squeek out, "Isn't there a way can get back to our lives without killing anyone?"

Somehow, having Davo as a friend was stressing her out more than having him as an enemy.

Davo went on, "Well, you can't go back to your house neither, because your house is almost certainly watched. And you can't contact your sister either. That's out of the question. How can you go back to your life? I mean, everything, they've got surveillance on everything. It's their contacts at the NSA, you see, they've got eyes on everyone."

Michelle was on more solid ground here – talking about what was and was not possible electronically. "There are some things I can do, Davo. We can do non-specific web searches, keeping them general. I can withdraw money from my bit coin account. And I can keep an eye on Natasha's dropboxes, the places she usually puts things on the Dark Net when she wants to get them to me."

Davo raised his eyebrows. "Really! You and your sister, into the Dark Net, hey? And there I was thinking you were both good Christian girls." He chuckled, but then the way he looked across at her, ogling her breasts and her tummy quite unashamedly, made Michelle feel very uncomfortable.

She steeled her nerve and spoke very firmly. "Davo! You are a married man. What would your wife think of you staring at my breasts?"

Davo shrugged. "Probably wouldn't mind so long as it didn't go any further than that." Then he shrugged again. "You know, there you are again, taking the high ground and all, being a good Christian girl, and yet when I picked you up you were completely sozzled, I mean, absolutely stonkered. I bet you put out. Come on, love, we've got a few weeks at least of lying low, maybe even months. I'll look after you – don't mind doin' that – but you know, you owe me and all. How about it? It's just a bit of fun in the bedroom. You and me. The wife doesn't have to know. What she don't know won't hurt her."

Michelle's throat tightened and a palpable pain began to burn in her chest. She realised she was not out of the woods yet. She began to pray again.

Thankfully a mood of quietness descended on Davo then and Michelle prayed about what to say to him. She had to take charge – she could see that now – it was no use simply trusting Davo's apparent affection for her was enough to keep him from harming her or even killing her if the wind changed direction.

CHAPTER 15 — GENESIS AND JANNAH

In those few days, while they were relaxing, Nathanael slept a lot. For a change, he had free time, 'down time', and he started thinking about everything that had happened. Questions and puzzles began to form in his mind, small details that he had forgotten about in the hustle and bustle that had been his life since Natasha had taken him from the hospital.

In the bedside drawer he found a Gideon's Bible — were they still doing that? The only Bible Nathanael owned had been given to him by Gideons when he was a small child, in Primary School. It had a red imitation leather cover and in the first few pages, one bible verse, 'For God so loved the world that he gave his one and only son, so that whoever believes in Him shall not perish but have eternal life,' had been translated into dozens and dozens of different languages. He had pored over those pages as a child, fascinated with all the different oddly shaped scripts and languages.

His Bible had only had the New Testament and Psalms. But the one in the bedside drawer was complete, with Genesis at the start. What was it Jannah had mentioned? The era of the patriarchs.

He began reading through Genesis. First, the creation story. "In the beginning God created the heavens and the earth. The earth was without form and void, and darkness was upon the face of the deep; and the Spirit of God was moving over the face of the waters." That was interesting in itself — the way this was written, it seemed as though the earth and the darkness were already there when God created them. He continued reading. Then there was the story of Adam and Eve.

"The man gave names to all cattle, and to the birds of the air, and to every beast of the field; but for the man there was not found a helper fit for him."

So God gave Eve to Adam, then the snake tempts them to eat of the fruit of the tree of good and knowledge, which they do. Then God "drove out the man; and at the east of the garden of Eden he placed the cherubim, and a flaming sword which turned every way, to guard the way to the tree of life."

He remembered Bruce had said something about there being oblique archaeological evidence for Adam and Eve. An ancient temple. Their hosts were out that day and they didn't mind them using the computer, and Peter and Meth were both sleeping right now in their beds. Nathanael moved his researches out to the other room and sat down on the swivel chair, at the computer.

He googled, "Ancient Temple Adam and Eve," and came up with nothing. Then he remembered the name Bruce had mentioned.

Gobeckli Tepi? Gobekle Tepe?

Nathanael googled his best guess — and an article came up on the Smithsonian Magazine website about an archaeological site called Gobekli Tepe.

Originally thought to be nothing more than a Byzantine cemetery, dismissed by archaeologists from the universities of Chicago and Istanbul, an archaeologist called Schmidt decided to check the site again. He had gone there and immediately knew it was important when he saw the shape of the hill. "Only man could have created something like this," he says. "It was clear right away this was a gigantic Stone Age site."

He started a dig there and found giant standing stones, with foxes, lions, scorpions and vultures, and many other animals carved on them. What was this? Adam and Eve's memorial to their time in garden of Eden, their cultural reminder that Adam named the animals?

Based on carbon dating of flints and other artefacts found at the site, Schmidt believes Gobekli Tepe to be the earliest centre of worship known to science.

And what was Romans one twenty five? He distinctly remembered Bruce mentioning that particular number (which is five cubed when five squared is twenty five times one.)

Perhaps it meant what the Romans were doing in one hundred and twenty five a.d.? He googled it. About the only notable event in that year was the construction of the Pantheon in Rome.

But then he typed in "Romans 125 animals" and it came up with a bible verse, Romans 1:25, "because they exchanged the truth about God for a lie and worshiped and served the creature rather than the Creator." Was this what Bruce had meant? After Adam and Eve had been expelled from the garden they had set up a memorial to Adam's deed of naming the animals, and instead starting worshipping those images? The beginnings of religion...

Nathanael kept reading. Cain killed Abel and had to wander the earth, then Cain had fathered Enoch, all those boring genealogies. He skipped that part.

Then there was a peculiar section then about the sons of God desiring the daughters of men and God sends the flood, and Noah, his wife, and his three sons and their wives are the only ones who survive.

He read onwards. After the next boring genealogy was the story of Abram, who became Abraham. The patriarch of the Jews. The age of the patriarchs. So was this what Bruce had been talking about? But wait a moment, he said this section had evidence — the laws and customs of the time were known — they matched.

What had Bruce been talking about? That Jannah thought there was proof of something? The age of the patriarchs?

No, no, she had said the age of the antediluvian patriarchs. Antediluvian — ante meant before in Latin. What did diluvian mean? He googled antediluvian.

"Of or belonging to the time before the biblical Flood."

So this is something about the period of time before Noah?

Clearly Bruce, along with a large proportion of the scholars, had always assumed that Noah's flood and everything before it was mythological, or at the most, that no one could find any proof for this age.

Could they have found proof?

And what did that have to do with the boy, Meth?

And Peter Lazarus-Fox, a palaeoanthropologist who specialised in working with DNA?

There were so many other puzzles as well.

Bruce's last words. The colophon. That's what Bruce had said. "I was wrong when I told you we have nothing. We have the colophons. The colophons. The toll of death."

What on earth was a colophon? Bruce knew what the word meant, it was that little copyright notice at the start of a book that told you who the publisher was. But did it have some special meaning in archaeology?

He typed in "Colophon, Genesis" into google and came up with a page describing something called the Wiseman hypothesis.

Apparently P.J.Wiseman was a British Air Commodore who visited Babylonian archaeological sites in the early twentieth century and had noticed something about the tablets they were digging up — (he must have been able to read the tablets, so he was more than just a military man, so who didn't they call him an archaeologist in the article?) — at the end of each tablet were found three standard pieces of information. The first states "this has been the history/book/genealogy of…", the second tells you the name of the person who wrote the tablet, and the third piece of information is the date it was composed, such as "the 3rd year of king so-and-so".

Wiseman had called these, 'colophons', and related them to the 'Tolodeth' in Genesis.

Ah, Bruce had not said, "Toll of death," a meaningless phrase, not in Bruce's character, he had said, "Tolodeth."

The genealogies that Nathanael had skipped.

So did this mean Bruce agreed with the Wiseman hypothesis?

He read through the genealogies carefully and noticed the extreme ages of the patriarchs. Methuselah was clearly the oldest, he had had his first son at a hundred and eighty seven years old.

"When Methuselah had lived a hundred and eighty-seven years, he became the father of Lamech. Methuselah lived after the birth of Lamech seven hundred and eighty-two years, and had other sons and daughters. Thus all the days of Methuselah were nine hundred and sixty-nine years; and he died."

Nathanael had read something about this somewhere, some people apparently thought this extreme longevity was explained by the fact that the numbers were measuring lunar months instead of years, or some other value.

Nathanael tried a few alternatives. The problem was, Enoch was 65 when he fathered Methuselah. And Methuselah was 969 years old when he died. Also, Methuselah was 187 when he fathered Lamech. (What was it about these figures — there was something familiar about them, Nathanael mused) So to make these figures work...

Let's say Methuselah was around 70 when he died, a reasonably old age. Well, then, Enoch would have to have been about 5 years old when he fathered Methuselah; he got there by dividing all the figures by approximately 14.

Okay, let's divide them by 12. That would make them lunar months of some sort.

So if that was the case, then Methuselah was 80 when he died, a reasonably old age. Well, then, Enoch would have to have been about 5 and a half years old when he fathered Methuselah. No better, really. Well, quite frankly, ridiculous.

Really, the youngest Enoch could have been when he fathered Methuselah was about 12 or 13, Nathanael supposed, and that would make Methuselah near enough to 200 when he died. And this relied on dividing all the dates by 5. It still sounded unrealistic.

Then he noticed something. Noah was 500 years old when he had Ham, Shem and Japheth. That would make him 100, when he fathered three sons, if we were dividing the figures by 5.

No, it was impossible to make these figures work that way.

Anyway, what was it about the antediluvian period that these scientists had discovered?

And what did that have to do with Cro-Magnon man?

Nathanael looked over at the room where Peter and the boy were sleeping. He didn't think Peter was going to be very forthcoming with his information. So far, what had he told him? Nothing much.

Then he remembered something else. Peter had been talking about something called the 4977-bp deletion — (Nathanael knew the number was 4977 because 4977 is 7 times 711, and "9" looks like "p" and "b" upside down. And 1659 times 3 is 4977, and 1659 has a 9 and a 6 in it, reminding him of the "p" and the "b".)

When Nathanael googled 4977-bp deletion, pages and pages of scholarly articles appeared. The top result was titled, "Mitochondrial DNA 4977-bp deletion is a common phenomenon in hair..." He clicked on it. In the abstract it said, "mtDNA deletions have been reported in various human tissues, e.g., the brain, heart, and skeletal muscle."

He looked at some of the other articles. Apparently 4977-bp deletion was the most common mutation in mitochondrial DNA.

What could possibly relate all these things together?

He looked at the first article again. "Mitochondrial DNA 4977-bp deletion is a common phenomenon in hair, and is related to age."

Did these scientists think that Cro-Magnon fossils were people from antediluvian times?

Suddenly Nathanael remembered why those dates in Genesis seemed familiar.

The three numbers that undid the lock on Meth's cell door.

187-782-969

187 was the age at which Methuselah fathered Lamech. 969 was how old Methuselah was when he died. And 782 was how old Lamech was when Methuselah died...

Meth.

The name had nothing to do with Methamphetamines.

Meth was short for Methuselah.

Was it possible?

What had these scientists done?

CHAPTER 16 — TAXI TAXONOMY

The taxi driver received a phone call on his hands-free. Natasha couldn't hear the other side of the conversation because he was wearing an earpiece.

He said, "Yes. Alright, sir. Yes, right away." He closed the phone connection and turned slightly to talk to Natasha in the back seat. "I'm very sorry, Ma'am. You have been polite to me and it grieves me to have to do this." And he pressed another button on the dash. All the locks clicked shut. Natasha tried the window button. It didn't work, either.

Natasha said, "What's going on?"

He said, "I don't want you to think I don't appreciate your tip, Ma'am, but do you see that car behind us? The one you asked me to get away from? They already tipped me... an awful lot more than you did." While still driving, he took the fifty pound note back out of his cash register and passed it back to her through the partition.

Natasha put the note back in her purse. No point knocking it back. "Do you want more money?"

"Well, quite frankly, this is my job, and I don't mean... driving the taxi. I can't accept bribes in one of these... situations."

"What's happening to me? Where are you taking me?"

"I don't know Ma'am. I'm just following instructions. But I would say… these are very powerful people, Ma'am, who have captured you. You ought to give up all thoughts of escaping the fate they have in mind for you right now."

Natasha ignored him. After setting the 'record' app to record everything that was happening, Natasha quietly stashed her mobile phone in her panties, doing the job beneath her laptop which was over her lap, while pretending to surf the web with her other hand. Even with a camera on her in here they'd find it hard to work out what she was doing.

He was watching what she was doing on some sort of dashboard camera. He said, "You realise you can't get an internet connection in here, even if we happened to be going past an open wireless network at a public library or something. The whole car including the windows is lead-lined. Not super healthy, I suppose, in the long run, but certainly succeeds in preventing my… customers from raising the alarm when I abduct them for… them."

"So how come your phone works?"

"External antenna. And why am I telling you this? I think we'll exercise the virtue of silence for a little while. I seem to find I… er… lose my customary reticence with you. And that could get me into trouble."

He pressed another button on the dashboard and a plexiglass screen came down between them. She could no longer hear him and, she presumed, he could not hear her.

~~~

One and a half hours later they reached London. They continued through London for another ten or fifteen minutes until they reached a single story block of flats
~~~

in West Drayton. The taxi turned off the main road into a driveway, through a set of gates that opened on their own as soon as the taxi coasted towards them and into a large shed in the backyard. The taxi driver got out and left Natasha in the car. He exited through a door at the side of the shed.

A few minutes later the two men she had seen in the black car, watching her, came through the door the taxi driver had exited through. The car locks clicked open. Natasha quickly tried to exit through the opposite side from which the men were coming, but that door was still locked. The men opened the door on their side, grabbed her laptop and then pulled her through by the leg.

Natasha decided not to make it easy for them. She kicked, punched, bit at them, but as soon as they had pulled her off the car seat one of the the men grabbed and held her arm in a painful hand lock, with her hand bent backwards the wrong way. She found she could not move without putting herself in considerable pain.

They walked her like this, bent over with the man holding her hand, out of the shed and into one of the units in the townhouse.

What on earth did the neighbours think when they saw things like this happening?

They shoved her into a room with no windows and only one door and locked the door behind her.

~~~

Natasha lost track of time then. She didn't know how long it was she was waiting, it could have been an hour, it might have been three or four hours, could have even been a day. It was not a short time.
~~~

A man came in wearing a nondescript suit. He brought a chair in with him and sat on it, wrong way around, facing the back of the chair, facing her.

"Miss Natasha Chase," he said in a gravelly voice that sounded like two heavy stones grinding together, in an accent she couldn't readily identify. She didn't think it was an English accent, actually, rather South African or Australian, but not the broad variety of either, but an Oxford or Cambridge educated version, if she was not mistaken. "Miss Chase," he repeated, "We are not with them, the people who have been troubling you. Rather, we are with an international group dedicated to discovering what they are doing. So I think you will understand, the more information you give us, the quicker we can let you go."

Natasha's pulse started pounding and a sick, nauseous feeling began in the pit of her stomach, rising up to her throat. What if they were with them, and were just trying to find out how much she knew? How could she possibly trust these people?

A tentative vocalisation came out of her mouth first, the sound of vulnerability, rather than words. Then she said, "Um... Mister...? Sorry, I find it hard to say anything without having a name attached to the person I am speaking to."

He said, "Mister Smith is what you may call me."

"Mister Smith. I think you will understand that in my present circumstances I don't know who to trust. And unless you can show me that you are trustworthy, you will appreciate that I can't share anything with you, much less any 'secrets' I may inadvertently be in possession of."

And one secret Mister Smith did not yet have possession of was the fact that her mobile was sitting rather uncomfortably in her underpants. All she needed was the opportunity to use it away from the prying eyes that were undoubtedly watching her through the camera that was certainly watching this room.

Mister Smith scrunched up his face in what appeared to be an uncustomary expression of uncertainty. "I don't really know how I can convince you that I can trust you."

"Well you could start by letting me use the bathroom. Or should I say, the lavatory. And perhaps afterwards, by giving me something to eat and a cup of tea in a room that has a nicer view of the outside world than this one."

~~~

A few minutes later she was sitting in a rather more comfortable sitting room, sipping a cup of coffee. After she had drunk her coffee, she walked around the room looking at things.

On the wall was a chart labelled, "Taxonomy of the Animal Phyla," with a list of the usual subdivisions in the animal kingdom. An unusual thing to have on the wall in a secret government organisation's safe house. Well, perhaps not, considering the strange byways of this whole affair. Perhaps it was more likely they were in a secret scientific organisation's safe house. The books on the book case looked to be mostly about biology and genetics, with odd, apparently obscure titles such as, "Cherokee DNA: Real people who proved the Geneticists wrong" and "Mitochondrial Dysfunction in Ageing and Diseases."

Nothing much she could use, except perhaps for the computer in the corner. She didn't know the password, but there were more ways around that little inconvenience than one.
~~~

For some reason no one had come to check on her.

What she wanted to do might not take longer than fifteen or twenty minutes. All she had to do was put the USB in her pocket into the machine, turn it on, and the trojan would do the rest. She had already uploaded everything else she needed to their account in the Amazon cloud, and even if she couldn't use their wireless network, with the internet connection on her mobile she might just be able to set the hack in motion.

The only thing that could ruin it was if someone interrupted before she had finished.

CHAPTER 17 — CRO-MAGNON KINGS

Nathanael didn't notice Peter looking over his shoulder at the computer screen, with its picture of Gobekli Tepe and the other search results in the tabs, the 4977-bp anomaly, book of Genesis, Wiseman hypothesis, so he almost jumped when Peter said, "You've worked it all out, haven't you?"

Nathanael breathed a sigh of relief when he realised it was Peter. "Yes. Yes, I believe I have. Meth is short for Methuselah. What you've done is… found some way to revive the longevity of ancient Cro-Magnon man. The… antediluvians." Nathanael still had problems with this part of the whole thing. "I presume it has something to do with Mitochondrial DNA."

Peter said, "Exactly. I came out here to fill you in while Meth was sleeping, but it looks as though you're already well on the way towards working it out yourself. Obviously I didn't want to talk about it while Meth was listening. He still believes he is an ordinary child and thinks he'll be able to find his parents. He thinks he has a rare chromosomal disorder that makes him age more slowly. He believes that might be the key to finding out who his parents are, wherever they are; the treatment they might be receiving."

Nathanael turned around in the swivel chair and said, "But he is never going to find them, is he?"

Peter shook his head sadly. "No, he won't. His 'parents' — or rather, the source for his DNA — was a group of Cro-Magnon remains that we were studying in 2002. We found soft tissue with intact DNA, enough to construct a complete sequence which we inserted into an embryo. Well, quite a few embryos actually. Meth was the only one who survived. He was 'conceived' (if you can call it that) on the 2nd January 2003."

Nathanael said, "Fourteen years ago? Meth is fourteen?" He stood up. He could not take such news sitting down, he had to be moving around.

Peter nodded. "Indeed. Yes. Fourteen."

"What does this mean? I mean — is that what Jannah was going on about? Proof that Genesis is historically accurate?"

Peter raised his eyes to the ceiling, as though he couldn't believe Nathanael's naiveté. He explained, "Legends of long-lived individuals in ancient times are not confined to the Bible, you realise. From China, Guan Chen Zi lived for 1200 years, Peng Zu lived for over 800 years and according to Chinese medical records, a doctor of the Qin dynasty lived for 300 years. The Greek seer Tiresias is said to have lived for over 600 years. The medieval Persian epic Shahnameh contains an ancient king list, perhaps sourced from other, older documents, in which the ages of the earliest kings range from 500 to 1000 years, quite like this list in Genesis. There exist numerous versions of a Sumerian King List in which the earliest eight kings had ages measured in shar, units of 3,600 years. The first ruled for 28800 years. Alaljar ruled for 36000 years. 2 kings ruled for 64800 years, and so on. Actually, if you assume a scribe mistakenly assuming the set numbers were written in sexagesimal notation, these ages can be shown to be directly based on the numbers in the Genesis account, if they were originally written in decimal — of course this doesn't establish the historicity of Genesis — just that the Genesis account was earlier than the Sumerian. And the length of the reign of the Pharaohs in the Egyptian time of Zep Tepi, or the 'first time', ranges from 1000 years down to 300 years. Following this dynasty the length of the reigns become more plausible. Actually, when you compare the lifespans of the Biblical antediluvian patriarchs with the reign of these Egyptian kings, one finds they are quite comparable, like the Sumerian list, as if all three had been compiled from the same source document."

Nathanael said, "But how did you get the DNA? I mean, these bones are supposedly forty or fifty thousand years old. Was it blood, preserved inside a mosquito, in amber, then?"

Peter laughed. "No, no, this isn't Jurassic Park! The fact is, for at least twenty years people have been getting soft tissue from dinosaur fossils as old as two hundred million years. Something very few people realise, though it has been in the scholarly journals. The first person to publish the recovery of soft tissue from a dinosaur fossil was a palaeontologist named Mary Schweitzer, she found soft tissue in a T-Rex and the results were published in 2005. But you know, people have been getting it since the late 1990s, it's just that no one wanted to try publishing it in case they were labelled a creationist. (One fellow did lose his job over it, actually.) Since 2005 a great deal of soft tissue has been recovered from dinosaurs. And an awful lot more soft tissue and mitochondrial DNA from human ancestors, you can be certain, and we discovered the soft tissue in the Cro Magnon fossils in the early 2000s. Paleoanthropologist Lee Berger of the University of the Witwatersrand recovered soft tissue from a 2 million year old Australopithecus. Under certain circumstances; for instance when the fossil has apparently been buried in just the right sort of material at death, the soft tissue simply doesn't decompose, even for millenia."

Nathanael grunted noncommittally.

Peter said, "And using the DNA we proved that the Cro-Magnons clearly were very long-lived. We discovered their longevity when we mapped their mitochondrial DNA and found an extreme mismatch between apparent age and mitochondrial age. Something that has often been ascribed to endocrine disorders and the like by other archaeologists studying the same data, in isolation, but we were studying a large group of fossils, so it was hard to deny the evidence before our very eyes. You see, the ratio of 4977-bp deletion to dental age seems to operate at a slower ratio in the Cro-Magnons. 4977-bp deletion in Cro-Magnon man we estimate to operate at about 25% the rate at which modern 4977-bp deletion occurs. Furthermore, 4977-bp deletion in Cro-Magnon samples ranges up to 0.35%."

Nathanael was having a hard time following him now. He said, "I'm not sure what you mean."

"Slower 4977-bp deletion combined with a much greater range of 4977-bp deletion! You know what 4977-bp deletion is, of course?"

Nathanael said, "Something to do with aging. That's what I gleaned already."

"Well I'll spare you the details. To cut a long story short, it indicates that Cro-Magnon man may have reached ages of up to at least three to five hundred years old, at least, in the samples we have had access to. Which is actually quite a few samples, thanks to the... ah... what we might euphemistically call museum appropriations. Many museums were decidedly unwilling to give up their Cro-Magnon skeletons for the sort of testing we were doing. It can be quite destructive to the fossil." He added, as though it could justify the thefts, "But our research explains an awful lot, though."

Peter sat down at the computer and typed something. A picture of a Cro-Magnon skull whose nasal cavities had apparently been eaten away appeared.

Peter explained. "This theory explains the prevalence of illnesses like these — a very bad fungal infection caused this pitting — in early modern human samples — our theory is that a simple sinus infection carried for over three or four hundred years will result in actual damage to the skull around the sinus cavities, this kind of pitting. Also, it explains some anomalies of bone regrowth as well."

Nathanael asked, "How long did they live, then?"

Peter said, "Potentially, Cro-Magnons may have lived up to ten times the life span of a modern human. Exactly what the Biblical record says — nothing more than a coincidence I'm sure — I mean, that doesn't really prove anything worthwhile, does it?" He scoffed, "Talking donkeys and pillars of fire and the sea splitting in two to let a whole nation walk through. Evil spirits and goats dedicated to Azazel. And people rising from the dead, honestly..."

"Peter, what have you done with this knowledge?" He wasn't sure he wanted to know.

"What we have done is isolated the genetic markers for extreme longevity, genes that have been absent from the human genome for millenia. Now we're going to put them back in, if we can. If we can't insert the genes into adults (it is theoretically possible using viruses but the practicalities are that it could all go wrong very easily) then we're going to construct progeny for our adult clients, hybrids, humans who are essentially Methuselah's children, with as much of the DNA of their prospective parents as we can without impeding their longevity. We have such power now, Nathanael. We have the power to make humans into gods. Can you imagine the medical advances we will have when a doctor can study medicine for five hundred years? The scientific advances? Incredible! This will be the dawn of a new era."

A new era? An era of two classes, the short-lived Morlocks, condemned to drudgery and slavery to try to make their brief, sorrowful span on this earth mean something, while their masters, the Eloi, lived lives of leisure and light and unnatural health, a lifespan of hundreds of years, doing all the research and the intellectual work. Of course, it would seem natural to everybody that such chronologically gifted people would rule the others. They would be like gods, after all. And only the rich would be able to afford these genetically engineered half-offspring.

"Ha!" said Peter. "God limited the human lifespan to one hundred and twenty years at the time of Noah. We're going to increase it to five hundred, seven hundred, a thousand years, who knows?"

Was this hubris? Nathanael wasn't even certain any god or Gods existed, but messing around with the human genome... Wasn't that the height of hubris? It was tempting fate, surely, particularly if... Well it wasn't worth thinking about... Nathanael changed the subject. "Who on earth has been funding all this?"

Peter said, "Who cares? I don't know. Wouldn't have a clue. The man in charge has been nothing more than a disembodied voice on the phone to me the whole time. Clearly someone very powerful, very rich, a billionaire, I'd guess, from the extent of his power and his ability to control things, but I couldn't recognise his voice from the news or anything like that. All my more immediate dealings have been with his minions. They all tend to conform to the same template — ex-bikies, people with criminal records who couldn't get jobs elsewhere, perhaps, because of their past."

"Was yours a paid position? When did you get involved?"

"It was the year 2000 when they initially offered me an unpaid consultancy in Eastern Europe, they just provided the airfare, food and accomodation, but I felt like a holiday and I had just bought my house so didn't have much spare cash and so I did consultancy that while I was on my long service leave. I was expecting a dirty, second rate place but the facilities were tremendous, and that was when I realised it must have been funded by some sort of international company. But when I showed some interest in the basic premise — using DNA from early modern humans to cure ageing — they flew me over to their top secret facility in California. That was in 2001. I took leave from the Museum for two years, which the Museum allowed — you understand, I am one of the top authorities in paleogenetics — so the Museum wanted me back. They told me they would keep my position open for as long as I wished. I worked at their facility in California until 2003, when Meth was conceived. I wanted to move back home and that was why they set up the house in Essex, for Meth, and also so that I could continue my work there from home, mostly, while still doing my work at the museum."

"And what happened afterwards? You seem to have had some kind of falling out with the company. You were patching it up when I got into the hideout and let the boy out..."

Peter's expression was a mixture of admiration and awkward embarrassment. "How did you know that? Did you and your cronies bug the place or something?"

"Your boss has cronies. I have friends. And acquaintances, I suppose, Andy would fall into that category. Tell me... Does the phrase 'Hesperus is Phosphorus' mean anything to you?"

"Nothing at all. Should it?"

"Why did you fall out with them?"

"Anyway, the falling out happened when I refused to go along with them keeping the boy in the dark, keeping him imprisoned, away from school, limiting his life so much for any longer. You know, they were treating him more like a lab monkey than the first-born prince of the new beginning of the human race! I demanded better treatment for him, access to knowledge, the internet, books to read, something to feed that hunger for knowledge that he has, physical exercise, open space, contact with nature, animals, pets, companions, everything we take for granted. Everything he didn't have. Dear God, a child in a United Nations refugee camp has a more fulfilled life than Meth had in that tiny room in that little house."

"So what happened when you disagreed with them? Why did you end up as a gardener?"

"I think the only reason they didn't kill me or make me disappear (as they did many others who had been involved) was that Meth was rather fond of me and they needed to keep him happy. So they had me fired from the British Museum instead, to show me who's boss, I suppose. It wasn't hard for them to do — a rumour here, innuendo there from a trustworthy source — instructions from above. It was all very shady and underhand. Then they offered me the chance to go and see him, in the middle of a work week, mind you. I had to compromise my gardening business to do it. I had all but accepted their offer to rejoin the fold — well, more of a pack of wild animals, really, than a fold — when you arrived and made me a better offer. Freedom for Methuselah. I really am rather fond of the boy, you know. I suppose it's his intelligence — I was a smart kid myself and that did not make me well liked among my peers. I see a little of myself in him; of course, I know that's totally ridiculous. But sometimes what one feels is not quite rational, is it? Even for intelligent people like you and me. What I worry about, though, is, how do we get a proper life for this boy? How do we get him into a school, friends, all the rest of it?"

Suddenly he stopped and said, "Oh, look at the screen. What's happening?"

Microsoft Word had just opened of its own accord and words had begun appearing.

Hello Nathanael. Natasha here. I'm in some trouble. Managed to hack British Telecom servers, though, a while ago, now I set a small trojan looking for certain web searches in all metadata throughput found your ip address. (Presuming it is you.) Easy hack from there. Of course, this implies they can find you too. In other words, flee! Run right now! Meet me on Saturday where it's better to suffer for doing good than for doing wrong. I will be there if I can. If not, leave a message for me. Have to go now. Someone coming.

Nathanael said, "I've been contacted — I think it really is Natasha — but she made the point that if she can find me so can they. Come on! We're back on the road."

Peter quickly went and woke up Meth. "We've got to go."

Chapter 18 — Heosphoros is Phosphorus

It was the man in the nondescript suit who walked in on Natasha.

The so-called Mr Smith.

His implacable voice spoke, grinding like two boulders of granite, "Well, one could not say you are completely unpredictable, my dear, could one? Just put a computer in front of you and you'll try to hack it."

He looked at the screen and clicked a few keys. Some sort of keystroke log came up. "Fascinating. This computer was supposed to be unhackable. And look at this — I wouldn't be surprised if you hadn't managed to upload some sort of program to the cloud and send a message to — who? Nathanael, I would say. Nathanael Wayfarer. Your partner in crime. That was very quick, actually. Why haven't you been snaffled up yet by one of the agencies? Quite a smart little pebble, aren't you? Wasted writing hospital databases. Up with the latest, you're using tools that are hard to find, even on the Darknet. Why, what you've just accomplished is analogous to building a castle, solid as rock, unbreakable, with nothing but sand and water as materials."

Despite Natasha's deep sense of insecurity, her heart began swelling at these compliments. She warned herself not to be fooled. Compliments were stones masquerading as bread; they wouldn't fill you up.

"Then again," he continued, "None of us accomplish anything on our own do we? I mean, even the greatest of men — and women — is only as tall and strong as the shoulders on which he or she is standing. And let's be frank: this is not your own work, but the extension of the prior accomplishments of the greats who stand beneath you. Gary McKinnon, Adrian Lamo, Mathew Bevan, Hector Montsegur, Jack Davis, not to mention Anonymous. Nonetheless, it takes exceptional talent to know which shoulders to choose to stand upon, even for an acrobat who truly rocks, let us say, just as it takes exceptional skill for the architect to know which ground to build upon, and you chose the best. You chose a fraternity solid as the rock beneath your feet upon which to build your own accomplishments."

Natasha rolled her eyes at the mixed metaphors. "Yes, technical knowledge is good, but every trick of the trade I learned, trojans, worms, programs, viruses, parasites, all these are merely tools, nothing more. And none of them are any kind of rock beneath my feet. If I have survived this far it's not because I'm standing on the shoulders of these people. It's not because any of them could be called rocks. And you forgot about Natasha Grigori, Jannah Rutkowska, Jude Milhon, Ying Cracker, Kristina Svechinskaya. No, I've survived this long because I'm standing on a rock much stronger and more long lived than any mere hackers. My rock is the foundation on which justice is built, the cornerstone on which I build is truth. And the truth I would like to know is, who are you, Mr Smith? And why have you kidnapped me?"

"Hmmm. You think perhaps that the truth will set you free? I hope it does. It will. I already told you that truth. I come from a group in the government opposed to those who have been troubling you. We are concerned that certain fundamental freedoms are being threatened. We are concerned that an international cabal of high value individuals and establishment figures in the governments of the Western Nations are cooperating to create a race of offspring genetically enhanced for longevity, intelligence and charisma. They want to end democracy and create an aeoneocracy, a society ruled by the eternally young. An exaggeration, perhaps, for their lifespans might range from five hundred to nine hundred years, but the term is a valid one, particularly because the Greek means, an aristocracy of those who are young for an era. Such dictators would treat multigenerational problems such as global warming as a concern to be dealt with for their own sakes, their own futures, not just for their children, and human beings are fundamentally selfish creatures — there is a certain twisted logic to their reasoning. Many in the intelligence services ridicule our concerns still, but now, this conspiracy, this cabal, seems to be on the verge of achieving their goal. Even now, according to our sources, a laboratory at their headquarters is creating the first batch of 'offspring', combining the genetic material from various sources to create these long-lived supermen."

Natasha frowned. "Let's assume you're right about all of this. What on earth do you want from me?"

Mr Smith was wandering around the room, tapping his fingers on furniture as he spoke, as though to accentuate his syllables. "How much have you discovered of this already? What do you know that we do not yet know? We need everything from you. We do not yet know where their headquarters are. We do not where to concentrate our intelligence."

"I didn't put any of the pieces together. It's not me who has been putting the pieces together. I've done the hacking, but..."

"Nathanael? Are you saying he knows more than you do, Natasha?"

"I should think so. Didn't you see the web searches he was doing? I think he's putting it all together. Surely you have access to Boundless Informant?"

"There was nothing in any of his recent searches that we were not already familiar with."

"Then I don't know how I can help you."

Mr Smith frowned then. "What if we set you loose? Let us say you manage to discover the... nest of the vipers, so to speak? We would then want to tell us where it is, so that we can come in and... clean it up. I am using euphemisms, Miss Chance. I don't necessarily want this on any record, you understand."

Did Mr Smith know she was recording the whole thing on her mobile phone? Though whether the app would make a decent recording while it was in her pants was another matter. The audio could probably be enhanced later, even if it turned out to be a little unclear.

It was very uncomfortable, though.

"I understand," said Natasha. "I think I could agree with that. How would I contact you?"

"I will give you a phone number, an email address. And some other methods as well. I will tell you how to

find our safe houses — we have them in nearly every city…
And please contact us if you're in trouble. We would like
to show you that you can trust us… We will help you if
you call on us."

"If this is the case, why did you kidnap me unwillingly
in the first place?"

"We wanted to do all this quietly. We had to make
sure that we were not being followed. And we also had to
assess you. There was some possibility in our minds that
you were with our enemies. We had to make sure that you
were on the right side of the fence, so to speak."

They brought her laptop out, her handbag and her
other things.

"Since we've taken you so far out of your way, we
will, of course, provide you with a car."

"Thank you," she said, slightly sarcastically. She
really wasn't sure yet that he meant anything he was saying.
She wasn't sure that this wasn't just another ploy to get
information out of her. Dangle the promise of freedom in
front of her and she'll start spilling her beans — is that
what they thought?

~~~

Nathanael, Peter and Meth were on the road again.
Peter took the wheel this time, Nathanael was quite simply
exhausted. He had been thinking and surfing the net for
longer than he'd noticed — quite a few hours — he slept
in the passenger seat and Meth talked with Peter softly as
they drove.

Nathanael woke up a few hours later.

Meth was asleep now.

Peter said, "I've been thinking of everything we've
been talking about. And I have to admit I am beginning
~~~

to think it was all a bit ill-conceived. How am I possible going to get a good life for Meth? The only way would be if we can bring them down."

Nathanael said, "I've been thinking the same thing. Natasha and I are not going to get our lives back unless we can publicise it all, break the news to everybody of what has been happening, who's been funding it."

They were driving into Leicester.

Nathanael needed the toilet, so they stopped at a McDonalds and he went. He bought some breakfast for them there.

As they sat in the carpark eating, Nathanael started feeling very depressed. Peter noticed something was wrong and asked him about it.

Nathanael said, "For the last three or four days I thought I would have enough information to do something about all this. I don't know what. Expose it. Send it to the media. And you and Meth were the key. I really felt, really believed that when I found you, Peter, when I got you to spill the beans, that that would be it. This whole thing would have a solution and I could go back to my stupid life. I really thought that-"

Peter said, "Well, hold on, rewind a little there. Why is your life stupid?"

Nathanael shook his head. "I've been married, Peter, for twelve years, and now it's ended. It was a total disaster to be frank, although there were happy times, but we were a mismatch. She married me because I'm smart but that meant something different to her than it did to me. I wanted kids, my wife didn't. She wanted my smarts in order to use me, in a sense, for material gain. I was just a tool to her. I liked just doing the things I do, but all the way along she wanted me to be a top dog, earning the big bucks, but that was never going to happen. You see I don't really fit in anywhere, never have. Always make people feel stupid without really meaning to, at least in the work environment, people feel threatened, they try to protect themselves against me. Debra left me for other reasons, too, though. But even without her in it I don't mind my life when it comes down to it. I mean, at least it is my life. It's the only one I've got. And now it's been taken from me. You know, I was completely deceived by my feelings in this matter. I thought, getting hold of you and the boy, knowing the truth, that this would be enough. But it wasn't. I'm supposed to be smart and I should have seen that."

Peter said, "Well... You're saying that in this instance your hopes deceived you..."

Nathanael said, "Yes, yes, they did. Completely. It was my feeling of hope that in this case finding out the truth would change everything. Yet I find we're still on the run. I really can't see an end to all this. I feel as though I'm falling into a black hole, a deep whirlpool. An abyss. Scylla and Charybdis. How can I rely on my feelings about anything?"

Peter put his hand on Nathanael's shoulder, a rather awkward gesture coming from him, but probably the best attempt he could make to console someone. "So, your feelings of hope deceived you. Well, isn't it just possible right now that your feelings of despair are deceiving you as well? Things were not as good as you'd hoped. Well, perhaps, right now, things are not as bad as you fear, as well? Is that possible?"

Nathanael said, "You know, you could be right. Thank you! I feel a little better with that thought." He said that, but he really didn't feel much better. But the thing is, he really couldn't take much more of Peter's attempts at consolation.

"No problem. Glad I could help. So… Where to now?"

Nathanael considered the problem. "I think… a public library, if possible. Public internet. I have one thing to look up. The one clue I haven't deciphered yet. Hesperus is Phosphorus. Some sort of Greek mythological reference, I guess. Come on, let's find a library."

~~~

Someone in the McDonald's directed them to the Leicester Central Library. Free computer use and internet was provided.

They got there and found a free computer in a fairly isolated spot. Peter said, "I'm going to find something for Meth to do. A video to watch, something to read, perhaps."

Nathanael searched 'Hesperus is Phosphorus.' He came up with a page about a philosophical problem called 'Frege's Puzzle.'

Apparently it referred to a puzzle to do with the philosophy of language.

Consider the following two sentences:

1)   Hesperus is Hesperus
2)   Hesperus is Phosphorus.

The first is clearly true. But the second is also true because it is a truth discovered by astronomers, as Hesperus was the evening star and Phosphorus the morning star, and they discovered that both were the same.

Venus — the evening and the morning star. Something nagged at Nathanael's mind. Venus was also something else, in mythology.
~~~

Something relevant to their discussions.

Once he knew what he was looking for, Nathanael's memory worked well. But in this case, he had to remember in reverse. He was looking for something that had something to do with Venus.

He looked up Venus on the computer. The other names for Venus were Vesper, for the evening star, and... Lucifer. Latin for 'light bringer.'

That was it. The Lucifer Institute. That was the name of the organisation Jannah had said was behind everything.

Nathanael looked up 'Hesperus Institute.' Nothing came up. Surely that would be it. But there simply was nothing called the 'Hesperus Institute.'

He looked up Hesperus again. Another name for Hesperus was 'Heosphoros.'

He googled, 'Heosphoros Institute.'

Nothing came up with that title, but when he googled 'Heosphoros and Lucifer Institute' he found something called the 'Heosphoros Foundation.' Nathanael looked at their webpage and found the page describing the history of the organisation now called the Heosphoros Foundation.

The Heosphoros Foundation was established by Roland Adamant as a research trust under the umbrella of the Adamantine Institute, dedicated to using all the resources of science and technology in the service of the higher spiritual principles known by those who are enlightened by the Inner Light. The Foundation was originally incorporated in the Washington DC, USA, on April 6, 1920, under the name Lucifer Institute.

Lucifer is the angel in ancient mythology who was the primordial bringer of light into the world. This was seen as an appropriate name for an organisation dedicated to the inner light, a name that was given to the Institute in honour of a theosophical journal edited for many years by the great founder of our philosophy, HP Blavatsky. Some Christian groups, however, mistakenly identified Lucifer with the Biblical figure of Satan, so to prevent bad publicity the Institute's name was changed in 1924 to the Heosphoros Foundation.

So, the original name of the Heosphoros Foundation had been the Lucifer Institute. Well, Heosphoros was simply the Greek translation of the Latin word Lucifer; was it just a coincidence, or was it a philosophical irony that tickled Roland Adamant's fancy?

Nathanael knew exactly who Roland Adamant was. He was the great grandfather of Richard Adamant, billionaire philanthropist, who was now number 16 on the Forbes 400 list of America's wealthiest men. Was Richard Adamant the one who was behind everything that had been happening? Could his foundation have funded the research, appropriated the Cro-Magnon skeletons, created Meth?

Was Richard Adamant still a Theosophist, a follower of this apparently harmless philosophy of inner light and higher spiritual principles?

Nathanael knew a little bit about Theosophism and Madame Blavatsky. He decided to find out some more. What was her view about the Lucifer of the Bible? He googled this, and fairly quickly found the following section in one of her books:

...it is but natural — even from the dead letter standpoint — to view Satan, the Serpent of Genesis, as the real creator and benefactor, the Father of Spiritual mankind. For it is he who was the "Harbinger of Light," bright radiant Lucifer, who opened the eyes of the automaton created by Jehovah, as alleged; and he who was the first to whisper: "in the day ye eat thereof ye shall be as Elohim, knowing good and evil" — can only be regarded in the light of a Saviour. An "adversary" to Jehovah the "personating spirit," he still remains in esoteric truth the ever‑loving "Messenger" (the angel), the Seraphim and Cherubim who both knew well, and loved still more, and who conferred on us spiritual, instead of physical immortality…

So she took the Biblical story, which he was now a little more familiar with, and turned it upside down. The villain, the snake who opened Adam and Eve's eyes, was actually the hero in her philosophy.

Well, perhaps there was something in that. The snake saying, "in the day you eat of the fruit you shall be as God, knowing good and evil" — this was the beginnings of science. Doubting the prevaling theory. Testing cause and effect. Not taking received knowledge for granted. It really was like a symbolic representation of the beginnings of science, if God was taken to mean, received spiritual knowledge.

Of course, if there really was a God… Well, things are a bit different, then, aren't they?

This was something Nathanael had not really given much thought to before his accident, but if Natasha believed it, and she was no fool, then he ought to at least consider the possibility. Indeed, he owed his life to her belief, something that made him see these issues a little differently now, to how he might have viewed religion beforehand.

And if the God of the Bible was real, well, then, if you have a direct message from Him, like 'don't eat from that tree', you hardly need science, do you, to test it? I mean, science is taking the long way round to truth. There are truths you can't get from science. You can sometimes get the 'what' and the 'how', but you can't really get the 'why', and if an omniscient, morally perfect, totally truthful being tells you 'don't do that, it will be bad for you,' well, doing 'that' is stupid, to say the least.

So if Natasha was right about God's existence, well, this Heosphoros Foundation was at the least misguided.

But the most interesting fact as far as Nathanael could see about the Heosphoros Foundation according to their website was that they were bare-faced liars. Nathanael was highly alert to deceptions and self-contradictions, and nothing annoyed him more than a liar. Once you caught someone in a lie, everything else they said was suspect.

And here these sectarians were, on the one hand, insisting on their website that their 'Lucifer' was not the same as the Lucifer/Satan in the Bible, when it actually was very plain from Blavatsky's writings that he was the very same figure, the snake in the garden, the tempter.

And that really was a bit creepy, Nathanael decided, to make the Satan figure the hero, just taking the story at face value. After all, clearly the snake didn't have Adam and Eve's best interest at heart, did he?

And if God was real, and Satan was real… Well, being caught in the middle of their little battle might not be the best place to be…

"God," Nathanael said into the air, "If you're there. Just… help me with all this, please? I might be out of my depth here…"

"Okay," said a voice. Nathanael started — it was Peter, standing behind him, he must have been watching him searching the web. Peter laughed, clapped his hand onto Nathanael's shoulder and said, "Sorry. Too good an opportunity to resist. In any case, now we may well know who the voice who told me what to do on the phone was... Richard Adamant. Billionaire."

Nathanael looked around for Meth. Peter said, "Don't worry, he's over there, watching a documentary in the video room. I felt he needed to know a bit more about this world he's suddenly found himself living in. Shocking, the holes in his education. Hadn't heard of John F Kennedy, the moon landings, communism, the list goes on and on"

Nathanael indicated the screen. "It's all a bit creepy, isn't it? Theosophy, Lucifer, the snake in the garden of Eden, Madame Blavatsky."

"Oh, she was part of what inspired Hitler, you know, that whole occult thing. There were books about magic in Hitler's personal library — with underlined sections to do with demonic seed, etcetera — the whole racist philosophy of Nazism owed a lot to her ideas about Aryans being a superior race. I once looked into theosophy — thought it might be a way to reconcile science and faith. But it was all rubbish. She said Jews, black people, non-Aryans were inferior. She said Hashem, the God of the Old Testament, was some second rate god, an imposter. I'm Jewish you know, Nathanael, by race, a little less certain whether I am one by belief..."

"You're Jewish?" said Nathanael. "But... I thought you were a complete atheist."

"Are you an atheist?"

Looking down at the ground, Nathanael idly scratched his forearm. A feeling of shame was making his brow feel hot, he didn't know why. "I don't know. Lately I've been… questioning my former stance… I might be a little less agnostic now than I used to be."

"I believe in my own rather cynical way. I suppose I'm a scientist first of all, and I have a sense of awe to do with this universe and the inexplicable fact of our existence which makes me think there must be something greater than ourselves. But all of that occult stuff — it's just creepy and… makes human beings smaller, more petty… For God's sake, trying to talk to your dead relatives — when, if they're in heaven, it's all good for them, isn't it? Why bring them back down to our level? Blavatsky, as you probably know, practised seances and was proven a fraud by the parapsychologist Richard Hodgson in the 1880s, she used table rapping techniques. And she used to drop letters through a secret compartment, claiming they had gotten there supernaturally and were written by a secret Tibetan Master, when it was all in her own handwriting. All a load of hogwash. I am sure there are nice theosophists who know nothing about Blavatsky's more odious views, just as there are nice Lutherans (Luther was another rabid anti-Semite you know) and perhaps there are even nice skinheads or Nazis too… But doesn't change the fact that Blavatsky was a liar and a fraud and her beliefs were odious and racist. Strange thought, to use science in the service of all that ridiculous superstition."

Nathanael said, "Anyway… The Heosphoros Foundation is in Washington DC — what are going to do? Are we going there?"

Peter nodded. "Let's. Let's go there and blow this whole thing wide open. You've convinced me. For Meth's sake, we need to publicise the lot, bring them right down. We'll need documentation, Nathanael, the proof that this is going on, everything they've been doing. Of course, it's not going to do wonders for my career, but, God knows, if I have to I'll go back to gardening. I just want a better life for Meth."

Nathanael said, "We need Natasha back, don't we…?"

"Yes! Hack their computers, photocopy the contents of their filing cabinets, something like that. We need to blow the whistle, get the whole lot published on Wikileaks or some newspaper, the Guardian perhaps."

"Well," said Nathanael, "Saturday night — tomorrow night — we'll go to the… ahem… place she indicated… see if she made it…" He didn't even want to mention where it was he was so paranoid about being surveilled now…

Peter said, "Hold on a second. Where's Meth?"

Nathanael said, "Where was he?"

"Just over there, at that desk. He was watching the video with headphones on."

They went over to his desk. The video was still going and the headphones were sitting on the desk, but Meth wasn't there.

Peter said, "Oh, my God."

Inwardly, Nathanael started to panic.

Peter looked around frantically. "I don't know what to do. Where do we even start?"

If Natasha was right and there was a God, then they needed HIs help, so Nathanael prayed inwardly, "God, if you're there, if you exist, please help us to find the boy.

Please don't let him fall back into their hands." It was more like throwing the dice, taking a chance on something that he was or wasn't sure of, than a trusting prayer, but who knows? Perhaps if God really was there He would even hear a prayer like this.

Nathanael happened to look down. There was a sheet on the table with some numbers on it. He said to Peter, "What's this?" He held up the piece of paper.

Peter glanced at it dismissively. "It's just a list of call numbers. Come on, leave that, we've got to find him."

Nathanael looked at it. "A list of call numbers? I don't think so, Peter..."

19.1.23   "19... That's the Dewey number for a dictionary catalogue. But why three numbers separated by dots?"

13.1.14   "13... There's another problem. 13 is unassigned in the Dewey Decimal System."

9   "9 is also unassigned."

11.14.5.23   "11 is bibliographies but again it has four numbers, almost looks like an IP address..."

9.14   "9 again."

3.1.18   "3 is systems."

14.15.23   "And 14 is bibliographies of anonymous and pseudonymous works, which seems to have nothing to do with the others. These are not call numbers. These might be.... words."

Peter was perplexed. "What do you mean?"

Nathanael said, "Well... 1 is A. See it's always in the middle of the three? And 15 is O. It might just be a simple alphabetic substitution cypher."

He decoded it.

"SAW MAN I KNEW IN CAR NOW."

They rushed out to the car. Meth was not out there either.

Two men came out from behind a nearby van. One of them had a gun in his hand.

The one without the gun said, "You can live if you just give us the boy. Where is he? Tell us where to find him."

The other one said, "Slippery little bugger."

Nathanael said, "We don't know where he is."

The one with the gun grabbed Peter by the hand and twisted his arm the wrong way. Nathanael cried out, "Stop!"

"We're not playing games here!" He held the gun to Peter's head. "Cough it up! Where is he!"

Nathanael heard a very quiet sound, like 'sput', and the guy crumpled. His gun fell out of his hand. He started moaning and writhing on the ground.

Peter was holding a gun with his other hand. He picked up the guy's gun and held his own gun towards the other man, watching him the whole while.

Peter said, "Now, you can live if you tell us who sent you!"

The guy gestured with his hand, both placatory and like a man holding his hands up. "Hey, hey, it's alright buddy, we're in a bikie gang. We're just bikies. We're just hired hands, thugs. Someone paid us to do this. We're just recovering this guy's child, that's all, they said you'd kidnapped him. I thought, good, something I can be proud of for a change instead of popping someone who's been selling rocks on our turf. Kill a couple of pedophiles. Me wife might be pleased with me for a change."

Nathanael rolled his eyes. "Oh, great. So that's what they're saying about us."

Peter shot the guy in the foot. He cried out and crumpled to the ground, groaning. "Take that message back to your bosses. We aren't the ones who were keeping the kid prisoner. Tell them to check their facts first. We're not pedophiles, we're saviours."

Nathanael looked at Peter. Was his affection for Meth more than just...? Surely not... Meth hadn't given any sign of having suffered anything like that. And his trust for Peter would be... more icky, surely, if their relationship was like that... But he did wonder if Peter was almost too fond of the boy... Could that be a problem?

All Nathanael wanted was his life back. But Meth got to your heart, somehow, and Nathanael did want to see Meth have a decent life too, for what it was worth.

The first one Peter had shot was writhing on the ground in pain, but he was still breathing.

Nathanael checked his pulse. Steady. He said to him in a quiet voice, "Relax, get in the accident position. We'll get you some help." He put the guy's limbs in the correct position.

Peter waved the gun at Nathanael. "Stop it! If he dies, your DNA is all over him."

Nathanael rolled his eyes. "Yeh, but if I do some first aid on him and he doesn't die, we won't have to worry, will we?"

The guy groaned, "Thanks. Thanks a lot"

Nathanael said, "How did you find us?"

"They told us you guys go to public libraries to abuse children."

Peter kicked the other one and said to him, "Hey. Stupid. I think you should ring an ambulance. I think your buddy is shot pretty badly."

The guy took out his mobile phone from his jacket with some difficulty, rang 112 and said, "Ambulance. Leicester Library. And police. We were shot by two muggers." He held his phone up to take a photo of Nathanael and Peter but Peter kicked it away from him. It smashed somewhere about three feet away.

"Dammit," said Peter. "Where's Meth, then? We've got to get out of here."

Meth crawled out from under the car. "I'm here! I'm alright! I recognised them from the house in Essex. You didn't have to shoot them, Peter."

Peter said, "Yes, I did! Come on! Get in the car."

Meth said, "By the way, what's a pedophile? I haven't heard that word before."

Peter glanced at Nathanael. "We'll... explain on the way. It's something very unpleasant, Meth, that older men do to children."

Nathanael hopped in the driver's seat and once they were all in their seats, he sped out of the car park as quickly as he could drive. Sirens sounded in the distance.

CHAPTER 19 — CHEAP AS CHIPS

"They seem to have dropped off the grid again."

"Look for her search patterns on the Dark net. She's fairly predictable isn't she?"

"There's been no activity since she left that safe house."

"What about him? And the boy, and the scientist?"

"There was some highly relevant search activity. It warranted a response, but whoever it was assaulted the respondent. There was no security camera footage and the respondents won't be talking to the police. But that was in Leicester."

"So they're playing it smart. They move around a bit. How come we didn't get that car? We know the plates already."

"They haven't come up. Could they have switched them?"

"I know, look for number plates that have been out of use for a while, you know, registration paid but not coming up on any of our databases, with a mismatch to the vehicle."

"Alright. May I say, that's a very smart search, sir. Very smart."

"Well you need to be specific. See what it comes up with."

~~~~

Nathanael was beginning to be a little concerned about funds as it was looking as though they would have to fund some plane tickets and accomodation in Washington DC, a place that he surmised was probably expensive to stay in, and some more identity documents might be in order too, perhaps even plastic surgery, so he was more careful to find a cheap place this time than he had been before. After an hour's drive, including some stops at other motor inns checking prices, they ended up in a cheap motor inn in Coventry. Nathanael had to park the car nearby in a multi-story carpark, but for five pounds for parking and thirty five for the room, it wasn't too bad.

Peter was unhappy with the room, though. "The toilet is dirty," he said. "That might not be good for Meth's immune system. After all, he's been virtually quarantined for years — hasn't been exposed to many infections — probably got an underdeveloped immune system — the wrong bug could kill him."

"Well then," Nathanael replied, being in a slightly vexatious mood and really not wanting to change hotels, since he had been driving for the past two hours. "Exposing him to the odd bug is necessary to strengthen his immune response."

"Hmmmph," said Peter, glancing at Nathanael with a sour expression, "Not all at once, that's all."

Meth seemed anxious to preserve the peace, and he said, "I'll avoid using the toilet or I won't breathe in while I'm in there."
~~~~

Nathanael said, "Look, I'll clean the toilet, alright? As well as I can using what's available here. Then he can use it if he needs to." This was the last thing Nathanael needed.

"Alright," said Peter grudgingly.

Nathanael's throat constricted, his palms began getting sweaty and his pulse quickened. He blurted out, "You really stuffed things up, you know. Shooting those guys. It could have really mucked up our chances of getting out of this."

Peter said, "I had no other choice, did I? We'd both be dead otherwise now. No way out of that, is there?"

Of course, if Natasha was right then there was. Nathanael went and found a mop and a bucket. He filled the bucket with hot water and soap scrapings and did the best he could with the toilet.

Then he walked up the road to find them something to eat. There was a cheap Kebab place a few hundred feet from the hotel and he bought three doner kebabs and some lebanese bread and took them back to their room.

Meth ate it slowly and almost reverently, treasuring every mouthful — clearly a kebab was something completely new for him.

After dinner they watched television for a short while. Peter had a set of cards and had clearly taught the rules of the games to Meth; they played Euchre, 500 Rummy and one or two other games. Meth had a phenomenal memory.

After the card games they talked for a while. Finally it was time to sleep.

Peter and Meth slept well, but Nathanael didn't. At 2am he found himself still lying in bed awake, at 3am he was pacing around, worrying. Somehow he was suddenly responsible for two people, one, a rather unique child, the other arguably a scientific genius. And he had lost Natasha. Where was she? Was she safe? Would she be there at the hotel tomorrow night? By 4am he was wishing he was smoking again, a habit he had long ago dropped but one that occasionally still caused residual cravings.

By 4:30am Nathanael had started planning his next moves. They needed new identities for Peter, Meth, him and Natasha. They needed a place for Peter and Meth to stay. Somewhere secret. Somewhere safe. And they needed plane tickets to Washington DC for Natasha and him.

It would be easier doing all of this with Natasha's help. She could surf the Darknet, find the new identities, book the plane tickets without the authorities knowing. All he had to do was keep Peter and Meth away from the people trying to capture Meth for another day, until he could get back together with Natasha in London, at the pub where she had said, "As Professor Fetherington's favourite book says, it's better to suffer for doing good than for doing wrong."

By 6am Nathanael was calm, ready to face the day. There was no point worrying. What had to be done, had to be done, and the main thing was to keep Peter and Meth away from any security cameras.

Nathanael asked around at a cafe across the road, to find something to do for the day.

Apparently about thirty five minutes drive away was a nature reserve. The fellow gave him directions. "Well… if you'd prefer to avoid the tollways, take the Chester Road. Head down Corporation Street, turn left onto Upper Well, then left at the roundabout onto Ringway Hill Cross. Then you get onto the A45, stay on that until you get to Holyhead. Then Pickford way and back onto the A45 at the airport..." The directions continued like this, onto this road, onto that road. At moments like these, Nathanael was thankful for his excellent memory.

So they went to Sutton Park Nature Reserve. Meth fed the ducks with the leftover lebanese bread, petted the donkeys, stood in awe watching the cattle grazing, and they spent the morning in quietness and peace wandering past the lake, through the forests and the fields. Meth's gratitude was almost palpable — it was a reward in itself. Nathanael vowed to himself that the boy was not going to be imprisoned again.

During lunch, which they had at the golf course adjoining the reserve, while Meth was filling up his plate for the third time at the buffet, Peter said quietly to Nathanael, "You know... This brings to mind something odd, that I'd all but forgotten. In the early days, when we... started work... When Meth was... born, there were some others. One or two others who didn't work out so well. They said they put them in Sutton Estate. I thought it was just a euphemism for euthanasia, but later I wasn't so sure. I think they might have thought it was easier to get extra DNA from living specimens, even though these ones were... the mistakes. We used chimpanzee DNA instead of human DNA to fill in the gaps. That was before we had sequenced the Cro Magnon DNA and knew they were fully human. You should look up Sutton Estate. It might be a real place, not a metaphor. Perhaps there are more children like Meth there. Perhaps the... mistakes are still there. It's the kind of evidence you are looking for. The kind of evidence we need to bring these people down, to make Meth and me safe." At that moment Meth returned and Peter stopped talking.

Straight after lunch, Nathanael made some enquiries. There was a manor house called Sutton Estate in the area, less than five miles from the Nature Reserve. A pamphlet from Sutton Park Nature Reserve had a photograph of the building, a huge double story renaissance mansion with three wings. The grounds comprised many acres of carefully manicured gardens and farmland.

Nathanael quietly told Peter he would look into it.

Peter said, "Fine. I'm sure Meth and I can find plenty to do here. He seems to enjoy the outdoors."

Nathanael drove to the mansion immediately. It took less than five minutes.

He parked on the side of the road, next to the high wall that surrounded the whole estate. There were two large gatehouses surrounding the driveway to the mansion. He could not see the estate from the road.

Nathanael thought about his options. To get in he would have to get past the guard house somehow - shouldn't be too difficult - either climb the wall or find some legitimate reason to get in. But he only had two or three hours now. He also had to get back to London to meet Natasha. He looked at his watch. He would give himself forty five minutes. If he hadn't found anything by then, he would give up and go back to his car.

He got out and climbed onto the car roof and from there managed to step right onto the top of the wall. The wall was about six foot high, and he figured he could probably have managed to climb it, but this was easier. Once he had his footing, Nathanael leaped off the wall onto the grass below, but he realised as he was falling that he had forgotten about his legs, that he was still recovering, so he changed his leap into a roll and nearly sprained his ankle. He stood up and rolled the ankle around — it seemed to be fine. He started looking about.

He was in what amounted to an extremely large well-manicured garden with grass everwhere and every possible variety of bush and tree, some straight and tall, some well knotted, some pine trees, others perhaps oaks or ashes, Nathanael wasn't terribly familiar with English trees.

He explored the grounds, following the wall at first so that he wouldn't get lost.

It was a very large property. Once he felt he had an idea of where everything was, he set off into the middle. He found himself behind the mansion in vegetable gardens. He went through a gate in an internal wall and found himself in a very ornate decorated garden.

The sky was darkening with black clouds. Was it going to rain soon? That could significantly hamper his way back to the car. He looked at his watch. He had been here for thirty five minutes. What was he expecting to see? He had almost thought that he might look in the windows of the mansion, or try to find some hidden room or other, but when it came down to it, he had been rather too timid to venture so close to the part of the estate that was almost certain to be inhabited.

A low, rumble of thunder sounded. Nathanael didn't want to get caught here in the rain. He set off back to the car.

It was then that he saw it. A white shape simply appeared next to one of the trees. What was it? At first it looked like a woman, in a dress made of some material that moved rather strangely, but the arms seemed altogether too long for the body.

Nathanael made his way closer to get a better look, walking as softly as he could on the grass, trying to avoid any leaves or sticks that might betray his presence. The thunder rumbled again and the figure appeared afraid, looked up at the sky. Whoever it was, she didn't like the thunder.

Nathanael ran towards it. Perhaps it was just a girl, a woman, but he couldn't tell from this distance.

As he approached the white figure turned around.

It was the red eyes he noticed first, then the fact that it wasn't a dress, the white substance was fur, long, white, beastly fur. The figure looked at him and opened its mouth and howled, a haunting, beastly sound, neither human nor animal but something in between, a sound that shook Nathanael to the core because of how close it was to being human, but it wasn't.

Nathanael took out his mobile phone. As quickly as he could he accessed the camera and turned it towards the creature. Even as he pressed the red button, the creature fled into the bushes. Had he caught it on the camera? Apart from Peter and Meth this was their first corroborating evidence.

Nathanael thought about following the thing into the bushes but surely whoever guarded or looked after this creature had heard its howl. They would be coming for him. Instead, he ran as quickly as he could back to the wall. It began raining as he approached.

He clambered uncomfortably up the bricks, falling and scraping himself on the inside of his wrists several times before he managed to get to the top of the wall. He slipped over, falling next to the car onto the gravel.

He felt nauseous. He fumbled his keys as he got them out of his pocket, picked them up off the ground and, as quickly as he could, unlocked the door and got in.

He drove into town. What he had seen had perturbed him considerably and his inital response was that he needed to know more.

He went to the Sutton library.

After fifteen minutes of fruitless searching through card catalogues the librarian, a tall, greying woman with permanently pursed lips and a nervous squint, asked him if he needed any help. Nathanael said, "I... just saw something on the grounds of Sutton Estate..."

The lady squinted at him, adjusted her glasses and said, "Wellll... There is this." She disappeared into the bowels of the building for a few minutes then emerged with several issues of the 'Sun' newspaper.

The first had a hazy picture of something resembling a Yeti, with the title, "Sutton Estate Bigfoot Strikes Again." The article was the typical vague piece of cryptozoological news, a man who had been walking through the garden, saw the Bigfoot for a moment then it disappeared.

Looking at the blurry photograph, Nathanael remembered the one he had taken on his phone. He quickly called it up.

It was no better than the one in the newspaper. The creature was already running away when he had pressed the button, a blurry figure that could just as well be a man in a suit, running into the forest.

The second newspaper had the title, "Sutton Estate Ghost Haunting Howl," and told the story of a man who had been visiting the Paradise Garden in Sutton Estate and had seen a strange woman roaming the grounds.Rumour had it that she had lost her child to diptheria in the late 1950s and had then committed suicide. Since then, she wandered the grounds, howling for her child.

"As you can see," the librarian said, "Whatever report you might make to the police or the media will have no more credibility than these two articles."

Nathanael thanked her slightly cynically and then went back to his car, crestfallen. Clearly they needed more evidence than this.

He drove back to Sutton Park and parked in the golf club, the prearranged meeting spot. Some time later Peter knocked on the car window.

Nathanael awakened with a start and opened the door.

"What's the time?" he said, shocked that he had fallen asleep.

Peter said. "About three thirty in the afternoon."

"Damn," Nathanael said, "I'd better start heading back to London. I've been thinking — it might be better if you two stay here for the night. If Natasha is at the pub, well, then, all's well and good, I can bring her back here or come and get you two, whatever we decide to do."

Peter nodded thoughtfully. "I concur. It's best to keep away from any place where there are security cameras, toll roads, such like. I talked to someone — there is a nice little bed and breakfast place less than two miles away — Meth and I will stay there, if you take care of the other business." He looked at Meth. "Look, we might start looking for something more permanent — a house to stay in. Won't make any decisions till we hear from you, though."

Nathanael said, "I know I'm going to Washington DC, to sort things out. Probably need Natasha with me, too. But Meth travelling — might be too much of a risk. Taking him through customs might raise all sorts of flags with the people who are watching everything. A child of his apparent age would be travelling with his mother and, to be honest, Natasha really can't pass as Meth's mother."

Peter said, "Alright then. Good luck, Nathanael. And thank you for everything you've done so far."

Nathanael dropped them off at the bed and breakfast then set off for London.

~~~

It took him two and a half hours to drive to the pub and a little while longer to find parking and a clean enough public toilet that he could tidy himself up a little. He couldn't go into the pub with dried blood on his wrists. Not a good look.

Despite these hassles, by a few minutes after six o'clock, he was sitting in the tavern consuming a pint of apple cider.

He looked around. It really was a pretentious place, more pretentious than he had remembered. There was very little on the menu that was simply good, solid food. Everything had to have a culinary justification to be there.

He was looking around for Natasha, but she wasn't there yet. Well, he was going to wait, it didn't matter how long. And he knew she would have left a message, or get one to him somehow, if she wasn't able to be here herself.

He looked around the crowd. Perhaps something had happened to her? Something clearly had happened — but she must have anticipated finding a way out, when she had sent him the message. Or was it just optimism on her part? Clearly Natasha was quite optimistic, or she wouldn't have tried to save him in the first place, from the two murderers in the hospital.

Had fate caught up with her at last? The thought chilled him.
~~~

Pretty soon, he was on his third pint of apple cider, and his eyelids were starting to droop.

"Nathanael," her voice breathed in his ear.

"Natasha!" He turned around. It really was her! For a fraction of a second he had thought he was just dreaming.

They embraced.

She was carrying a drink, white wine, and was wearing an evening dress. She fitted in well at that venue, while Nathanael felt he was not quite dressed well enough — his shirt was slightly crumpled — too long on the road. How did she manage it? Nathanael held her by the shoulders and looked at her, as if afraid that she might escape his grasp again. "Where were you? Did they capture you?"

"I escaped them. But some other people were watching — people from the intelligence services — or they said they were. They wanted to know what I knew. They are onto the whole conspiracy, apparently."

"Well I found out who's behind it all. It's an organisation called the Heosphoros Foundation. It was originally called the Lucifer Institute; it was founded by Richard Adamant in the 1920s. To avoid the negative connotations of the name, 'Lucifer', they changed the name soon after founding the group."

"Richard Adamant. Is that...?"

"Yes, it is. The billionaire Roland Adamant's grandfather. They are an organisation dedicated to the theories and ideas of Madame Blavatsky — strange, really, that their whole goal is scientific research, when Blavatsky herself was so unscientific. Anti-scientific, really. The Heosphoros Foundation's headquarters are in Washington DC."

She arched her eyebrows and said, "Well done," and patted him on the side of his arm.

Despite himself, Nathanael was swelling up with pride. It was just the shock of seeing her again, of course, it would be ridiculous to assume that he craved Natasha's attention and approval. Completely ridiculous.

Nathanael said, "So what are we doing? I believe Washington DC is where we need to be."

Natasha nodded, "We need access to their computers. We need to be able to get hold of the incriminating documents. We need to publicise what they're trying to do. To genetically engineer the human race, to increase the possible age…"

Nathanael looked around. The pub was filled with people of all ages, from eighteen, nineteen, early twenties, up to seventies and even eighties. But there was one common denominator, something he'd never really thought about much. Not till he'd started getting a few grey hairs himself. He said to Natasha, "Ha. Look at all these people. So much normal social interaction is about concealing age. Women's makeup, foundation to make their skin look young, soft, flawless, new skin, shading cheeks to make them look more child-like, waif-like, the whole keeping slim thing is about looking like a teenager, even plastic surgery — the purpose of it all is to make a woman look younger."

Natasha laughed. "Not just women. What about hipster beards, so trendy these days? Men dye them to make themselves look younger. No grey hairs. Do you pluck yours? Every now and then I see one, and it's gone the next day! And what about working out, lifting weights?

Vanity for both sexes is all about seeming younger than your age."

Suddenly Nathanael's collar felt uncomfortably tight. He tried to loosen it. He was sure he wasn't a vain person, but the thing is, nobody wanted to get old. What was wrong with feeling that way? "So to that extent let's just — ah — ignore the murders and thieving and the other thuggery for a moment. I'm going to be the devil's advocate... If they are able to increase human lifespan, what's wrong with doing that? I mean, clearly it is what everybody wants? Doesn't the end justify the means, at least, in this case?"

Natasha shook her head vigourously. "But they're only giving this technology to the elite..."

"Well I suppose it was expensive to develop. Why shouldn't people pay for it? ...To have children who will live for hundreds of years?"

"But who are they to decide on the contents of the human genome? There is already a process that decides what the genome contains."

Nathanael said, "But that process is random. It's like the lottery. Some people win. Extra intelligence, physical strength, beautiful faces, figures, those people who never get fat no matter how much they eat. Some people lose. Alzheimer's disease, heart disease, Parkinson's, Huntington's, cancer, Down's syndrome, diabetes, dementia, all of these diseases and many others have components or causes that are genetic, some of them are all genetic causes. Wouldn't it be better for everybody if these diseases could be eliminated for the next generation?"

Natasha went very reflective for a moment. "My grandfather died of lung cancer. Part of that was undoubtedly caused by the fact that he smoked. But at the same time, he must have had a genetic susceptibility to lung cancer. Not everyone who smokes dies from lung cancer. But the odious element of the Heosphoros Foundation's approach is that they want to only give these benefits to the elite. People with money and influence. It's disgusting."

Nathanael shook his head. "Haven't you heard of the trickle down effect? Eventually those genes would enter the general population-"

"-diluted by the number of generations away from the ones with all the longevity genes. Each generation of normal genes would dilute the longevity genes by fifty percent — at least, that seems logical, doesn't it? I suppose unless they're recessive or something and need to be activated. No, Nathanael, if these genes are going to be inserted into the human genome, they need to be made available to everyone. And the big question is, who is it that gets to decide what humanity is? What humanity becomes?"

Nathanael said, "Well… everyone should. Shouldn't they? It could be some sort of democratic decision."

Natasha saluted with her white wine glass, sipped it and said, "Indeed. That's why we need to publicise this. And also, to stop them from trying to stop us from publicising it. And why are they trying to stop us, Nathanael? Because what you're talking about is surely just the tip of the iceberg. We already know they are wrong-doers."

Nathanael swirled his Guinness in the glass. "We already know that they are murderers, thieves, liars, blackmailers." He took a swig, finishing it off.

Natasha nodded. "The murders, the thuggery, threatening people, bullying academics — if that's what we know about, what have they been doing that we don't know about? We need to find out everything and expose it. That's why we need to go to Washington DC."

Nathanael said, "And what about Meth and Peter? Should they come too?"

A concerned expression flitted over Natasha's face. "Where are they? I was a little worried when I saw they weren't with you."

"They're hiding out in a national park, called Sutton Park, it's in Birmingham, about two hours north. So do you think they should come with us or not?"

Natasha considered this. "On the 'yes' side — I think it may well be a lot easier to crack their computer system with Peter's help. I mean, he may already have an account. On the 'no' side, it seems far more likely that Meth might be noticed or captured if he is with Peter. Maybe it would be sufficient if we have a mobile phone number or two that we could reach them on."

"Well, we need to decide. I think the quicker we get on to a plane to DC, the better chance we'll have of winning out."

"Let's go to Sutton Park, then, and make the decision with Peter's input."

~~~

That night they stayed in the same hotel they had stayed in before. They set off at about five o'clock in the morning, which was a little too early for Nathanael. He gave Natasha instructions and then slept till six, then took over driving after that.

They got to Sutton Park by eight o'clock in the morning, having taken a route that avoided any toll roads.
~~~

They found the guest house and knocked on the door. The owners identified Peter and Meth by Nathanael's description and a few minutes later, they were with them in their bungalow, in a pleasantly casual sitting room, seated around a small wooden table with cups of tea and coffee in their hands.

Meth had a cup of hot chocolate, something that had apparently become a fast favourite with him.

Nathanael noticed a strange reticence about Natasha — a reticence towards the boy. As though she was uncomfortable around children. He wondered idly why, but he promptly forgot about it when Natasha asked Peter what he thought about going to Washington DC.

Before Peter could answer, Meth said, "Are we going there to find my parents? That's what I thought we were doing here, but I realised they don't live here in this national park, do they?"

Peter said softly, "No, they don't, Meth." Peter suddenly bowed his head and held it, as though a migraine had just hit. He continued, "Oh, dear God. I have to tell you the truth about this, Meth. I've been avoiding the subject, almost hoping you might forget about it, which I suppose is impossible. I don't want to tell you, but I know the truth is better. And you are twelve years old now — old enough to understand — old enough to know. Those men in that prison-house were lying to you. We will not find your parents either here or in the United States, or anywhere else, Meth. Your parents lived a very, very long time ago."

Meth said, "What, was I formed from very old sperm and a very old egg? How were these preserved?"

Peter said, "Do you understand that process? It's about your DNA, Meth..."

"Yes," he said, "I understand. Sperm and egg each contain half the DNA."

"Yes. But... In your, case, no," said Peter. "You were not made from one sperm and one egg. Your DNA was sequenced by taking some very old DNA and reconstructing it into a complete sequence. You are, effectively, a clone of someone who lived a very long time ago, with a few parts recombined from other ancient individuals."

Meth considered this for a while, almost as though he was trying hard to digest it. "So is that why I grow so slowly?"

"Exactly," said Peter. "You grow slowly because all the people did in those ancient times. Something happened to the human genome in the early part of our pre-history, that cause people to age more quickly. A mutation, really — I mean, you are the living proof that it wasn't an environmental change."

Meth sounded broken, completely broken. "I thought I would be able to find my parents. That was all I wanted. Now I find I really am a freak. There is no one like me in the world."

Peter said, "Meth, I am the closest thing to a parent that you have. I was one of the people who formed your genome, who made you what you are."

"Why?" Meth said, "Why did you make me like this? I will never be like other children. I will never have a normal life."

"You will have a very special life." Peter tried to hold his hand, but Meth pulled his hand away, clenching his teeth angrily. He looked away from Peter as though embarrassed by his anger.

"You're very special," Peter said, his voice breaking. "You will be able to live for at least five hundred years. Whatever field or endeavour you take on, you will have the time to make a long-term impact. Who knows — with such a long lifespan, imagine the medical advances you could make. You already have a way of thinking far beyond any twelve year old in many respects, because your infancy has lasted so long. You are still at the stage where you absorb every stimulus, every fact, every piece of information, and with the proper education that I give you, you will certainly learn more and more deeply than other children. Imagine — you will have what so many people envy — eternal youth — well, if not eternal, then a youth that lasts for hundreds of years. If you study science, you will have a much larger knowledge of every aspect of science than anyone else. You could become an expert in many fields, finding the connections between them, or an expert in one field, deepening and broadening human knowledge."

"I know what it means," said Meth bitterly, "It doesn't mean what you're saying at all. I'm surprised at you, Peter, at your age, not even knowing what is important in life. It is not what you achieve, how big an advancement in science you make. It is your friends, your family. Everything I have missed up till now, imprisoned in that tiny room, believing their lies." Meth started to shout, "Everything that was taken from me, and now I learn, it was never even mine in the first place!"

Peter said, "Shhh! Shhh! People will hear!"

Meth quietened his voice. "Don't you see? It means I don't even have a family, never can have one. I can never know my parents because they've been dead for millions of years. It means, if I become friends with anyone, they'll die before I do, unless of course, they happen to be... a person stuck together out of bits of the past, like me. But there is no one else like me, is there, Peter? If I love anyone, they will be doomed to die before I do. If I have a family I will have to watch my son die, and his sons, too, maybe. If I marry a normal woman and have children at fifty, then my son will die when I'm three hundred, his son will die when I'm four hundred and fifty, I will see his son die at five hundred and seventy five. I will watch the whole world die, ten times over, perhaps, before I myself die. You have constructed me to be different to other children, but in doing that you've doomed me to a world of death, watching everyone I love die, over and over again. But who asked me if this was what I wanted? Did you consult with me, before you created me to be different from everybody else, every other human on this planet?" Meth turned his sharp gaze onto Peter.

Peter folded his hands over Meth's hands and said, "Think about it — how could I possibly do that? How could I ask you, before I created you? Would you rather I didn't make you at all?"

Meth pulled his hands away. "Exactly. So you shouldn't have done it, should you? Who are you to play at being God?"

Peter squirmed uncomfortably on his chair. "It wasn't my choice anyway. I was coerced into it. The question of how to create you, whether to create you, Meth, it wasn't really up to me at all. It was the decision of the people who run the company. It was Roland Adamant's decision, if Nathanael is right, though I didn't even know who the voice on the phone was, telling me what to do, supervising everything. Roland Adamant is the one who decided to play God, not me, if it really was him. I was just an... unwitting part of the process. I only knew my little part of the procedure — the genetic component — even the final splicing and inserting the genetic material into a foetus at conception, even that was done by someone else. If you want to rail at someone, you should rail at him. Of course, once I found out that my work had contributed to such a marvel — as you — a living being — a son, if you will, the closest person I've ever had to being my own child, Meth — I started to care about you. You are like a son to me."

Meth looked at Peter with something approaching pity, mixed with combined compassion and revulsion. It seemed strange, seeing such ambivalent emotions vying on the face of a child apparently so young. But when Nathanael thought about Meth as a twelve year old, it made a little more sense. It was still incongruous, neither one nor the other, neither infantile nor mature.

Meth said in a strangely mature tone of voice, "You've been the closest thing to a father I have known. I do care about you, too, Peter." Nonetheless it still sounded somewhat begrudging, as though he was saying it because he didn't want to disappoint Peter.

Surely Peter realised that as well. Peter's tone of voice was more business-like, "Perhaps you do need to confront Roland Adamant at some point. After all, he is the one who was responsible for your existence."

It was time to say something. Nathanael said, "Not while he has power over you. We must ensure that he is brought down first — so that no one can hurt you, Meth. You need to have a proper life — up till now, you've had the life of a lab rat, nothing more."

Peter scowled. "I object to that description — really, after all, it's not as if-"

But Natasha interrupted, "It's a very apt description, Peter. I'm surprised you didn't try to spring him out earlier."

Meth looked at Peter, his intense gaze slightly hostile. Peter looked away guiltily. It was amazing to Nathanael that the child had so much power over the adult.

Nathanael continued, "I think we need to hide you away. I'm not sure England is the best place for it. Perhaps somewhere in Europe, or even Eastern Europe. I know that will be a little hard since Brexit, but the fact is that England is simply so over-surveilled that the chances of them discovering you here are particularly high. We need to get you out of here, preferably into a quality English language school somewhere — although you could probably thrive in a school that uses any language."

Peter nodded. He seemed far more cheerful talking about practicalities. "He could. He could learn a language far more easily than any other twelve year old. It would be like a second mother-tongue for him. His brain still exhibits an extremely high degree of neuroplasticity. While in normal children this degree of plasticity endures to about six or seven years old, I believe that in Meth it may even last until he's twenty or thirty."

Meth sighed and said, "I love how you talk about me sometimes as if I'm not even here. Back in that nasty house, I learned more from listening to that sort of talk, than just about anything else, except of course, searching the internet."

Nathanael shrugged. "How come you didn't work out that you didn't have parents, then?"

Meth's face took on a pained expression. His voice was small, far away. "I... don't think I wanted to know that."

Peter said, "We did talk about it — if I'd realised he was listening I wouldn't have."

Meth said, even more distantly, "They did talk about it in front of me, I remember it now, but I always explained it some other way to myself."

Natasha said, "I think it's time. I think we know what we have to do. We have to get him to a place where the Heosphoros Foundation cannot reach, somewhere where even their tentacles don't have the power to grasp hold of him. Then Nathanael and I need to go to Washington DC and expose everything they are doing, bring them down."

Then she added, "I wonder how many other children there are like him?"

Peter said, "That's odd. I hadn't thought of that. Do you really think he might not be unique?"

Natasha said, "Why would they only create one, if they could make more?"

Nathanael was about to mention the creature he had seen on the grounds of Sutton Estate, two days before, but he glanced at Meth. The poor boy already had enough to deal with. What would it do to him if he found out that he had... half-brothers who were beasts, half-animal, half-human?

Natasha was still talking, "Do you really think Roland Adamant doesn't have some sort of redundancy calculation in his plan? There could be labs like this all around the world, couldn't there? Any hospital, any clinic, might be the sort of place where they find surrogate mothers?"

That seemed like a strange leap of logic. How did she know they used surrogates? Perhaps they had some means of growing the foetuses outside of the womb?

Peter said, "You're right, we were using surrogates; we called them clients. I never got to meet them. But you see, we had trouble with our technique, in the early days. Before Meth, when, you know, Nathanael, we weren't using the same DNA, the Sutton Estate..." Clearly Peter didn't want Meth to know either.

Nathanael nodded. "I... saw him."

Peter raised his eyebrows in astonishment. "Really? You saw him? He's still around then — well, actually, he is a she. That's good. She wasn't very talkative, though, although clearly intelligent."

Natasha looked from one to the other. "What are you talking about?"

"Explain later," said Peter. "But you see the procedure worked fine with Meth — we had an almost complete DNA sequence to work with (God alone knows how, I mean, according to the palaeontologists it was a sample at least forty thousand years old, but it had been well preserved in mud of a particular composition, apparently, I don't know the details.) But when we tried to transfer the relevant genetic sections across to modern foetuses, we got nowhere. Ultimately we were trying to combine Meth's DNA with the DNA of some of the donors, the clients as we called them. So the other thing we were trying was to essentially to create a virus that could spread the new DNA throughout an adult's genome. The fact is, we failed rather catastrophically with that one. Killed a few test subjects at the start, caused widespread cell rejection in others; they would have to be on anti-rejection drugs the rest of their lives, just to stop one half of their body from killing the other half. But I suppose that wouldn't preclude other labs from working on other sides of the problem. Creating more Methuselah's — why not? It could be. For the whole time I never even saw many of the other people I was working with, never knew who was doing what. It was very secretive, very secretive indeed."

Natasha said, "Well, let's work out where Meth is going. We'll need identity documents, a school, somewhere with a good education system but a favourable exchange rate, to make whatever money we can rustle up last as long as possible. You'll need to get a job there, Peter."

Peter said, "I will, even if it's teaching in a high school. Even if it's gardening."

"And I need to pick your brains as well," Natasha continued. "Nathanael and I need to know everything you can tell us about passwords, pass codes, computer access codes, that sort of thing."

Peter nodded. "Alright. Let's start with that, then."

~~~

"Sir, we found a set of plates in London today, matching the description you asked for. They were on the M1 last night, but we can't seem to determine where they got off. Somewhere around Birmingham we suspect but we can't be certain."

"Well, look for Dark net activity on any of the networks in Birmingham. Surely you can narrow it down. Who was in the car? The boy?"
~~~

"No. A man and a woman."

"Well I need more than that. We need something more specific. Keep trying."

~~~

After two hours of probing Peter's memory, Nathanael had memorised every pass code, password or computer access code that Peter could remember. Rather more helpfully, however, Peter had recalled the default passwords for some of the systems, and they were rather predictable in their own way — usually something like 'cro-magnon' or 'palaeo1' or 'genesis' or 'dna1', depending on which part of the system they were for.

"I was there from the beginning, you see, working for them," Peter said. "Right from the start."

Meanwhile, Natasha had gone into into Birmingham City Centre and found a mobile and computer store. She had bought ten prepaid mobile phones and a couple of laptops, as well as an extra internal hard drive, and replacement chips for the CPU and the GPU, and then had driven back. Using one of the new laptops (after taping over the camera and microphone) accessing the internet through the one of the mobiles, she started looking for a school for Meth to go to. Justifying her caution, she said, "Even this could be something they might use to find us."

She found several International schools in Budapest. The typical term fee was about 1000,000 Hungarian Forint, which equated to around three thousand US dollars.

She discovered that the currency of Iceland was quite low as well, but the school fees were a little too high, comparatively speaking. Even South Korea was another possibility; the fees were slightly more expensive than
~~~

Budapest but probably still manageable, but Budapest was closer, so that was why they decided Budapest was the best place to send Meth to. The train fare from London to Budapest wasn't too expensive, either. Natasha still had to find someone to give them identity documents. She took out the second laptop and a different mobile phone. "I'll need to go somewhere else to do this part, but first I need photos of everyone."

They took the photos, unsmiling against the white wall.

Peter and Meth stayed behind. Nathanael and Natasha drove into Birmingham City Centre. They found a car park with no visible cameras and parked there. Natasha opened Tor and searched the Dark net for identity documents in Birmingham. She found one they could afford which she contacted.

This time it was a lovely cottage on the outskirts of town with an exquisitely tended garden. They arrived half an hour later as arranged.

And when they rang the doorbell the man who met them was an old fellow, in his late seventies, wearing a tweed jacket and sporting a pipe that he puffed on once every few minutes. The pipe appeared to be empty.

He had the documents ready for them already. "These are Jamaican passports," he explained. "Fairly easy to fake and I have intact computer codes. I wouldn't use them after six months, however; that tends to be the typical lifespan of documents like these. I won't ask you what you want them for. I've done four passports — one a boy of five years old, a man in his fifties, a man in his forties, and a woman in her late twenties, and inserted the photographs. The boy looks a bit young — are you sure you want him to be five?"

"He talks like a seven year old," said Nathanael. "Any younger than five and it would be odd."

"Odd, either way," the old man said, arching his eyebrow. "Still, it's your business." He handed over a small satchel. "In here are the other identity documents. I may have gone a bit overboard, but I like to be thorough. You said the fellow's a scientist, university educated? Well, there's some academic records there, if they check them too thoroughly they'll find out, but I have a friend in Jamaica at that University who is a hacker — well, let's call him a sub-contractor. He's ensured that everything is hunky dory. But as I say, if anyone starts asking questions, like, 'Which lecturer will remember you personally?' or 'What building was that in?', you know, every fabrication has holes in it, ultimately, that someone could find if they were determined enough."

"These are good," said Nathanael. "Do you think we could pass for Jamaicans?"

"Of course you could," he said. "Plenty of ex-pats living there these days."

Natasha said, "If we ever need to get more documents, would you be available later if we need them sent overseas?"

"Of course. For a fee. Speaking of which-"

Natasha and Nathanael reluctantly shared the expense; it was a very large fee this time. Still, his thoroughness appeared to be worth the extra.

On the way back to Sutton Park Nature Reserve she stopped at the side of the road on a fairly deserted road. She had already taken out the mobile phone battery. After taking a hammer and smashing the phone's hard drive, she chucked the wreckage into the bushes. Then she took out some tools she had in her purse and quickly replaced the hard drive, the CPU and the GPU on the computer, then destroyed the old components, stabbing the hard drive with a screwdriver then frying the integrated circuits one by one with the cigarette lighter from the car until they started to cook with a distinctive plastic smell, then stomping them one by one into the mud in different places.

Nathanael said, "Wow."

She said, stomping the last part into the mud, "No point making it easy for them."

~~~

"Yes, sir. A laptop using Tor in Birmingham. No cameras, unfortunately. They were on the mobile network. That particular mobile phone went blank soon afterwards — we suggest the battery was taken out. No, the computer hasn't been used again. Well, we're still looking for the car number plate. At this moment we've narrowed down the appearances to Birmingham and surrounding areas. Well, Eugene in analysis is suggesting Sutton Park Nature Reserve as the most likely scenario. Alright, Sir, we'll organise an expedition tomorrow afternoon. Yes that's the earliest we can do it. Well, Thompson won't be back from Washington DC till then. Alright, Sir."

~~~

Knowing it was their last night together, there was an air of melancholy in the room. After dinner Natasha briefed Peter as to what was happening. Then after ensuring that Peter had enough cash for Meth's first term and their living expenses in Budapest Natasha gave Peter two of the unused mobile phones.

After that the four of them played cards, Gin Rummy and Bridge. Meth wanted to stay awake until after midnight, but Peter made him go to bed at about eleven. He said, "You don't want to be grumpy on the train," and Meth agreed, after all it was his first time going on a train.

Peter, Natasha and Nathanael kept playing cards into the early hours.

After Peter went to bed, about one thirty, Natasha brought out a small bottle from the bar fridge. "Share a Kahlúa?"

They each had half, just a taste really, but it was sweet.

Nathanael said, "You're a wonderful girl, Natasha. Smart. Where would I be without you?"

Natasha said, "Dead. But do you know, I'm really rather glad I saved you from those thugs at the hospital?"

They talked for a while about this and that, then Nathanael said, "Nice boy, that Meth. Strange kid, really. Always wanted kids myself, but, you know, Debra didn't want to have them. She was such a…" He didn't want to say the word he had thought of in front of Natasha.

Natasha looked slightly pained, and for a moment Nathanael wondered why. Perhaps she didn't like him talking about his ex-wife. She wasn't Catholic, was she? Didn't like divorce, perhaps. But then Natasha yawned and said, "I'm really exhausted, Nathanael, it's been a very long day. Didn't really realise how tired I am — the Kahlúa has brought it on, though. I think it's time for bed, really," and he put it down to tiredness.

She kissed him on the cheek as she went and said, "Thank you."

He said, "What for?"

"Just for being who you are."

~~~

The following morning they drove into London and farewelled Meth and Peter at Waterloo Railway station, then Natasha booked two plane tickets, using the refurbished computer. They then parked the car in a dark alleyway and took off the number plates and took them to a self-storage place nearby, where they stored all the things they didn't think they would need. Natasha paid for six months. Nearby was a Post Office, where she put the key in an envelope and sent it to "Andy the Sound Engineer, c/o Saffron Music Store," etc., with a short note inside saying thanks.

She also sent another hand-written letter to the hire car company, apologising about the number plates being taken off and telling them they had parked the car near such-and-such street in the alleyway behind the warehouse.

After a cheap meal of fish and chips at a little place near the train station they caught the tube to Heathrow airport.

The fake documents worked fine — there was no problem with the airport security, which was the main thing Natasha had feared up until then.

It was an eight and a half hour flight, and neither of them slept. They sat quietly, keeping their thoughts to themselves.

Both of them were wondering what awaited them in Washington DC.

Both of them were asking themselves if they were up to the challenge.

~~~

"Well, they were definitely there in Sutton Park. One of our operatives talked to a couple who own a bed and breakfast there. Left this morning, unfortunately, before we got there. Even we can't be everywhere at once, sir. We're going through all the train footage and the footage at Heathrow airport. I suspect we might know where they're headed within say, eight hours. There is a lot of footage to go through, sir. Yes, I know, sir, it will be too late if they've already left the country. We can only do our best sir. Oh, yes, we've already told the Americans. Well, Eugene says, Washington DC is the most likely destination. No, he can't say whether the boy will be with them. It's unlikely, Eugene says it's more likely the boy and the scientist will go to ground. Yes, sir, we're still listening. We never stop listening, you know that."

Chapter 20 — Seeking Disclosure in DC

It was just after eleven o'clock in the morning when they arrived in Washington. They collected their luggage and made their way to the hire car rentals. Not having a credit card in the name of any of their aliases made it a little difficult this time, but by paying a fairly hefty cash deposit they were able to hire a car. Nathanael was a little concerned — his money was disappearing faster than he had hoped. Peter had given them a few thousand extra from his own funds, but that wasn't going to last at this rate.

None of the mobiles she had were equipped with roaming — it was rather hard to get without a credit card — which meant she would not be able to use the internet to find a place to stay.

There was a road guide in the car, however, and Natasha used it to find the Heosphoros Foundation, which they already had the address for. Helpfully, there was also a yellow pages, which she used to find any home stays, small motels, hotels nearby. Home stays were always preferable as they were less likely to have cameras.

They got some lunch at a corner store and sat in the car eating it, then found the homestay. They arrived at about two thirty in the afternoon. Natasha knocked on the door and the owners answered. Luckily the room was free for the next three days, but after that it was booked, so they could stay for the next three days, anyway.

Dinner was included in the homestay and it was a good square meal.

After they had eaten, Nathanael said, "Our money is disappearing fast. I suggest we try to find a place to rent. Overall it would be cheaper."

Natasha nodded. "I had noticed that. Sounds good. I'm exhausted, though. Let's take care of that in the morning. By the way, I have some bit coin I haven't cashed in yet. I bought quite a few blocks back in 2012 when the price was around eleven dollars. Depending on what the exchange rate is at the moment, it might be worth quite a lot."

~~~

The following day Natasha got up and during breakfast said, "Did you notice if there's a phone book here?" Nathanael said, "Yes. In the cupboard next to the bed." "I've got some things to do — will you remember to put it in the car?" "Sure."

The first thing she did was buy a prepaid mobile. Her Jamaican identity documents were sufficient. She used the mobile's internet connection to search for the nearest bitcoin exchange where she could sell bitcoins for cash.

There was an actual bitcoin ATM in 18th avenue. They drove there. It was in an industrial part of the town, near a fairly nondescript park. She looked at the bitcoin exchange rate. It was over $800. "That's the best it's been for a few years at least." She took out five thousand
~~~

dollars in cash. "There's a lot more there, Nathanael. I hadn't realised how much the value has gone up."

~~~

They returned to the bed and breakfast place. It was about one o'clock in the afternoon by then. Natasha said, "I want to see if I can hack their website. But the thing is, if I do it from here it's like lighting a flare, saying, 'Here I am,' to anyone who is watching the internet."

"So why do you get rid of all your computer gear after you've done a hack like this?"

"Once I've used a computer for something like this, the manufacturer's serial number on the hard drive, the CPU serial number, the computer's serial number, all these things become neon signs advertising who I am, and the whole computer can be accessed by clever hackers with a back door. And the one with the biggest back door key into everybody's computer is the government. Come on, let's go for a drive. Find me somewhere reasonably remote that probably still has mobile phone access."

"How do I do that?"

"Look in this." She opened the glove box and pulled out the street directory, whilst still watching the road.

"Oh. Alright."

She simply drove for a few minutes, while he flipped through the book. "Do you know what... I think we need to go to Maryland. There's a national park called Wooton's Landing, looks to be about half an hour away."

~~~

It took them forty minutes to get there. They parked on a side road into the park, about ten metres from the main road. She looked at her phone. "Four bars on 4G!" she said. "That's fine, then. Let's get to work."

"Anything you want me to do?"

Natasha said, "Swap. You drive, in case we need to make a quick getaway. I can't imagine we will, but best to be prepared."

Nathanael got out and she moved across to the passenger seat and began opening windows.

On the Heosphoros Foundation website there was a login page. She started trying to hack it.

"I'm using the ftp site. It's suspiciously easy," she said. "I didn't think it would be this easy. It just accepted 'username' as the username and 'password' as the password."

A list of folders appeared on the screen.

She shut down the page and said, "I'm very suspicious about this. I'm going to do it another way."

For several hours she sat at the computer.

Eventually Nathanael had had enough. He said, "What are you actually doing?"

"I'm… setting up a fake computer, essentially. A long time ago I used some of my bitcoin to purchase some space on a server in Brazil. They have fairly lax internet laws. I've set up a fake server on their server. It's fairly rudimentary — but I'm going to monitor what happens when my fake server tries to mess with their server. I suspect their server is a honeypot. Hm. Funny — to be able to run a proper webpage that is also a honeypot — it's pretty clever, really, if that's what they're doing…"

"What's a honeypot?"

"Ever hear the expression, 'you catch more flies with honey than vinegar?' Well, in computer parlance a honeypot is a fake webpage for catching hackers. Only this really is the company webpage but when you look at the code, it's so full of intentional holes it can only be fake..." She now had several windows open. One of them showed the server login page, another one of them had a bunch of diagrams and a list of numbers — Nathanael was proud, he knew now that they were ip addresses — groups of 4 numbers separated by decimal points.

To show his superior knowledge, Nathanael asked, "What are those ip addresses?"

Natasha said, "Oh, they're the ip addresses of people accessing the website I created, the representation of the fake server. I think they're all bots, actually, surfing the net to find people to deliver advertising to. But watch what happens..." She typed something in the username and password field of the Heosphoros Foundation website.

A whole row of new ip addresses appeared. "Look at that. They're virtually flaming me. I'd better end this simulation."

She clicked on something and a new message appeared. 'All ports closed to traffic.'

Natasha said, "Damn. I can't keep this up for too long — perhaps we should have done this in Washington. I've got to find a way in quickly. They'll already be trying to track us down."

She screwed her eyes shut, as though by effort of concentration she could make an idea come. It seemed a long time before she looked up at Nathanael and said, "Well... Essentially I need to treat this as a black box test. But to do that I need at least to analyse the specifications and documentation for the system, do a proper flaw hypothesis methodology... Starting with html injection, sql insertion..."

She threw up her hands. "Oh, God, this is useless. Did you have that phone book I asked you to bring?"

"Yes, I do," Nathanael said, handing it to her.

She shook her head. "Look up Heosphoros Foundation in there and tell me the number."

He found it and did so.

Natasha balanced her computer on her knee and while Nathanael held her mobile and rang the number. He held the mobile up to her ear.

Someone answered the phone.

Natasha said, "Oh, hi, um, I'm so terribly sorry I've forgotten your name… Oh, Sophie, listen, could you do me a favour? I just need to be put through to that secretary in the IT security, whats her name?… Yes that's right, Angelique…"

Natasha held her nose and spoke in a deep voice. "Oh, Hi, Angelique, it's Michael here in admin. Yeh, I do I have a terrible cold, losing my voice. Listen, you couldn't do me a big favour? I've forgotten my password…" Natasha typed something on the server screen on her computer. "No it's still not working. Oh, yeh, just spell that username for me? MikeH505? No, still not working."

She tried again. It didn't work. With the phone handset covered she told Nathanael, "They must have a different web address for the admin."

Someone on the phone said something. Natasha said, "Oh, yeh, what's the admin website again?… Oh, I know, I've been with the company for a while, but look, someone spilled a cup of coffee on my computer. Still works just a little sluggish, and for some reason I lost all my bookmarks." Natasha covered the handset again and whispered to Nathanael, "No reason spilling coffee should make you lose your bookmarks! It's ridiculous but they'll buy it."

The other voice said something on the line again. Natasha replied in the deep voice, "Oh, I have no clue why my bookmarks went missing. Nothing to do with the coffee, I'm sure. No, I didn't mean to imply that it was."

Then Natasha screwed up her face a little, still holding her nose, which looked a bit funny, especially when she began talking in the fake deep voice again. "No, I'm not in Brazil. Why on earth would I be in Brazil? Look, I… honestly don't know why my IP address says that — no, I've been in the same place the whole time. Can you please tell me the web address? Honestly, I need to get in to get back to work. It's really imperative — you know — security updates — the whole database is in danger of being corrupted. Well, don't be ridiculous — if I wasn't Mike, how the hell would I know your real name, er, Angelique? Yes, well, luckily I remembered today, it must be your lucky day. Oh, okay, heosphorosfoundation.com forward slash admin forward slash login. Gee, that's easy, how could I possibly forget? Been stressed lately. Alright, thanks a lot, you too."

Natasha looked smug. "Well, everything that could go wrong did go wrong but I still got everything I needed from them. Admin access."

She typed in 'heosphorosfoundation.com/admin/login' and immediately the login page came up. She typed in Mike's username and password and immediately got through to the server dashboard.

It was an entirely different operating system, something she had never seen before, inside the web window, with some sort of 3D graphical interface. It reminded her of the old Mac Time Machine interface, but it was much fancier.

Nathanael said, "Wow."

"Yeh," said Natasha, smiling at him. "Human fallibility. The hacker's best friend. If all else fails, ask someone in the know. Let's see if I can get the maps of the building and the list of authorised personnel, plus passwords." To her surprise the interface was surprisingly easy to navigate. "But there's just too much there, I can't sort through it all at once." She clicked a few things, and a bar appeared in the window. Some sort of data upload, Nathanael guessed. "I'm going to be quick about this. As if the Brazil thing won't be raising enough flags for them, the fact that I've requested this data, if they're watching, will be a dead give-away. Damn it, I'm just going to pilfer as much as I can then run. Let's see if two Mike's can log in at once."

She fiddled around for a while, and soon she had twenty Mike accounts all logged in together, siphoning out data onto her external hard drive. "That will probably do. Don't want to max out the server in Brazil or they'll close down my account there. My God, this really is like sending up a flare. Look at how much information is being uploaded from their servers. Gigabytes. I'd hardly be surprised if someone tapped on the car window in a few minutes time. The only saving grace is it might take them a little while to get here."

While she waited for the files to upload, Nathanael said, "Why did you choose the name Mike?"

"Most common first name in America from 1954 to 1999, in a straight run for forty five years except for one year. About 1 in 44 men of working age will be called

Michael. So chances are, in a large organisation, someone in the office will be called Mike or Michael."

"Impressive," Nathanael grudgingly admitted. He really didn't like anyone else being smart.

Natasha shrugged. "It's just the sort of thing we used to work out when we were hacking at college. We had this little group, see. There were some pretty smart guys in that group. And girls. Me, for instance. Oh, no, they're onto me."

The list of ip addresses expanded, running down the page.

Natasha said, "Well, that will have to do." She pressed the same button as before and the message appeared, 'All ports closed to traffic.'

She said to Nathanael, "Well, let's get back to home base and start going through this. See if any of it is any use."

At that moment, someone tapped on her car window.

Natasha said, "Oh. I was right."

It was a man in a black suit. Was he one of the Heosphoros ones, or one of the ones from the British intelligence services?

He must have been in his forties, because he gestured for Natasha to wind the window down by turning his hand in a winding gesture. She whispered to Nathanael, "Get ready to drive," and pressed the window button.

The window came down and he waved a small pistol in Natasha's general direction said, "You accessing the internet? Heosphoros' servers through some Brazilian thing? Yes? Get out of the car. We need that computer."

CHAPTER 21 — INTERCEPTED TRIP TO BUDAPEST.

As soon as Meth opened his mouth on the train it was inevitable that someone would put a picture or even a video of him on Facebook, and so he tried, very, very hard not to talk.

Especially once a video of him was on Facebook, it would not be difficult for whoever was chasing them to do a computerised search for Meth's face, but it might even be easier than that. They may just have to search for tags or labels on the videos such as, 'Young toddler talking like an adult', or 'Baby who can already talk.'

And while Peter did his best, he couldn't watch Meth every hour of ever day.

It would be an understatement to say Meth enjoyed the train journey — he completely loved it. The view from the window, the scenery speeding past, the luxurious seats, the beds that folded out from the wall, the oh-so-civilised meals in the dining carriage, the various drinks (the ones he could have, lemon lime and bitters, ginger beer, Sprite.) And the butlers and ticket inspectors and serving staff and bartenders and maids impressed him with their efficient and crisp manner of servitude, something that almost seemed to have been bred into them.

In fact, the train staff really took to Meth, too. He tried so very hard not to talk to them but once they knew he could talk they began to consciously try to drew him out of his shell, and when they did manage to trick him into talking they loved his loquacity and penchant for large words, despite his apparent youth.

And so, it was only a matter of time before a video was posted on someone's Facebook page, of him babbling about the food or the drink on the carriage, using language far more mature than his apparent age.

That happened as they were approaching Paris.

The man in the black suit got on the train in Munich, one nondescript traveller to Budapest among so many other men who wearing black suits.

Had they seen the man in the black suit they would have thought nothing of it, even if he had been staring at them. Meth's eyes, so intense for such a young child, were enough to catch the attention of many who passed through the dining carriage while they were eating.

When they got off at Budapest, he was there, watching them alight from the train with their luggage. He was watching them at the taxi stand, and caught the next taxi in the rank.

A tracking device had already been placed in their luggage, so the man in the black suit hadn't even needed to tell the taxi driver to hurry. He simply told him to head into the city centre, and when Peter and Meth arrived at their hotel, an SMS informed him which hotel to tell the taxi driver to go to.

He watched them lugging their suitcases up the stairway laboriously until a porter arrived and helped them. He watched until the lights went on in one of the rooms, and waited until they both came to the window and looked out on the city that they thought was going to be their new home.

Their new home.

Indeed, it was, thought the man in the black suit.

But only for a few more hours.

Chapter 22 — States and Estates

Nathanael pressed his foot down all the way to the floor and turned the wheel. The car turned in a small turning circle, creating a huge dust cloud in the dirt road. The man started shooting at them, but the dust must have been obscuring his aim. Some of the shots pinged as they hit the car body, others thudded into the ground, but none of them even broke the glass or hit the car anywhere near Nathanael or Natasha. Nathanael swerved from side to side, trying to make the car a difficult target to hit.

He breaked a little to turn then floored the accelerator again as they hit the highway and they roared onto the main road, screeching out past a bunch of other cars doing a reasonable speed. The man was running out of the dirt road behind them, waving his pistol, still shooting at them. For such a little gun it seemed to have a lot of shots.

Natasha was shouting, "How did they do that so quickly? Is it government? I think it must be Heosphoros — they must own every server between here and Brazil! Man, that was quick!"

Nathanael looked in the rear view mirror. A black car pulled into the side road, from the wrong side of the road, facing against the traffic, and the gunman hopped in. Nathanael looked around for a side street.

He couldn't do this on his own.

Nathanael said, "Get the road guide, Natasha. Get us out of here, away from them."

She picked it up — it was already open on the right page. She quickly scanned the page. "There's nothing much until Prince George's county. No, we have to go the other way. Queen Anne Estates — confusing enough roads to maybe get away. Turn around!"

Nathanael slowed a little as they rounded the corner. He couldn't see the black car any longer, so they couldn't se him. He estimated his positioning based on the distance the black car was behind them and their speed, when they were coming up to the same corner, and quickly turned against the traffic, switching to the other side of the road.

The black car roared past them. Had they even seen that it was them? He wasn't sure.

Natasha said, "Good work. Keep going, though. Have we got enough gas?"

"Yeah, I filled it up last night. Three quarters of a tank at least."

They sped for about ten minutes along the same twisting and turning road. Nathanael was doing at least ten miles an hour above the speed limit. As they came up to a T-junction Natasha said, "Take the left fork. Patuxent River Road. I'll guide you from there — onto the highway — and if we exit at the Queen Anne Estate Road it'll give us the option of going back where we started or getting back on the highway. I don't think they're following us, though."

There was no sign of the black car behind them.

Natasha opened her window. The breeze rushed in, disturbing the pages of the road directory and making her hair billow up. She grabbed the street directory and put it open-side down on the floor beneath her feet.

Nathanael said, "What are you doing?"

She took her seat belt off and sat up, looking out onto the outside of the car door.

She reached out and grabbed something on the outer body of the car door.

It was a small circular object.

"It's a GPS tracking device, I would bet," she said. "What we need to do is not just dump it — we need to put it on something else to fool them. A gas station, maybe."

They came to another T-junction. She said, "Left. I'll bet there're some gas stations on the highway. We can just transfer it onto a truck or something."

They passed an auto repair shop. "Stop there?" Natasha said.

"No, none of those cars will be moving til they've fixed them. We want someone who's driving off."

"Look," said Natasha. "Ahead — there's a liquor store."

They stopped in the carpark. She surreptitiously got out and put the tracker on the SUV next to where they were parked. Just at that moment a large, big-boned man wearing a hunting jacket came out of the liquor store. "Hey! What are you doing to my car? You trying to steal it? You thieves? Gonna steal my SUV?"

"We're not doing anything to your car!" shouted Natasha.

The man shouted, "What? You call my SUV a car? I'm gonna show you!" He lumbered towards them like a murderous giant, taking massive steps on boulder-like legs, his big boots thumping on the asphalt.

Natasha clambering back in clumsily to her seat. "Drive, Nathanael, drive!"

Nathanael floored the accelerator again and they screeched out onto the road.

"Oh no," he said, "What's he going to do with the tracking device?"

Natasha said, "Just my luck! How stupid. How could that be — just when the man is coming out of the store! What idiotic luck!"

The man got in to his SUV, swearing and cussing, and gunned the engine. He didn't even see the tracking device. The SUV leaped out of the carpark to follow them.

"Oh, no," said Nathanael, hitting his forehead with his fist, "He's following us. That couldn't have gone more wrong than it did."

Nathanael pressed the accelerator to the floor as if that could make them go any faster than they already were. The little car was already going as fast as it could but the man in the SUV was getting closer, its engine whining like an over-wrought jet.

Nathanael started trying to weave away but the man thrust his SUV forwards, jolting them from behind.

There was a road, an intersection, coming up and briefly Nathanael considered going that way. But a flash of black caught his eye, making him hesitate. Then they were already there and it was too late.

One of the black limousines, just like the one that had been following them, was careening down the road, straight towards them. The SUV shoved them from behind once again and their car leaped forwards, past the intersection.

The black car was going incredibly fast. The bad guys probably hadn't seen the SUV — the limousine ploughed right into the side of it. Both cars left the road diagonal to the intersection, the SUV rolling over and over and the black limousine following into the scrub on the side of the road. Nathanael slowed right down and looked in the rear view mirror to watch, to make sure neither of them would be turning around to follow any more.

The SUV was still rolling unevenly, snapping small trees like twigs, ba-da-bump, ba-da-bump. Finally it came to rest about seven metres from the road. The limousine, still buffeting along on the undergrowth like a cartoon car, thudded rather lamely into the SUV's axle assembly. The entire bonnet crumpled.

Then they'd rounded a corner and he couldn't see either car any more.

They were on their own again.

"Let's get back to that bed and breakfast and check out the damage," he said.

No reply.

He glanced at Natasha.

Natasha was sitting, eyes wide, clinging to the seat with clenched fingers, swearing silently over and over again. Nathanael noticed that somehow in the middle of all of that she had gotten her seatbelt back on.

She stopped swearing and said, "I don't know how I'm going to go back to normal life again after this."

Nathanael said, "Yeah. It was a bit... exciting, wasn't it?"

She looked at him. "Yeh, right."

Then she sat there for a minute staring at the road almost hyperventilating. Then, finally calming down a little, she said, "You know, you are right. That was a thrill ride and a half. Only I hope we don't have to do it again any time soon."

They turned onto the highway interchange.

Nathanael said, "Damn."

"What?"

"There's one of those black limos, at that service station, parked on the off ramp."

She looked. "What's a — you mean that gas station?"

"Yeah." The black limo pulled past the trucks that were also parked there and slowly went past the gas station and followed them onto the highway.

Nathanael said, "It's got to be one of theirs. Who would give up their spot, when he was only one truck away from the bowser, to get back on the highway?"

He was only about fifty metres behind them.

Nathanael nodded, "I'm going to have to lose him in that place — Queen Anne — like you said."

Natasha groaned and put her head out the window. Her breakfast came back up, leaving a trail of puke on the highway behind them. "Oh, there was so much of it," she groaned.

Nathanael had an idea — it was a long shot but it was worth it.

"Now," said Nathanael, putting the brakes on.

The limo braked behind them with the two wheels on the left slipping in the puke. It was interesting to watch — the limo sort of shuddered, clearly the brakes were going on and off on the puke side of the car — some kind of computer error. It was exactly what Nathanael had anticipated — the computer that managed the brakes in the car was programmed for water, or ice, or oil, but the viscosity of vomit was something different that hadn't been anticipated.

They were still sitting at a dead stop in the middle of the highway and the black limo was approaching them. Nathanael said, "Brace yourself." Natasha grabbed the sides of her seat again, readying for the impact.

But the limo stopped, a dead stop in the middle of a highway, with the trunk on the wrong side of the road. A truck loomed in the rear view mirror, over the top of the limo. It changed lanes but too late. As it careened past them the trailer clipped the rear of the limo, throwing it end over end into the tiny embankment into the ditch on the side of the road.

The truck went past, a car passed them, then another truck, and finally Nathanael gathered his wits and gunned the engine again and they were away. As he accelerated he looked in the rear view mirror.

The limo was upside down in the ditch by the side of the road. He imagined he could see bits of diced carrot still spinning off of the one wheel that was still turning.

Natasha said in a slightly wan voice, "Well done, James Bond."

"But how did he know we'd be here?"

Natasha said, "This is a hire car. There's probably a tracker in it, put there by the hire company. The guy before got our license number, I would guess, and passed it on to the others. Unless of course they're following us on the highway surveillance cameras."

"We have to get organised, get in and do what we have to do as quick as we can. We can't fight this kind of universal surveillance for much longer."

"I agree." Natasha closed the street directory. "At least we can get rid of the GPS tracker, though. Maybe at some point we can swap cars again too."

They pulled over at the next gas station and found the GPS tracker underneath the wheel rim. It was a much more bulky model, a big black box with a red light on it to show the battery was still working. Nathanael was going to throw it into the bushes by the side of the road but Natasha said, "Wait." She took out the battery then put the unit and the battery into the trunk of the car. "It wouldn't be right to throw it away. After all, that's someone else's property."

When they got back in the car Natasha said, "Back to DC then. Just turn right when we get to the Stephanie Roper Highway. Then we'll be headed straight for Pennsylvania Avenue. I'm going to sleep for a little while. Wake me when we pass another car hire place. We'll use your details this time."

How exhausted Nathanael was. Natasha's deep, slow breathing next to him as she slept strengthened him. Despite this weariness, he'd rather be here, right now, driving in this car, than anywhere else he could imagine.

He wasn't sure if it was the challenge of the whole thing, or just... Natasha's presence with him in the middle of it. It was all worth it, though. He was sure of that.

He hadn't had so much fun in ages.

Chapter 23 - Rescued from Budapest

Peter locked the door to the hotel room but he still didn't feel safe. Meth was asleep as soon as his head hit the pillow. Peter watched him sleeping, his chest rising and falling gently. Someone had been following them, Peter was sure of it.

He let him sleep for half an hour, then he gently shook the boy's shoulder to wake him up.

"What? What is it?"

"We have to go," Peter said. "I'm sure we were being followed. I've felt someone was watching us, ever since we were on the train."

"Alright." Meth got up without complaining and put some clothes on over his pajamas. Peter already knew where the fire escape was, he was in the habit now of getting to know his options wherever he was, wherever they went.

He packed all the luggage again and wheeled it to the door. Meth was putting his shoes on. Peter opened the door. No sign of anybody yet.

They crept out, down the corridor. Then Peter heard the footsteps, coming from the other corridor, the one that led to the lift. "Hurry!" he said to Meth.

They started running. The footsteps behind them sped up too - was it just an echo? Or was someone following them?

Meth and Peter reached the exit door, that led to the fire escape. Peter opened it and pushed Meth through with the luggage, then went through himself, leaving the door open just a crack to see if someone really was following them.

Two men in black suits came running around the corner. As quietly as he could Peter closed the door, trying not to alert them to the fact that they were out here.

Meth said, "Peter."

Peter said, "Shhh."

Meth said again, "Peter," then, "Dad."

He looked up.

He couldn't make out the shape looming in the darkness, a sort of blob. As his eyes adjusted he saw the bald head and the ear first, then the barrel of a gun. A man in a black suit standing on the iron staircase, holding a gun. "Methuselah, we're here to rescue you."

Meth said, "What if I don't want to be rescued?"

The man said, "You don't have any choice in the matter. In fact, I'm not sure you have any human rights either, because you were not born, you were made. You are the property of Adamant Corporation, and you will be returned to the Adamant offices in Washington DC."

As the other two men came through the door behind them, both wielding guns, Peter said, "What about me?"

"You'll be taken to Washington DC to face a Federal Court where you will be charged with identity theft and kidnapping."

Chapter 24 — Is Lucy4 not Lucifer?

About fifteen minutes later, Natasha woke up. They were a few minutes away from crossing the state lines.

She said, "Any more black cars? Anyone following us?"

"Not so far."

"We haven't been careful enough. We have to stay off the grid."

"So, what do we do….?" Nathanael had some idea, but Natasha seemed to know more about this than he did; best to let her take the lead.

"I don't think we can use my fake identity again. We can still use yours. We need to change cars, that's the main thing. Any time we go through a freeway camera it's uploading our number plate to their servers. I'm looking through the data — you find somewhere to hire a car."

While Natasha began looking through the data they had downloaded, Nathanael pulled over and looked up the road directory.

The nearest car rental place was Washington Union Train Station.

It didn't take long to get there, and there was plenty of parking behind the Station building. Natasha snapped the laptop shut and they went in. She quickly dealt with the insurance over the damage to the car, paying a six hundred dollar excess. In the fine print in the contract there was apparently an extra two hundred dollar excess for bullet holes, something Natasha quibbled over, but it was there.

Nonetheless, even though this was a different office from the one where they had hired the car they returned her deposit, which surprised her because she had thought they might all be separate franchises. They spent about forty five minutes in a café in the train station having something to eat before hiring another car from a different company in Nathanael's name.

It was now about seven o'clock at night.

They drove back to the bed and breakfast place and parked about a block away.

Once they were back in their room, Natasha continued perusing the data she had downloaded.

After fifteen minutes of watching her doing this, Nathanael was starting to feel impatient.

He asked her, "Isn't there anything I can do?"

Natasha said simply, "No, nothing, not yet, I'm sorting," and continued working.

To his relief, after about half an hour she said, "Get your new smart phone out." He did. She said, "Look, I'm using one of my spare cloud accounts — I set it up earlier, under your alias, which is the only one they haven't got yet. I used bitcoin — it's highly secure, only accessible through Tor."

"But didn't you say Tor would be like a beacon?"

"I suspect there's more people using encryption in Washington than most other cities. It will take them a while just to get onto checking us. And it's all encrypted.

Hard to crack. They have to identify the ip address first, to use the back door. Hand me your phone."

She fiddled for a few minutes.

"I've set up Tor on your phone. Just copy this link into your browser." He copied the link and opened up the page. A list of links appeared. Natasha said, "That's the database, I've uploaded the whole lot, the folders are ordered by subject rather than alphabetical. If you want to help, just download everything to your phone, then look through those files for anything we can use, particularly architectural plans or anything to do with security in the Foundation Museum. I've put Autocad 360 on your phone too, so you can view .dwg files."

Nathanael nodded. He was familiar with Autocad, which is software for designing in 3d, he knew architects and engineers use it.

Natasha said, "Disconnect from the wireless network and close Tor as soon as you've finished downloading everything. I think we're safer here than usual but no point tempting fate."

Nathanael nodded. It took about fifteen minutes, then he disconnected from the network and closed Tor.

He worked through the folders fairly systematically. If it was a text file or a .doc, he read the first few paragraphs to make sure it wasn't important. If it was an image, he viewed the thumbnail. Autocad files he looked at more carefully.

Anything that looked like it might be useful he copied to another folder, which he labelled, "extracted files."

Gradually he made inroads into the massive database. Some sections were clearly missing, but there were historic plans for the Foundation as .jpg image files, from when it was called the Lucifer Institute, as well as the .dwg files for the current plans. He put them in the other folder.

There were also some email accounts that seemed significant. It looked to him like Roland Adamant's email account, and another one was the computer administrator's email account. He copied the whole lot to "extracted files."

Natasha was still going when he finished perusing them in his systematic fashion at about three o'clock in the morning. She finished about half an hour later.

She said, "What did you find?"

They compared the contents of their folders.

NATHANAEL	NATASHA
1921plans.jpg	
heosphorosinstituterenovations.dwg	heosphorosinstituterenovations.dwg
emails (folder)	
roland adamant (folder)	roland adamant's emails (folder)
administrator (folder)	
heosphorosrenovations2.dwg	
encrypted files (folder)	
GWT8hSlZpjYEdVqUuEJdePg.zip	
XNJzmrK1F5gM3HO3gt3czIj.zip	
BSHVIWTEf4roDYkDiIQwfM.zip	
FWdLHKsbx63F1HNcnnCMDYo.zip	
ukfnUaeUeyRQI2m0kGFiSE3.zip	
Staff_Quarterly_2016October.pdf	Staff_Quarterly_2016October.pdf
Staff_Quarterly_2016June.pdf	Staff_Quarterly_2016June.pdf
Staff_Quarterly_2016April.pdf	Staff_Quarterly_2016April.pdf
Staff_Quarterly_2016January.pdf	Staff_Quarterly_2016January.pdf
Heosphoros%20Institute%20History.docx	Heosphoros%20Institute%20History.docx
Map%20for%20Newcomers.jpg	Map%20for%20Newcomers.jpg
New%20Staff%20Handbook.pdf	
Layout%20All%20Surv.pdf	
PasswordList.frm	
PasswordList.ibd	

Natasha said, "Well done. You found a few I hadn't noticed. Where on earth did you find 'Password List'?"

Nathanael recited the file path.

"Found\No_longer_needed\Trashes2016\To_Delete\Documents\Old_invoices_stationary_etc\Backup\ProgramData\MySQL\MySQL_Server_5.7.17\data\Passwords\mytable.frm and mytable.ibd. The Layout All Surv was in the same Backup file too."

Natasha said, "That's pretty clever. How did you remember that?"

Nathanael admitted, "The file path? I don't really know. Sometimes I try to remember stuff, sometimes it just sticks in my head."

Natasha said, "So you went through all those little folders… Pretty thorough. More thorough than I was. Interesting that it's not encrypted. Must have been some sort of oversight… It's the latest version of MySQL, so… pretty recent. Well done. Alright, let's start going through these. You look at the building plans, reconcile the renovations. Then memorise all the admin passwords. Then, if I'm still going, read through the doc files and pdfs. And I'll try to decrypt the encrypted ones."

~~~

Two hours later, Natasha said, "I've decrypted them." It was about eleven o'clock at night.

"What are they?"

"Pretty strange, some sort of data file. I think they might be DNA sequences."

"Can I have a look?"

"Sure," said Natasha.
~~~

Each zip file contained 46 files. Each of the 46 files was labelled with the same identifier that the zip file had, plus the number of the file, from 1 to 46, added at the end. Each file contained nothing but different iterations of the letters, C, A, G, and T, in long rows. "CAGACGTGTCAGTCGACTCGATATACTGAG..." etc.

When he'd finished reading through them Natasha said, "What do you think?"

"Yes, I've seen sequenced genomes before, that is certainly what it looks like," said Nathanael.

"What did you get?"

"I've got some... suspicions about something. I'll show you."

He opened up the 1921 plan file and the contemporary floor plan file. Carefully he changed the magnification and positioning until they were both the same size, in the same place on the screen. Then he switched between them.

"Look at this section," he said, pointing to the left hand bottom corner. A room in the basement was disappearing and reappearing, a room that was represented in the 1921 plan but missing in the modern version.

"What do you think it is?"

Nathanael said, "I think the particular geometry of the architecture is actually designed to conceal the existence of this room. And whatever might be beyond it."

"Hmmm. That might be some sort of secret lab, do you think?"

"Maybe... There was nothing much that's helpful in Staff Quarterlies or the Handbook. The Map for Newcomers was just very basic, no good really. Oh, I've memorised all the passwords, too." He opened the Layout All Surv file. Nathanael continued, "The Layout All Surv file is the location of all the surveillance cameras and other types of surveillance. There are alarms on some of the exhibits, protecting them." He pointed to the bottom left hand corner of the basement plan. There was a small diagram next to the door. And next to the diagram was a label showing a fingerprint and the iris of an eye. And Nathanael said, "And I think this is some sort of biometric scanner. At the door to the hidden room."

Natasha said quietly, "Wow."

Nathanael said, "The only thing I haven't looked at yet is the emails. But let's leave that til tomorrow morning. I know you're still firing on all cylinders, but I'm completely knackered now. Just can't keep going."

~~~

The following morning after a quick breakfast they divided the emails in half, Nathanael read half, Natasha read the other half. Most of the emails were fairly routine, supervising the renovations, hiring and firing staff, authorising payments, organising meetings at the Museum and any matters concerning the board of directors. But there was a series of emails to someone called Lucy4@heosphoros.org that didn't fit the pattern of the other emails.

After Nathanael read through them he said to Natasha, "I think the emails to Lucy4 are about the genetics program. They're rather sparse on details, but I noticed that the expenses never seem to go through the normal budgetary channels." He flipped through the emails, showed her a few of them. "And look, there're things here about recent acquisitions, names of staff, things like that. I think if we can go through these and cross-reference them with the passwords files, perhaps we
~~~

can work out which of the staff work in that program. With any luck, those passwords will still be current."

Natasha said, "Maybe. Just maybe."

And Nathanael said, "Natasha, I think we need to get into the hidden room, the labs, whatever they are. And I believe that in there we will find the records that we need to blow this whole thing wide open."

"When I was at Uni and my hacker group used to hack things, we'd set a timetable, a target date for the hack. Kept us on our toes. Let's make a target date, start setting the timetable for our... incursion into the Heosphoros Foundation."

Nathanael agreed. "How about next Wednesday, Seventh of December?"

Natasha said, "Do you think one week is enough?"

"What do you think?"

Natasha said, "Yes, I think it is."

"Agreed, then. On the Seventh of December, we're going in."

~~~

Their week was spent making plans, looking for more helpful files and gathering resources. One thing Nathanael found in the same backup file that had held the password database and the Surveillance layout was the night roster for the security guards. He couldn't find the day roster. That led to their decision to make their incursion at night.

And Natasha went shopping and spent more of their money on things they would need when they made their incursion. The main point was to remain anonymous, so she found woolen caps they could make into balaclavas and some black clothes.
~~~

She also got guns, easy enough to buy even in DC. She bought spray cans of mace, water canteens, orienteering equipment and a small step ladder, and more computer gear. She also bought fingerprinting kits, masking tape, and one or two other bits and pieces. Also she bought some cardboard boxes and some printable labels, and some black gloves. And a large flashlight, big enough to use as a weapon.

With everything she bought, Natasha exercised abundant caution. She used only cash, left no fingerprints or DNA on anything, and tried to avoid buying anything in shops that had security cameras.

They surveilled the Foundation, watching to make sure the changes of the guard conformed to the roster they had, and checking to see whether any of the staff worked at night. As far as they could tell, they didn't.

Natasha also thought about emailing the Foundation, telling them that the such-and-such was arriving on the 7th December, but she was worried that if she did that they would trace her ip address or work out somehow that it was not from a genuine supplier. No, it was only worth attempting an email as a last resort, on the night itself, if they were in real trouble.

They spent the last two or three days going through their plans and practicing the various steps, as well as playing, 'what if' with their own plan. 'What if' someone walks in while we are opening this door here, 'what if' they don't change the guard at the same time as the guard roster we have, 'what if' we forget to bring something.

And on the day of the incursion, they relaxed. Nathanael went swimming at a nearby health centre and Natasha went to the gym and did a workout then had her hair and makeup done. They ate a decent lunch. As the sun was going down they began packing the two boxes, marking them with 'Heosphoros Foundation' stickers, then carrying them into the hire car. All of this they did with gloves on and hair covering, to prevent their DNA or fingerprints from getting onto anything they were using.

Once the car was packed, they had dinner — a simple salad with pitta bread.

They tried to sleep or relax for at least half an hour, then, to make sure they were fully awake for the incursion.

Then they started getting ready. Natasha tied her hair back and covered it with a transparent plastic hair covering, to prevent stray hairs from escaping and identifying her. Nathanael covered his hair also. They put their clothes on, neat, professional clothes as well, with 'Museum Transport Couriers' on the pockets.

At eight thirty exactly, Nathanael took the wheel. The security guard shift changed at 8:38 pm exactly, and they had timed the trip to seven minutes. If they got there at exactly the right moment and the second guard was slightly late (he had been on the two nights they had been watching) then the guard station would be unoccupied for about thirty seconds.

They had to go south along the main street for about one and half miles. There was one set of traffic lights, but it changed fairly quickly, and they were back on the road. Then they had to turn right. The main entrance was on their left. The guard station was unoccupied. Nathanael cruised past with his lights off.

Even at night there was one or two people walking in the park around the Museum.

They had planned for this, and Nathanael put his parking lights on and simply backed into the loading bay. With the boxes marked, 'Heosphoros Foundation' they would have an excuse for being there.

They chose this particular loading bay because Nathanael had worked out it was in a blind spot of the surveillance. Nathanael had wondered if this was intentional — the door they were going to try to break into was the closest door to the hidden room. Perhaps they didn't want surveillance on that door, when they were taking things to the secret lab.

They both put their gloves on.

There was a keypad next to the door. By a process of elimination they had identified one or two of the staff more likely to be workers in the secret lab.

Nathanael had memorised all the passwords and passcodes. He typed in that particular worker's passcode, 122587, and the door clicked open. They pushed open the door and Nathanael lodged it open with a doorstop. Then they carried in the two boxes, then closed the trunk and Nathanael locked the car.

It was particularly quiet in the Museum. Every sound they made echoed accusingly through the hallways. They brought the boxes into a conference room to the left of the entrance, hugging the left wall, another blind spot for the security cameras.

They opened the boxes, put on their balaclavas and black shirts, took their guns, the spray cans of mace, water canteens, Nathanael carried the orienteering equipment and the small step ladder, and after strapping the flash light onto her belt, Natasha took out the computer gear and the other things and put them in a small back pack, which she put on.

Nathanael quickly returned the empty boxes to the trunk of the car, locked the car again, closed the door behind him and joined Natasha, who had been busy while he was gone. She had taken out her mobile phone and computer and had shared the internet connection on her mobile phone with her computer. On her computer she had opened a login page and accessed Bushguard. In the caching buffer she had inserted some pre-prepared numbers.

As they set off into the building, the lights went off inside and outside the building. Through a window Nathanael could see the park outside. It was completely in darkness. The whole Heosphoros Foundation block had been affected by the blackout.

They had no clue as to whether the cameras had backup battery power but it seemed logical to Nathanael that the monitors the security guards were watching would not. While they kept to the blind spots as much as possible, they moved with greater urgency now. Quickly and quietly they made their way through the maze of hallways to the centre of the Museum, where the entrances to the lifts and the stairwell were. They went down the polished wooden stairway to the basement in a tiptoeing sprint, quickly and quietly.

Quite a few of the doors were locked in the basement. The code, 122587, worked in each case. The door locks seemed to be on a different power network to the rest of the building. Perhaps they had battery backups, Nathanael didn't know.

They came to the door with the biometric scanners. They were glowing, it seemed that they were also on the same power system as the door locks.

Natasha took the fingerprint kit and dusted the wall to the right of the scanner for fingerprints.

Four fingerprints showed up. Natasha took the masking tape and ripped off a piece about three centimetres long. She pressed it gently onto the clearest of the fingerprints, then stuck the piece of masking tape to the door frame temporarily. Then she ripped the iris scanner out of the wall.

There were four or five wires on the end of the iris scanner. Carefully Natasha stripped the plastic covering from the brown, blue and yellow wires. She had a device that had three wires, each with a clip, coloured brown, blue and yellow. On the other end was a small box and a usb connection. She attached the clips and plugged the usb connector into her computer, opened some software, then chopped the end of each of the wires attached to the iris scanner.

Then Natasha took the piece of masking tape. She placed the part of the tape with the fingerprint on it onto the fingerprint scanner. After a few seconds a computerised voice said, "Verified. Hello Miss Thorndike."

Natasha typed a command into the computer.

Nothing seemed to be happening.

Nathanael said, "What's going on?"

Natasha said, "The computer is decrypting the connection. Should take about half a minute. The iris scans are all stored on the central computer — the iris scanner simply accesses the scans in the computer and compares them with the real iris, then returns a positive result. If I can access the hard drive on the computer, I can feed back one of the scans to the computer."

A window appeared on the computer, showing a set of files as graphic thumbnails. Each of them was an iris scan. Their names were quite simply the names of the people whose scans they were. Natasha clicked on the file named, 'EMMA_LOUISE_THORNDIKE,' and it opened up. Two buttons showed up on the window, 'FEED,' 'CANCEL,' and Natasha pressed 'FEED.' A horizontal bar appeared with a blue line travelling slowly across it.

When the light reached the right hand side, the same computerised voice said, "Verified Iris Scan. Welcome Miss Thorndike."

And the door clicked open, revealing a thin line of light in the crack.

Natasha clamped the wires back on the iris scanner then detached her computer and all the other bits and pieces. Nathanael opened the door and they went in.

As the door closed behind them a light went on in the small entry room. There were white coats of various sizes, small hair covering hats, gloves and shoe coverings.

The computerised voice spoke. "Put on your lab coat before entrance can be allowed into the laboratory."

"So we were right," said Nathanael. "It is a lab."

They both grabbed a lab coat, hat, gloves and shoe coverings and put the items on. The elastic hats looked particularly strange on top of the balaclavas. As soon as they had finished, the door into the laboratory clicked open.

They walked in.

The lights had clearly been dimmed for night-time and that only made the sight that confronted them more eerie and unsettling. It wasn't just the fact that they were foetuses, preserved inside bottles in formaldehyde. It was the sheer magnitude of them. The corridor stretched on for at least fifty metres, with row upon row of human foetuses, each with a label on it.

Except, of course, that the first ones were clearly not quite human. It was the long arms, the pre-natal hair, that betrayed the fact. "Chimpanzee DNA," said Nathanael.

"What?" asked Natasha.

"I didn't tell you what I saw at Sutton Estate, did I? Well, it was a lot less definitive than this." He took out his mobile phone and started snapping pictures of the place.

Natasha shone the flashlight at the label on the first of the bottles.

Nathanael examined it. It had an identifier, "1NMw8ffnch4eWS9h9JbNJ4j", a set of 23 letters and numbers, just like the names of the zip files. He said, "Let me see?" and she handed him the flashlight He looked further along. "They're arranged in alphanumeric order," he said. "Each of these is a unique identifier. I think you were right — those zipped folders contained the genetic codes of some of their experiments."

Beneath the identifier was another label.

On the first bottle, it said:

"SURROGATE: Emma Louise Thorndike.

AGE: 39

DATE: 2 February 1999

ADDRESS: 3212 5th Street SE Washington DC

PROFESSION: Scientist

SOURCE: Lagar Velho 1, modern Chimp 32A"

Natasha said, "Isn't that the name of the scientist whose identity we used to get in?"

Nathanael nodded. "She must have been the first surrogate mother."

Natasha took some photos with her mobile phone. "I'm uploading these to our cloud account," she said.

They followed the alphanumeric codes along, until they got to 95MWw3oDJy8Dj7XpGWstH, the last to begin with a number. After this were the capital letters, AmE0FBhUMPzqLSPc8nDm4, and Nathanael kept following them until he got to 'B'.

"It's missing," he said.

"What is?" said Natasha.

"Well, look at these. We have BMJqGiwSxwUVC4CtUzEx0 then BZbjgaMe6uycQGOVJH87. Where is BSHVIWTEf4roDYkDiIQwfM?"

Natasha said, "What do you mean?"

"Well, that's the title of the zip file lowest in alphanumeric order. BSHVIWTEf4roDYkDiIQwfM. It should be here, between these two. It's not."

"You memorised that?"

"Yes, and the others. Chicken feed, easy as pie. Just a matter of mnemonics. Come on, let's check."

Nathanael checked. The foetuses that should have had the same codes as the zip files were all missing.

The last one of the zip files, ukfnUaeUeyRQI2m0kGFiSE3, should have been between ueoba6m6AQTWAuSeAI6Q and uxPamhqh2xTIzTrxfWRJ. "Look at the dates on these," said Nathanael. "This year. So they're still continuing with these experiments."

"SURROGATE: Jemma Yvetta Tremillion.
AGE: 26
DATE: 2 February 2016

ADDRESS: 99 Maple Leaf Dr, Boston, MA 02136
PROFESSION: Nurse
SOURCE: Satsurblia SLC24A5"

Nathanael continued to peruse the names and codes on each of the bottles. Natasha said, "Come on, let's go. Let's see what's... in the next room."

"No," said Nathanael, "Wait. I just want to..." Then he stopped. "Natasha, what's this?"

He was shining the flashlight on one of the labels.

"What? Come on, let's go. Don't stick around here I don't like it."

"This here," said Nathanael. "What does it mean?"

In the circle of light formed by the flashlight's glow was the following information:

"SURROGATE: Natasha Charlotta Chase.
AGE: 26
DATE: 2 February 2009
ADDRESS: 213 E Marlettes Ave, Phoenix, AZ 85013
PROFESSION: Computer Programmer
SOURCE: La Quina 5 & La Quina 18 & Sidron Beta-192066 resequenced with M3."

Natasha went very quiet. She pressed her lips together and stood there, uncomfortably, as though she had been caught out. Which Nathanael supposed she had.

Nathanael said softly, "I don't know what it is that you haven't told me. All I can say is that... I won't be angry with you. Perhaps you were embarrassed about it, perhaps it was something you didn't feel... up to telling me. But the thing is, Natasha, you saved my life... Let me guess what happened. You were part of some kind of...

in vitro fertilisation study. You conceived a child and then lost it. And you wanted to know what happened."

Natasha started weeping. Nathanael clasped her to himself, let her cry on his shoulder. "It's alright, Natasha, it's okay."

She said, "I never thought I'd meet anyone. I wanted children. The doctor told me I had low ovarian reserves, and some other problems. He said I needed to get pregnant relatively young if I was going to have children. The expense of IVF with donor sperm at that stage was beyond me — you wouldn't believe how much it costs — and anyway, I had to find a willing donor. I was single and had no boyfriend, I'd been looking for someone smart, I guess, perhaps I was being too picky. Three months before that I had only lost my programming job because of the 2008 financial crash. I had very little in the way of financial reserves, and most of the programming jobs in Arizona were being farmed out to India, and I had no health insurance. I was living at Mum's and Dad's at the time and when the advertisement appeared in the newspaper, it seemed too good to be true. A study into IVF. Women under 35 accepted. Sperm and egg donations provided if necessary. And the best thing was, it was at Flagstaff, close enough to drive to. Despite my medical condition they accepted me. The scientist told me low ovarian reserves would not be a problem with this experiment. I went into premature labor at twenty four weeks, they took me into the hospital and I gave birth, but the baby died. They didn't even let me hold her. When I asked to see her, they said, 'Check the contract you signed, if the baby died before birth, it belongs to us.'"

He said, "My God. That's not so good, is it?"

She said, "No. I went through the contract. It also said, if the baby shows any genetic abnormalities they would have possession of it. I started looking into things. The thing is, I couldn't find a single woman who had been through this program who had kept her child. I was poking around at the hospital in Flagstaff when I noticed the position open for computer administrator — I went for the job and was quite over-qualified, actually, so they accepted me immediately. There were certain people at the hospital involved in the research and I was watching their email addresses, all their communications."

Nathanael said, "So when I turned up it was just a coincidence?" He wasn't sure he was buying it.

Natasha said, "No. This research has been happening at a lot of different hospitals. Flagstaff is just one of at least nine hundred hospitals and clinics involved in it. But the fact is, it was your lucky day when I found the email to one of the administrators saying that there would be two men coming to the hospital, please make everything available to them. Everything I said about their emails, that they came from a bikie gang, all of that was true, basically. It was just that I didn't tell you how I first got onto them — it was that email to the administrator, the sort of clandestine thing I was looking for."

Nathanael nodded. "Anything else you need to tell me?"

Natasha shook her head, low, as though she was ashamed. "No."

Nathanael lifted up her chin. "Don't be ashamed. You hardly knew me. I would hardly expect you to tell me this on our first meeting. These sorts of things, they're...

difficult subjects, Natasha. Conception, IVF, birth, miscarriage. Come on, lift up your spirits."

"I'm a coward," she said. "I should have told you earlier."

"You're quite simply the bravest woman I've ever met in my life. So gird your loins — bad expression perhaps," he handed her back the flashlight. "Put on your sword, mighty warrior!" She laughed a little and rolled her eyes as she strapped the flashlight back on her belt, and Nathanael's heart swelled in his chest. He wasn't totally useless. He added, "Let's go and make those murderers pay for everything they've done."

They made their way through the hall. At the very end of the hall was another door, white and nondescript. It had a sign on it saying "Laboratory 1-25."

They went through and found themselves in a massive complex with glass walls everywhere. The lights here were also dimmed, perhaps because of the power blackout or perhaps because it was night time and none of the staff were here.

As they stood at the doorway looking out, they could see further into the massive complex, containing many, many laboratories, each with corridors between them.

Clearly some of the rooms were genetics laboratories. There was more than one. These had lots of test tubes with blue caps on them, various bits of equipment that Nathanael couldn't identify, centrifuges, perhaps, or DNA analysers. Some of the other rooms must have been for autopsies, others were places where people could be examined or perhaps even be operated upon, with a bench for the examinee to lie down on.

At the top of the corridor there were letters and numbers, they probably represented rows and columns in the grid. Nathanael looked around for a map or key.

A few feet from the door, in darkness, was a map of the complex. He asked Natasha for the torch again and shone it on the map.

"Here," he said. "I think that would be where the computers are." The label said, 'ITD' "Information Technology Division, or Department, if I'm not mistaken." The grid location was H13.

He handed the flashlight back to Natasha and they set off for row H, column 13 in the grid.

It was actually quite a long walk to get there.

Natasha shone her flashlight into the room. There was nothing in there except for three screens, each with a keyboard and mouse, a mini-tower and about thirty hard drives, stacked neatly in shelves.

Natasha nodded. "This looks like it."

The room needed a pass-code. Natasha typed in 122587 but it didn't work. "Nathanael — quick! Another code. One that's likely to be an IT worker." He thought quickly. IT worker — most probably a male, 17 to 40 years old. Natasha had already worked out the most common name — Michael. He recited, "Michael Ostraca — 357645." She typed that in. It didn't work. "Michael James Athelas — 398502."

It worked. The door clicked open.

Natasha went in. To start up the computer required a biometric scan again, only for fingerprints, no iris scan, so she quickly took out the fingerprinting kit and defeated the scanner the same way as before. There were plenty of fingerprints on the table and she simply hoped that she got the right one.

Nathanael was standing behind her.

As she started the computer up, it said, "Fingerprint scan for login."

She placed the piece of masking tape on the scanner.

The computer said, "Welcome Frederick Lieberman. Type in pass code to enable keyboard."

Nathanael said, "Frederick Aaron Lieberman. 644885."

Natasha typed 644885.

A new window came up on the computer screen.

'Frederick Lieberman. Password:______"

Nathanael said, "His password is Kermit585, with a capital K."

Natasha typed the password in.

The home screen appeared. It was the same operating system that Natasha had hacked using the server in Brazil. She was reasonably familiar with it, more so since they had gone through the files they had downloaded before. This time she found it much easier to find her way around.

She needed the records of this facility. All the records.

"Nathanael. Tell me some of those zip file numbers."

He said, "Capital B, capital S, capital H-"

Natasha said, "No, no, I forgot there's capitals, lower case and numbers, come over and type it in to the search field here."

He did. BSHVIWTEf4roDYkDiIQwfM

A list of folders came up. The top one said, "Methuselah."

She clicked on it.

It contained everything about Meth. The details of the neolithic sources for his DNA, a file called 'Conception BSHVIWTEf4roDYkDiIQwfM' that had information about his conception, a folder called 'Surrogate Mother' that contained all the details of his surrogate mother, as well as the details of everyone who had been looking after him and the places he had been imprisoned in. Also, the latest folder was called 'Abduction,' and contained an article, 'Budapest Train Operation.

"Oh, no," said Natasha. She clicked on it.

Methuselah's rescue operation took place on Tuesday 29th November in Budapest. The scientist Peter Lazarus-Fox, involved in the attempt, was also taken into custody. The details of the operation are as follows. Facial image and video initially located on a Facebook page, Leon Lukas Müller, the result subsequently turned up on twelve more Facebook pages, enabling us to narrow down the location.

The file continued in this way.

Nathanael said, "Where are they now?"

Natasha scrolled down to the bottom of the file.

Peter Lazarus-Fox and Methuselah 1 were both transported to Washington DC to the facility at 344 M Street SE, where they currently reside as at 3rd December 2016. It is planned to keep them here until a more suitable accomodation can be found. Despite his treachery, it has been decided that Lazarus-Fox must be kept with the child, to pacify him.

Natasha said, "Quick, I've got to start uploading."

She found the Command Prompt and typed a few commands in. "Oh, no," she said. "I can't access the cloud. They must have traced it back and disabled the accounts somehow."

She typed a few other commands in.

"None of my cloud accounts are available."

Natasha moaned. She typed some more commands in.

"Nothing. Even my server at home seems to have been compromised."

"I have a USB?" said Nathanael, pulling one out of his wallet. Natasha laughed. "We need at least 100GB of space, Nathanael. These are not small files. Anyway I was going to use this." She brought out an external hard drive from her back pack and put it on the table. "But I still want to upload them to the cloud. Safer when they're remotely stored. Keep two copies of everything, three if you can. Maybe, just maybe, there's one more thing I can try..."

She found a web server and opened it.

She went to dropbox.com, and typed in some account information.

A dropbox folder opened up. 'Welcome Natasha Chase. You are sharing this folder with Michelle Chase.'

Quickly, Natasha began choosing folders and dumping them into the dropbox page. They began uploading.

She said, "Oh, give me your phone, too." She took his phone and copied all the photos he had taken across to the dropbox and her computer's hard drive as well.

Then she plugged in the external hard drive she kept with her computer as well, and copied the same files across that she was uploading to dropbox, including the ones from Nathanael's phone.

She did some more searches, on the surrogate mothers' names, on some more of the foetuses, and also on various figures, such as Bruce Fetherington, Piers Enderen, Milton F. Dryford. The details of the murders, the blackmail cases, the various dirty trick were fully described in their case files, along with the agents responsible. Everything she found, she uploaded and copied onto her hard drive.

"The only thing missing seems to be the command structure," said Nathanael. "See if you can find out who's in charge here."

Natasha searched, but there was nothing about any board of directors or persons or people in charge. Roland Adamant's name didn't even come up. Natasha said, "Roland Adamant, and the others, if there are any, seem to have kept their names out of these files."

Nathanael said, "Still, with all this evidence I think it will be hard for them to exercise plausible deniability."

Slowly the files uploaded.

Nathanael said, "Well… we've been here for at least an hour already. I wonder when we'll be discovered? Hadn't we better start thinking about leaving?"

Natasha said, "Oh no… Look at this one."

The file said, 'Michelle Chase.'

Chapter 25 — End of file.

Natasha opened the folder.

She scrolled to the end.

The last file in date order was called, 'Abduction of Michelle Chase.'

She opened the file and scrolled to the end.

Agent David Hustings contacted us to confirm that Michelle Chase had been terminated on Tuesday November 22nd 2016. Evidence was disposed of in a deserted area in Utah. He is returning to DC to take on his next assignment. Special note: see case file Kade Karl Kelly, unfortunately Kade Kelly was shot in an accident with a gun in the operation. End of file.

Natasha gasped and tears began to fall down her cheeks. "No, no, no. Michelle. Oh, no, it's all my fault. It's completely my fault."

Nathanael said, "It isn't. It really isn't your fault."

"I got her involved, Nathanael. She'd still be alive if it wasn't for…"

"It's not your fault. They are responsible for what they have done."

She started weeping, sobbing, "No, I can't believe she's gone." Nathanael didn't know what to do or say, he put his hand on her shoulder and she grasped hold of it and began to calm down.

Strangely enough it made him feel strong, the thought that she needed his strength.

She almost seemed to be praying now, "Dear Lord in heaven, I have to get justice for her. Help." Then she turned to him. Calmness had descended on her features. "Let's get out of this place. They're so good at tracing things, perhaps even now they're tracing what I'm doing, about to delete my dropbox folder or something. Come on, Nathanael, let's go and download the lot onto a hard drive, make a few copies, disseminate them. I can't let them get away with it."

"Yes, I was thinking that — we've stayed here too long, I think. They might even have the power up again outside."

She copied the last folder across to the dropbox and the hard drive, the folder named 'Michelle Chase', in a strangely tender, reverent way.

She watched it finish copying and then went to the command prompt and typed something in. She said to Nathanael, "I found this virus on a darknet page. It will erase from the computer any evidence of our activity for the last two hours, then it will erase itself." After it had finished she shut the computer down.

"I'm getting them," she said, as she picked up her hard drive and the other things and put them in her back pack. "I'm going to get them back. I don't care who they are. I am going to get them back."

They walked out of the computer room and closed the door behind them, then made their way back through the glass corridors to the entrance. They left that room and walked through the hallway, full of foetuses. Natasha shivered as they went past hers, then put her hand on the glass for a moment.

They came out into the entrance room, the airlock, and the computerised voice said, "Return laboratory coats, gloves and coverings. Door will open on receipt." They took off the white lab coats, the gloves, the head coverings, the foot coverings, and returned them to their places quickly.

The computerised voice said, "Laboratory clothes returned. Press exit button to exit."

Natasha pressed the exit button. There seemed to be no security on the way out, presumably in the case of fire or some other disaster.

But the exit button didn't work.

Natasha tried it again. It still didn't work.

She said, "Maybe when the power went down, this button reset, or something."

Nathanael tried the other door, the one that led into the lab. It didn't open either. "Maybe there's another way out."

Natasha shook her head. "You don't think they've locked us in, do you? Could they have discovered us already? I mean, we haven't been here for longer than an hour. Perhaps a guard discovered the car and the boxes?"

Nathanael said, "I doubt it. We chose that parking place because they don't watch it that carefully, and sometimes people park there and leave their cars there overnight. Anyway, would they really be likely to check? I doubt it, somehow. It doesn't seem to have been usual practice. Perhaps they're smarter than we thought, though?"

They tried the doors again, but they wouldn't budge. For at least ten minutes, they kept trying the doors, but nothing happened.

Nathanael said, "You must be right. They know we're here. They've caught us, Natasha, red-handed."

They both sat down, back to back, on the floor.

"What now?" said Natasha.

Nathanael said, "I really don't know. But I don't think it's going to be good."

Natasha bowed her head and started praying, whispering, Nathanael heard her say the name, "Jesus," more than once. But he couldn't hear what she was saying. He bowed his head as well.

When she finished, he said, "Amen," and she said, "What?"

"Well, you were praying. I presume you were praying for us — for us to be rescued or something. I just said, 'Amen,' because I would like that to happen too."

Natasha said, "Okay. I didn't think you believed in all that? That's why I prayed silently."

"Well... I'm still not sure I do. But let's say I have a... few more doubts about my agnosticism than I had before..."

Natasha said, "Nathanael. I can't believe Michelle is dead. I really believe she's still alive. I think that file is wrong."

Nathanael wanted to say something, you're deluding yourself, she's gone. Surely it would be better to have no hope when there was no hope? He didn't want Natasha's hopes to be crushed — but he simply couldn't bring himself to say anything. He couldn't bring himself to crush her hopes himself.

At that moment the door opened.

Three security guards came in.

Two of them had guns in their right hand, and were holding jackets neatly folded in their left hands. One of the guns was pointed at Natasha and the other at Nathanael.

The third one seemed to have more authority than the other two. He stood differently. He had nothing in his hands, no gun, no jacket and when he spoke he had an air of command as though he expected people to obey him. "You're coming with us. He wants to see you. You need to come quietly. We will use the guns if we have to, but we really don't want to. Not out in the open. But I am sure we can come up with a story as to why the guns were necessary. We've done it before, in my time, more than once. We can do it again."

The one with the gun pointed at Natasha waved it towards the door. "Walk in front of us, both of you."

They walked out of the door. The men walked behind them and told them where to go, carrying their guns underneath their jackets. They walked along a small pathway, past their car, to another building. It was an impressive building, old, some sort of old house, but it had crenelations on the roof like a castle and a turret.

They told them to go into the house.

They went into the back door of the house.

They told them to go down the corridor. They ended up in some sort of sitting room at the front of the house. The two goons with the guns stood with their guns exposed now, pointed at Nathanael and Natasha. The other man walked out of the room.

They heard his footsteps. He was going up a stairwell. Probably into the little tower. Then they heard muffled voices. Two sets of footsteps were coming down the stairwell now.

A man in his sixties walked into the room, well groomed, wearing a suit that fit him perfectly. His hair was silver at the temples but his skin was perfectly tanned, despite it being winter.

Nathanael knew him. Roland Adamant. The billionaire.

So he was the one in charge.

His gut began to ache and he couldn't shake the sensation that he was sinking into the floor.

How long would Adamant let them live, now that they knew everything that was going on, and that he was behind it?

CHAPTER 26 — ADAMANT IS ADAMANT

Nathanael noticed Natasha was doing something in her pocket, fiddling around in there. What was it? Then she took out a tissue and started dabbing at her eye. Something seemed odd about the behaviour to him — was she trying to send a message to him? But she didn't look over. Then again, she was grieving the loss of her sister. Who knows what might be normal behaviour in that case?

"You two have been the bane of my existence," Roland Adamant said, going to the liquor cabinet and pouring himself a neat scotch. He sipped it for a moment, with his eyes closed. "Fifty year old single malt Speyside Whisky. Nothing better on the tongue that I know of, anyhow. Do you know, I've been trying to catch up with you both for months now? First, I have you, Natasha Chase, fossicking around the hospital records, trying to find out everything you can about the surrogate mothers. What an intrusion of my privacy. Then I have you, Nathanael Wayfarer, at the British Museum, buggering around with my acquisitions. Then you both get together and it's a free for all, hacking my systems, disturbing my operations everywhere from Sussex to DC." Roland Adamant sipped his glass again. "Where are my manners? I feel as though I ought to offer you both a drink. After all, you are my guests. Please be seated."

Natasha said, "What, when you're going to kill us both? You're just going to treat us like guests beforehand? Are you some kind of psychopath?" Nathanael rolled his eyes. Didn't she realise she was just making things worse?

"Kill you?" said Roland Adamant. "Why, that item is on the agenda, I admit, but before I do that, I need to wring every last bit of usefulness out of you. And there is the pleasure of gloating to be considered. After all, we have been at war and I have beaten you. Victory is far, far sweeter when you have the opportunity to completely humiliate your opponent. And who is the more humiliated? Someone who is done away with quickly? Or the one who is treated as so far beneath the victor, that he (and I say he advisedly, for I am not gender neutral); he may treat them politely before their demise — in a sense, it shows his upbringing. In another sense, it shows that they (I mean you) are so far beneath me that I have no need to posture in order to show my superiority. I am like a god to you, you are like slaves or possessions to me. I can elevate you or destroy you, with a wave of my hand." He lifted his hand, as though about to wave them away.

"You want us to shoot them now, sir?" asked one of the thugs.

"No," said Roland Adamant. "Not yet. Let them sit down, though."

"Sit down," said the thug.

Nathanael sat down on the lounge chair.

Natasha refused. The thug grabbed her wrist and forced her down.

"Thank you," said Roland Adamant. "You can wait outside the door. Don't worry, I can take care of myself."

They clearly believed him, for they went outside and closed the door without comment.

"Now. Do you have any questions for me?"

Nathanael said, "Questions? Why would we have questions? You're going to kill us. Why should we care?"

"Come now," Adamant replied, "Surely there are gaps. You can't have found out everything. And it would satisfy me more to know that you are going to your graves knowing the full truth, the whole truth. I will sit in my bed at night and imagine your regret and disappointment, the last feelings you will feel, knowing that you knew everything and yet could not tell anyone before you died. Knowing that injustice has triumphed over justice, as you would see it. This is a satisfying thought to me."

Natasha said, "Why did you do this? The whole thing, getting Cro-Magnon DNA, reconstructing the ancient genome?"

"Obvious isn't it? I want to live longer. I want my children to live longer."

Natasha said, "No, no, not that. I mean, the whole thing is predicated on a part of the Bible being true — a part that is not really believed by many people these days. The ages of the antediluvian patriarchs is something even some evangelical parishioners would not take seriously, let alone serious scholars. Do you believe the Bible is true, Roland Adamant?"

"Ah. You do know who I am. Yes indeed, I am Roland Adamant, the billionaire philanthropist. Ha! I hadn't realised you'd even got that far. Very clever, my girl, very clever." He clapped slowly and sarcastically.

Natasha's eyes flashed. "I asked you a question, Mister Adamant. I think you're avoiding it. I think you know the Bible is true. I think you fear God's judgement."

Adamant sneered, "God. Jesus. You true believers make me sick. Look at you, willing to do just about anything in the cause of making me pay. Lying, cheating, hacking, stealing, deceiving." He sniffed his scotch again and sipped another gulp down, then sighed a deep, heavy sigh. "But… You asked me a question. And I vowed to tell you everything. Oh, I am a man of my word. And yes, you could say I have funded the Adamantine Project because I believe the Bible is true. Parts of it are definitely historical, much more of it, I would say, than many Episcopalian theologians believe. I just take… a different point of view from the Judeo-Christian one, you could say, about who is the protagonist and who the antagonist in that book. After all, where would we be if the snake had never given the fruit of the tree of knowledge to Eve? And what about these Sons of God in Genesis chapter 6? In every version of the story except for the one in the Bible, these divine figures come to bring benefits to the sons of mankind. They go by different names in different cultures — Zeus, Baal, Jupiter, Krishna, Zarathustra, the Buddha, Gabriel."

Natasha said, "So you celebrate evil? You think the snake was good?"

Adamant nodded, swirling the last of his scotch. "The essential moral question of our age was enumerated by Socrates to his foe Phaedrus. 'And what is good, Phaedrus, and what is not good—need we ask anyone to tell us these things?' Hahaha. Socrates was right, in this case. Clearly humanity does need people to tell us what is good and what is not good. People like me. Superior people. People who know the Ascended Masters."

Natasha rolled her eyes and said under her breath, "Now we're going into nutcase territory."

Adamant seemed not to have heard her. He wandered over and poured another half glass of neat scotch. "And so, Natasha — that is the sort of thing I've been funding. We need people to tell us what They say is good and what is not good. The Heavenly Council. The Ascended Masters. The Sons of God. They go by many names, but all humans throughout history agree that They are the friends of mankind, except of course for those who wrote this one book, the Bible. And look at me — have I not received the benefits of Their friendship? Money, power, privilege, sexual satisfaction, all the benefits that this world can bring. So we must encourage humanity to worship the creation instead of the creator, indeed, this is the wonderful religion of green environmentalism that we have been spreading! (Of course, we try to distract them from the real problems — let them put their efforts where its not going to bear fruit — let them not try to save the orang-utan or the Sumatran tiger.) No, men must learn to despise themselves, for they are made in the image of a divine despot. Thus we encourage one world government, abortion, euthanasia, and eventually, eugenics — for our goal is complete control, from birth to death over the whole of humanity."

Natasha said, "What about the present president? Surely he has rocked the boat somewhat."

"Him? Hahaha! He is one of ours, too. You don't think he got into the Oval Office without compromise, do you?"

Natasha said, "Well what about Jesus? He died on the cross, rose again. He is Lord even over you."

For a moment Adamant seemed very angry. A vein in his neck bulged and he hissed through his front teeth, like a snake, "Sssss." It was very disconcerting to Nathanael.

Roland Adamant struggled with himself then seemed to regain control. Then suddenly he spat his words out, "Jesus? Jesus? Because of him, the Roman Empire fell. His pale, deathly influence destroyed the finest civilisation our world had ever known and replaced it with the childish, infantile Middle Ages, with their multi-coloured flags and ridiculous ideals of chivalry and courtly love, saints and monks and princesses and piety. And then the Reformation, with their ridiculous, hypocritical stance on the Bible. No, the Ascended Masters have been curtailed in Europe by Christianity, if not Christendom, their power to influence men has been limited by that restraining power, for thousands of years now. But at last, with the fall of Palestine and Jerusalem to the Jewish money-lenders, the Masters have been set free again, to create a new world order where mankind is free at last to create his own destiny."

Natasha said, "And to this end, you have killed, ordered people to be murdered, you have committed fraud, you have deceived innocent women, exploited their desire to have children, you have lied and thieved and taken what is not yours and committed blackmail and many other crimes? Is this not so?"

Roland Adamant snickered, he actually snickered. "Yes, yes, I have. A secret you will take to the grave with you. How pleasant the thought will be to me that you are lying on the ground, bleeding out, thinking to yourself, 'If only I could have told someone, if only I could have got that dropbox out there, if only I could have given that hard drive to someone, I could have made Roland Adamant suffer for his crimes.' But we found the dropbox and emptied it. We have you hard drive, in your back pack. You want justice. Justice. But there is no justice. Justice is a pipe dream of the naive. I am going to live, a long life, like all my ancestors (except for that stupid bishop) and I am going to die on my bed at an old age, satisfied with all I have achieved. But you will die all too soon, and you'll take it all with you, my dear, all of this knowledge. The knowledge of my misdeeds. Everything I did, I did it for Them. My Masters."

Natasha shook her head violently. "No!" she said firmly. "Jesus Christ will ensure that you are punished for what you have done. He won't let you get away with all the murders, all the lies, all the hypocrisy. No. It cannot be. If you refuse to repent, and who knows, Mister Adamant, this might be your last chance? If you refuse to repent, you will die, one day, and then you will face justice. God will demand an accounting of your life from you. God is real, you know."

"Phhhh," Roland Adamant scoffed, "Well, of course God is real! If Lucifer is real, doesn't that imply God is real? Stupid, stupid little girl. Don't you see, I can get the best of both worlds? I can have my cake and eat it too. Who could deny that I have benefited greatly from following the Light-Bringer, Lucifer, the angel who benefited mankind and was punished for it. I worshipped him as my father did and his father before him. But what you don't see is the obvious fact — I'll have plenty of time to repent! You do realise I'll live to a ripe old age, evil people like me always do, only the good die young. Hehe.

Like you two are going to. When I'm on my death bed I'll call the local priest in, perhaps the bishop, even, repent of my sins and receive remission, cleansing, and everything will be fine in the afterlife for me. I will have had my fun and then it will all be fine. That God you worship is naive, like a naive old man, and I can outsmart him. You see, I know how he thinks." Grotesque, the way he was tapping his head with his forefinger. Roland Adamant was completely insane. Horrifying thought. A crazy man in charge of a global empire, his finger in so many pies, controlling governments and business interests all around the world.

Contemptible fool. Despite how rich, how powerful, how intelligent he was, he was no better than an animal, really. An out of control animal that needed to be put down. "You're just totally insane. You've lost your marbles, mate. You should be in a mental asylum. You barely have any humanity left in you, do you?"

Adamant looked at him through eyes that now seemed to Nathanael to be completely irrational, like a raging beast's eyes. Or crocodile eyes. Nothing human left in them. Adamant growled at him for a moment — it seemed as though his real nature had revealed itself, as though the mask had come off. Then Adamant paused as though putting the mask on again. He said, "Nathanael Wayfarer, that hurts, I mean, really, it does, that you could say such a disrespectful thing to me, speaking in such a manner to someone who is greatly superior to you — you, a mere gnat — an ant that I can step on at any time if I wish. You are a very offensive person, a person of bad upbringing, who is so ill-bred he cannot even recognise his betters. You are... deplorable." He waved his hand in a dramatic gesture that wouldn't have been out of place in a melodrama. "And so, having had enough of this conversation, I say to you, that's it for you, then! Meeting over. I'm going to have you both exterminated right now like the pests you are. Men!"

The men came into the room and Nathanael closed his eyes for a moment. It was his fault. He could have managed to gain a few more precious moments of life for them both if his bad temper hadn't got the better of him. They pointed their guns at Nathanael and Natasha. Their boss came in and said, "Out of here. Roland doesn't want blood on his carpet, do you sir?"

"No, definitely not. Take them to the usual place."

Chapter 27 — Turning the Tide

As the men were walking them out of Roland Adamant's sitting room, Nathanael saw Natasha's back pack, sitting in the hallway. But all he had to do was get the back pack — he could make a run for it — get justice for Michelle. Perhaps in the melée Natasha could get free as well. And if she couldn't then he would at least have something to bargain with.

It was a split second decision and he made it.

He kicked one of the men in the ankle, ducked down as the other one shot at his head. The shot thudded into the wall behind him. The one whose ankle he had kicked had dropped his gun. Nathanael kicked it out of the way as he reached across and grabbed the back pack. The other one had trained his gun on Nathanael's head, but Natasha hit his forearm with both hands, grasped together, enough to make his aim go awry. The bullet thudded into the wall. Natasha cried out, "Run! Get that onto the internet! Run! Save yourself! Leave! Go!" The man swore and grabbed her and, to his immediate shame, Nathanael did run.

He sprinted out of the door, through the morning crowd. (Had they been imprisoned for that long?) Their car was still parked where Natasha had left it. The keys were jangling inside the back pack. Nathanael opened it as he ran and jumped in the car.

He was used to this car by now. He put it in reverse and gunned the engine. The wheels span as he reversed onto the grass, then accelerated through the crowd of people walking on the grass. They jumped out of the way, some of them cursing him, then in moments he was on the road, getting out of there.

He knew his way around Washington now, a little better, and he went down to the foreshore near the Jefferson Memorial. It seemed appropriate — Jefferson once said, "A nation cannot be ignorant and free." And Nathanael was about to ensure that everyone's ignorance was ended. And Nathanael would be the one to end it.

All he had to do was upload everything on this disk to Wikileaks, or the Guardian newspaper, and he would put an end to Roland Adamant's injustices, exposing them all to the light.

But something just didn't feel right.

He couldn't stop himself from wondering if there was anything more he could have done to save Natasha. He imagined himself there, in the room, with her shouting, "Leave! Go!"

Could he have at least looked around for the other gun? It was on the floor somewhere at that moment. Surely he could have got it, shot the guy, saved Natasha.

He knew what she would say. "My life isn't as important as freedom. I give it away gladly for you, Nathanael. I give it away gladly for everyone." She wasn't selfless. She didn't value her life, she had faith in God.

But how would he ever live with himself? For the rest of his life he would be asking, was he a coward? Had he run because he was afraid? Could he have stayed there, fought for a little longer? Perhaps he might have saved her.

He looked at the hard drive in his hand. It was his life. He could get his life back. All he had to do was upload it onto Wikileaks — which he could do right now, with Natasha's computer and her mobile phone. Or his mobile phone. And that was why he'd started on this journey. To get his life back.

But what was his life worth if he had to live with the guilt of having left Natasha behind, to get killed? He would always be wondering if he had done the right thing.

Oh, he could upload the stuff to Wikileaks and hope that, once it was all exposed, they wouldn't have any reason to kill Natasha any more. But that ball was already rolling.

How could he live with himself?

He would always be wondering, what if? What if Natasha was the one he was supposed to be with? What if she had been his destiny and he had stuffed it up by letting her die? What if they were just supposed to be friends?

The longer he sat there in the carpark, the more desperately his thoughts revolved around that single moment. That moment when he had run away. That moment of cowardice, desperate, selfish cowardice.

He should have stayed and fought.

But he still had the hard drive.

He could exchange it for Natasha's life.

He took the phone and rang the Heosphoros Foundation.

A man answered. "Heosphoros Foundation, a division of the Adamantine Institute. Mike Gunter speaking."

Nathanael said, "I have something that Roland Adamant wants, and I am willing to trade."

"Ah. Mister Adamant said someone would be ringing with some sort of business proposition. Would you believe it, he asked for you to be put right through to him? That seldom happens — a real privilege."

Hold music came on for a moment, then Adamant answered. "Yes? You're willing to trade?"

"The hard drive for Natasha."

Adamant said, "They're on the way to Maryland, to the Bayside Beach. It's forty five minutes drive."

Nathanael said, "How do I get there?"

"You're so good on the internet. Look it up on google maps." He paused for a moment. "By the way if even a whiff of this makes it onto social media, Wikileaks, the Guardian, any other place online or offline, in the next forty five minutes, I will order them to kill her. It's inconvenient for me, I admit, if you do that. But I do have my contingency plans in place. But if I have to use those contingency plans I guarantee you, I will make her pay."

Adamant put the phone down.

Nathanael looked up Bayside Beach on google maps. It was actually forty nine minutes drive.

He revved the engine and took off. Speeding didn't matter so much as getting there in less than forty five minutes.

He was almost wishing a police car would see him speeding and chase him. It would be the best way to get some assistance down there. He starting praying, "God, let a police car chase me. I need help, I'm pretty sure I can't salvage this situation on my own."

Then he started thinking, after this, Natasha would never respect him. She'd say he sacrificed the truth, just to get her back. She'd say he compromised.

He couldn't stop thinking like this. His thoughts began going round and round in circles, as though some dark, oppressive force was trying to make him turn around or stop driving. Eventually he cried out, "God help me!" He felt a sense of peace. Was it just psychological, or something more?

Google maps said, "Turn left," and he turned left. Google maps said, "Turn right," and he turned right.

When he was about five minutes from the beach, his thoughts were at their worst, incriminating him, blaming him. You're a coward. You won't be able to do anything. You're doomed. You have stuffed it up. Nothing you do ever works out right. You're stupid. You're going to die and it's all going to be pointless.

He turned the radio on to get his mind off it all. The news had just started.

"Wikileaks has made a historic public announcement in the last half hour. 'Wikileaks has just received a large amount of incriminating data from Roland Adamant's private servers. At this stage we are sorting through it, but we anticipate releasing some of the files in the next two or three days. This is the first time a billionaire of his calibre has had his personal affairs revealed to the light of day, and it is not a pretty picture. Apart from clear evidence of tax evasion, we are certain Roland Adamant is going to be charged with crimes, but we also wish to ensure that no innocent people's names are dragged into his mess, so we are not going to release the files unedited, except to one or two responsible news outlets that we can trust to do their own editing.'"

Nathanael groaned. Things had just gotten worse, much worse, when he didn't even think they could get any worse. They'll think it was me who released everything on the hard drive! Who else would Adamant blame?

Yet I didn't and that's the truth. Someone did. Did Natasha have a contingency plan? Nathanael couldn't work it out.

But his bargaining chip was gone. How would he get her back?

He parked at a resort, not far from the beach. Then he got out of the car, looked up at the overcast sky and whispered, "I hope you really are there."

He walked down to the beach, ready to ring Adamant, or whoever he needed to.

As he approached the beach, though, his mobile reception went down to two bars. Then one bar. Then it said, 'Out of range. No reception.'

Perhaps there was still hope - perhaps the thugs didn't know.

Nathanael came down a small pathway and saw them standing there, the two thugs and Natasha, on a small beach surrounded by rock cliffs about twenty foot high. The beach was sandy, but there were rocks all around them, and the ocean in front of them. Completely insulated from the rest of the world. Any sound they made, no matter how loud, would just reflect back off the cliffs into the vastness of the sea.

One of the two thugs had his gun on Natasha, the other had his gun pointed towards Nathanael.

Nathanael said, "Put your gun down. If you don't, you won't get the hard drive."

The man put his gun down.

Nathanael said, "You as well."

The other man said, "No. We get the hard drive then you get the girl."

Nathanael shook his head. "No guns. At the same time. That's the way it's going to be."

He put his gun down, grabbed Natasha's arm and guided her forwards.

"Far enough," said Nathanael. "Let go of her."

"Only when I've got the drive."

Nathanael reached forwards with the hard drive and the man grabbed it. Natasha ran forwards to Nathanael and he said, "Let's go then."

"Not so fast," said another voice. Their boss. He was behind Nathanael on the pathway.

Nathanael said, "We had a deal."

Their boss said, "Yeah, well, that deal didn't suit Roland Adamant and he's made a new deal. Get down onto that beach."

As they were walking down, Natasha said, "Don't worry, it's going to be alright. You did the right thing by coming back for me."

Nathanael looked at her. She was to the north of him and they were facing the ocean. He said, "I'm sorry I couldn't make it work."

Natasha said, "It's alright. It had to happen this way. It's just the way it is."

Their boss said, "Alright, shut up now. Get your guns, goons. You two, turn around and count to three."

"One... Two..."

A gunshot sounded. For a moment Nathanael thought it was over, but when he looked down and saw his legs and the pebbles in the beach-sand below his feet he knew he was still standing. He looked to his left. So was Natasha.

He looked around.

The boss was lying on the sand in a pool of his own blood. He had been shot in the shoulder and it wasn't a pretty sight, he was grasping his shoulder and moaning in pain.

A voice said, "Why did you shove me gun hand like that? I had a clear shot to his head." Then the voice added, "Drop the guns, goons." Nathanael looked around to see who had spoken. A stocky man, dressed like the others, stood there with a pistol that was still smoking from the barrel.

The other two dropped their guns immediately.

Michelle walked out behind the stocky man and said, "Davo, I bumped you because I told you already not to kill anyone. Just disable them."

Davo shot the two goons in the leg, one after the other. They crumpled. "Like that?"

Michelle rolled her eyes. "Davo — they just surrendered! You just shot them, and they'd surrendered."

Davo turned to her and shouted, "Look. I'm doing the best I can. Just — don't be too hard on me!"

Michelle put her hand on his shoulder and said, "I'm sorry Davo, I know you're just learning. Just don't kill people, alright? Even if they're very bad people. Don't kill them."

Nathanael quickly gathered their guns up before they could crawl over to them to use them. Those two were lying on the ground, moaning in pain as well. Nathanael put their guns in the back of his jeans, tore off his shirt into three pieces to make tourniquets to stem the bleeding. He did that for the two who had been shot in the thigh, then he went and tended to the one who had been shot in the shoulder. Fortunately Davo had a few luggage ties in his pocket and with those they tied the men's hands and legs together to stop them from running away.

Natasha embraced Michelle and wept. "I thought you had died. But how did you know we'd be here?"

Michelle replied, "I read those files you posted last night. But I already knew where it was all happening. Davo was one of them. He told me all about their operations. He and I were watching the Heosphoros Foundation for the last two days. Then we saw you and Nathanael go in, then we saw them taking you down here, and we followed all the way here. Nathanael passed us on the last stretch — he must have been going about a hundred and twenty miles an hour."

"It was you," said Nathanael. "You posted the files on the internet. How did you get them?"

"I did," said Michelle. "That was me. I got the dropbox link immediately when Natasha posted it and I started posting them on Wikileaks, while I was still downloading them. Just after I finished they all disappeared from dropbox, but they were too late. I had already got everything. Nathanael, is that phone in your name?"

Nathanael shook his head. Michelle called the police on Nathanael's phone, told them to come to the beach, that some men had been shot and they might need an ambulance, and then she threw the phone into the ocean as far as she could chuck it. It sailed out like a frisbee and landed in the waves, a long way out. It meandered for a while on some sort of rip-tide on the surface, a tiny black thing, floating further and further away, until it disappeared.

Davo said to the men on the ground, "Do you know who I am?"

One them groaned, "You're Davo. I know who you are."

"I'm not a nice fellow, am I?"

"No, Davo, you're not."

"I'm not a good Christian bloke, am I?"

"No, Davo, you're not."

"Well that shows how much you know. But if you blab anything about these people here or me, what do you think is going to happen to you?"

"Something not very nice, Davo. You'll shoot us worse."

"Got it in one. So keep those tongues from wagging."

Michelle said, "Come on, we should go now."

Police sirens were wailing in the distance.

Michelle said, "I want to know what's happening to Roland Adamant. And I really don't want to be here when the police get here."

Michelle, Davo, Natasha and Nathanael sprinted up the stairway into the carpark. They leaped into the hire car. As Nathanael started the engine he looked up at the roof of the nearby lodge — there was a camera there but someone had already shot it out — there would be no record of this trip to the beach.

Nathanael drove.

~~~

Forty nine minutes later, they were at the Heosphoros Foundation. It was getting quite dark now, must have been about five o'clock in the afternoon at least.
~~~

Michelle said they had an appointment with Roland Adamant. The secretary said, "There's no record of such an appointment." Michelle said, "It's not that sort of appointment. Davo, tell him."

Davo said, "It's not that sort of appointment."

The secretary nodded. He knew Davo and he knew what sorts of appointments they were. Ones that Roland didn't want people hearing about. But he said, "I understand. But unfortunately I simply don't have any idea where Roland Adamant is right now."

One of the other staff spoke up then, though, and said Roland had gone to the other side of the park, to his uncle's memorial. He sometimes went there when he was in a thoughtful mood, apparently. "It's the big monument, a big statue of an Episcopalian bishop, at the other end of the park. The statue's face looks kind."

"Here," said the secretary, and threw a Heosphoros t-shirt to Nathanael. "Wear this when you meet him. He's got… particular ideas about manners."

Nathanael put the t-shirt on, not for that reason, but because he was feeling rather cold.

As they walked out Michelle said, "We have to make sure he faces justice."

Davo said, "You bet. Justice." He fingered the trigger on his gun.

Michelle said, "That means, not killing him. Not letting him get away with it, but not killing him."

The four of them bundled back into the hire car and Nathanael gunned the engine. They crossed the park and ended up in front of a large, kindly-faced statue of a bishop. There was a seven foot long hole in the ground, that looked like an empty grave, in front of it, and Roland

Adamant was standing in the grave, looking thoughtfully up at the statue.

He turned around and saw them coming. Nathanael and Davo both held guns. He smiled at them, apparently unperturbed. "Come to gloat, have you?"

"Why come here, Roland?" asked Nathanael, anxious to buy them a little more time, so that the computer files could disseminate more widely. Hopefully Adamant did not yet know that Michelle had uploaded them. Nathanael wanted to draw him into a conversation and he knew Adamant loved nothing more than a good monologue. "Why in front of the statue of your uncle? A bishop? A Christian, apparently?"

"I hated him. The rest of my family were faithful — they kept the faith. But he — he was the only one who abandoned Lucifer, the Light-Bringer, the Philosophy as we liked to call it. Uncle Robert was in charge of some kind of Biblical translation exercise. It was all supposed to be bringing rationality into the whole thing — you know — using the Alexandrian texts as definitive — to try to sneak a bit of healthy heresy into the mix.

"Uncle Robert was classically educated, as we all were in those days, knew his Greek and his Latin, but the thing is, the more he read that book, the more he began to say things like, 'Do you know, there really might be something in all this New Testament stuff? The Alexandrian texts say pretty much the same thing as the Textus Receptus — no major differences really — and the more I read it, Richard, the more I begin to think it's all true.'

"My father tried to argue him out of it, but within a year Uncle Robert had become a priest, then a bishop, but that would have been fine if he was the usual useless

Episcopalian sort. But you see, he really believed in it all. He was a thorn in my father's side until the day of his death. Even father began to weaken before the end. Had this statue built above my his grave, after Uncle Robert died. Well, I've fixed him. Taken Uncle Robert's bones and had them moved to a toxic waste disposal site. Next I'm going to be rid of this ridiculous statue." He waved his hand carelessly at it. "I come here when I need someone to curse. Someone to harangue. Something to shout at. Don't quite know what I'll do when it's gone."

To Nathanael's eye, the statue seemed to have a bit of an unhealthy lean.

"That statue," Nathanael said. "It looks like it's leaning over a bit. Doesn't look very stable. Are you sure it's safe to stand right under it?"

"What do you mean, it's leaning over?" He glanced back at it. "Nothing wrong with it. Oh, I get it, it's a metaphor for the Adamantine Institute, or perhaps the Heosphoros Foundation. You think my empire is leaning over? You think you can gloat over me? You think you've defeated me?" His glee was palpable and very galling. Nathanael felt like saying to Davo, 'shoot him now.' But he didn't — Michelle wouldn't have been happy with that, nor Natasha, probably.

Roland Adamant was still blabbering on. "You realise there won't be anything to gloat about. I may not be able to stop the files from being released now, but I have a contingency plan! A good one! They can hardly charge me if there is no concrete evidence of any of this, can they? It was just the ravings of an insignificant computer programmer, a conspiracy theorist, one of those nuts you read about on the internet, someone who thinks the moon landings were faked."

"What do you mean?" said Nathanael.

"In about, oh, five minutes time, the gelignite in the basement laboratory will be ignited. The men are ready right now to seal off the door to the hidden room — it will be as though it never existed. And all anyone will find is rubble, even if they have the cheek to start digging down in the Heosphoros Foundation grounds. And, by the way, you have no evidence whatsoever that I personally was involved. I have been very careful to keep my name out of everything. Good luck proving that."

Nathanael said to Natasha, "He's got a point."

Adamant continued, "Haha! You think I'm the one who's done for? But it's you. You four. Yes, you too, Davo, you're going down. The police are on their way. That's why I decided to keep talking — to keep you here. They will arrest the four of you for wire fraud, fraud, and blackmail. Who do you think they will believe, you or me? Hahaha, you're done for. You are done for."

The ground rumbled slightly, then a slightly louder rumble sounded, like distant thunder.

"That's it starting. The evidence is all being destroyed. Listen for another one, a louder explosion."

The ground rumbled again.

"You've got nothing on me!" he shouted over the rumble of the explosion. "Nothing! That's the third blast! That means it's all on it's way."

For a moment the rumbling stopped.

"Oh," said Adamant. "There should have another blast. Oh well, doesn't matter anyway, does it? I can just blame it on my underlings, even if they can find a part of the lab still there underneath the building. But there is no way they can ever pin any of this on me!"

Then Natasha took out her mobile phone.

"What are you doing?" said Adamant.

Natasha said, "It's been in my pocket the whole time, Roland."

She keyed in her code. The phone opened up on the Sound Recorder app.

It was still recording.

She stopped it.

"Luckily I had the 256 Gig model. Plenty of space for long recordings. It's been going since your goons took us into your sitting room."

She pressed Play.

Roland Adamant's voice came out of the phone.

'You two have been the bane of my existence.'

Then the sound of Scotch being poured into a glass.

'Fifty year old single malt Speyside Whisky. Nothing better on the tongue that I know of, anyhow. Do you know, I've been trying to catch up with you both for months now? First, I have you, Natasha Chase, fossicking around the hospital records, trying to find out everything you can about the surrogate mothers. What an intrusion of my privacy. Then I have you, Nathanael Wayfarer, at the British Museum, buggering around with my acquisitions. Then you both get together and it's a free for all, hacking my systems, disturbing my operations everywhere from Sussex to DC. Where are my manners? I feel as though I ought to offer you both a drink. After all, you are my guests. Please be seated.'

Then Natasha's voice, saying, 'What, when you're going to kill us both? You're just going to treat us like guests beforehand? Are you some kind of psychopath?'

Roland Adamant's voice came out of the phone again. 'Kill you? Why, that item is on the agenda, I admit."

Natasha stopped the recording. She said, "I have it all on here, Roland. And believe it or not, I've already uploaded it to dropbox and five different cloud accounts, as well as Facebook. Organised that on the way here, you can do it while it's still recording, did you know that?" She remarked to Nathanael in a sort of aside, "Pretty good hey?"

"Pretty good," Nathanael admitted. "I'm impressed."

Roland was silent.

Then another rumble sounded.

Roland laughed. "Thank goodness. I am going to get away with it. That's the last corner of the laboratory to be obliterated. How will you prove any of this without evidence?" His voice suddenly changed, "Give me that phone!"

"I don't think so," said Natasha.

Roland snapped, "Give it to me." A gun appeared in his hand. Nathanael wasn't sure where it had come from. Had it been there all along? It was pointed at Nathanael's chest.

Damn.

Roland said, "Give it to me, or he gets it."

The rumble got louder.

Behind Roland the statue started to tip forward slightly. The ground was rumbling even louder.

Nathanael reached forward involuntarily. He cried out, "Roland! The statue — behind you — it's starting to fall."

Roland scoffed, "You're just trying to make me turn around, so that she can shoot me in the back while my gun isn't on you."

But Nathanael said, "No! I'm trying to save you!"

Natasha said, "He is trying to save you! Look, the statue is leaning down, really badly. It's that explosion — it must have weakened the foundation."

Roland laughed, "Oh, very clever of you. Weakened the Heosphoros Foundation. A marvellous pun." Then his voice got more serious and he waved the gun at Nathanael. "I'm just going to shoot him, then, if you don't give me the phone. Don't try these stupid games."

Natasha said slowly and carefully, "Roland Adamant. There is time for you to repent. There is even time for you to save yourself, to save your life. But you have to listen to us. You have to believe us. The statue is falling."

Roland sneered, "Oh, shut up. I know, it's his life you're trying to save. And your own. Nobody cares about anybody else in this world."

Natasha said, "But it's going to fall over. You won't have time to repent."

Michelle said, "It is. It's leaning over. It's about to squash you."

Nathanael reached out his hand. "Roland, take my hand, I'll pull you out of there. You just have to reach forwards. Grab my hand! Clasp it! Let me save you!"

Roland laughed even louder. The rumbling was louder and it drowned him out for a moment. "I'd have to take the gun off you to do that! You don't think I'm that stupid do you? You must think I'm completely stupid! Give me the phone. I'm going to count down, when I get to one, if you don't give it to me, I will shoot him. Ten. Nine. Eight."

The rumbling was louder than thunder, completely deafening, and it drowned out their pleas to him and all their shouting, and his countdown, for a moment.

The tall statue leaned forwards, slowly, ever so slowly. "Six. Five. Four." It was like watching an action replay on a football game. "Three. Two." It really wasn't worth reaching forward to try and save someone who refused to be saved. Nathanael stepped back and pulled his arm back, just in time. As Roland Adamant formed his mouth to say the word, "One," the statue plummeted down into the open grave and obliterated all sight of the intransigent billionaire.

Blood welled up and gradually stained the statue from beneath. Nothing more of Adamant was visible beneath the stone bulk, except for one hand that had been thrust aside by the full force of the stone monument, now dismembered, its knuckles pressing against the side of the grave.

The hand that was still holding the gun.

They all stood there, silently taking in the gruesome sight.

Finally Natasha said, "It reminds me of something I once read — a Bible verse — 'anyone who falls on this stone will be broken to pieces; anyone on whom it falls will be crushed.'"

The police arrived soon afterwards and Natasha told them she had Roland Adamant's confession on her mobile phone.

While all of this was going on, Nathanael's heart suddenly thumped up into his throat. "What's wrong?" said Natasha.

Nathanael said, "344 M Street East."

The policeman said, "What's 344 M Street East?"

"That's where he is. Quick!"

"Who?"

"The boy. Meth. And Peter. There's a boy they kidnapped... And his father, Peter Lazarus-Fox, a prominent English palaeontologist. They're imprisoned in a place — 344 M Street East. Please send someone over there, to let them out." Nathanael was wringing his hands. "I hope they're all right. I hope he didn't dynamite that place too. Please send someone right away."

The policeman nodded. "Okay. I will. Look, if there was any other places dynamited I would have heard of it. I'm sure they're still okay." But he quickly got onto his radio and called a couple of cars out to that address. "Are they likely to be armed?"

"Yes," said Natasha. "They will be."

He warned the other officers to be prepared to use force.

Nathanael said, "Thank you. Can we see them when you get them out?"

"Yes, oh, yeah. We'll be bringing you all into the station to make your statements. I think from the looks of it this might end up being an FBI case, in which case we'll assist where we can, but... for now it's in our jurisdiction, so... Look, afterwards, I'll get you taken wherever you wish. But I just need those statements while it's fresh in your minds. By the way, I just heard. Once the other members of his criminal gang realised that Roland Adamant was dead they gave themselves up. I wouldn't be surprised if many of them were working for him under coercion, threats of blackmail or harm to their families. "

CHAPTER 28 — AFTERMATH AND METH, AFTER.

Giving their statements at the police station was fairly painless — they weren't too interested in the whole history of what had happened, just the last few hours. They wanted to take Natasha's phone as evidence, which she allowed, but not before insisting they make a copy of the phone's hard drive and store it in at least two other places, one inaccessible from the net, just in case they got hacked. She showed them how to do it.

Davo, who was expecting to get off scot-free now that he had changed his ways, was arrested instead. Michelle told him softly, "Davo, you committed a bunch of crimes. You need to come clean - tell the police everything. Help them with their inquiries. Then maybe you'll get to see your sons again."

As they took him away in handcuffs, he looked at Michelle with hostility, as though she had betrayed him.

Some FBI men arrived soon afterwards and interviewed Natasha and Michelle about Davo, mostly. They told Natasha Davo was wanted in twelve states for murders, they had suspected Adamant's organisation's involvement but had not been able to prove anything and had also had problems with NSA surveillance files going missing.

Michelle made them aware of Davo's wishes. "I think he'll only talk to you if you can reassure him that he'll get to see his sons again." They thanked her and said they would take that into consideration.

Meth and Peter arrived at the police station half an hour later accompanied by the policeman who had rescued them.

Since Meth and Peter didn't have any accomodation the police paid for them to stay at a motor inn that night. After going back to the bed and breakfast place and getting their possessions, Natasha and Nathanael booked the room next door to Meth and Peter. Michelle booked the next one along.

They all went to Meth and Peter's room and played Five Card Draw, for several hours, laughing and talking and betting matchsticks from the motel bedside drawer. After a while, the mood quietened and the game ended.

Nathanael said, "What about the help Adamant was getting from the security agencies? I mean, both in England and here, he clearly had aid from some people high up in the NSA, the MI5, who knows who? What are we going to do about that?"

"It's all coming out in the computer files," said Natasha. "That's what the FBI are here for — once they're involved, they are probably the only ones who have enough power to look into things like like that. At least, that's what they told me."

Meth yawned. "It's past your bed time, young man," said Peter. It was broad enough hint; Nathanael and Natasha went back to their room and Michelle and Davo went back to theirs.

Nathanael sat on the bed while Natasha changed in the bathroom.

"Natasha," he said, when she came out. "I've wanted to ask you this. Do you ever think… there could be anything between you and me? I mean, more than this…?"

She said, "You mean, more than this marvellous friendship? Nathanael, honestly speaking, while I find you to be a very attractive man, although perhaps a little old for me, though that wouldn't stop me if… The thing is, you're not a Christian, and I simply couldn't marry someone who isn't a Christian."

"Well, why? What's the difference?"

"Jesus Christ. My life is… like a house I'm building. All our lives are, like houses, I'm building mine on Him. He's the foundation, a firm foundation. An adamantine foundation, you might say. How will it work if you're not building on the same foundation? How can we build a house together, like that? If you're not building on Jesus, you're building on insecure sand. Your half of the house will fall over when there's any trouble, any storms, leaving mine still there, but broken."

Nathanael took the couch and Natasha took the bed.

He was starting to feel grumpy as he laid down.

"You know… You say you're a Christian, and I've just seen you lie, cheat, steal (information, but isn't that just as bad?) And you enjoy drinking, too. Quite a lot. You know, you haven't really behaved like a Christian. No more than me, really. I mean, and how can a computer hacker be a Christian as well?"

"Nathanael," said Natasha. "If you were simply trying to convince any girl to go to bed with you, this would probably not be the right way to begin. Flattery might work better. But if you're trying to convince me of anything more than that, i.e. some sort of long term commitment, then that was probably the worst start you could possibly make."

"What's your point?" A bitter taste came into his mouth. Didn't she realise she was his hero? Couldn't she see how much he respected her?

Natasha leaned on the end of the bed, looking down at him on the couch. "The thing is, Nathanael Wayfarer, I don't have to justify myself to you. Not in the least. Because I am already justified in God's sight by Jesus Christ. My sins are forgiven."

"What about mine?" said Nathanael, remembering at the same moment how comforting the thought had been that his sins were forgiven, when that person was praying for him when he was in the hospital, after the accident.

"Yours are too," said Natasha. "Your sins are forgiven, Nathanael. You can know that, because Jesus died for you, freely, out of his love for you. But if you don't accept that, if you don't believe it, how are you any different from Roland Adamant, standing in his uncle's grave, refusing the help that was offered to him?"

Somewhere, outside, in the distance, a woman's voice started singing,

> "Rock of ages cleft for me,
> let me hide myself in thee.
> Let the water and the blood
> From Thy riven side which flowed
> Be of sin the double cure
> Cleanse me from it's guilt and pow'r.
> Nothing in my hand I bring
> Simply to Thy cross I cling..."

APPENDIX I: TRUTH OR FICTION.

I wrote this appendix because I thought the reader might want to know what was real research and what was fiction in this book.

Early European Modern Humans, Soft Tissue, Aging and Genetics.

It is indeed true that the boundaries between Cro-Magnon man, Neanderthals and modern humans have been made redundant by DNA testing of the mitochondrial DNA, which has shown that Cro-Magnons and Neanderthals were both completely human. Indeed, a lot of DNA has been recovered from fossils, and the mitochondrial DNA is apparently the easiest to recover because it contains more redundancy.

For DNA analysis, soft tissue — blood, skin — is extremely useful — and for scientists to recover DNA from early humans in enough detail to reconstruct it in entirety does not seem completely implausible, for not only has soft tissue been recovered from two Australopithecus fossils said to be 2 million years old by paleoanthropologist Lee Berger of the University of the Witwatersrand, but in 2005 it was announced that soft tissue was recovered even from a 68 million year old T-Rex by Mary Schweitzer, a molecular palaeontologist at North Carolina State University, and she also subsequently recovered soft tissue from about half of their other dinosaur fossils going back to the Jurassic period, 150 to 200 million years ago. Subsequently more soft tissue has been found in dinosaur fossils elsewhere.

Susannah Maidment, a palaeontologist who conducted a study at Imperial College in 2015, told the Guardian, "It's really difficult to get curators to allow you to snap bits off their fossils. The ones we tested are crap, very fragmentary, and they are not the sorts of fossils you'd expect to have soft tissue." Yet they also found soft tissue even in these fossils.

The method of estimating age from the 4977-bp deletion anomaly is also true. However, to my knowledge this kind of experiment has not been done on Cro-Magnon skeletons. Everything about the extreme age of Cro-Magnon skeletons is my own invention, except for something I found on an old archaeological discussion board on the internet, the skeleton found in China with most epiphyses unfused but still with a dental age of around 29-33 years; this was real but was ascribed by the discoverer to an endocrine disorder.

As far as I know, no one has ever used the genes of early humans to create a long-lived person today.

Historicity of the Old and New Testaments.

Regarding the historicity of the Bible — everything that Professor Bruce Fetherington says about the New Testament being historically verifiable, the excellent archaeological evidence, the 70AD destruction of

Jerusalem and the fact that the documents reflect the Jerusalem of Jesus' time, and the four gospels' similarities of style and editing method with Plutarch, all of this is true, as is the fact that the archaeological evidence for the Bible gets sparser the further back in history we go. The early part of Genesis, from before the time of Noah, evinces no archaeological evidence at all, insofar as I know. Although Gobekli-Tepe, the mysterious ancient temple found on a hilltop in Turkey, the earliest human construction ever found, is in fact real, and contains stelae of many sorts of animals, snakes in particular, but whether this has anything to do with Adam and Eve is complete, unfounded speculation.

Surveillance, Privacy, Darknet and Tor.

But what might be surprising to readers is that the information about surveillance, and the ability of the NSA in the United States and three of its Five Eyes partners, the ASD in Australia, the GCHQ in the United Kingdom (GCHQ), and the CSEC in Canada to surveil them is completely true.

What is apparent from the existence of this surveillance is that there are no international agreements in place governing surveillance. Thus, when these services are sharing intelligence, it would be quite legal for the NSA to spy on Australian phone calls, then tell the ASD, or for the GCHQ to spy on something and tell the NSA, etc. There really needs to be some limits on their invasion of our privacy — even if it is all in the good cause of preventing terrorist acts.

Everything about back doors into computer systems, the transferal of phone calls to text and their storage in the

NSA data centre, the ease with which the US government can hack almost anything, the potential for hacking video surveillance, tracking and hacking mobile phones, all of this was revealed in the Edward Snowden leaks, although it was suspected as far back as the early 2000s that the US government might be capable of doing some these things, and possibly actually doing them.

All one needs to do to verify what I am saying is to google NSA surveillance, or Edward Snowden leaks.

Everything about the Darknet and Tor is true as well, more or less, and also the fact that if the computer at the end is hackable, then it doesn't matter, unless you can remain completely anonymous and hidden, as Natasha tries to do. Just google 'Darknet' or 'Tor' to find out more about these subjects, too. Of course, if one finds one's computer has a few glitches, runs slow, or opens random windows in the hour or so following such web-searches, one should not be surprised. I did not make any of this up. It happens.

The great power these organisations have for surveilling people makes the thought chilling that even one or two people in those organisations might have nefarious reasons for wanting to spy on supposedly free, private citizens in their own countries and others.

Theosophy, Occultism, One World Government and Jesus.

Nonetheless, the global conspiracy in my book is not based on truth, insofar as I can determine it. Unless you can call a broad agreement among a wide variety of progressive leaning politicians, that individual governments are bad and a world government would be a good thing — unless you can call such a broad agreement a 'conspiracy.' I do not know.

However, it is an undeniable fact that scholars and politicians on the ideologically progressive left would like a One-World government and have been working towards that goal, and the efforts to suppress the ethics of the Biblical religions and promote abortion, euthanasia and eugenics, gay marriage and various other matters, all of these are undeniable facts of the political landscape.

And as most people would realise, there really do exist cultish groups and new-age religions promoting a One-World government, whose philosophy specifically opposes Jesus Christ's uniqueness as the Son of God, while claiming to be in harmony with everybody and claiming to teach tolerance and a universal truth.

The idea for the Heosphoros Foundation being originally named the Lucifer Institute, came from a real organisation, though, the Lucifer Publishing Company founded by the writer Alice Bailey. They actual later renamed their company, 'Lucis Trust', supposedly to prevent confusion between the Lucifer of their theology and the Satan of the Bible. However, the philosophy of Madame Blavatsky, Alice Bailey's teacher, seems to have purveyed just this confusion, a kind of upside-down philosophy where God is evil and Satan is good, for thus she wrote about God and the snake in the Garden of Eden:

> The Beings, or the Being, collectively called Elohim, who first (if ever) pronounced the cruel words, "Behold, the man is become as one of us, to know good and evil; and now, lest he put forth his hand and take also of the

tree of life and eat and live forever..." must have been indeed the Ilda'baoth, the Demiurge of the Nazarenes, filled with rage and envy against his own creature, whose reflection created Ophiomorphos. In this case it is but natural — even from the dead letter standpoint — to view Satan, the Serpent of Genesis, as the real creator and benefactor, the Father of Spiritual mankind. For it is he who was the Harbinger of Light, bright radiant Lucifer, who opened the eyes of the automaton created by Jehovah, as alleged; and he who was the first to whisper: "in the day ye eat thereof ye shall be as Elohim, knowing good and evil" — can only be regarded in the light of a Saviour. An "adversary" to Jehovah the "personating spirit," he still remains in esoteric truth the ever loving "Messenger" (the angel), the Seraphim and Cherubim who both knew well, and loved still more, and who conferred on us spiritual, instead of physical immortality — the latter a kind of static immortality that would have transformed man into an undying "Wandering Jew."

The Secret Doctrine, the synthesis of science, religion and philosophy, Volume 2, p. 218, Madame Blavatsky, 1888, Theosophical Publishing Company, Ltd, London.

It is very interesting how Madame Blavatsky takes her opposition to Christianity and turns it into hatred of

Jews as well. Some people will excuse this, saying, 'Many people were racists/anti-Semites, in those days', but the fact is, many were not. The great missionary endeavours of the eighteenth and nineteenth century treated all human beings as valuable in God's sight and equal in his love, even if they might have been culturally blinkered in other ways. Madame Blavatsky's racism in evidence:

> No amount of culture, nor generations of training amid civilization, could raise such human specimens as the Bushmen, the Veddhas of Ceylon, and some African Tribes, to the same intellectual level as the Aryans, the Semites, and the Turanians so called. The 'sacred spark' is missing in them and it is they who are the only inferior races on the globe, now happily – owing to the wise adjustment of nature which ever works in that direction – fast dying out.
> *The Secret Doctrine (ibid.), Vol. 2, p 377 footnotes*

> But now Judaism, built solely on Phallic worship, has become one of the latest creeds in Asia, and theologically a religion of hate and malice toward everyone and everything outside themselves.
> *The Secret Doctrine (ibid.), Vol. 2, p 421*

Of course, I am not meaning to suggest that the Lucis Trust is anything like my fictional Heosphoros

Foundation, which is clearly a criminal organisation, a sort of conglomeration of every evil. But it would be foolish to follow any sect or ideology that replaces Jesus' light with 'Inner Light of Self.' Which, in Blavatsky's philosophy, it is quite plainly stated, means the light of Lucifer, Satan.

There seems to be a lot of confusion these days, among Christians, treating such ideas as though they are equivalent to sound Biblical theology regarding the Holy Spirit. The differences are quite simple for those who have open eyes: Jesus Christ and the Bible. Where Jesus is worshipped as Lord, any other ideas or bringers of dubious light have to be seen for what they are: half-truths and lies that get in the way of knowing Jesus Christ, who alone is Way, Truth, and Life.

The Biblical Testimony About Jesus Christ

Yes, there is a historical witness in the Bible about Jesus, but there is also a spiritual witness about who Jesus Christ is, in relation to God. Some people may say Jesus was merely a wise teacher. But the Bible says He was much more than this: He was the unique Son of God, and is the only way to God. There never was anyone else like Him and there never will be.

Many people today see the claims Christians make about Jesus being the only way to God to be intolerant and exclusivist. But these claims are completely biblical and anyone who claims to be Christian but preaches a more 'tolerant' Christianity is not being honest about what the Bible actually says. Yes, God is love, but human beings can be stubborn like Roland Adamant — standing beneath a falling stone, unable to believe that the people who are trying to help them (by telling them about Jesus, in this case) are actually telling the truth.

Here are some of Jesus' claims about Himself:

> When Jesus spoke again to the people, he said, "I am the light of the world. Whoever follows me will never walk in darkness, but will have the light of life." *John 8:12*

> Jesus answered: "I am the way and the truth and the life. No one comes to the Father except through me." *John 14:6*

> Jesus said, "All who came before Me were thieves and robbers, but the sheep did not listen to them. I am the gate. If anyone enters through Me, he will be saved." John 10:8-9

> "My sheep listen to My voice; I know them, and they follow Me. I give them eternal life, and they will never perish. No one can snatch them out of My hand. My Father who has given them to Me is greater than all. No one can snatch them out of My Father's hand." *John 10:27-29*

And here is what the Bible says about the meaning of Jesus' death on the cross:

> For God so loved the world that He gave His one and only Son, that whoever believes

> in Him shall not perish but have eternal life.
> *John 3:16*

The forgiveness of sins is given alone through the shed blood of Jesus on the cross:

> In Him we have redemption through His blood, the forgiveness of sins, in accordance with the riches of God's grace. *Ephesians 1:7*

Places and people.
The various places in the story are always described as accurately as I can manage using google maps, streetview and images from the internet, at least, those places I have not visited myself in the recent past, though I have changed the names of some of the shops and organisations, etc., simply because they might not want to be in my story. If I have made any mistakes in the descriptions of various places, I assure you it was not through want of trying as hard as I could to be accurate.

Nonetheless, despite all the true facts and information that inspired this novel, please note that all the characters in my work are, of course, fictional, and none of them are based on real people.

APPENDIX 2 — NSA BOUNDLESS INFORMANT

FAQ

This is the NSA's Frequently Asked Questions file about Boundless Informant, their program for accessing metadata from any country about internet sites being surfed. This really is chilling reading, as it basically describes a system where the software user can click on any country, select any type of website or organisation, see how many people are looking at a particular website, and then select a single user to see what their IP address is. It is important to note that this computer program is used in collaboration with their other computer programs, such as PRISM which allows court ordered access to GOOGLE and YAHOO accounts.

This was revealed in the guardian newspaper, here is the link.

https://www.theguardian.com/world/
interactive/2013/jun/08/boundless-
informant-nsa-full-text

And here is the document:

OFFICIAL USE ONLY BOUNDLESS INFORMANT -- Frequently Asked Questions 09-06-2012

Questions

1) What is its purpose?

2) Who are the intended users of the tool?

3) What are the different views?

4) Where do you get your data?

5) Do you have all the data? What data is missing?

6) Why are you showing metadata record counts versus content?

7) Do you distinguish between sustained collect and survey collect? 8) What is the technical architecture for the tool?

9) What are some upcoming features/ enhancements?

10) How are new features or views requested and prioritized?

11) Why are record counts different from other tools like ASDF and What's On Cover?

12) Why is the tool Is there a releasable version?

13) How do you compile your record counts for each country?

Note: This document is a work-in-progress and will be updated frequently as additional questions and guidance are provided.

1) (U) What is What is its purpose?

BOUNDLESS INFORMANT is a GAO prototype tool for a self-documenting SIGINT system. The purpose of the tool is to fundamentally shift the manner in which GAO describes its collection posture. BOUNDLESS INFORMANT provides the ability to dynamically describe GAO's collection capabilities (through metadata record counts) with no human intervention and graphically display the information in a map view, bar chart, or simple table. Prior to BOUNDLESS INFORMANT, the method for understanding the collection capabilities of GAO's assets involved ad hoc surveying of repositories, sites, developers, and/or programs and offices. By extracting information from every DNI and DNR metadata record, the tool is able to create a near real- time snapshot of GAO's collection capability at any given moment. The tool allows users to select a country on a map and view the metadata volume and select details about the collection against that country. The tool also allows users to view high level metrics by organization and then drill down to a more actionable level — down to the program and cover term.

Sample Use Cases How many records are collected for an organizational unit?

How many records (and what type) are collected against a particular country? Are there any visible trends for the collection? What assets collect against a specific country? What type of collection?

What is the field of view for a specific site? What countries does it collect against? What type of collection?

2) (U) Who are the intended users of the tool?

Mission and collection managers seeking to understand output characteristics of a site based on what is being ingested into repositories.

— -- at -- .--

organization/office level or seeking to answer data calls on NSA collection capability.

BOUNDLESSINFORMANT -- FAQ Page 1 0:

OFFICIAL USE ONLY OFFICIAL USE ONLY BOUNDLESS INFORMANT -- Frequentlv Asked Questions 09-06-2012

looking for additional sites to task for coverage of a particular technology within a specific country.

3) What are the different views?

Map View -- The Map View is designed
to allow users to view overall DNI,
DNR, or aggegated collection posture
of the agency or a site. Clicking on a
country will show the collection posture
(record counts, type of collection, and
contributing SIGADS or sites) against
that particular country in addition to
providing a graphical display of record
count trends. In order to bin the records
into a country, a normalized phone
number (DNR) or an administrative region
atom (DNI) must be populated within
the record. Clicking on a site (within
the Site Specific view) will show the
viewshed for that site -- what countries
the site collects against.

Org View -- The Organization View
is designed to allow users to view the
metadata record counts by organizational
structure GAO -- SSO -- -- SPINNERET)
all the way down to the cover term.
Since it's not necessary to have a
normalized number or administrative
region populated, the numbers in the Org
View will be higher than the numbers in
the Map View.

Similarity View -- The Similarity
View is currently a placeholder view for
an upcoming feature that will graphically
display sites that are similar in nature.
This can be used to identify areas for

a de-duplication effort or to inform of additional SIGADS to task for queries (similar to Amazon's "if you like this item, you'll also like these" feature).

4) (U) Where do you get your data? BOUNDLESS INFORMANT extracts metadata records from GM-PLACE post- FALLOUT (DNI ingest processor) and (DNR ingest processor). The records are enriched with organization information SSO, FORNSAT) and cover term. Every valid DNI and DNR metadata record is aggregated to provide a count at the appropriate level. See the different views question above for additional information.

5) (U) Do you have all the data? What data is missing?

The tool resides on GM-PLACE which is only accredited up to TS/SI/NOFORN. Therefore, the tool does not contain ECI or FISA data.

The Map View only shows counts for records with a valid normalized number (DNR) or administrative region atom (DNI).

Only metadata records that are sent back to NSA--W through FASCIA or FALLOUT are counted. Therefore, programs with a distributed data distribution system MUSCULAR and Terrestrial RF) are not currently counted.

Only SIGINT records are currently counted. There are no ELINT or other records included.

6) (U) Why are you showing metadata record counts versus content?

(Q) Do you distinguish between sustained collect and survey collect?

The tool currently makes no distinction between sustained collect and survey collect: This feature is on the roadmap.

BOUNDLESS INFORMANT -- FAQ Page 2, OFFICIAL USE ONLY OFFICIAL USE ONLY

BOUNDLESS INFORMANT -- Frequently Asked Questions

09-06-2012

8) What is the technical architecture for the tool?

Click Eg for a graphical view of the tool's architecture

DNI metadata (ASDF), DNR metadata (FASCIA) delivered to Hadoop Distributed File System (HDFS) on GM-PLACE

Use Java MapReduce job to transform/filter and enrich data with business logic to assign organization rules to data

Bulk import of data (serialized Google Protobuf objects) into Cloudbase (enabled by custom aggregators)

Use Java web app (hosted via Tomcat) on MachineShop (formerly TurkeyTower) to query Cloudbase

GUI triggers queries to CloudBase -- GXT

9) What are some upcoming features/enhancements?

Add technology type JUGGERNAUT, LOPER to provide additional granularity in the numbers

Add additional details to the Differential view

Refine the Site Specific view

Include CASN information

Add ability to export data behind any view   Add in selected (vs. unselected) data indicators

Include filter for sustained versus survey collection

10) How are new features or views requested and prioritized?

The team uses lawmill to accept user requests for additional functionality or enhancements. Users are also allowed to vote on which functionality or enhancements are most important to them (as well as add comments). The BOUNDLESS INFORMANT team will periodically review all requests and triage according to level of effort (Easy, Medium, Hard) and mission impact (High, Medium, Low). The team will review the queue with the project champion and government steering committee to be added onto the BOUNDLESS INFORMANT roadmap.

11) Why are record counts different from other tools like ASDF and What's On Cover? There are a number of reasons why record counts may vary. The purpose of the tool is to provide BOUNDLESS INFORMANT -- FAQ

OFFICIAL USE ONLY

Page 3 0:

BIBLIOGRAPHY

DNA FROM CRO-MAGNON SHOWS THEY ARE HUMAN:
Caramelli, D; Lalueza-Fox, C; Vernesi, C; Lari, M; Casoli, A; Mallegni, F; Chiarelli, B; Dupanloup, I; Bertranpetit, J; Barbujani, G; Bertorelle, G (May 2003). "Evidence for a genetic discontinuity between Neandertals and 24,000-year-old anatomically modern Europeans". Proc. Natl. Acad. Sci. U.S.A. 100 (11): 6593–7.
http://www.pnas.org/content/100/11/6593.long
Jones E. R., Gonzalez-Fortes G., Connell, S., Siska, V., Eriksson, A., Martiniano, R., McLaughlin, R. L., Llorente, M. G., Cassidy, L. M., Gamba, C., Meshveliani, T., Bar-Yosef, O., Müller, W., Belfer-Cohen, A., Matskevich, Z., Jakeli, N., Higham, T. F. G., Currat, M., Lordkipanidze, D., Hofreiter, M., Manica, A., Pinhasi, R., and Bradley, D. G. 2015 Upper Palaeolithic genomes reveal deep roots of modern Eurasians (Journal Article). Nature Communications volume 6 2015 Nature Publishing Group
http://rdcu.be/m0U1

SOFT TISSUE FOUND IN HUMAN ANCESTORS:
http://popular-archaeology.com/issue/september-2011/article/preserved-flesh-of-2-million-year-old-human-ancestor-found
Keeling R., and Berger, L.R. 2013. Potential soft organic tissue preserved in association with the Australopithecus sediba fossils from the Malapa cave site, South Africa. (Paper). 82nd Annual Meeting of the American Association of Physical Anthropologists, Knoxville, Tennessee, United States of America. American Journal of Physical Anthropology. Wiley Blackwell. Supplement 56: p. 163.
http://www.palaeontologicalsociety.co.za/Palnews%20
19_2%20Jul%202013.pdf

SOFT TISSUE FOUND IN DINOSAURS
Schweitzer, Mary H.; Wittmeyer, Jennifer L.; Horner, John R. (2007). "Soft tissue and cellular preservation in vertebrate skeletal elements from the Cretaceous to the present". Proc Biol Sci. 274 (1607): 183–97.
https://www.ncbi.nlm.nih.gov/pmc/articles/PMC1685849/

Bertazzo S, Maidment SCR, Kallepitis C, Fearn S, Stevens MM, Xie H-N et al., 2015, Fibres and cellular structures preserved in 75-million-year-old dinosaur specimens (vol 6, 7352, 2015), NATURE COMMUNICATIONS, Vol: 6, ISSN: 2041-1723
http://hdl.handle.net/10044/1/23666
https://www.theguardian.com/science/2015/jun/09/75-million-year-old-dinosaur-blood-and-collagen-discovered-in-fossil-fragments

USING 4977-bp DELETION OF MITOCHONDRIAL DNA TO DETERMINE AGE

Meissner C, Bruse P, Mohamed SA, Schulz A, Warnk H, Storm T, Oehmichen M. The 4977-bp deletion of mitochondrial DNA in human skeletal muscle, heart and different areas of the brain: a useful biomarker or more? Exp Gerontol. 2008 Jul;43(7):645-52. doi: 10.1016/j.exger.2008.03.004. PubMed PMID: 18439778.
https://www.ncbi.nlm.nih.gov/pubmed/18439778

EPHIPHYSES UNFUSED BUT WITH DENTAL AGE OF 29-33 YEARS

https://www.researchgate.net/post/What_is_the_best_way_to_determine_age_in_skeletal_remains NEW TESTAMENT HISTORICITY AND PLUTARCH

The prologue of Luke:
http://www.perseus.tufts.edu/hopper/text?doc=Perseus:text:1999.01.0156:book=Luke
The prologue of Herodotus' Histories:
http://www.perseus.tufts.edu/hopper/text?doc=Perseus:text:1999.01.0126
The reliability of the New Testament:
The Resurrection of Jesus, A New Historiographical Approach by Michael R Licona, Apollos 2010
Why Are There Differences in the Gospels?: What We Can Learn from Ancient Biography 1st Edition by Michael R. Licona (Author), Craig A. Evans (Foreword) Oxford University Press 2016
http://www.str.org/articles/is-the-new-testament-text-reliable#.WDqpKTJ7Hvw

http://www.christianitytoday.com/edstetzer/2012/february/ closer-look-historical-reliability-of-new-testament.html

OLD TESTAMENT HISTORICITY

I have not read this book, though it's on my 'to peruse' list, but I have been reading about the Archaeology of the Old Testament for years, and it sounds from the reviews as though KA Kitchen's conclusions agree broadly with Professor Fetherington's in my book:

On the Reliability of the Old Testament, by K A Kitchen, William B Eerdmans Publishing Co 2006

Regarding the Colophon/Tolodeth equivalency: https://en.wikipedia.org/wiki/Wiseman_hypothesis

THE SUMERIAN KING LIST AND GENESIS

I believe the line of argument in the following article to be very credible, despite it coming from a journal many people would a priori distrust. If it does not quite establish the historicity of the flood or the genuine longevity of the antediluvian patriarchs, it certainly appears to establish the priority of the genealogy in Genesis, and also that a Sumerian scribe far closer to that time in pre-history than *we* are believed the Genesis genealogy to be a historical record of the antediluvian period.

The Antediluvian Patriarchs and the Sumerian King List by Raúl Erlando López, Journal of Creation 12(3):347–357, 1998

http://creation.com/the-antediluvian-patriarchs-and-the-sumerian-king-list

GOBEKLI TEPE

Curry, Andrew (November 2008). "Gobekli Tepe: The World's First Temple?". Smithsonian.com.

http://www.smithsonianmag.com/history/gobekli-tepe-the-worlds-first-temple-83613665/

J. Peters & K. Schmidt: "Animals in the symbolic world of Pre-Pottery Neolithic Göbekli Tepe, south-eastern Turkey: a preliminary assessment." Anthropozoologica 39.1 (2004), 179–218

http://sciencepress.mnhn.fr/sites/default/files/articles/pdf/az2004n1a13.pdf

EDWARD SNOWDEN AND ELECTRONIC SURVEILLANCE

https://www.theguardian.com/world/2013/jun/08/nsa-boundless-informant-global-datamining

https://en.wikipedia.org/wiki/Edward_Snowden#Global_surveillance_disclosures

The Wikipedia page contains a great plethora of references and the section on Global surveillance disclosures, to which I have linked, is fascinating and chilling reading.

DARKNET AND TOR

https://en.wikipedia.org/wiki/Darknet

https://en.wikipedia.org/wiki/Dark_web

https://en.wikipedia.org/wiki/Tor_(anonymity_network)

WORLD GOVERNMENT AND OCCULTISM.

The history of the organisations and names:

https://www.lucistrust.org/about_us/history

Enumerating that Madame Blavatsky was Alice Bailey's teacher and inspiration for using the name "Lucifer":

https://www.lucistrust.org/arcane_school/talks_and_articles/the_esoteric_meaning_lucifer

The quote from Madame Blavatsky:

The Secret Doctrine, the synthesis of science, religion and philosophy, Volume 2, p. 218, Madame Blavatsky, 1888, Theosophical Publishing Company, Ltd, London.

https://www.theosophytrust.org/Online_Books/The_Secret_Doctrine_Vol_2_V2.0.pdf

The Lucis Trust's connections with the UN:

https://www.lucistrust.org/blog_wgun

Madame Blavatsky's fraud:

Proceedings of the Society for Psychical Research, Volume 3, p. 216 onwards. Society for Psychical Research, 1885, National Press Agency, London.

https://archive.org/stream/proceedingssoci00britgoog#page/n216/mode/1upEvans (Foreword) Oxford University Press 2016

CGT
CCTAG
CCT   AGAGGCAGCCCAGTTCCTGTACTC
GAGCATTTAGAAGCACTGATACAGCTGGGTGCGGTGGCTC
TCC AGCACTTTGGGAGGC   GGTGGATCATGAG
AGCCGATCCTGGCTAA   GCG
TA   GAGGTG GTGGCGGGC   ACT
CTGAGGCAGGAGATCACTTGAACC   GGCAG
AGATCGCACCAG C CT TC
AAAAA
CGATGACCTTT TTC TGC

www.ingramcontent.com/pod-product-compliance
Lightning Source LLC
Chambersburg PA
CBHW070801120726
47910CB00001B/257

9 780992 368159